I0715663

DENGUE

Also by Millicent Eidson

MayaVerse Series Titles

Microbial Mysteries: A Story Collection (Book 0)
Anthracis: A Microbial Mystery (Book 1)
Borrelia: A Microbial Mystery (Book 2)
Corona: A Microbial Mystery (Book 3)
Ebola: A Microbial Mystery (Book 5)

Short Works

Monuments: A Ten-Minute Play
Red Thread
Pariah

DENGUE

A MICROBIAL MYSTERY

Millicent Eidson

Maya Maguire Media - Vermont

Dedication

To all those whose health and safety are threatened by a changing climate, including the people of Lahaina, Maui

Praise for Millicent Eidson

"Millicent Eidson's unparalleled talent shines through in this remarkable work, ensuring a thrilling reading experience. I confidently predict that this offering will be warmly embraced by the literary world, solidifying Millicent Eidson's place among the most esteemed authors of our time."—**Midwest Book Review**, *Anthracis: A Microbial Mystery*

"Dr. Eidson's medical thriller serves up unique and carefully drawn characters, fascinating and chillingly realistic threats, and enough Happily For Now resolutions to satisfy any women's fiction or romantic suspense fan. You won't want to miss this new entrant into the genre."—**Amazon Reviewer**, *Anthracis: A Microbial Mystery*

"This 2nd book in the Maya Maguire series follows the intrepid CDC veterinary detective as she tries to track down the mysterious tick microbes causing *Borrelia* infections. Her travels lead her from her home in New Mexico to the European sites of other outbreaks. Meanwhile, Maya is dealing with her own professional and romantic issues. This is a fascinating insider's look at the increasingly menacing diseases arising from animal microbes worldwide."—**Amazon Reviewer**, *Borrelia: A Microbial Mystery*

"The author's background as a scientist working for the CDC gives you an insider's view of this public-health agency at a time of crisis. I recommend Corona to all fans of medical mysteries."—**Amazon Reviewer**, *Corona: A Microbial Mystery*

"The mystery, the characters, the setting, and the uncanny timing of this book make it a compelling read. I would recommend it to anyone who loves medical thrillers, mysteries set in Hawaii, mysteries with diverse characters, books with a strong female protagonist, and fictional tales related to climate change."—**A.M. Reade, USA Today Bestselling Author**, *Dengue: A Microbial Mystery*

Author Note

Dengue is an important emerging public health threat. This novel conveys accurate information about dengue virus and the tools to combat it for 2021, the time period of the novel.

Most locations and organizations are real. Plot incidents are inspired by actual outbreaks in various settings and time periods. However, the characters are fictional. Character actions are scientifically based but do not necessarily reflect the decisions of actual agency personnel. The MayaVerse is a world of imagination that provides insights into the science and practice of public health related to zoonoses, diseases from animals and insects.

Written and spoken Hawaiian words may include an ʻokina (glottal stop), as represented by a left single quotation mark. An example is Hawaiʻi. A kahakō elongates vowel sounds and is represented as a macron over a vowel. Hawaiian agencies and tourist information vary on their use of these spellings, which impact pronunciation and meaning. Although inconsistencies may seem confusing, these words are spelled to reflect character pronunciations and written agency documents.

To keep updated, join the MayaVerse Reader List at https://drmayamaguire.com/. For a universal link to all MayaVerse formats and distributors, see https://books2read.com/millicenteidson/.

Readers who would like to consult on future stories or provide feedback are encouraged to email: drmayamaguire@gmail.com. Ratings and reviews are critically important to help others discover the MayaVerse. Add them to your favorite bookseller or to https://www.bookbub.com/.

INCEPTION

Las Piedras, Puerto Rico—Monday, June 28, 2021

First-graders burst with glee out the summer school's wooden door. Their hot carbon dioxide exhalations tempt the female *Aedes aegypti* mosquito, but a smaller male tracks her down through his bushy antennae and they adjust their wing beats in harmonic convergence.

His abdominal pincers seize her dark, white-spotted torso and he inserts his aedeagus to secrete sperm into her genital chamber. The seminal fluid triggers a passion for blood so she circles back to the playground. Too many targets entice, but high carboxylic acid wafts from the skin of a teacher, recumbent on a patio bench and wiping his brow with his handkerchief. A mosquito magnet— she's bitten him several times starting last Tuesday. The teacher's body is permeated with dengue virus that alters his microbiome to grow more *Bacillus* bacteria emitting acetophenone. Much more attractive than the uninfected children.

The mosquito lands on the back of the teacher's bald head, then pierces his skin with her needle-like proboscis. She sucks up blood tainted with microscopic viral particles which will travel to her midgut for replication. He swats and misses.

Students scream with noisy rounds of tag. *Aedes aegypti* selects a girl whose cartwheels expose tanned legs under a pink skirt. The mosquito bites the back of the child's knee, regurgitating dengue virus from her earlier meals of teacher blood. The multiple feedings provide enough energy to find the ideal location for egg laying.

Mold-encrusted tombs beckon from a cemetery at the end of the block. A cement flowerpot with a plastic lily and blocked drainage draws the mosquito close to an obelisk topped with a marble cross. The water-clogged crack in the mausoleum's base looks perfect. She deposits more than a hundred white eggs which adhere to the edge, just above the liquid's surface. During Puerto Rico's rainy season, the drizzle will provide moisture for the eggs to hatch, then turn into wriggling larvae, pupae, and finally new adults, all within a week.

She hangs for a moment on a cherubic carving that honors a much-loved baby boy, then spots a discarded beer can for her next deposit. After a few more days guaranteeing life for her offspring, she'll join the other dead in the graveyard.

ONE

Santa Fe, New Mexico—Tuesday, July 6, 2021

At sunrise, the moon was on its way to dying. Only a sliver floated over the purpled mountains as Maya supervised her vacationing friend's dog. In Erika's backyard, Rojo orbited the fence line with puppy energy. Dog duty done and Rojo snoozing in the kitchen, Maya dragged herself into her Prius for a fifteen-minute drive to the New Mexico Department of Health. Braving a gauntlet of staff she hadn't seen in almost ten months, she went through the motions of smiling during a barrage of greetings.

"Hey, Dr. Maguire, happy to have you back."

"Didn't recognize you with that new hairdo—like it!"

"How ya doing, kid, conquered that long COVID yet?"

She'd only restarted her Preventive Medicine Residency on July 1. Yesterday's revisit to Harvey Cornell Rose Park, the site of her wedding, triggered a sob each time she touched a velvety flower petal. With the three-day holiday weekend, many in the office still knew little of the momentous last year since her marriage to Manolo.

The cheerful office voices filtered down the hall and eased Maya's heartache as she answered calls about dog bites. All routine, no monumental public health challenges, just what she needed. But the masks and staggered work schedules provided a stark reminder of the pandemic, even with its summer lull.

All day, she rehearsed what to say if someone acknowledged her anniversary. Under COVID restrictions, only three local friends had attended the July 6 ceremony last year, with her family and her supervisors joining on Zoom. Dr. Grinwold and Stephanie, his secretary, would remember. But like Erika, they weren't in the office.

At five-thirty, Maya closed the office door and hurried back to Erika's house, praying that the two-month-old Labradoodle hadn't made a mess. As she released Rojo into the yard again, she cleaned up a puddle of urine on the kitchen tiles. He'd missed the puppy pad.

When Erika was planning a camping trip to celebrate her son's eighth birthday, she'd approached Maya for help. "You're a vet, my ideal dog sitter." Their campervan, a grandparent pandemic gift, was too small to include an untrained twelve-pound puppy.

The paper towel Maya swiped over the damp floor also collected strands of her red-streaked black hair. Like the dog breed, she shouldn't be shedding, but extreme stress had multiple impacts. Preventive medicine—that was the intent in getting away from the apartment she had shared with Manolo until his COVID death. Without mentioning Manolo or the wedding anniversary, Erika had offered Maya a place to recuperate with a consoling animal.

Maya slid open the patio door and Rojo bounded in, then curled up with her on the couch. As her fingers caressed his silky red fur, bumps of his warm black nose on her arm soothed her soul. Rojo's brown eyes darted toward and away from hers. She was always a sucker for dark eyes, and the dog's expression appeared to mirror the pain in her own.

"Rojo, don't worry." Maya's tone was soft—she wanted to calm both their nerves. "Kyle will be home Saturday, full of Smokey the Bear and Billy the Kid tales. If you work on bladder control, I bet you can join them next trip."

The abrupt musical note and flashing screen of her phone laid waste to her meditative state. Rojo leapt to the floor, headed for his cushion. "Hi, Mom, thanks for calling. I knew you guys wouldn't forget."

She moved to the kitchen table and rested the phone on its adjustable case. Flagstaff's San Francisco Peaks framed her mom's head, crowned by flaming dyed hair. Then her dad's balding pate poked into view. Her parents looked better in their early seventies than she felt at twenty-eight.

"I still can't get used to your haircut," her mom said. "You've never had it so short."

Maya plastered on a smile. "I tried to match your color—not easy for a Chinese American to look Irish."

"Men like long hair on their women," her mom answered.

Her dad cut off the awkward discussion begun two weeks earlier when Maya returned from China. "Barbara, Maya's decision on hairstyle isn't important. She made it home—they could have locked her up longer in that dangerous COVID hotel, or even worse, a Chinese prison."

"If Manolo were alive, he'd never let her do something so stupid."

Her dad redirected the conversation. "We've been looking at the wedding pictures and video that your colleague Dr. Schwartz put together. We thank God for those enduring memories."

"Me too," Maya answered. After visiting the park yesterday, she'd gone through the electronic album on her laptop, the first time since Dave sent it. Manolo's ebullient personality was reflected in his embroidered Guayabera shirt honoring his Puerto Rican heritage. His face was ecstatic and loving, goatee grown in for her personal preference even though he'd have to shave it later for the Public Health Service uniform requirements. Seeing his kisses on the video triggered sense memories of his persuasive lips and his earthy smell. Could she ever love or be loved so passionately again?

"I wish you had stopped here on your way home from China." Her mom continued her chiding. "Hypatia misses you." She rotated the phone to take in the black Persian cruising their legs.

Maya's patience snapped. "Dammit, Mom, I needed time to prepare for my CDC training. I was lucky they let me postpone it after Manolo and the baby died."

She couldn't remember cursing at her mother before. Adoptees were supposed to be forever grateful, her conscience chastised. But her mom was right—she should have squeezed in a quick visit to Arizona after her return from Hong Kong.

"I'll make you a solemn promise. The first vacation days I

earn will be prioritized for you guys. Or if Dave and I go back to northern Arizona to investigate COVID-infected mink, we'll stop by your place."

"All right, dear." Another first, her retired-astronomer mom backing down. "We just hate you being alone on such an important day. But Manolo's with you in spirit."

Maya felt his presence, too. She wasn't spiritual but his light burned so bright in their two years of dating and the brief marriage, even death couldn't extinguish it. Many people had been touched by his brand of confident caring. His friends at the Indian Health Service had started a scholarship in his name for public health physicians working in areas of scarce resources.

"I've been thinking," she told her parents. "A good time to hold a memorial service for Manolo and the baby would be the anniversary of his death, Oct. 6. Maybe his family can travel here from New York."

The words were leaden, hard to form and share, but nine months after their deaths, she released them. She didn't know the date of her miscarriage while in the COVID coma, or if the baby had been a boy or a girl. Not knowing allowed the short pregnancy to seem unreal, like a dream that happened to someone else.

"I love you, Mom and Dad. Rojo's scratching to go outside again. Thanks for checking on me."

Maya hooked a leash to Rojo's collar and headed to the arroyo behind the neighborhood. Slanted light rays were colored by suspended particles of New Mexico dust. She'd never seen better sunsets during undergrad and vet school in Colorado or while working toward her public health degree in New York City. During her early years in Flagstaff, the ponderosa forests had blocked distant views. But on this clear, cool evening, mountain ranges to the south and west provided a rough bottom stroke to a Bierstadt landscape, with the closer peaks a darker hue.

Rojo sniffed at every plant while Maya kicked over some rocks, looking for the lizards Kyle loved. Erika had told Maya that caring for the dog would make her feel useful and calmer. Having her own pet might be a good idea, but with her demanding job and COVID recovery, Maya avoided any commitments.

She rubbed her arms with the rapid drop in temperature. The shivers might be related to her prolonged depression, perhaps from the time on a respirator and coronaviral effects on the brain. But she focused on gratitude for regaining most of her strength.

Breaking into a slow jog, she guided Rojo back to Erika's patio door. Once he nodded off on his dog bed, she opened her laptop and clicked on the Chinese wildlife biologist's email, sent over his secure channel.

<Glad to hear you're back to work. I apologize for persuading you to cross into China as my pretend sister so we could capture bats. I am not allowed to work on COVID so I seek our giant salamander before it disappears with heat waves and Yangtze drying up.>

Maya was still furious with Mu Jian and Stefan Duda, her World Health Organization colleague, for the risks they took in organizing the expedition. Her birth in China and return visit at age twelve had lulled her into a sense of security and curiosity. Jian and Stefan counted on those good feelings to rope her into a trip that was too dangerous with the People's Republic of China COVID-paranoia. Her mental processing wasn't a hundred percent, and they took advantage. But the adventure had snapped her out of mourning and reoriented her brain to epidemiology. And they both appeared to be genuinely sorry, so she couldn't hold a grudge.

She typed a reply. **<So much in common—we're science and medical detectives born in Tongling, Anhui Province. What are the odds? I have pictures from my 2005 visit—could you share some recent ones? My parents said in the twelve years between their trip to pick me up and our return, the provincial capital became unrecognizable. Hefei had no traffic lights the first time, then transformed into a bustling city a few years later.>**

Maya was surprised to get an immediate response from Jian,

until she remembered it was midmorning the next day in the PRC. <I will send photos for both cities. My grandparents want to meet this lost daughter of Tongling. They miss my mother so much, another casualty of COVID like your husband. Take a picture with your mobile so I can share it.>

Jian had taken selfies of them on a tour boat before they got caught, but she took one more and texted it. With the weight loss and pixie haircut, the only thing she recognized in the photo was the small flat mole near her left eye.

The headshot didn't expose her body damaged by accidents and disease investigation misadventures. With Manolo's love, she'd tried to move beyond embarrassment about the missing baby finger next to the wedding ring, and scars on her head, arms and legs. Some might be put off by a Chinese girl less exotic and perfect than their imaginations. Fortunately, any future commitments to another man were off the table.

As the sun vanished and gloom of night settled in, she reached down to give the sleeping Rojo a final pet. She envied the dog's untroubled dreams. Hers about Manolo could be consolatory or fictional monstrosities. Black waves of his hair gleamed in the sunlight or twitched like tarantulas. Eyes invited her to swim in soothing cenote pools or swirling maelstroms. Lips puckered, supple with desire or obliterated by leprosy. She flung her tea cup into the sink and it shattered.

"Fuck my fucked-up mind," she exclaimed to the dog who cocked his head before falling back into his trance. All alone again, she cleaned up the mess. Memories to cherish, and memories to loathe.

TWO

Queens, New York City—Wednesday, July 7, 2021

From the Citi Field seats in the upper right section, Faye Simpson checked her text message. Heart racing, she anticipated meeting up with one of her favorite hookups. She maneuvered her bulk to the aisle and down to the entrance, nostalgic for the gaudy blue-and-white Shea Stadium. A highlight had been the 1986 World Series championship during her early years as the City's Public Health Veterinarian.

Scanning the crowd, she almost didn't spot Taylor, a towering bronze goddess. After almost two years apart, the mask and shaved head threw Faye off.

"Dr. Lewis, you look wonderful." Faye leaned on the irony of a formal greeting. "I wasn't sure you'd make it."

Taylor stretched out one bare arm, glistening with the ninety-degree heat. "You look marvelous too, dear, including your enhanced curves with pandemic pounds."

Faye accepted the handshake, warmed by the memory of their barbed banter. She was certain Taylor was flirting, not offering an insult. With luck, the evening would advance to further contact.

"It's hotter than Hades," Taylor said, "but I got in a practice run for the marathon."

Faye smirked. "You've got more energy than me."

As they headed to the stadium gate, Faye flushed with the realization of how much she didn't know about Taylor even after eight years of intermittent interludes. An accomplished physician but an amateur athlete as well? She should have guessed by Taylor's sculpted physique, although running might be a pandemic hobby.

Her initial attraction to Taylor at the Village Halloween parade was Taylor's resemblance to Robert, Faye's veterinary externship mentor and long-lost love.

The spectacular day when she congratulated Robert at the end of the 1984 marathon flooded her memory. Under crisp blue skies, his sandalwood cologne had mixed with sweat as he twirled her in joy, stirring up the orange and yellow leaves painting the fading grass. Faye's favorite time of year.

Then Robert collapsed and died two weeks later from AIDS and a brain parasite, so she never got to see him in his late forties like Taylor. The crinkles around Taylor's dark eyes made her wonder if Robert would have aged as gracefully.

Faye flashed her phone for the ticket taker. "I arrived before my guest. Can you still scan their ticket?" Taylor, as a trans woman, had requested the gender-neutral pronoun when they first met.

On the upper deck, Faye again shoved past fans wearing blue-striped Mets jerseys and blue caps. Heads jerked up as they passed— her roly-poly body with its sagging freckled skin contrasted with her statuesque Black companion. This was their first time out together in a social setting. Most previous encounters were in the Staten Island hospital where Taylor served as Chief of Staff, or in Taylor's lower Manhattan apartment.

Once seated, Faye pulled out her beer from under the seat and offered it to Taylor. "When the guy comes around again, we can order a fresh one," she said. Fingering her graying strawberry-blonde curls, she eyed her dimply thighs. The two of them didn't look like a couple—she was old enough to be Taylor's mother.

In the bottom of the inning when Dominic Smith hit a groundball to right field and took first base, Faye shouted to make herself heard over the roar of the crowd. "I'm sweltering. Let's ditch these masks."

"Governor Cuomo eliminated the mandates two weeks ago. This Flushing Bay breeze will waft away the cooties."

Faye glanced at those nearby, uncertain if anyone would be offended by Taylor's quip. In tense pandemic and political times, everyone was on a hair trigger. As they removed their N95s in solidarity with other beer-guzzling patrons, Taylor's ambiguous gender with purple nail polish and matching lipstick drew quick glances. Faye's conservative Colorado parents would be rolling over in their graves. But on her rare Thanksgiving visits to the ranch before their deaths, they'd given hints of suspecting Faye's eclectic tastes.

Public health and medical small talk were kept to a minimum. Faye concentrated on the game rather than the palpable yearnings generated by their bare leg contact. After the Milwaukee Brewers scored two runs in the top of the second inning, she followed Taylor down to grab dinner. While standing together at one of the round metal tables, her chin dripped butter from her lobster roll. Taylor snaked a long finger to wipe it off, then took bites from Vegan City nachos with jackfruit.

"A far stretch from the Nathan's hot dogs I used to get here," Faye said. "I'm overwhelmed by the food choices, especially when I should cut back."

"Is this our first official date?" Taylor lifted a Brooklyn Lager with two fingers.

Faye laughed. Their occasional hookups and work meetings didn't qualify. "Maybe. We haven't discussed any epidemics yet."

Taylor set the bottle on the table and laced hands with Faye. "Will you forgive me if I consult about a single case?"

The energizing shock of Taylor's caress sent Faye's mind spinning. Three thousand touch receptors in each fingertip. To distract from the sensations, she grabbed her lobster roll and directed her brain to diseases from animals and insects. "Which zoonosis is it this time?"

Taylor leaned in close. "Dengue fever. The state texted me lab confirmation while I was on the train. It's a little girl visiting from Puerto Rico."

Faye noted no one loitering nearby but lowered her voice. "It's unlikely she caught it here—we don't have *Aedes aegypti* mosquitoes. However, our *Aedes albopictus* can transmit it. That would be a first—we've never had local transmission."

"She's got mild cystic fibrosis which may complicate the prognosis. Dengue wasn't on the initial rule-out list because her signs were nonspecific."

"I bet you're more attuned to dengue with your overseas work."

A wide smile broke Taylor's angular features. "The chance to volunteer in the Philippines dengue outbreak was life-changing."

"Do you know I represent states and cities on the Dengue Vaccine Work Group?"

"Of course. I follow your career closely."

Faye was surprised that anything made her blush at sixty-six. "I definitely want the details of your case, but this isn't the best place."

Taylor nodded. "You can visit the patient with me tomorrow."

Faye's mind went wild with dengue virus speculations, insufficiently distracted by a ball game with few runs. At game end, they joined the throngs of dejected Mets fans headed to the train. "I hate losing five to zip," Faye said, "but we can get home early."

Masks back on, Taylor draped an arm over Faye's shoulders, keeping them close.

An hour later, they had negotiated the subway to Faye's one-bedroom condo at the border of Little Italy and Chinatown. Both of them had skin beaded with moisture, so she closed the drapes and turned on the A/C.

Taylor dropped to a shredded couch covered with a blue Mets throw blanket.

Faye grimaced. "Sorry for the furniture. The cats had a field day before the last one died of renal failure."

Taylor's aquiline nose wrinkled for a sneeze. "Guess I should have expected a vet to have pets. This is only a slight allergy."

A cat had slept in their bed during their first tryst in 2013 at an apartment belonging to Taylor's friend, and all subsequent meetings had been catless. Taylor's revelation of a problem only reinforced Faye's decision to keep their assignations casual.

Taylor reached out to undo the button and zipper of Faye's yellow shorts. "This ungodly heat—we're stinky pigs." Taylor's lips twisted in a tentative grin. "Can we start with a shower?"

Faye allowed Taylor to finish undressing her before she returned the favor with stroking fingers.

Naked, their contrast in age, stature, and skin color was even more prominent, but Faye had dimmed the table lamp. She knew Taylor took female hormones which formed small breasts but had not started any surgical transformations. It just provided more love-making options.

Staten Island, New York City—Thursday, July 8, 2021

They rode the Staten Island ferry the next morning. With Taylor at the railing of the open deck, Faye stretched like a cat in the filtered sunshine. An incoming text confirmed that her boss, Dr. Moskowitz, had approved her plans.

She glanced around. The area was uncrowded with most travelers going into Manhattan for work, not their direction. "Tell me more about your patient," she said.

"Juana came into the ER on Monday with a high-grade fever, severe headache, vomiting, gum bleeding, and a rash. Tuesday, we moved her to the neuro ward."

"I never heard of neurological problems with dengue."

"She has diminished tone in both lower limbs, incontinence, and absent perianal sensations."

The boat docked as summer storm clouds blocked the sun. "I often jog from here." Taylor's eyebrows were raised in a question.

Faye squirmed. Wearing tennis shoes, there was no reason she couldn't join Taylor, except that she didn't run.

"Have you ever seen me exercise?" she joked. "Well, except for what we do in bed."

Taylor dabbed a raindrop from Faye's nose and hailed a cab.

Thirty minutes later, they had gowned and huddled at the door to the ICU room. Faye looked in at the small child, dark hair fanned over the pillow and face marked with a diffuse rash. The girl opened her eyes and rubbed them, moaning in pain. Then she seemed to recognize Taylor and grinned, waving one hand.

"Juana, this is Dr. Simpson," Taylor said.

"Hi. When can I see the Statue of Liberty?" Juana twisted to scratch at one knee. A strangled groan emanated from her lips and a nurse adjusted what Faye assumed was a pain drip.

Faye turned to Taylor and whispered. "Her discomfort is extreme. What got dengue on your radar before the lab results?"

"Routine tests for other diseases came up with nothing, and no place in the US is more dangerous for dengue than Puerto Rico." Taylor turned to the centralized computer and opened the medical record. "Last night's MRI found a spinal epidural hematoma. They plan to operate."

Faye wracked her brain, realizing she was out of her league on some human disease complications. "How did her infection cause blood to compress the spinal cord?"

"The rash may reflect a bleeding disorder. Listen, I have to page the surgeon."

"Of course. Is there anything I can do to help?"

"We need to rule out New York for her exposure. Can you nail down the family's travel details?"

Faye blanched. With COVID's impact on the public health and medical infrastructure, the last thing they needed was a swarm of blood-sucking mosquitoes spreading breakbone fever.

"No problem, there must be a relative nearby." She stepped closer to Juana. "Hang in there, kiddo. Dr. Lewis mentioned you want to be a gymnast—I can't wait to see your moves."

Juana reached out a hand toward Faye. "When I get out, I want hair highlights like yours."

So someone appreciated her multitoned natural color—an advantage of not dying it. "I'll pass that along to your parents."

She asked the clerk to page the Lopez family to the cafeteria. Stepping into the elevator, she scratched at a mosquito bite on her arm. She'd been too excited about meeting with Taylor last night at the ballgame to remember bug repellent.

THREE

Santa Fe, New Mexico—Friday, July 9, 2021

Water in Maya's ears muffled other sounds as she pounded out the laps, alternating her strokes in the pool just a block from the health department. When her pace lagged, visions of loved ones stolen by COVID haunted like brief rainbows. Her grandmother, the baby, Manolo. Then she kicked it into gear and refocused on speed until she stood up at the shallow end, gasping from the intense thirty-minute workout.

After a quick shower, she munched a tuna salad sandwich as she walked across the park. She hesitated next to a massive black steam locomotive surrounded by a chain-link fence and hedges. Manolo had told her it was donated in 1959. If he and their child had lived, she could imagine a family outing with him expounding on every detail of its capacity.

A songbird's sweet, clear notes counteracted traffic noise when she paused at the crosswalk. Her phone rang with a call from Dave Schwartz, her US Department of Agriculture colleague.

"I'm at the Rodeo de Santa Fe this afternoon on a USDA inspection. Any chance you can join me?"

Maya headed to her car. "I can't pass up a chance to see you in person. Give me about fifteen minutes."

When reaching the open-air fairgrounds on the south side, she spotted Dave leaning against one of the metal chutes, dirty brown cowboy hat low over his chiseled face. In his mid-thirties like Manolo, he was built like a lean rodeo cowboy, but she didn't recall he'd ever tried it.

"Break any more government regulations?" Dave's droll sense

of humor came on strong. "Not that I should criticize your China debacle. I got a speeding ticket yesterday."

"You're such an outlaw." She bumped his chest with her fist. "By the way, my parents are still gushing over the wedding photos. Thank you."

"You're welcome. Must be a hard time, with your anniversary and all."

"Mixed feelings, but I'm okay."

Dave led her over to hard metal seats in the grandstand. "The haircut and weight loss suit you." He gestured to the young woman kicking her horse into high speed as she raced into the arena. "Maybe healthy enough to compete with these barrel racers."

"I've been on a workout plan for COVID recovery, but I'm not ready to ride." Dave's personal remarks could have been intrusive but after three years of working together, she was tolerant of his good-old-boy ways. Nobody was more dedicated to his role as a family man and USDA veterinarian.

"Why are you visiting Santa Fe?" she asked. "Need an infusion of culture and charm from the City Different?"

"Everyone's getting in practice for the upcoming rodeo so I'm reviewing animal health." The cowgirls and cowboys lining the fence whooped in encouragement as the horse and rider went into a steep lean, hugging the barrel through the turn.

Dave turned back to Maya. "We haven't connected in more than a month. How are you really doing?"

"Peachy keen," Maya said, unwilling to dump her mental health challenges on him. Then she switched to work. "I have a question about deer and COVID."

"USDA is planning to release our study analyzing deer antibody levels in four states. Thirty-three percent were infected."

The news triggered a rapid heartbeat—she hoped the China trip hadn't amped up her fight-or-flight response. "How did it spill over to deer? We feared that mink would be the first natural reservoir here."

"Don't go batshit crazy—we've got no evidence of clinical

illness in the deer, nor reason to think they're spreading it to people. Probably the other way around, perhaps through wastewater or an intermediary species."

She didn't appreciate him insinuating that she was hysterical, but ignored his dig. "Like everyone, I've got pandemic fatigue."

He wrinkled his hat in his hand. "It's not only deer we have to worry about. Remember those stray cats we saw at the Arizona mink farm?"

"I was distracted by the beefy guards throwing us out."

"Well, a Utah mink farm was more cooperative, where we captured some free-roaming cats. GPS collars tracked them to neighborhoods where they could contact people, as well as other domestic and wild animals. A few of the cats were infected with corona, apparently from eating virus-contaminated mink feed."

"When did you do all this?"

"While you were in COVID recovery—we're still analyzing the results."

With all the drama she could muster, Maya placed her palms together and raised her hands toward the metal roof of the grandstand.

"God, please send me something *different* that's scary and fatal to work on!"

"Gal, don't go makin' stupid wishes like that. I'm hearing the voice of my religious wife—she'd be appalled at your request."

Maya knew he was right. It was just too tempting to joke around—no one else was able to get in that groove with her. Except Stefan Duda, but her resentment over his luring her to China still burbled like a hot spring.

"Dave, tell Emilia she can drag me to church next time I visit. I have a whole lot of sins to confess."

"Come stay with us soon. The kids will be happy to show off their latest horsemanship skills. Have you been to a real rodeo? Let's plan on a family night here when the show's scheduled."

Maya shook her head. "Seeing people or animals get hurt isn't my cup of tea."

"Ah, but it's the glory of athletic courage." He pointed to the rider in a black cowboy hat and green-checked shirt taking her practice run around the barrel closest to them. "They use a cloverleaf pattern to circle the three barrels—not easy to pull off. One rider did it in 16.63 seconds last year."

Maya grinned. "Anything with the Schwartz family is fun so I'll consider your offer. Can you email that COVID deer report?"

"Of course."

The rider knocked over the final barrel and the spectators groaned as Dave led Maya toward the gate. He paused with arms wide in an invitation for a hug. "We skipped the masks—think we can take another risk?" He stooped for an embrace.

It felt wonderful to have his arms around her. Not a sexual thrill, but comfort—she longed for Manolo's exuberant, revitalizing hugs.

By the time Maya arrived at the health department, she had the USDA report in her email. Dave's attitude sometimes mimicked a lazy lion under a baobab tree but he was always on top of his game.

She forwarded the information to Dr. Grinwold, along with an invitation to meet whenever he returned. He poked his head in at two-thirty and led her to his office.

"I've got big news." He settled into a large, cushioned chair. Perhaps it was a new purchase as he continued to add pounds. She knew he had diabetes and tried to control it with weightlifting, difficult with the gyms closed until recently.

He removed thick-lensed glasses and rubbed the expanding bald area on his head, only a few brown-gray strands remaining. "Nancy's giving up the job and joining me in Santa Fe. The moving van picks up her things in Phoenix on Sunday—I'm flying there tonight to finish packing."

The news was momentous—the culmination of a lifetime dream of being together after decades working in adjacent states. Maya was tempted to leap up and give him a congratulatory hug, but they never had that kind of relationship.

"That's fantastic! Who's her replacement?"

A wave of dizziness washed over her. Surely not Enzo? Her aggressive Arizona counterpart had accepted a federal position after his training ended in June. The further away he worked, the better. It was almost two years since his sexual assaults and his blackmail to keep his position.

"Your friend Lila Becker got the job. She finished her Preventive Medicine Residency in California and wants to stay in the Southwest."

Maya stomped on a centipede of envy that Lila had completed her PMR while Maya was starting over, derailed by her COVID infection. And Lila had met another physician on the job, with the two women exchanging engagement rings on a TikTok video. Her fiancée appeared as sedate and serious as Lila was loud and proud.

"Arizona couldn't be in better hands," Maya said, "now that Nancy's here with you." She looked forward to working with Lila on cross-border outbreaks.

Dr. Grinwold smiled, something Maya didn't see often. "Everything's falling into place. We're all thrilled you're back working with us. I know it's been rough for you lately."

The classic poster of a kitten hanging on for dear life from a tree limb, that's how Maya felt. "This place is a second family."

"Good, and thanks for the deer update. Let me know when the mink/cat study has any official results. CDC reports you're doing an excellent job managing the reportable disease database this week in Erika's absence."

Maya brushed her skirt, thrown off guard by the unfamiliar compliment. "Happy to take care of it." She stood to leave. "I need to check on the latest reports."

"Nancy and I will have you over to dinner once she's settled in."

That would be a first—Maya didn't even know where he lived. Although COVID had spread its tentacles to multiple living creatures, US human cases had plummeted from more than a quarter million a day in January to only ten thousand a day in July. Many believed the pandemic was over. Things were looking up for all of them.

FOUR

Manhattan, New York City—Friday, July 9, 2021

Faye's back was in agony from hours at her desk. Finally at home, she wondered why she killed herself working past typical retirement age. She placed the phone call, eager for a shower and bed.

"Maya, are you sitting down?" she asked.

"That sounds ominous. What is it?"

"Dengue virus, possibly in your state."

"One second." Maya went silent and Faye heard clicking keys.

"New Mexico hasn't had local transmission," Maya said, "but there's *Aedes aegypti* near the Rio Grande River."

"We have confirmed infection in a child named Juana Lopez. She stopped in New Mexico on her way here from Puerto Rico."

Maya sounded tentative. "Are you concerned that she became infected in New Mexico, or was a source for infecting other people while here?"

"Both. I'm sorry to dump this on you when you just started working full time again. Should I talk to Fred?"

"Dr. Grinwold's helping Dr. Bingham move from Phoenix to Santa Fe this weekend, so I can take the lead. Where in New Mexico did the girl visit?"

An alarm blared and Faye looked down the street, slick with an evening rain shower. Beacons on an ambulance and firetruck flashed—her neighborhood was never quiet.

She turned her attention back to the phone call. "Juana's dying grandmother lives in Corrales, which I understand is in the Albuquerque area. She was there June 29 to July 2."

"My colleague Dave Schwartz lives in Bernalillo, next door to

Corrales. He's probably up on mosquito issues in that area. I'll also check with Albuquerque Environmental Health."

Sirens finally silent, Faye moved back to her kitchen table. "Juana is in critical condition—she had surgery this morning to remove a blood clot pressing on her spine."

She paused before continuing. Might as well be honest.

"The rumor mill says that CDC wasn't too happy about your China expedition. Are you sure you're ready for this?"

Maya sounded irritated. "CDC rehired me so we're beyond that. I won't let you down."

As she wolfed down a chicken pot pie, Faye flipped through the Living Arts section of the *New York Times*. She felt guilty about the trees sacrificed to print it but she couldn't adjust to reading it online. The sky outside the window was a gloomy gray with limited visibility at sunset.

The emergency vehicles had left. With fifty-five apartments in the ornate former Police Building, populated by numerous senior citizens, there were plenty of candidates for getting sick.

The buzzer interrupted and she spoke into the old-fashioned wall speaker. "Geraldo, what is it?"

"Dr. Simpson, there's a Dr. Lewis here at the front desk."

When Taylor stayed over Wednesday night after the Mets game, they'd gone straight up to Faye's apartment and didn't interact with the doorman. No love interests had ever shown up in her lobby uninvited. Maybe it was a major mistake to spend the night at her place rather than Taylor's.

Geraldo cleared his throat. "Uh, for Dr. Lewis, do you want me to send him, er, her, up?"

"Yes, they know the way."

At the rap from the lion's head knocker, she yanked the door open and fixed her fiercest scowl to dissuade such behavior.

Taylor was dressed in scrubs and wore a black wig of wavy hair. The color of the lilies in Taylor's hand matched Faye's pink pajama gown covered with white bunnies.

"Dr. Lewis," Faye said in an imperious tone. "You didn't call or text to say you were dropping by."

Her guest leaned a muscled arm on the door jamb and flashed a brilliant smile. Taylor's magnetic charm likely worked wonders in hospital personnel disagreements.

"I thought you might enjoy a surprise." Taylor proffered the flowers with a curtsy. "Guess I was wrong."

Faye didn't respond. How much should she torture Taylor for assuming their relationship was to the level of drop-ins? The two of them staring in silence on her doorstep wasn't a discreet option, so she opened her door wider.

"Can I put these in water?" Taylor gestured at the kitchen door as Faye settled on her couch.

Minutes later, Taylor returned with the flowers in a vase. "I apologize again. I'll call and check with you in the future. Can I update you on Juana Lopez?"

Faye scooted over to make room. She vowed to let her displeasure go if Taylor didn't show up like this again.

"How's she doing after the procedure?"

"We removed the blood clot and she's responsive, but still no improvement in her lower limbs. And she's not breathing on her own, so she's getting air through a tracheostomy."

Taylor's fingers interlaced with her own. "Thanks for the email about your interview with the Lopez family."

Faye withdrew her hand, attempting to keep their exchange on a business level. "Maya Maguire will try to identify dengue-infected mosquitoes in New Mexico where Juana visited. I plan to do the same here. The number and type of mosquito traps, their locations—all that is yet to be determined."

"Good. Has anyone contacted Puerto Rico?"

"I gave them a heads-up this afternoon. Would you like a cup of herbal tea?"

Taylor nodded and Faye headed to the kitchen for the chamomile. When she returned with the steaming mugs, she said, "I'm preparing an Epi-X report. That's how CDC alerts other states."

After a sip, Taylor reached out to play with Faye's pale gray curls. "Did you recommend anything to the family members?"

Aroused, Faye tried to remain focused. "They'll be checking temperatures twice a day and we'll facilitate rapid lab testing if anyone develops signs or symptoms."

Taylor's fingers drifted down to Faye's bare neck, making feathery circular strokes on her skin. "Glad to hear I only have one patient to worry about and you're on top of everything else."

With flames of fire from Taylor's tender caresses, Faye eked out a minimal response. "No problem."

Taylor glanced around the apartment. "I got a good look at this grand Baroque palace while cooling my heels in the lobby. Chandeliers gleaming in the tile floor, the building's copper dome—it reminds me of Paris."

"I lucked out with my purchase." Faye leaned back and gave into the tactile sensations, forgetting her vow to throw Taylor out as soon as possible. "I'd make a killing if I sold it now."

Taylor's lips feathered the arch of Faye's jaw. "Please don't sell. I want to do this here for a long time."

If Faye were a cat, she'd start to purr. "No commitments, except for tonight." Her hands grabbed for the drawstring on Taylor's pants.

FIVE

Santa Fe, New Mexico—Saturday, July 10, 2021

Rojo bounced up and down in Erika's kitchen as if on a trampoline. His eight-year-old owner adopted a stern stare beneath the stiff-brim black hat. "I'm Sheriff Kyle. Is anyone acting up?"

Maya popped both of her hands into the air. "Oh, no, Sheriff, we're all on our best behavior." She smiled at the contrast between Kyle's pose and his Only You Can Prevent Wildfires t-shirt. Smokey cuddled two baby bunnies, surrounded by a skunk, a fawn, fox cubs and baby ducks. Kyle tumbled to the floor when Rojo jumped at his legs.

"With all the souvenirs, it looks like you helped out New Mexico's stagnant economy," Maya teased his parents.

Erika put her arm around her shorter husband's waist. "Billy the Kid made a big impression."

"The reenactment with Sheriff Pat Garrett reinforced the 'crime doesn't pay' message." Rolf unloaded food from the cooler into the refrigerator. "So I don't think we've created a little cattle rustler."

After yanking her blonde hair back into a ponytail, Erika started separating the whites from the dark colors in the pile of dirty clothes she'd dumped on the kitchen table. Whiffs of campfire emanated with every toss of a sock. "Speaking of the international criminal in this room, did you ever discover who sprung you from your COVID jail in China?"

Maya shook her head, exhausted from trying to figure it out. If she had to hear one more jibe about her law-breaking—she forced a laugh. "No, but I have a theory."

She checked the time on her phone. "I'd help you unpack but

there's a New York child with dengue. She spent time here in New Mexico."

"You don't have to hang around—we came home early to allow time for cleaning up."

Handing over a Santa Fe-themed mug, Maya said, "I broke one of your old ones so I replaced it with this. Turns out I made the biggest mess, not Rojo."

"Don't worry about it." Erika grinned. "We can always use more stuff decorated with red chiles. Need any help with the dengue?"

"Monday will be fine. Dr. Grinwold says there's a lot to plan with multiple agencies. The kid's exposure was likely in Puerto Rico where she lives."

"You look a bit deflated. Are you sure Rojo didn't give you any trouble?"

"Not at all, he was my major source of fun. I forgot the joys of living with a pet that's young and rambunctious." Her mind again slipped into work mode. "This girl with dengue—she's close to Kyle's age and in bad shape."

Erika held the screen door open. "You've got to depersonalize. When I work on our reports to CDC, I can't get invested in every sick or dead human."

Maya tossed her bag in her Prius. "You'd think I would have learned that lesson. But COVID dragged me through the gutter." She headed around to the driver's door and waved goodbye. "Thanks for giving me a mini-vacay with the dogsitting. I needed an excuse to escape from home."

Maya opened the front door of her apartment for the first time in a week. Her jaw tightened—she hated the place.

Popcorn ceiling and yellowing walls were all she could afford when she started as a CDC Epidemic Intelligence Service Officer three years earlier. After she completed her EIS training, Manolo had moved in his higher-quality furniture. Near the kitchen, his intriguing black-and-white photo of Acoma Pueblo reminded her that he was gone.

She flipped open her laptop to scrutinize the questionnaire she'd worked on all night for Juana's local family, then clicked over to her summary of mosquito collection techniques. Dr. Grinwold had promised to review the drafts in between packing Nancy's things for her move from Phoenix.

On its own, Maya's right foot tapped the floor. Unfinished business. She moved to the couch and pressed **<Zielinski, Mark>** on her phone contact list.

"Maya, how the heck are you doing?" His cheery and confident words blared through the cell speaker. "I'm placing bets we're only a mile apart."

"Are you back in New Mexico?" She hesitated. "I apologize for not being in touch. The first week at work has been hectic."

"Crazy here, too. I'm in my office downtown, catching up on New Mexico court cases. I flew in from Phoenix last night—couldn't stand the temps above a hundred anymore."

"I'm glad Manolo left those behind." Maya pulled at the couch cushion tassels. When would she stop referring to him as if he were alive?

"In your email from Hong Kong, you planned to come by my Phoenix office when flying home to visit your parents. What happened?"

"My sponsoring foundation only covered a ticket back to Albuquerque. I promised my parents a trip to Flagstaff next time I'm off work."

"But surely you have time for a local break. Come out to the ranch for dinner tonight."

Her muscles tensed as she anticipated a confrontation. She adopted a formal tone. "That fits my schedule. I can be there by six-thirty."

"Looking forward to it." He hung up without additional pleasantries, perhaps picking up on her businesslike attitude.

She dropped the phone onto the end table and closed her eyes, intending only to rest them after hours trying to become a dengue expert.

When she opened them again, the phone flashed 5:15. The drive was at least forty-five minutes and she hadn't showered. Rapid swipes of the washcloth over her breasts triggered memories of Manolo's sensitive fingers and tender lips. Steamy spray had enveloped them in a world of their own, protected from medical demands and microbial mysteries. Her body yearned to prolong the sensations and re-enact orgasmic bliss, but there was no time.

She stepped out of the bathroom only partially dry. A sliver of low-angle sunlight illuminated the urn on the bookshelf with the cremains of her husband and baby. The swashes of earth and sea colors said *hold me*, but she couldn't do it. Instead she focused on the closet. She should look nice but didn't want to lead Mark on. He was always a friendly, protective bear of a man, but he'd admitted an attraction. Not in a frame of mind to pursue it, she'd turned him down.

A blousy red shirt over a pair of dark pants would be fine. No need for a sweater with evening temps dropping only to the low seventies. When did Santa Fe at seven thousand feet of elevation get so warm? With the new pixie cut, she didn't have to worry about her hair getting tangled so she kept the Prius window rolled down as she headed east on I-25. Fly away, troubles, fly.

The soothing swish of the Pecos River countered Maya's trepidation as she drove across the small bridge. She parked outside the two-story adobe home, all rounded curves like a New Mexican church. When she exited her car, the gentle bleating of sheep drifted over from the barn. Hops used in animal feed tickled her nostrils as Carmen, Mark's house manager, waved from the shade of the front portal.

"Maya, it's so good to have you again. When were you last here, April?" Just past fifty like Mark, Carmen always appeared warm and composed, as if she couldn't imagine a better life. Did their close work relationship ever cross over into something more intimate? Neither provided any hints. "Mr. Zielinski is eager to see you."

She led Maya through the front hall past a Georgia O'Keeffe

flower painting that evoked a woman's vagina. Fixing a wide smile, Maya greeted Mark, still in his wheelchair. Beneath a high forehead traced by strands of thick black hair, his dark eyes brightened and he held out both hands. Maya grasped them with affection and strength, eliciting a spark.

"I'm sorry you didn't escape this chair," she said. "We both worked so hard with your physical therapist."

"Still spinal weakness from my fuckin' horseback injury. The rattler should have spooked him on someone else's property—then there'd be a person to sue."

Maya covered her mouth with her hand, cracking up at his threat. Mark was respected as a major donor to cultural institutions in two states, nothing like an ambulance chaser.

He lifted a glass of his favorite single malt Scotch. "You look awesome. Can I pour you a drink?"

"Not tonight, thanks." She needed a clear head to get him to admit what she suspected. But the discussion could wait until the end of dinner when both were more relaxed.

Carmen played hostess but refused to join them while they ate a salad from the garden and elk steaks from an animal Mark had hunted last fall. He bragged about a lawsuit he'd just won on behalf of teenagers who suffered lung damage from vaping. "Even after all those hospitalizations, the manufacturers still didn't change the package warnings."

"We're working on the same side." Maya's tongue luxuriated in the sweetness of homemade apple pie. "I developed consumer warnings and you nailed the companies' carcasses to the barn wall."

Mark leaned against the chairback etched with a pine tree symbol. His hair gleamed under the elk antler lamp hanging from the ceiling. He adjusted his silver belt buckle. "I ate more than I intended, drowning stress with food. No more business tonight."

After Carmen helped him transfer to the wheelchair, he gave her the rest of the evening off. Back into a familiar routine, Maya pushed him to the front porch where she perched on the wooden bench next to his chair. The sun had dropped behind the mountain peaks and changed the western sky to a creamy yellow. Clouds dotting the east were lit up like puffy pink candies. Maya settled into a tranquil mood as a contented whinny drifted over from the horse barn.

"You just won a big case, so why are you stress-eating?" she asked.

He rested his arm on the wheelchair close to her own but didn't touch her. "Perhaps I'm guessing what's behind your somewhat distracted manner tonight."

Maya gulped—no better time. He was begging for the question. "Did you pay the ten thousand dollars to get me released from China?"

But he didn't fess up. "Your family—they were so worried about you. They likely raised the funds."

"They don't have that kind of money sitting around, and I can guess who they might turn to."

He sighed. "Will you hold it against me if I admit to arranging it?"

"Of course not, I didn't want to spend another night in that COVID hell. You can't imagine how awful it was—no air conditioning, no toilet or clean water, little food."

He grimaced and turned away. "You were terribly stupid, amiga. Sneaking into China to test bats and people to discover COVID origins. How did you expect their government to react?"

Maya couldn't sit still. She stepped to the edge of the brick pavers, arm around a portal post. He was right, but she hated hearing the words from his lips.

"I didn't sneak. I used my real name and passport. Mu Jian did the lying—he told them I was his half-sister visiting for the Dragon Boat holiday."

Mark wheeled closer. "I was surprised to see you go along on something so reckless."

"I surprised myself. It's my birth country and I was eager for a change, making a contribution to science after so much time off."

His voice was gruff. "You should have considered the worst-case scenario. Your parents were apoplectic. I could never have left you stuck over there."

Maya's legs weakened with a wave of remorse. "I'll pay you back. I can pull it together by Christmas."

He reached for her left hand, his squeeze sparing the scar from her missing baby finger. "You're wearing your rings. I assume you're still not ready to explore a personal relationship."

The electric current between them flashed on, then off, like someone flicking a switch. "Mark, it's nine months since Manolo's death but nothing's changed. I'm attracted to you, but it could be just missing a man in my life. Not any man, but someone strong and kind, like you and Manolo."

"We connected so well on every level while you convalesced here. I'd be fine with serving as his substitute, even for a short time to help you ease your grief."

Maya stepped away again. "Even if that were possible, the money changes everything. I'd feel like a hooker, getting paid for sex. I can't escape into a physical relationship while obligated to you."

"Shit, I was afraid of that." His expression turned rueful. "But I couldn't leave you a prisoner on the other side of the world."

Maya leaned down and kissed him on the cheek. "Expect monthly checks in the mail."

SIX

The Bronx, New York City—Sunday, July 11, 2021

The grandfather of the child hospitalized with dengue attended the eleven o'clock Mass at San Simon Catholic Church every Sunday morning, so Faye waited until noon before heading to the South Bronx. On a hot, sunny afternoon when she emerged from the subway, the streets were lively with car traffic, honking horns, and brassy music.

A bicyclist avoided piles of trash bags on the concrete path between the multistory brick buildings of public housing, then zoomed around Faye as if she were a ski slalom gate. She retreated to a bench, enjoying the shade of overhanging trees and the little kids climbing the jungle gym.

Several minutes after her phone call to let the family patriarch know of her arrival, he opened the building's front door.

"Señor Lopez," Faye said, "thanks for letting me stop by to see where Juana stayed before her hospitalization. I'm sorry she's so ill."

Inside the apartment, she scanned the screenless open windows, one with a small air conditioner. Documenting Juana's potential opportunities for mosquito bites was critically important in identifying the source of her dengue infection. "When I talked with your son at the hospital, he mentioned a picnic in the park last week to celebrate your birthday and the holiday."

He motioned to the couch and its two pillows with the New York Yankees logo.

"Makes sense you're a fan, living so close to the stadium," she added. In hopes of promoting cooperation, she didn't bring up her loyalty to the Mets.

"The Red Sox are here Friday and I had planned to take Juana." He rubbed his forehead with a wrinkled hand, then pivoted for the kitchen. "Dr. Simpson, may I offer you a Malta Goya? It's carbonated with no alcohol. Very cooling on a sweltering day."

"¿Por qué no?" The City's gastronomic treats tempted her into accepting the hospitality. Pulling her mask to her neck, she cradled the frosty, damp bottle with her fingers. Thick and sweet with a bitter aftertaste, the drink provided a comforting fullness to her stomach. She replaced her mask and set the bottle on a wooden coaster. COVID cases were dropping, and she refused to stress out over his lack of a mask.

"Señor Lopez, I visited Juana yesterday. She was smiling and engaging with the hospital staff. Such remarkable courage."

Beneath heavy brows, his deep-set eyes held a hint of sadness. "She insisted on summer school after missing classes for a surgery. They removed polyps in her nose 'cause they made it hard to breathe. We pat her chest to loosen the gunk."

"Her dad told me she wants to be a gymnast—quite ambitious."

"Unlikely with her cystic fibrosis, but no one has the heart to tell her." His voice was low and pained.

Faye redirected the discussion. "Are you aware of anyone else who's not feeling well?"

He shook his head. "No one's sick, just Juana."

In an attempt to reassure him, she said, "You can't catch dengue directly from her, which is a relief after coronavirus. The risk to your family and friends only comes from mosquitoes that bite her, then you."

"Sometimes they get in here." He turned his arm to show off several welts.

"How often do you leave your windows open? *Aedes* mosquitoes, the type that spread dengue, live close to homes."

He crossed his arms as his dark eyes flashed with anger. "Are you accusing us of doing this to Juana?"

Faye dropped her mask and took another sip while composing her response.

"Not at all, Señor Lopez. The first time she vomited was the day after the picnic, July third, correct?"

"We already told the doctors that."

"It takes at least three days after a mosquito bite for the virus to spread enough in the body to show signs and symptoms. Sometimes a week or two. We call that the intrinsic incubation period."

The man uncrossed his arms. "Juana arrived here on the day of the picnic."

"Thanks for verifying those dates," Faye said. "So the mosquito bite must have been in Puerto Rico or when Juana visited her abuela in New Mexico."

He grabbed his second Medalla Light from the refrigerator. Despite a flash of guilt that she stressed him enough to guzzle beer so early in the afternoon, Faye pressed on.

"Leaving the windows open without a screen is still a problem. A mosquito biting Juana could infect someone new within a week when it's in the upper eighties like today. That's the extrinsic incubation period."

"You've lost me."

"I apologize for the technical terms—this is a complicated disease. The virus can multiply in the gut of any mosquito that bit Juana, then spread dengue to another person."

"So you'll blame my granddaughter if more people come down with it."

"Of course not, it's not her fault. And it's unlikely she infected enough mosquitoes to do that."

In disease detective mode, Faye knew the value of retracing the scene of a crime. "Señor Lopez, can you show me the area around this apartment complex?"

He grabbed his keys and led her to the stairway. Outside, water pooled in soil indentations next to the building and one of the flower pots on the step was filled with an inch of dirty water. She flipped it upside down. "This kind of mosquito loves to lay its eggs in areas of standing water. I'll send you and the building manager more information on control."

On the three-block walk to the park, they dodged skateboarders and parents pushing baby strollers. Faye abhorred exercise but was energized by the buoyant shouts and light breeze fluttering the trees. The park revealed attractive spots for a female *Aedes* to start her family. Mr. Lopez helped her turn over a water-laden broken tire swing on the ground.

Resting on a bench, she told him, "Using a helicopter, we apply environmentally friendly larvicides to kill young West Nile virus mosquitoes in marshes and wetlands. If we find *Aedes*, the mosquito that carries dengue, maybe we'll do that here."

He leaned back and wiped away a tear. "When I look at these kids, all I can think of is Juana fighting for her life."

Faye's heart snapped like a rubber band. Without any long-term relationships, she never missed having kids until moments like this. She was similar in age to Mr. Lopez but they had nothing in common—his family tree overflowed with relatives. Faye had no one. But many other female professional friends traveled the same work-focused path. And there were the exciting nights with Taylor and a few others. Her life was full, just not with the joy of children.

Faye glanced again at Juana's grandfather whose torso was bent almost to his knees. His shoulders shook with sobs. When he glanced up, his facial wrinkles glistened like tidal bays.

She reached out a hand to his arm. "Dr. Lewis, the chief medical officer, has an impressive staff. Juana's getting the best care."

The man's grief was a sharp reminder that having loved ones to lose was the price of family. She shoved up from her seat in frustration, uncertain how to console him. "Señor Lopez, should we head back to your apartment?"

Along a new route, her nose twitched with the warm odors of searing meat. A silver truck at the curb was emblazoned with the bright red, white, and blue of the Puerto Rican flag. "Es un genio chef borinqueño," Mr. Lopez said.

Faye had grown up in Colorado and studied Spanish in school, but her use was rusty. "What kind of genius chef?"

"Lo siento," he apologized. "Borinquén is the former name of our island." He gestured toward the black oven on the sidewalk with the aromatic steam. "You must try adobo-pork. I've seen him out here at three in the morning roasting it."

The two men greeted each other in Spanish like old friends. With a sun-leathered arm, the cook whipped out a machete and whacked off a hunk of meat. He diced it into a paper bowl on top of golden rice, then crowned it with a banana.

Mr. Lopez bowed and handed it to her. The first bite coated her mouth, throat, and nose with a piquant flavor. But he didn't take any food for himself and she remembered the ancient furniture in his apartment. Perhaps he was worried about medical bills.

"Gracias, this is heavenly." Pulling out cash, she said, "How about you? It's my treat."

"Guineo, por favor," he instructed the vendor, and the man mashed a banana with sauce into a cup.

Faye leaned against a graffiti-scrawled building as they finished their lunch. What was it about food? *Cocoon me with comfort, calm my core.*

Faced with the elderly man's slumped body and troubled face, she shared a benediction from her Pentecostal roots. "Let your unfailing love be with us, Lord, even as we put our hope in you."

She tugged up her cloth mask, back into her protective but stifling fabric of separation.

"Juana will be just fine, I know it." Her reassurance was built on faith, not any clinical information, and she prayed it wasn't a false hope.

SEVEN

Bernalillo, New Mexico—Monday, July 12, 2021

Maya raised the rear hatch of her Prius as a woodpecker's rat-tat-tat echoed through the Bosque, the cottonwood wetlands of the Rio Grande River adjacent to Dave's ranch.

Tugging out one of the dark, round containers, he said, "You must have been mighty persuasive with the local health department to get these so quickly." He dropped it into the arms of Braxton, his fourteen-year-old brother.

"What are they called?" Braxton asked.

"BG-Sentinel mosquito traps," Maya answered. "The staff only grumbled a bit."

Dave hauled the remaining three containers to the packed dirt of his driveway. "What did they complain about?"

"Odds are low for Juana getting infected by an *Aedes* bite here, then developing illness so soon after she arrived in New York. It's also unlikely there was enough dengue virus in her blood when she was here to infect local mosquitoes."

"But not impossible." Dave slammed her hatch closed.

"Yup, that's why they gave me the traps. These wetlands are a hotspot for mosquito activity. We'll familiarize ourselves with the equipment today. Juana's family said we can collect mosquitoes on their Corrales property tomorrow."

"Can I help too? My friends will think this is so badass." The lanky teenager bounced on his toes until Dave cuffed his dirty-blond hair.

"Slow down, pardner. This needs to be on the Q-T. Right, Maya?"

She removed her mask. Damned COVID protocols—wearing one outside was overkill. A game of probabilities, like her beloved statistics. Impossible to eliminate risk but worth trying to reduce it some of the time.

"Our work's confidential for now, Braxton." She carried the first trap to the front portal. "*Aedes* mosquitoes feed on people so this is a good spot close to the door, protected from the elements. Where's everyone else, by the way?"

"Emilia's picking up the girls from summer camp with Bo. Like every good dog, his favorite thing is riding in the car with his head out the window."

Maya pulled out the lure cartridge to show Braxton. "Mosquitoes are drawn in by the chemical mix which mimics the odors people give off."

Dave adjusted his weathered cowboy hat, the accumulated dust matching the light brown of his hair. "Not to brag, but yours truly helped with some USDA studies on the best attractant."

Maya took a drink from her bottle. "I'm surprised—dengue is primarily a human threat."

"Hah, so typical." Dave's face displayed his disdain. "You public health guys think the world revolves around human health. But USDA and state ag manage horses and cattle affected by mosquito-borne diseases."

She grinned. "The One Health concept—the health of humans, other animals, and the environment are interrelated. Thanks for the schooling."

Each of them carried a trap as Maya led them to Dave's back portal. Then she placed the third in the barn near the water trough. Teresa's and Lydia's gelding ponies whinnied in anticipation of food while Braxton patted the neck of a larger bay mare.

"Give me a second," he fake-whispered in the horse's ear. "I'll get out under the thumb of these old farts and we'll go for a ride." He shoved the fourth container beneath a bush.

Dave draped his arm around Braxton's shoulders. "All right kid, you're released from duty. Is this a good location, Maya?"

She shifted it to a spot under the cottonwood shadowing the back corner of the corral. "Mosquitoes need to see this—it was designed to be visually appealing."

Emilia's sedan pulled up next to the barn and disgorged two whooping elementary-school girls and one woofing black Lab. All three jumped on Braxton and knocked him to the dirt. "We got ice cream today and you didn't," Teresa screamed.

The adults moved to the back door where Emilia embraced Dave. "The camp's treat came too close to dinnertime. Maya, I didn't realize you were stopping by." Then she noticed the container. "What's this?"

"Mosquito trap." Dave held up the lure cartridge with a posture of pride. "I helped develop this chemical attractant to bring them in."

Emilia frowned. "The kids get enough bites—why would you want to draw them to the house?"

"I'm sorry, it was my idea," Maya said. "I'm investigating a case of dengue fever. The mosquitoes lay eggs in standing water and seek out humans near their homes."

Dark braids flying, Emilia pivoted back to Dave. "So you're luring them in where they could kill our kids!"

Maya flushed—she'd never seen the couple argue, and she was the cause of it. "Dengue is rarely fatal but we're trying to figure out whether to do mosquito control along the Bosque."

Dave rested a hand on Emilia's arm. "The li'l buggers get captured in the trap for testing."

"All of them?" Emilia's voice volume increased to rival her six-foot height. "Number one, you could put them somewhere else on the property. Number two, you need to discuss it with me first, hombre."

She jerked open the back screen door. Within minutes, the banging of pots and pans filtered to the patio.

Maya hugged her arms in exasperation. "We didn't have to do this here. I should have waited until tomorrow to distribute them in Corrales."

He scuffed the dirt. "We've got stuff going on—she's under a lot of stress."

"You didn't mention anything at the rodeo practice on Friday." Maya checked the time on her phone. "It'll take me an hour to get home and I'm still cautious about driving after dark."

"Don't leave yet. I'll help Emilia pull together leftovers for dinner."

Dave and Emilia were among her closest friends. Getting drawn into their fight reminded Maya of the issues associated with having friends who were also work colleagues. Sharing a meal might heal a festering wound.

She headed to the barn while Dave sorted out his marital disagreement. The hay gave her nose a warm tickle. Thank goodness she didn't have allergies like some vets who got overdosed in large animal vet practice. All three kids were feeding their horses apples.

"Get those at camp?" she asked.

"Yeah, Aunt Maya." Teresa, the eight-year-old, was a carbon copy of her mother's dark beauty.

"We brought an extra for Braxton." Lydia, younger by a year, looked more like her dad, rusty-brown hair and lean planes to her face.

Maya was encouraged by Lydia's thoughtfulness. Dave had worried about insertion of his half-brother into the family dynamic. But every time she saw the kids together, they appeared bonded. Braxton had lived with a big family of siblings in a polygamous sect on the Arizona-Utah border, and now he was nurturing his nieces, treating them like sisters.

After twenty minutes of stories about the ponies, Maya heard Dave shout "Food's ready" from the portal. The kids raced each other to the back door, always competitive. While they washed up, Maya removed her mask and set out the earthenware plates painted with horses.

"I'm sorry to be short with you earlier." Emilia removed a steaming bowl of ground round from the microwave. She set it on the knotty pine table as Dave spread out containers of lettuce, sliced tomatoes, and shredded cheese.

"Dave explained more about your study," Emilia said. "Dengue virus freaked me out—one of those exotic diseases we don't think about happening here."

Bo crawled under the table and nestled around Maya's feet, black tail thumping the floor planks. Maya held Dave's and Braxton's hands as Emilia led them in a recitation of grace.

Maya's first family meal with kids since the deaths of Manolo and the baby. Grief's lightning flashed through her body. She took slow abdominal breaths.

Her psychiatrist had warned the first year would be hardest with its reminders of loss. Don't let the feelings hold you back—that was the important thing. Keep going, make new memories in the new normal and the painful ones would hurt less. Eventually.

Everyone assembled their tacos. "We went to the BioPark today," Lydia announced. "My favorite animals were the penguins."

"Those were boring," Teresa interjected. "They don't do anything except squawk and swim. The male lion roared like he was going to break out and attack."

Maya chuckled. "He's just announcing he's king of the zoo. That reminds me of the lion at the religious-themed wildlife park. I never heard of any more animal deaths there from COVID."

"They're going strong," Dave answered. "With all the exhibits outside, people feel pretty safe there."

At dinner's end, Braxton helped Emilia wash the dishes and the girls saddled their ponies for a ride around the arena.

Dave followed Maya to the Prius. "You could spend the night on the couch." The temperature dropped as the sun slipped behind the house and the sky pinkened.

"I should drive more often to get comfortable with it again. My reaction times are slower since COVID."

Dave's laconic, masculine posture often hid any deeper turmoil. But they'd weathered many storms together and he might not get pissed if she pressed him on his marriage.

"Wanna talk about Emilia's stress?" Maya asked.

"We started court proceedings to adopt Braxton." Wings whistling, a dove flapped by, its sight and sound smoothing the mood. But Dave's expression was fierce.

"The sect is fighting it, and there have been occasional strange vehicles pulling into the drive, then leaving when we look out. Emilia's finding it difficult to sleep—me, too."

Maya's stomach clenched in sympathy. "Maybe someone was just lost. You've had no break-ins, no one approaching Braxton?"

Dave shook his head. "Our mother sends letters to him, not me. It's crazy they would fight this. They're the ones who tossed him out for bad behavior, when we know the real reason they eject the lost boys is to reduce competition for the females."

The breeze cooled Maya's bare skin. "It freaks me out for people to live like that in this modern age. I can't believe it's legal."

"Civilizations shifting backward—'end time' approaching, as they would say."

Maya leaned her weight on the Prius hood. "The world's become too scary. Maybe it's better my child never lived."

"Jesus Christ, Maya, don't ever say that!" Dave wrapped a long arm around her shoulder and squeezed. "I shouldn't burden you with our troubles."

She attempted to wrest her mind away from her own losses to her friend's dilemma. "What does Braxton think? He must miss his other brothers and sisters—he's so good with your girls."

"Of course, but he has no desire to return." Dave's laughter sounded like a mature version of Braxton's. "Who'd want to give up TV and video games?"

"You still have those surveillance cameras? You're so isolated back here—I worry about you all."

Dave puffed up his chest. "We're armed and ready for anything, no need to fret."

Maya climbed into her front seat. "I'll install additional mosquito traps in Corrales tomorrow, then I'll swing by. This time, make sure to keep Emilia in the loop."

"Will do. I'm going for positive thinking. I predict no *Aedes* mosquitoes in this area or dengue virus, and you won't continue as the Queen of new zoonotic disease threats in the Southwest."

Uncomfortable with his label, she pulled out to the main road toward the interstate. His optimistic attitude might be half-right. With the warming climate, *Aedes* had already begun to encroach on New Mexico and Arizona. But a locally-acquired dengue infection? That was a bullet they'd likely dodge.

EIGHT

Queens, New York City—Tuesday, July 13, 2021

Dr. Moshe Moskowitz, Faye's boss, prioritized formality and order above all else. The haphazard arrangement of old photos from cat calendars on Faye's three cubicle walls violated his unwritten expectations. She assumed her favorite position—leaning back in her office chair, tennis shoes on the edge of the desk, jumbo coffee in her hand. Only seven AM, but her brain and muscles felt the torpor of a tortoise, following a long Monday assessing the department's dengue guidelines, then connecting with Taylor for their first dinner date at a local restaurant.

Like *Lady and the Tramp*, they had shared every morsel of linguini in vodka sauce, washed down with too much Riesling. But the romantic atmosphere and flavors lighting up her tongue didn't stop her from pumping Taylor for details on Juana.

Taylor's dark eyes, accented by eyeliner, shifted from the food to Faye. "I wish I had better news. She's having problems with chest fluid and breathing. We may need to put her on a ventilator."

"I showed Mr. Lopez places where mosquitoes could lay eggs. It made his grief worse, like it was his fault Juana became deathly ill."

"Her exposure is still likely Puerto Rico." Taylor offered a spoonful of soursop ice cream. "You'd think she was your kid, you worry so much. Spend the night with me and I'll distract you."

Faye declined the invitation, planning an extensive review of dengue virus. Taylor offered to walk her home, leading her out the back way to cut off several blocks from the route.

Halfway down the narrow alley, passion unleashed feverish kisses and frenetic clothing adjustments. Faye was lifted into the air, her legs locked around Taylor's waist. Their conflagration peaked, then left them panting as Taylor lowered her to the ground. Lips bruised like a ripe tomato, limbs limp like noodles—Faye yearned for another bite.

"That was unexpected, and nice." She stroked Taylor's dexterous fingers. "An advantage of your not getting any male-to-female surgery."

"I prefer to maintain all options." Taylor adjusted the wig and kept an arm draped over Faye's shoulders when they reached the street.

But Faye refused a chaperone for the rest of the walk home. "Don't forget, I'm a Broadway baby who went to musicals alone until the pandemic."

Moshe raced into her cubicle, interrupting Faye's memories of the ardent after-dinner blaze. "I don't know why you're proposing any guideline changes. In five years, we've had over two hundred imported dengue cases. This little girl, no matter how tragic, won't change our policies."

Faye dropped her feet and spun in her chair. "Nothing major." She'd learned long ago to act deferential, on occasion, to her younger supervisor. He needed to experience respect from others, although the times he didn't give it were too numerous to count.

"I updated the list of labs to include the Mayo Clinic," she said.

His skin and eyes were so light in color, he could have been taken for a corpse, except for the scents of eucalyptus aftershave and coconut-infused hair conditioner. He'd bragged about his favorite grooming products during a slightly tipsy holiday party. Not being chemically sensitive, Faye didn't mind. The odors were pleasing, compensating for his occasional Napoleonic outbursts.

"Did the Wadsworth Lab in Albany approve adding a new one?" he asked.

Faye twinged with a slight crick in her neck. "Yes, and I checked with CDC. When you authorize this update, we'll post it on the website and distribute it to medical providers."

Next she handed him their *Fight the Bite* pamphlet. "This only mentions West Nile and Zika viruses. I'd like the health educators to squeeze in dengue, too."

"All right, but it stays on the shelf until we have more local cases." His eyes narrowed. "Don't go jumping the gun on me."

She flashed a twinkling smile. "Ah, come on, Moshe. When have you known this staid old lady to be impetuous?" Other than last night, the devil on her shoulder whispered.

He seemed to miss her joke. "You dashed off to London and Saudi Arabia for a single imported case of Middle East Respiratory Syndrome."

Irritated with his holding a grudge for eight years, she countered, "MERS was a new coronavirus. We didn't want it spreading person-to-person here. Luckily it's not as contagious as COVID, but we didn't know that then."

The discussion flashed her back to Kareem, her investigation host and momentary fling. He didn't list Faye as a coauthor but included her name in the acknowledgments—that was enough. Mixing work and play—never a good idea.

So why was she breaking her rule for Taylor?

The Bronx, New York City—Tuesday, July 13, 2021

Faye and Daniel Toussaint from the Office of Vector Surveillance and Control took the subway to the South Bronx. By the time they walked up to the housing complex where Mr. Lopez lived, Faye discovered Daniel's parents had been teachers killed with their students in the 2010 Haitian earthquake. An aunt in Queens took him in, and he did well in school.

"The wife of one of our CDC field supervisors is from Haiti," Faye said. "Her accent is easy on the ears, like yours. I wish I knew more French, but growing up in Colorado, I only studied Spanish."

She envied Daniel's wide smile. Her family couldn't afford braces so she often smiled with her lips closed to hide her crooked teeth.

"French is used by educators like my parents," he said, "or the elites. Haitian Creole blends French with Taíno, the language of our indigenous people, and some languages from West Africa."

"Well, as long as you speak mosquito, I'm happy." She showed him the areas at the building perimeter where water accumulated.

He crouched and examined the surface of a small pool, then raised the brim of his Mets cap. She felt a ripple of fondness for him at their common sports fandom, on top of their shared concerns about vector-borne diseases.

"With dengue," Faye said, "I'm worried about *Aedes aegypti* and *Aedes albopictus*, but I know your primary focus is on the West Nile virus *Culex* species."

He pulled a ladle from his backpack and pointed to the pool. "See those wigglers?"

The tiny larvae hung down from the water surface, breathing through their siphons. After Daniel skimmed them up, Faye grabbed a pipette to suck them out of the ladle cup and transfer them into an empty jar in his other hand.

He marked the location on the jar and held it up. "These look like *Culex*—they have longer siphons than *Aedes*. We'll make the final ID in the lab."

"Others might be hiding at the bottom. I heard they sometimes dive when people approach."

"We could wait for ten minutes to see if they come back up." He dug in his pack and pulled out a package with a donut-shaped larvicide. "Or we can obliterate the little suckers."

"That's a mosquito dunk, right? Can you remind me how it works?"

"It has a soil bacterium with toxins to target mosquito and blackfly larvae."

Faye appreciated his preparation, but had children on the brain. "If we drop it in here, we can't keep kids from seeing it or handling it."

"It's sold over-the-counter to homeowners and isn't a risk to humans, only slightly irritating to the skin or eyes." He kicked at the packed dirt to bury the mosquito pool and smother the larvae. "But we'll take a more old-fashioned approach. I'll get the Housing Authority to improve landscaping on the entire property."

Faye followed his example until the water disappeared, then led him the few blocks to the broken tire swing still lying on the ground. Kids in an apparent parkour race ricocheted off the tire's surface.

Daniel waved his hand. "Hey guys, give me five minutes." He reached inside the rim and pulled up some water with his pipette.

"Can I try?" one wide-eyed boy asked, appearing in awe of the scientist with dark skin like his, and much closer in age than Faye.

Daniel was patient and guided him in the technique, coming up empty most of the time without being able to see the water hidden in the tire. But when they sucked up a larva, the kid danced and screamed to the others, "Look, I got one!"

Faye's phone chimed with a FaceTime call and she separated herself from the group of enthusiastic kids.

"We lost her." Taylor's stricken face reflected the awful news. "Neurologic function deteriorated and we couldn't counteract her failure to clot. Also secondary sepsis—lab tests are pending to identify the bacterial overgrowth in her system."

As a light drizzle began, raindrops on Faye's bare arms felt like the tears of the universe. "It's not possible. The dengue mortality rate should be low." She grabbed a tree for support and glanced down the street. "We're not far from her grandfather's apartment—does he know?"

Taylor grimaced. "Yes, he was at her bedside with the family. We had a couple hours' notice that things were going south, so they had time to arrive."

"Okay." Taking a deep breath, she pushed on. "My field investigation feels kinda wasted." She rubbed her fist against her breastbone. Her day's activities weren't nearly as important as the grief of Juana's family and her hospital caregivers.

"How are you doing, Taylor? I can cook dinner to help you decompress. That's one thing we haven't done yet. Being raised on a ranch, my mother taught me a few tricks."

Taylor swiveled, ICU sign coming into view. "I'm not sure when I can get away. We need to confirm what went wrong. I'll keep in touch."

The video cut out before Faye had a chance to say goodbye. She remained leaning against the tree until Daniel came to find her.

"You think you have your whole life ahead of you," she muttered. "I'm like an armadillo caught on the highway with traffic racing toward me in both directions. Juana just died and I haven't a clue which way to turn first."

NINE

Albuquerque, New Mexico—Tuesday, July 13, 2021

In the ninety-degree heat, Dave helped his youngest daughter cast her line into the Children's Pond at Tingley Beach. Maya adjusted her cap to block sunrays from her dark hair, then put a worm on his older daughter's hook.

Teresa wrested her rod away. "I'm eight, I don't need no help like my baby sister."

"You go, girl." Maya flashed a big smile. "Next time, you can do the worm, too."

"I'm bored." Braxton's long limbs spread like a Daddy-Longlegs from the folding chair. "Why can't I fish here?"

"See that sign? It's twelve and under, kid." Dave tossed him his keys. "Get your rod from the truck and head over to Central Pond. But keep in touch with your phone and don't leave the area."

Maya and Dave stood back as the girls jiggled their rods. "Wait for the catfish to come to you," Dave called out. "Don't reel it in until you feel a jerk."

"Are you comfortable with Braxton going off on his own?" Maya asked.

Dave pulled out an additional chair and invited Maya to join him. "He's fourteen and lived on the streets of St. George before we brought him home. He knows how to take care of himself. Nobody's gonna kidnap him in such a crowded area."

Maya shivered despite the intense sun. "I can't imagine living with the possibility of losing any of your kids."

"I don't think the sect wants Braxton back. The Prophet's just mad I've got him now, corrupting his soul."

"I'm not sure I'll ever take the risk of having children again. They're too vulnerable, and we can't always protect them."

Dave rested his calloused hand on her arm. "Maya, it's less than a year since you lost Manolo and your baby. You've got plenty of time for a new family."

"Well, I appreciate this little fishing distraction. I'm tuckered out from mosquito collection. COVID's cut back my stamina."

"Papa, I got one!" Lydia called out and Dave ran to help her.

FaceTime on Maya's phone chimed and she saw Faye's stricken face. "What's going on?" Maya asked. "Did something happen?"

Faye rubbed her reddened eyes. "Juana didn't make it." She paused for a sip from the soda cup, then went on. "We're developing a mosquito surveillance plan to include in tomorrow's press release."

A mini-volcano erupted in Maya's stomach and pushed up through her esophagus. She swallowed hard to counter the acid taste. Never having met Juana, she shouldn't feel this gut punch. But Faye's attachment to the girl was a revelation. Her older mentor had never shown any particular fondness for children.

The burning in Maya's throat spread throughout her chest. It was only two hours since she met Juana's cousin and grandmother when she placed mosquito traps at their Corrales home. They must have been called about her death after she left.

"I, uh, thanks for the heads-up. I'll retrieve the traps around their home tomorrow." She hoped for the strength to help the Lopez family with their grief.

Dave and his daughters strolled back along the bank of the pond, Lydia carrying a bucket.

"Faye, keep me posted." Maya stumbled over what to offer a much-older mentor. *I'm sorry for your loss* didn't quite apply to a situation that clearly affected Faye but wasn't personal.

"Shoot me any recommendations for dengue surveillance or control steps we should take here in New Mexico."

Faye nodded and the screen turned to black. Lydia shoved her bucket into Maya's lap, revealing a whiskered catfish.

"A three-pounder, I think," Dave said. "Perfect size for dinner.

And it's not large enough to accumulate much mercury from the water."

"Way to take the fun out of Lydia's catch," Maya groused.

Dave frowned. "What's got the bee in your bonnet? You know our risk assessment brains never turn off."

Maya glanced at the girls. "That situation I'm working on—the index case didn't make it."

He winced, then ruffled Lydia's hair. "Let's get on home and show Mom your prize."

"Aw, Dad, what about me?" Teresa whined. "I want one too."

Dave pivoted from his older daughter to Maya. "Join us for dinner—this one's big enough to share. Teresa, we'll come back again next week for your turn."

Maya hesitated, unwilling to impose her morose mood on the Schwartz family. Her psychiatrist had advised against letting grief cut her off from friends.

She forced a grin and took Lydia's hand. "That's quite a catch—I'd love to help you eat it."

After folding up her chair, she handed it to Dave. "I can retrieve Braxton while you get the girls to your truck."

Central Pond was crowded but no dirty-blond teen. How many fishing areas could there be? Panic flooded her limbs until she found him at the catch-and-release pond. "Hey Braxton, you didn't want catfish for dinner? Lydia got one."

He turned and smiled. "Hi, Aunt Maya, trout are more fun."

"Good, you take after Dave. He never saw a mountain he didn't want to climb."

Braxton's face screwed up with confusion. "I don't remember him doing that."

Maya laughed. "Sorry, I was being metaphorical. He's courageous and likes taking on new challenges. We should all be like him."

Braxton reeled in his lure. "I think you're brave, too. Dad told me some of your adventures. The time you guys were looking for sick antelope and got busted by the border patrol—that was dope."

His referring to Dave as Dad startled Maya but the family had been open about adoption plans. "Well, I'm here to corral you. We're headed home." The pull of the Schwartz ranch contrasted sharply with the dread of going back to her own apartment, desolate without Manolo.

Corn-on-the-cob and pan-fried catfish coated with creole seasoning—a delicious dinner. Maya had planned to drive the fifty miles to Santa Fe until Emilia offered the couch. She handed Maya a cotton gown.

"Short on me but full-length for you, just right on our cool evenings."

"Thanks, I'm exhausted—I should have passed on the wine."

Maya cleaned up in the bathroom, then jumped onto the couch as Bo nestled in his dog bed on the floor. She adjusted the down pillow and pulled the blanket up to her chin.

Fresh air wafted in from the nearby Rio Grande and Maya recognized the deep trill of an acrobatic nighthawk diving to impress his mate. The nature cues and Emilia's faint giggle behind the bedroom door flashed Maya back to tent camping a year earlier with Manolo.

Maya had suggested a backyard reenactment of their first time making love in Chaco National Park. They prioritized a break from the chaos of his relocation from Phoenix.

Manolo unfolded the nylon tent as she tried to distract him, tracing the abdominal muscles above his cargo shorts. He glanced at the wood fences on either side of the grassy yard and lowered his voice. "Wait 'til we have this erected—then you can start your foreplay."

"Can't wait to work on another erection." She spread out the tarp. "Do you wish we were in a campground?"

He grimaced. "No time, we're still moving my stuff."

She kissed his furrowed brow. "The weekend before we get married should be fun, not stressed out. We can rent a storage locker and postpone the final decision about what to keep."

The tent pole dropped to the grass and he pulled her in for a deep kiss. Then he cupped her face as their dark eyes locked. "My brain's on a racetrack with dying patients."

She reached for a tent pole. "I'll get your mind off everything."

When Maya unrolled two foam pads on the tent floor, Manolo joined the sleeping bags together. "It's too warm to zip these up like at Chaco," he said.

She spread out a single sheet and light blanket retrieved from the couch. Seconds later, her clothes were crumpled in the corner and she knelt in a provocative pose, arching her back.

His own shorts joined hers and he tugged her down on top of him. "I'm looking forward to a lifetime of this, skin to skin. Don't ever think of wearing pajamas, even when you're eighty and wrinkled."

"I promise." She adjusted her position. "Your months of training me to ride my favorite Puerto Rican stallion are going to pay off, mi amor."

A heavy weight on Maya's legs yanked her out of the sexy memory and she reached down to feel Bo's fur. "You're crazy, there's not enough room on the couch for both of us."

But she didn't have the heart to give up a fuzzy cuddle. She drifted off with her hand on the Labrador Retriever's head, a chorus of whinnies from the barn, and a faint hoo-hoo-hoo-hoo from a Great Horned Owl.

Corrales, New Mexico—Wednesday, July 14, 2021

A young man in his twenties opened the carved pine door when Maya rang the bell at ten AM. "Mr. Burgos, I'm so sorry to bother you after the news about your cousin, but I'm here to retrieve the mosquito traps."

He reached back to rub his neck. "Uh, yeah, go ahead. They took Grandma to the hospital last night—losing her only granddaughter hit her hard."

Juana had visited because her grandmother was dying of lung cancer. "This is a rough time," Maya said. "I won't need your help."

With her own losses, she ought to be more proficient at

a comforting response, but stumbled over her words with a sudden brain freeze. "I'll email the dengue results, I mean on the mosquitoes…as soon as I get them."

She examined the catch bag on the first trap near the front door and verified mosquitoes. After moving the trap to her Prius, she headed around the side of the house to the goat corral. On her way back to the car, the young man came out to help.

"Thanks, Mr. Burgos, but I can manage by myself."

"Grandma had a bad headache and some eye pain when they took her in last night, but they told us that fits with her cancer. I've got the same thing today. I kinda ache all over—my muscles, bones, and joints."

Maya tried to keep her voice steady. "Did you take your temperature?"

"No. I'll do that."

With no local cases ever reported from the Southwest, Maya tried to convince herself it wasn't dengue, but she still needed to follow up.

"If you develop fever, vomiting, or bleeding, call your doctor and mention we're testing your property for dengue-infected mosquitoes. They're the threat, not your couple of days in contact with Juana."

"Thanks, Dr. Maguire. The sun's getting to me—I'll head inside."

She shifted the second trap into the hatch of her car. "Please call with any questions. I want to help your family any way I can." After escorting him into the cave-like living room kept cool by massive adobe walls, she retrieved her final two traps from the back porch and the farm's milking parlor.

Two Holsteins relaxed in the hay, chewing their cud as a barn cat pounced on the twitching tails. The animals were oblivious to the risk of death—death that stalked their human companions after each *Aedes* mosquito bite. Animals like the barn occupants had little to worry about, unless something changed.

TEN

The Bronx, New York City—Wednesday, July 14, 2021

"Got one." Faye swung the hand net toward the family photos in the Lopez apartment.

Daniel Toussaint picked up the battery-powered aspirator. "Keep it against the wall so it doesn't escape." He lifted a corner of the net, sucked up the mosquito into the small collection cup, and snapped on a lid. With a black marker, he labeled it with 'living room,' the date, time, and address.

Faye took a quick slurp from her coffee. "I'm glad Mr. Lopez could stay with a friend so we're not bothering him so early."

Spiky dreads pulled back into a high man-bun, dark skin pearled with sweat, Daniel radiated a picture of youthful energy and concern. "You live in Manhattan, right?"

"Yes. Thanks for bringing the equipment." Tugging open the drapes, she corralled another mosquito against the window. "My alarm went off at five but I was already awake."

She flushed with a woozy memory. After a warning text, Taylor had appeared at midnight with Sparkling Pointe 2015 Séduction Blanc de Noirs Méthode Champenoise. First they shed tipsy tears and cheers to Juana's courageous life cut short, then smothered each other with gliding strokes and tender kisses.

Having missed breakfast, Faye concealed a burp tasting only of fruit-flavored alcohol. "Growing up on a Colorado ranch, I'm imprinted by early morning chores. But I'm lazier in my dotage."

Daniel labeled a second container. "I'm glad you're still excited about the work—tells me the job won't get boring. Do you think about retirement?"

She reflected on her grief over Juana's death. The inevitable illnesses and deaths of friends and family were bad enough. When she turned sixty-five at the start of the pandemic, it wasn't the time to bail. But like a police officer who spent her career fighting crime, bad days tackling microbial villains took their toll.

"If the President lifts the COVID public health emergency—that'll be my cue to spend time on kitties and Broadway shows."

"I sure won't mind ditching these masks," Daniel said.

A mosquito buzzed close to Faye's ear. Her net flashed in a rapid reflex to catch it.

"Three for three," Daniel complimented. "You're either a mosquito magnet or have a knack for vector control work, if you want to get out of the office more often."

"We'll see," she answered. "COVID's hunkering-in-place has me itching to break free."

"The protocol says two hours of collection so let's keep going," Daniel said. "Then I'll treat for a coffee break." He looked in her open paper cup. "I think you'll be ready for a refill by then."

The Bronx, New York City—Friday, July 16, 2021

The Requiem Mass was traditional and poignant. Faye coughed when the priest in white vestments waved incense as he circled the closed coffin, granting Juana absolution from her sins.

Not that Juana could possibly have any sins to be forgiven, but Faye kept her thoughts to herself. She was already self-conscious about their standing out as a short, drab older woman alongside her taller escort, muscled form hidden under a conservative dark men's suit. No makeup, no wig, nothing to indicate Taylor's transgender identity.

Everyone else appeared to be a relative or neighbor, most having spoken to each other in Spanish before the service. When the funeral concluded and pallbearers carried out the white-draped casket, a pianist played *On Eagle's Wings*. Faye remembered lyrics about the loved one being borne to the sun on eagle wings, to shine forever like the sun.

"I want to say something to Mr. Lopez," Faye whispered to Taylor.

On the front steps, she popped open her floral umbrella as the firmament drowned them in sorrow. Not having a black one, she rationalized the vivid color as an homage to Juana's exuberance in the few times Faye met her in the hospital.

Juana's grandfather shook hands with everyone, and no one except Faye and Taylor wore masks. "Señor Lopez, we're so sorry for your loss."

Faye wasn't familiar with the Catholic ceremony but remembered her Pentecostal traditions from her parents' funerals. "I know she's with God in a state of immortality." Her own beliefs about an afterlife were muddled, but if anyone went straight to Heaven, it was Juana.

"Muchas gracias," Mr. Lopez answered. "You each went beyond your duty in helping our family."

Taylor cradled the man's hand. "We're hoping for more test results soon. It won't ease your suffering, but perhaps understanding what happened will bring some closure."

"God needed another angel—that's the only explanation." Mr. Lopez turned away to comfort a sobbing older woman.

Faye tucked into a small corner table next to an expansive mural of an Italian cathedral. "I should be healthy and order a Caesar salad," she told Taylor. "But all I'm craving is comfort food."

"The manicotti with spinach is good."

Faye raised her eyebrows. "I wonder if there are any culinary opportunities in the City you haven't tried."

Taylor smiled. "I don't have time or inclination to cook. Besides, eating out alone is a good chance to check out the ladies."

"Okay…"

She should have expected Taylor had other ways to find dates beyond the Halloween parade. She didn't like the reminder that she wasn't Taylor's only hookup, but couldn't expect more given her own lack of commitment to the relationship.

They both ordered the manicotti. When the waiter turned away, Taylor said, "I'm teasing you. I told you my pickups are rare. There was something irresistible about your off-key belting of *No One Mourns the Wicked* at the Greenwich parade."

"Almost eight years ago—I'd never inflict that on someone today. I guess everyone's voice deteriorates with age, except maybe Tony Bennett."

"As long as he keeps doing duets with Lady Gaga, I'm happy." Taylor handed Faye the bread basket.

She buttered a piece, then considered whether to bring down the mood. But she needed to understand what went wrong with Juana. "Tell me about the autopsy."

"Nothing definitive. Tuesday morning before she crashed, her serum ferritin levels were high, suggesting hemophagocytic syndrome or HPS."

"I don't remember enough to understand that." Faye was reminded that she didn't have the bandwidth for clinical medicine.

"It's an intense form of inflammation especially in the bone marrow, which increases the iron-containing protein complex, ferritin."

"So that's what killed her?"

"Unsure. The blood clot in her spine led to the paralysis, and liver deterioration was documented on autopsy. Sequencing from bone marrow confirmed she had the DENV-1 serotype."

"Did her cystic fibrosis play a role?"

Taylor twisted a napkin. "Uh, one doctor started a platelet transfusion to deal with the bleeding. But that can increase fluid in the lungs, particularly bad for someone who already has a compromised respiratory system."

"Is that doc in trouble?"

"We can't fault him for not being on top of all dengue complexities—it's too rare here. Each treatment choice is a balance between risks and benefits."

After the waiter delivered the pasta, Faye took a bite. "Anything else to help explain her death?"

"Dengue is more severe the second time. But as far as we know, this was her first infection."

"So I guess it was her cystic fibrosis."

"It likely played a role," Taylor said. "Juana's parents could barely stand up for the readings at the funeral. I'll call her grandfather tomorrow morning."

"Perhaps at his age—my age—he's a bit more realistic about the threat of death."

"Anything back on your mosquito tests?"

"Not yet. I hate to eat and run, but I promised Moshe I wouldn't take a whole day of annual leave. Plus I need to check in with Daniel on those results."

Taylor leaned over the table for a kiss. "No problem. I realize it's bad timing with everything going on, but when can we plan a second official date?"

Faye blushed, remembering the Monday night dinner and sex in the alley. She dropped her purse and felt stiff when bending over to retrieve it. "You mean a third date. Doesn't the Mets game count?"

"You only called me last-minute because one of your health department colleagues bailed."

"Who's counting?" Did she want to encourage Taylor's push for a date or keep it more to business? What the hell, Monday's brief romp in the alley still glowed deep in her private areas.

"Let me find out if our mosquitoes indicate Juana's dengue has spread," Faye said. "Then I'll know if I have the weekend free."

"All right, but this time I want to surprise you with something more than just sharing a meal."

She shrugged and smiled her acquiescence. The mosquitoes were likely to be negative and Taylor was creative enough to plan something diverting.

ELEVEN

Santa Fe, New Mexico—Friday, July 16, 2021

"It's painful for me to know that nearly every death we are seeing now from COVID-19 could have been prevented. I say that as someone who has lost ten family members to COVID-19, and who wishes each and every day that they had had the opportunity to get vaccinated."

Maya's skin prickled as the Surgeon General's interview was broadcast on *Washington Week*. Chilled by his warning and the cool evening, she got up from the couch and closed her kitchen window. Ten family members—she'd lost only three. Yet he continued the fight, so she had no excuse not to do the same.

FaceTime flashed on her phone with a call from Manolo's sister and Maya turned off the TV. Her stomach pinched. Ramona had started the habit of communicating with Maya's parents when she was in the COVID coma, and rarely checked in as Maya recovered. She had considered the Mirandas her second family, and missed them with an ache deeper than the Grand Canyon.

Should she answer the call? They never answered hers. She propped the phone on the table and swiped her finger. Ramona and Sebastian both came into view, neither smiling.

"We understand your travels are over and you're back to work full time," Manolo's father said, creases around his dark eyes framing them with hardened heartache. His face was a preview of Manolo's, if he'd lived long enough to turn sixty. Maya was tortured by the thought and rushed on to break the ice.

"Sebastian, thanks for checking in. I'm trying to get my feet under me. Are you calling to schedule Manolo's celebration of life?"

"In time with his birthday, we want a funeral service here." Ramona's hair, pulled into a tight ponytail, made her expression more severe. Only thirty-six, Ramona looked much older, new white hairs streaking the black.

Maya had considered something more uplifting for the ceremony in Manolo's beloved Southwest. "I, uh, do New York's COVID rules allow funerals now?"

"Yes, they were updated last month," Sebastian said.

Ramona added, "At limited occupancy with people masked and distanced."

Knocked back by their stern expressions, Maya tried to explain her thinking. "I understand, but some of his friends and colleagues suggested honoring him on the anniversary of his death."

"That's too late." Ramona's words were the texture of tiny pebbles. "Delta variant is spreading and hitting younger people."

"As you're aware," Sebastian said, "COVID risk increases in the fall. Approval for public events could be rescinded again."

Maya brushed her bangs from her eyes. Of course she knew that, but had been preoccupied with making sure Manolo was remembered on the day he died.

"And we will bury his remains here in a local Catholic crypt." Ramona stated their intent with no hesitation or discussion.

Maya twisted away. She didn't want to reveal her distress but couldn't stop the reflex reaction. As Manolo's wife, she had the legal right to decide. How far would they push this?

Time to confront the elephant in the room. "Sebastian and Ramona, I don't know how much of this is coming from your continued concern that I caused Manolo's death."

She recalled their handwritten letter in January.

We're starting a New Year without him. You didn't need to go to Europe, then spread your infection. We rejoiced that he survived anthrax, and never expected this. How can any of us go on without his bright light?

Maya tried to keep any complaint from her tone. "As I replied to your note this winter when I could write again…I'm grieving to the depths of the ocean that I made him sick. Of course if I could turn back time and not go to Denmark, I would."

She wiped tears leaking from her eyes. "I'm sorry…truly, deeply sorry…for what I took away from all of us. But he wouldn't want us locked in place, overcome with misery." She straightened her spine and forced a fierce gaze, tossing the words in their letter back at them. "That's not honoring his bright light."

"Regrets won't bring them back," Ramona said.

They were finally acknowledging the baby's loss. Maya had to find a compromise.

"Let me figure out a way for your service this summer and a fall ceremony with his friends. I'll call you back soon. Give my love to Abdi and Johnny."

She hoped that mention of Ramona's husband and son would remind them of her close connection with all of Manolo's immediate family.

They didn't respond and she hung up, then pulled the drapes to block the outside world.

Turning into bed early, she slipped on a sleep mask but it didn't deter Manolo's voice from echoing in her head. "Of course you won't go overseas."

His words were as clear as the late August day when she informed him of the European mink investigation. When he relented and dropped her at the airport, he told her, "I don't want you to endanger our baby." His final warning when kissing her goodbye was "Please be careful."

She'd been scrupulous about wearing full personal protective equipment around the infected animals. Her strain matched the UK variant—apparently her exposure was the time she removed her mask to eat in Heathrow.

The association of infection with food had killed her hunger ever since, although the problems with taste and smell didn't help. Like Mom always said, gluttony was one of the seven deadly sins. She could have held off eating until she was in a less crowded area.

"Careful, be careful." Manolo's words repeated in an endless loop that tightened around her stomach, squeezing it down to a marble.

Santa Fe, New Mexico—Saturday, July 17, 2021

A night of Manolo's imaginary recriminations eliminated her appetite. She sipped a cup of peppermint tea and waffled on how to use her day off. The dengue test results for her mosquito collections were still pending, and she'd heard nothing new about Juana's relatives in Corrales.

A trill drew her to the sliding glass door, and a small gray bird flitted off the fence. Now that Nancy was living together with Dr. Grinwold in Santa Fe, perhaps they could take her out on a birdwatching trip to learn the local species.

The phone ring startled her away from enjoying the morning outside. She rushed back in to grab it from the bedroom, the name of the epidemiology secretary flashing on her screen. "Stephanie, are you home from your national park tour?"

"Yes, it was fabulous," the older woman answered. "How's Dr. Grinwold handling the office and Nancy's big move?"

"Well, he's crotchety. I'm guessing he missed having you as his office wife."

Stephanie snickered. "He can't survive without me. Hey, after my five-hour drive yesterday from Mesa Verde, I need to get out and stretch my legs. Want to join me on a hike?"

Exploring the local trails was something Maya had planned to do with Manolo. Other than the Rail Trail near her apartment, she'd barely scratched the surface of the beautiful areas to explore. "Sure, where should we meet?"

"Let me give you a ride. We'll do the Two Mile Pond Loop. Can you be ready soon?"

An hour later, they took a break on a bench overlooking the pond, a mirror of the sky's brilliant blue. From shores hemmed in by dense bushes, rolling hills of junipers and piñon pines rose away on all sides.

"Look, it's a beaver." Stephanie plucked at Maya's sleeve.

The brown body created a small wake; its black eyes hovered at the surface. As a couple with a babbling infant in a carrier joined them at the overlook, the animal slapped its tail and disappeared.

Maya wasn't sure which tugged at her heart more. She never tired of magical moments with animals in nature, but the family who quickly headed out on the trail reminded her of precious adventures stolen by COVID. Her child would have been about two months old, and she had imagined excursions like this.

"You look rejuvenated by your vacation," Maya said.

Stephanie combed her gray-streaked dark curls with her fingers and adjusted her straw hat. "It was my first time in Bryce and Zion after Tony's death. I wasn't sure if I could enjoy them without him, but it was just different."

"What do you mean?" Maya had visited the same parks with her parents.

"This time, I was more outward-oriented, open to meeting strangers. The rangers, the tourists—without my husband, I engaged more with others."

Maya sipped from her water bottle. "That's one reason I went to Thailand and China after Manolo's death, to turn my focus outside myself. But if my attorney hadn't paid my fine, I might still be stuck there."

"No risk, no reward. And you're functioning at your usual max level, according to Dr. Grinwold. He mentioned you were out of the office to investigate dengue virus."

"I'm just worried about keeping up. My insomnia's knocking me back a bit."

Should she ask if Stephanie's dead husband visited her in dreams so real that even her senses of smell and touch were stimulated? But despite their close friendship, they were work colleagues. Stephanie had seen Maya's anxiety disorder and its consequences. It wouldn't be wise to have the office think she'd gone off the deep end one more time.

"I used to spend free time watching old movies," Maya

continued. "There's a horror film called *Fear of the Dark*, about how fear impacts people. Those images, and others, haunt me at night."

A mated pair of ruddy ducks glided into view. The male's dark tail and cap feathers rose as he beat his blue bill against his red neck. Creating a swirl of bubbles, he completed his display with a sound like a belch. Attracted, the tawny brown female floated closer.

Maya and Stephanie both pulled out binoculars from their packs and the ducks dove under water.

"We weren't quick or quiet enough," Stephanie said. She swiveled to face Maya. "You need to erase those types of films from your menu."

"I don't watch them anymore, but they're cemented in my brain."

"I recommend distraction. I used to fall asleep to the TV but the changing images woke me up. Books on tape worked for a while, but physical movements to change cassettes or CDs interrupted my drowsy state. Now I listen to podcasts on my cell phone."

Maya wondered why that hadn't occurred to her. "Any particular ones?"

Stephanie's lips stretched into a tentative grin. "I'm watching *The Bachelorette* on TV and my favorite podcast is *Bachelor Happy Hour*. Too low brow for you?"

Maya giggled. "I wouldn't have guessed you're a romance fan."

"Hun, when you've gone as long without a spouse as me, you become one. But there are others—news, short stories, even erotica."

Pivoting away to hide a blush, Maya placed her water bottle in her pack. "On that note, we should head back. I've got to get in some phone calls for dengue today."

Stephanie pulled into Maya's parking area as dark slabs of cloud raced each other to slam against the peaks to their northeast.

"Glad you dragged me out early so we missed the summer storm," Maya said.

"Happy to do it. I'm always available to talk."

Maya swiped at her eyes. "Last night, Manolo's family called. They insist on a Catholic funeral in New York and burying him there. I'd been slowly working my mind up to an outdoor ceremony here on October 6."

Stephanie put her hand on Maya's shoulder. "Forgive me if I'm saying too much. The cremains…can you split them in half so they can do what they want?"

"Maybe. It's hard to plan anything with them. They still blame me for Manolo's death."

Stephanie's usual sunny expression turned angry. "That's ridiculous. He spent all his time caring for COVID patients. He could have come down with it at any point."

"I know, but our variants matched the UK variant, lineage B.1.1.7, which wasn't reported in any numbers in the US until later last fall. If only he'd lived long enough to be vaccinated, he might have survived infection."

"You can't go down that path of thinking." Stephanie undid her seatbelt and rotated to face Maya. "Tony and I used to be smokers. Did he get his lung cancer from his smoking or mine? I'll never know, and it torments me. But he'd be pissed as hell if I blamed myself and stopped living."

Raindrops pelted the windshield as Maya unbuckled her own belt. "I need to hang around you more often—you're great at advice and pep talks. Thanks again for the hike. Just what the doctor ordered."

"Good luck with Manolo's folks. In their hearts, they still know you're a good person."

Maya dashed for her apartment door and dug out her house keys. Stephanie rolled down her window and shouted over the increasing din on the roof of Maya's small porch. "Have dinner with me soon. Quetzy misses you."

Raindrops dripped from Maya's hair to her face. "You think your macaw remembers me?"

"You know that animals are smarter than we think. Stop by and we'll find out." Stephanie waved and her sedan rolled away.

Once inside, Maya dropped her pack to the table just as her phone rang. "Armand, I was about to call you. How are you doing?"

The young man was so quiet, Maya could hardly hear him. "I'm at the hospital. Grandma just passed away."

"Armand, I'm so sorry to hear that." Maya wracked her brain. What kind of cancer did Mrs. Burgos have? Then she remembered. Lung cancer, like Stephanie's husband. That was likely her cause of death, not dengue.

"I haven't talked to you since Wednesday," she continued. "I assume you never developed a fever?"

"Not until this morning. My muscle and bone aches are worse, and I vomited. Before that, the hospital let us be with Grandma, all suited up, one at a time. I was holding her hand as she said her final goodbye. I thought I was feeling shitty from her death, but the doc says my temp is 102.3."

Vertigo hit with the unexpected news. "Armand, are you getting tested for dengue?"

"I'm going to the lab now. They said they might admit me. Dengue's got them freaked out."

Maya carried the phone as she headed for her bedroom. "We don't know for sure that's what we're dealing with, but we'll be on top of it. Do what the doctors tell you and I'll be in touch."

She stripped off her damp clothes and jumped into a hot shower. Her quiet weekend evaporated with the steam.

TWELVE

Manhattan, New York City—Saturday, July 17, 2021

The portly Falstaff, bedeviled by dancing and drumming West African spirits, moved down the aisle of Central Park's Delacorte Theatre, close enough for Faye to touch. Characters on stage in Ankara print dresses and red grass skirts revealed all the secrets of the *Merry Wives* before breaking into hip-thrusting leaps and bows as the audience clapped.

When the cast disappeared and the crowd rose to leave, Taylor led Faye out an exit of the open-air arena. Swept along by hundreds of other jubilant patrons, Faye clung to Taylor until they found some protection under a tree from misty showers.

She lifted Taylor's fingers to her throat. "Feel that? My pulse is still beating in rhythm to the performance. Shakespeare didn't write musicals but this adaptation sure set my ocean in motion."

Using one end of Taylor's red print sash draped over a gold sleeveless blouse, Faye dabbed raindrops from the bangs of Taylor's Cher wig.

In response, Taylor reached down to feather Faye's frizzled curls. "You look like a drowned rat. But one cute enough to tuck in my bag and keep next to my heart forever."

"Squeak, squeak." Faye feigned insult. "Our forgotten umbrellas wouldn't fit with your African queen look. You should have joined the cast on stage."

She stroked Taylor's full-length patchwork skirt of blue and green panels. "How did you pull this off? I thought attending this performance was last-minute."

"A patient got tickets through the digital lottery, then couldn't attend. But my family's from Ghana, so these clothes were in my closet."

"You never talked about your heritage before," Faye said. "This is kente cloth, made of silk and cotton? I heard the colors have meaning."

Taylor guided Faye's fingers along the fabric. "Green means renewal—I'm thrilled that we renewed our relationship. Blue is harmony—our planets are aligned."

Faye glanced around their verdant alcove, then caressed Taylor's small breasts. "And the gold?"

"My status as a medical leader." Taylor's breaths came like the brush of a breeze. "My red sash represents passion, so you better cut that out or we'll be forced to re-enact our alley scene in front of Shakespeare-in-the-Park fans."

Faye shivered as sprinkles penetrating the canopy transformed into a heavier downpour. "You're right, let's head home. Beat you to a cab." As if she had any chance of besting Taylor in a footrace.

Manhattan, New York City—Sunday, July 18, 2021

Faye poured two cups of coffee while Taylor thumbed through the Sunday *Times*, bare feet on the ottoman. Both wore Faye's full-length fluffy robes, Faye in pink and Taylor in blue, hem barely reaching the knees. Taylor tugged Faye down on the couch for a kiss and embrace.

"When did we get domestic?" Taylor's dark eyes glowed, even more arresting in a bald head. "Not that I'm complaining."

Faye shrugged. "Sex and mysterious microbes—that's been our primary connection for years. Maybe I'm ready to move on."

At Taylor's stricken expression, she clarified. "Take the next step in our relationship, I mean. You mentioned family from Ghana last night. Tell me more about them."

Taylor's eyes narrowed with a hint of moisture. "They were physicians—met here during surgical residencies at Columbia. They were flying home from a conference in London and died in the Lockerbie bombing."

Faye reached out to hold Taylor's face. "My God, I'm so sorry. I was the newbie public health vet here—I've forgotten the year."

"1988. I was sixteen, and my parents' friends took me in. I drowned my sorrows in my studies and became a Columbia premed."

Turning away for a bite of almond croissant, Faye remembered Daniel sharing a similar story when they collected mosquitoes. So much tragedy in young lives—she'd been blessed by long-lived parents, even with their revulsion toward her lifestyle.

"I should have been more interested in your background. Guess I was too distracted." She stretched her leg to rest between Taylor's, loving the contrast in their skin color. "When did you realize you were trans?"

"Slow process. I seemed to identify more with my mother. Gender dysphoria, they call it now, but not back then. Mama's boy, or maybe gay. But I wasn't turned on by men, so nothing made sense."

"And you didn't have family to help sort it out. Admittedly, mine was useless on anything related to sex. Abstinence outside marriage, or I'd go straight to Hell."

Taylor shook their head. "Sounds awful. I obsessively followed my parents' professional examples. But the World Trade Center tragedy hit emotionally close to home, and I decided to let in a little personal reality."

"Is that when you started taking female hormones?"

"Yes. I gravitated to the Ballroom Scene—drag queen pageants for Blacks and Latinos. The contests are divided into categories. Femme Queens for trans women, that's where I landed."

Taylor jumped up and struck a pose, legs crossed but feet apart, arms and hands at dramatic angles. Faye giggled as the blue bathrobe slipped down, exposing the anchor and rose tattoo on Taylor's bicep. "Are you voguing?" she asked.

Taylor's answer displayed pride and humor. "Damn right, sista. I won an award."

"I'd vote for you," Faye flirted. She patted the cushion, inviting

Taylor to rejoin her. "So if you're trans, why did you dress like a man for Juana's funeral?"

"Gender fluid—that's the new trend, and I like it. Nobody's shoving me in a box. My driver's license still says male but my work records say female."

"Maybe we'll get to a point where you don't have to pick," Faye said. "Why does the world have to be binary?"

Taylor's index finger traced Faye's lower lip. "This conversation's pretty one-sided."

For Faye, the delicate touch triggered Fourth of July sparklers. "I was always a bit of a tomboy, growing up on the ranch. I'm attracted to guys and gals, and refuse to be locked in, either."

There was an uncomfortable silence, then Taylor brushed Faye's curls behind her ears. "Anyone besides me, at the moment?"

Faye beamed reassurance. "Are you kidding? Between COVID, dengue, and contemplations of retirement, there hasn't been much time for someone else."

Then she sighed, stabbed by sorrow. "I was involved with a CSU faculty member on Colorado visits. But she's in an assisted-living facility now, with moderate dementia."

Taylor squeezed her shoulder. "I'm sorry, Faye. But I don't regret being your only current suitor. I've been fairly preoccupied by you, my lively strawberry-blonde."

Faye shook her head. "You're generous. Silvery strawberry-blonde, at this point."

"Regardless," Taylor said, "I'm going to thank my patient for the tickets and a chance to lure you out to the play. I wasn't expecting us to turn this corner."

A happy glow permeated Faye's skin and warmed her muscles, a reward for allowing someone else to get closer. "We're medical geeks attuned to the same wavelength, addicted to musical theatre and Shakespeare."

The high-pitched beep-beep of a truck backing up in the street broke the spell. Taylor jumped up, waving toward the digital clock in the bookcase. "Damn it, I lost track of time. I have a presentation at Columbia tomorrow. Their pandemic preparedness seminar had a cancellation so they asked me to talk about my Philippines dengue work and Juana's case. You should come."

Faye gulped more coffee and followed Taylor to the bedroom. "I'll need approval from Moshe—Dr. Moskowitz."

Taylor donned the wig and colorful clothes from the night before. "I seem to remember you butted heads with him when we worked on MERS."

"We've grown to accommodate each other. He likes control, but who doesn't."

"Would he approve your talking about the public health aspects of dengue, including your work on the vaccine taskforce?"

"Maybe, although he's not convinced about my particular involvement with vaccine approval. 'Not a high priority here,' he muttered on one occasion."

Hand on the apartment door, Taylor paused. "Give him a call— I'll carve out time from my lecture for you."

Faye wrapped her arms around Taylor's waist. "I like to strategize with partners, academic or otherwise," she said with a suggestive grin.

Manhattan, New York City—Monday, July 19, 2021

Taylor, lecturing from an auditorium podium in a conservative blue suit but the same wig from Saturday night, caught Faye's eye as she perched on the edge of her front-row seat.

"The Philippines has a nationwide push to empty all potential *Aedes* breeding containers daily at four o'clock," Taylor said. "We're not sure if it's working, but infections have dropped since the 437,653 cases reported when I was there in 2019."

A young man in a white coat raised his hand. "Dr. Lewis, I heard they used Dengvaxia vaccine—could that account for the success?"

"Thank you to my audience plant," Taylor joked. "The short answer is 'no.' The vaccine has become controversial, leading to lawsuits and an immunization backlash. I invited a colleague from the city health department to talk about that issue. Dr. Simpson?"

Faye took three steps up to join Taylor on the platform, then gazed out at several hundred attendees, all masked. Taylor's talk had been scheduled for the end of the day, yet the seats were mostly full. COVID helped increase the visibility of a day-long event on preparing for emerging infections.

Taylor pointed to the computer camera and Faye remembered that the presentations were beaming out on Zoom. She didn't get nervous when speaking publicly. But sharing recommendations of the Advisory Committee on Immunization Practices before their formal release caused a pounding pulse in her forehead.

Reminding herself that she had verbal approvals from Moshe and the ACIP Chair, she took a few quick breaths. "Our Dengue Vaccine Work Group met bimonthly for two-and-a-half years to review vaccine data from clinical trials. The ACIP and the CDC director approved Dengvaxia for anyone living in an endemic area who is 9-16 years old, if that person had a prior infection confirmed by a lab."

The previous questioner stood to respond. "What does the ACIP think of the vaccine opposition in the Philippines? We have the same problem with COVID vaccine, so what can we do about it?"

"More information will be available with publication," Faye said, "probably by the end of the year. So I can't say definitively—"

The questioner persisted. "A small number of young men develop heart inflammation after COVID vaccines, so some people are more frightened of vaccines in general. How can we do our jobs in the face of those fears?"

Brown-nosing resident-in-training. Faye tried to quash her judgmental thought.

Before she could answer, Taylor jumped in. "Two weeks ago the ACIP concluded that COVID vaccination benefits outweigh the myocarditis risks, and that's a separate issue from dengue vaccine concerns. But of course you should send reports to VAERS, the Vaccine Adverse Event Reporting System, so we can keep on top of this."

Faye pulled the microphone back and rocked up to the balls of her feet, trying to portray authority as the only ACIP consultant on the podium. "Dengue vaccine is a more complex issue than COVID vaccine. A second dengue infection increases the risk of severe outcomes. In children never infected before, the vaccine mimics the virus in causing a more severe reaction—the exact opposite of our intent."

"Sounds too dangerous." A middle-aged woman with a ponytail to her waist stood from the back right. "Cynthia Wong here from the *New York Post.*"

Faye's eyes locked with Taylor's in an unspoken question. She thought this was a scientific seminar, not open to the press. But she was on the spot, literally, and couldn't defer her responsibility to Taylor. "For those who've had prior infections and are at high risk of hospitalization with future exposure, the vaccine is very effective."

Cynthia Wong waved her hand. "Given the vaccine risks, why would anyone consider it?"

Faye swallowed her sigh. "The evidence for safety in the previously-infected 9-16 age group is high. More than a third of the world's population is at risk, and that's projected to increase to sixty percent by 2080 with climate change. An estimated twenty thousand people die from dengue hemorrhagic fever every year, primarily children."

Taylor leaned down to the microphone. "Remember that dengue disease is the most common mosquito-borne viral disease in the world. As Dr. Simpson said, public health preparedness requires us to be on top of this emerging threat."

Faye tried to find another hand in the air but Ms. Wong kept talking. "With the death of a child here in New York, is the vaccine under discussion at the health department?"

"No." Faye adopted her most assertive voice. "The vaccine will only be approved for endemic areas. Despite our recent death, we have no evidence to-date that dengue is endemic here."

"What does 'to-date' mean?" came from another questioner.

"Initial adult mosquito and larval collections have been negative, and there are no more reports of human cases. We have ongoing surveillance for *Aedes* mosquitoes, the type that can transmit dengue, although we only have *Aedes albopictus*. *Aedes aegypti*, which prefers warmer areas, is more likely to spread viruses like dengue, Zika, and chikungunya. But some studies show that the longer lifespan of *albopictus* may lead to greater vector competence."

"Translate that from doctor-speak into English," Ms. Wong said.

Faye hadn't anticipated a need to interpret for the press, but decades of experience kicked in. "Disease vectors, the living organisms that transmit pathogens, vary in their success rate for infecting humans. If a mosquito lives longer like *Aedes albopictus*, then it has a greater opportunity to spread viruses."

The elderly session moderator tottered across the stage with his cane. "Everyone's stomachs are likely grumbling this late in the day. Let's give a round of applause for Dr. Lewis and Dr. Simpson. Check our website for transcripts and video."

Faye grasped the podium and shook each leg to calm her nerves. "Don't do this to me again, Taylor. Dengue's way too complicated to shoehorn in at the end of the day."

Taylor appeared nonplussed. "You did fine. Should we follow the advice and grab dinner?"

Faye pressed the button on the side of her phone to turn it back on. "Have to take a rain check. Maya texted an hour ago—New Mexico has dengue."

THIRTEEN

Santa Fe, New Mexico—Monday, July 19, 2021

Maya slammed the office phone down in frustration. Faye was her go-to expert on dengue and for some reason she wasn't responding to texts or voicemail. The Albuquerque lab had confirmed dengue infections for Juana's cousin and dead grandmother. Transmission only occurred through arthropod insects like mosquitoes, so if Juana was the source, it was indirect.

She rounded the corner on her way to Dr. Grinwold's office.

"You look like you've been bitten by a ratón volador," Stephanie said.

Maya shook her head in frustration. Still stunned by the news of dengue in the state, she couldn't switch gears. "Manolo helped me refresh my Spanish, but I don't know what that is."

Stephanie laughed, the glow on her cheeks matching the desert-themed mask and tangerine pantsuit. "Sorry, New Mexican dialect. I was referring to the bat that bit the poor policeman directing traffic around a car accident."

"I took care of it—he's getting rabies treatment. Murciélago, that's the only name for a bat that I learned."

"Ratón volador is a flying mouse." Stephanie pointed to Dr. Grinwold's closed door. "He's not here."

"Let me know right away when you see him." She couldn't get over how cheerful Stephanie appeared. "What's up with you, win the lottery?"

"I'm stoked that we're all in the office today, with COVID counts down."

Maya wasn't as addicted to human interactions as Stephanie,

but she relished escaping her haunted home. "This feels empty with staggered schedules. I hope COVID doesn't surge again in the fall."

Stephanie waved her finger. "Don't go raining on my parade. I enjoyed getting out with you on Saturday."

Their leisure outing had been wonderful, but that was when dengue was only a theoretical problem. Now, the virus had nailed two of Juana's relatives who hadn't left the state. Maya twisted her hands with irritation over Dr. Grinwold's absence. "Let me get back to you. Is Erika around?"

At Stephanie's nod, Maya spun and hurried down the hall to the surveillance coordinator's office. Despite a loud knock on the partially open door, Erika remained fixated on her monitor.

Maya knocked again, harder, and Erika turned, yanking out her ear buds. She embraced Maya before motioning to the guest chair.

"I'm so sorry—Sibelius helps me focus. It's a calming counterpoint to hundreds of reports about sick or dead people."

In the confined space, they both kept their masks on. Maya glanced up at the green grass peeking through the narrow window at the top of the opposite wall. A tiny glimpse of the spectacular outside world in the Land of Enchantment rescued her from the gloom of their basement suite.

"Did you see the reports of two confirmed dengue cases from the state lab?" Maya asked.

"On my screen now. Abril Burgos, age 61, and Armand Burgos, age 22. I assume they're related?"

"Mrs. Burgos is Armand's grandmother, and Juana's too—the New York case." Maya rubbed her arms with a sudden chill. "Does the record include Mrs. Burgos's death?"

Erika nodded. "These are the first dengue cases I've seen. I didn't know it could kill."

Once again, Maya wished Faye had returned her call. "Many dengue infections can be asymptomatic, so with Mrs. Burgos's lung cancer, her test results might be incidental."

"I'll make my usual routine electronic report to CDC, but you should talk to someone there by phone."

Maya uncrossed her legs and pointed to Erika's printer. "Can you give me a copy of everything in the system about both cases?"

When Erika handed her the pages, Maya stepped for the door. "I wish I could check with Dr. Grinwold."

"You're a CDC employee—I'm sure it's fine for you to alert them. Do you know anyone in their dengue program?"

Maya's heart hammered with the realization she should have been talking to them already about Juana passing through New Mexico. Having two bosses, one in Atlanta plus Dr. Grinwold as the local authority, complicated chain of command.

No one came to mind at the Dengue Branch in Puerto Rico. Then she remembered Keegan Williams, the PhD epidemiologist in Vector-Borne Diseases, the higher-level division in Colorado.

"I trained one of the Fort Collins team during his Atlanta orientation."

By the time Maya reached her own office, her stomach growled like a grumpy cat and her legs cramped. She'd missed both lunch and her daily swim. As she lifted the receiver to contact Keegan, her phone rang with a call from Faye.

"Hi Maya, I was tied up on a dengue vaccine update at Columbia. You have cases there?"

"Juana's grandmother died Saturday and her cousin is hospitalized. Dengue confirmation just came in. I'm consulting with CDC in case they want to come down. You still have nothing brewing in New York, correct?"

"No positive mosquitoes, no other human infections." Faye's sympathetic sigh filtered through the phone. "I've handled imported cases before, but all of this must be new for you."

Maya shifted in her chair and rubbed her aching back with her free hand. "That's the thing—these two didn't travel with Juana from Puerto Rico."

"Holy cow, that's even bigger news. Well, I'm guessing when Juana opened her suitcase in New Mexico, some infected blood-seeking missiles escaped."

"You're kidding." Maya wrote a note to set up more mosquito

surveillance. "Infected travelers can get diagnosed in new locations. But hitchhiking mosquitoes?"

"It happens—we had a local infection once related to a container ship from Brazil. Thanks for letting me know, Maya. We'll continue our monitoring here. Get your CDC colleagues in the loop."

Albuquerque, New Mexico—Tuesday, July 20, 2021

Dr. Grinwold had authorized the official Epi-Aid invitation for CDC assistance. Inside the hospital's front entrance, Maya spotted Keegan immediately.

Several years older and a couple inches taller, he'd bonded with her as a fellow introvert and statistics nerd. Also like her, he was part of the increasing diversification of CDC trainees. He'd grown up in the shadow of CDC headquarters in Atlanta and attended Morehouse College, then Emory University. Beneath a puff of tight curls, his scalp was shaved in an attractive geometric pattern between his ears and forehead. A small diamond sparkling in his left ear flattered his bronze skin.

"Maya, good to see you again," he said with a slight Atlanta drawl. "Looks like we both have some new hair styles."

"Good thing you didn't join the Public Health Service Commissioned Corps. I don't think they'd allow that earring, but I love it. Thanks for coming so quickly."

"I'm excited to work with you again. In the arboviral branch, I've mostly helped with West Nile studies, but also COVID like everyone else."

"Did your family lobby for relocation to an Atlanta assignment?"

"They've got a full household with my brother and sisters. They're impressed by that coronavirus pet study I did in Arizona."

Keegan had emailed Maya a preliminary draft of the paper he coauthored with Lila Becker, the new Arizona State Epidemiologist. He had collected blood, nasal, and fecal specimens from companion animals in households with human infection. In March, a dog and cat were detected with the same SARS-CoV-2 lineage as the symptomatic owner, although they never showed any clinical signs.

"Those are important results." Maya hoped her tone conveyed the depth of her compliment despite the mask hiding her smile. "Let's review our two dengue patients and see if we can piece together the puzzle of their infections."

A clerk alerted the pathologist of their arrival and led them to a conference room. Ten minutes later, a large woman burst through the door like a derecho, strong winds just short of a tornado. Beneath a bob helmet of tinsel-streaked black hair, her piercing dark eyes contrasted with the pink of her mask and scrubs.

"Dr. Williams, welcome. Dr. Maguire, your dragonfly earrings look very familiar."

"Thanks, Dr. Neha." Maya followed the pathologist's example and didn't offer her hand. "These were a gift from my late husband."

"Small world—perhaps they were made by my mother, who's a Zuni artist."

Dr. Neha placed an x-ray on a light box. "The white nodules indicate the patient's lung cancer, which we confirmed on her autopsy. Her prognosis wasn't favorable even if not infected with dengue, so it's difficult to sort out which played a role in her death."

She displayed MRI scans of the woman's spine. Maya shuddered at the gray mass obliterating the darker color of the spinal cord. Even with the coldness of black-and-white images, the irregular borders brought the tumor to life, as if it were an alien invader in a horror movie stretching its tentacles through the screen to grab and absorb them.

"The thoracic spine is a common area for lung cancer metastases because it's so close," Dr. Neha said. "Her doctors discussed removal of her right lung to be followed by spinal surgery, but cancelled when she deteriorated last week."

Next she displayed two photomicrographs. Maya recognized the images as organ sections.

"We fast-tracked histopathology." Dr. Neha pointed to the left image. "This is the heart magnified four hundred times. Can you see inflammatory cells between the muscle fibers?" Maya nodded and Keegan shrugged his shoulders.

"I'm at a disadvantage compared to Maya, not having a medical degree. Give me some data and I'm your man. But with this," he peered at the screen, "I'll take your word for it."

Frown lines on Dr. Neha's forehead deepened but she continued. "Hemorrhagic necrosis of the liver may be harder to see, but aligns with the patient's elevated liver enzymes prior to death. Our tests detected dengue RNA in the liver and heart."

"So you believe the tissue damage was from dengue, not the lung cancer?" Maya asked.

"Yes. We have so few dengue deaths in the US, we thought it essential to complete a rapid and thorough postmortem. This will be an important article for my pathology resident to coordinate."

Maya understood the emphasis on scientific publications for academic teaching hospitals. Dr. Grinwold constantly pushed her to write up her disease investigations. "Can't prevent something if there's no information on how it started," he pronounced on more than one occasion.

But Dr. Neha hadn't mentioned Mrs. Burgos's name once. Was Juana's grandmother now reduced just to tissues and scans for a report?

Diplomacy at all times with interagency relations—Dr. Grinwold's warning came to mind. After all, Dr. Neha was just hyperfocused on her job. "Impressive work in such a short timeframe," Maya said.

Dr. Neha's eyes narrowed. "CDC needs to understand that writing up these results is our baby." Her voice increased in volume. "I'm doing you the courtesy of sharing our early findings, but as feds, you can't expect to take over."

Uncertain whether she could speak for Dr. Grinwold or CDC, Maya glanced to Keegan, who raised his eyebrows.

"Of course, we respect your expertise in this area," Maya said, heart fluttering with the sudden conflict. Why did different agencies pull together in an emergency but then fall apart when it was time to take credit? "There will be multiple aspects of this disease outbreak and I'm sure we can work out authorship as we proceed."

Keegan cleared his throat. "Can we visit the grandson now? We're trying to determine his dengue exposure."

Dr. Neha opened the door. "I understand he's on the third floor."

Maya took the hint that the pathologist was too busy to lead them there. "Thank you again."

She guided Keegan to the elevator. "I didn't expect her to turn frosty."

"Remember our summer course when Enzo Russo bullied his way to take charge? You taught me how to navigate those personality minefields. I heard he moved to Washington. At least we don't need to bump into him on southwestern outbreaks any more."

"Thanks for the credit," she said. Keegan didn't know that Enzo had sexually assaulted her. "But I dealt with Enzo more by avoidance than any skill."

The elevator door opened and they headed up to the clinical wards in silence. Who should she blame for Enzo's continued federal employment? It was mostly her fault due to her delay in reporting him, although Manolo's parking lot fight allowed Enzo to negotiate down disciplinary actions. Nancy might have dismissed Enzo if not so strapped for epidemiology experts in the pandemic. Because Enzo's assault had stopped short of rape, Maya didn't push for punishment. She hoped she hadn't enabled a predator on the loose.

A clerk at the nursing station directed them down the hall. Maya lightly knocked. With no answer, she eased open the door a crack. Armand was asleep, looking more like a teen taking a nap than a college student with a tropical disease that had robbed him of a cousin and grandmother.

"I don't want to disturb him," she whispered to Keegan. "Maybe we should grab lunch in the cafeteria and swing back a bit later."

Before she stepped out, an alarm went off and she saw the EKG go into an abnormal rhythm. In less than a minute, a team with a crash cart brushed past her as she held the door, panic flooding her nerves with an electric shock.

FOURTEEN

Queens, New York City—Tuesday, July 20, 2021

Faye buttoned her light sweater, cursing the lack of individual climate control in the health department's cubicles. She clicked on the Zoom link she'd emailed to Dr. Siti Rahim, CDC Dengue Branch Chief. Through previous discussions, they had bonded— both single women in their sixties who prioritized public health above their personal lives. Siti was based in Puerto Rico, far from her Southeast Asian Muslim roots. But Faye's almost forty years in New York was also a world apart from hauling hay on the Colorado eastern plains.

Twisting to study her calendar pages pinned to the cubicle walls, Faye lingered over one of her favorites. The longhaired tortie kitten lay on its back in a blue blanket, eyes closed, paws extended but curled. When would she bring another cat into her home? Taylor's slight allergy complicated the decision.

Then her monitor displayed a square face the appealing color of aged parchment. Gold-framed glasses rested on a wide nose, magnifying lively dark eyes. A surprise was the cropped hair, a dramatic swash of pink.

"It's been several weeks since we touched base." Siti smiled. "Thanks for arranging this."

"Your new 'do' is a striking change—my compliments." Faye indicated her approval with a thumbs-up.

Siti's thin fingers raked through her bright coif. "My retirement date is set for this month. Might as well go out with a bang. Any fallout with your New York case?"

"No, but did you hear about New Mexico?"

"Yes, I authorized Keegan Williams from the Fort Collins office to help. He should be there now."

Siti leaned in closer to her camera. "Faye, do you know about the program to reactivate Public Health Service Commissioned Corps officers?"

"Of course, but I've never done it."

"We pulled in a lot of retired folks for the pandemic. Dengue had been lower in some areas but that's starting to change. I have to head to the Far East."

"Well, you have family in Malaysia. Good excuse to stop in for a visit, right?"

"Not the reason I'm headed there, but I'll try to make time for them. Bangladesh has over two thousand dengue infections this year and COVID's million cases have collapsed their healthcare system. With beds full, there's no room for the severe dengue patients."

"You have a lot on your plate," Faye said. "I hope you can make a difference."

"Singapore's also exploding with DENV-3 and DENV-4 and the population doesn't have immunity to those serotypes. *Aedes aegypti* can be day biters and people working from home during the pandemic are more out-and-about than when confined to their offices."

Faye chugged her Coke to fuel a caffeine rush. "I'm not up for extensive travel like you, but if you need help closer to our shores, let me know."

"I'll keep your offer in mind," Siti said. "I appreciate your mentoring Maya Maguire with the New Mexico dengue."

"No problem. We first met when she helped on a MERS investigation in London. Even in vet school, her brilliance and attention to detail were impressive."

Siti's laugh trilled like a wind chime. "Well, we only hire the best for the Epidemic Intelligence Service, haven't you heard?"

Faye wondered if Siti was paying her and Maya a compliment to butter them up for a big favor. She silently agreed that the EIS selection process and intense program created exemplary public health leaders. And on top of that, Maya had just restarted her year of preventive medicine residency, an added credential Faye never applied for.

"I don't know how Maya does it," Faye said. "Last fall, she miscarried and lost her husband to COVID. I've never faced those obstacles to my work."

"I'm sure New Mexico appreciates her but hasn't she been there for three years? Many trainees branch out to different geographic areas."

Were Siti's pronouncements pointed in a certain direction? "Maya has overseas experience with disease outbreaks," Faye said. "She created some strong international ties. Well, except for a dustup with the Chinese government."

Ashamed that she'd revealed too much, Faye reconnoitered. "Siti, the main reason for my call is to find out more about Juana's dengue exposure in Puerto Rico—"

Siti's phone on her desk rang and she picked it up. Her head turned away as she listened for a moment, then spoke into the receiver. "Hang on."

Brow furrowed, her eyes focused back in Faye's direction. "I've got to go. Good to touch base." Siti's image blinked off before Faye had a chance to say goodbye.

Her attention to the computer screen was interrupted by Moshe's huff at her cubicle opening. "If you're talking to the head of the CDC Dengue Branch, I should be on the Zoom."

With both hands, she rubbed her temples. Fuckin' open office. Her authority to talk to CDC had been worked out years ago. But Moshe had been stomping the halls since yesterday.

Despite an increase in COVID cases, the mayor announced he wouldn't reinstate a citywide mask mandate, hoping to rely on vaccinations. Faye sympathized with Moshe's frustration at having his public health decisions overruled by politicians, but didn't appreciate his taking it out on the staff.

She took a deep breath. "Moshe, you know I keep you updated."

He waved his hand in her face, finger pointed. "And what's

up with all this extra mosquito testing? Daniel's collecting day and night and the lab's complaining. One dead girl doesn't justify this."

His crass words stabbed Faye in the heart even as she understood his right to be concerned about priorities. Squeaky wheels of a chair from the next cubicle reminded her of their lack of privacy. "Moshe, why don't we move to your office?"

The contortions of his frame threatened an Incredible Hulk explosion through his mask and clothes. "You don't give me orders. I'm fed up with your insubordination." On the final word, his voice rose to the timbre of a siren.

Faye wanted to be the bigger, more mature person. But years of pent-up deference to a government agency's protocols roiled her stomach like lighter fluid. "Moshe, I've been in this department since you were born. I'm sixty-six years old and fuck it if I'll take another minute of this."

His body finally relaxed and his eyes crinkled—Faye recognized he was smiling under his mask. That's when she realized she'd played right into his hands. Her next wise move—apologize for bad language and bare her throat like a subservient wolf. This time, it wasn't going to happen.

She leapt to her feet and shoved past him. Bug-eyed heads poked out of other workstations as she stormed by. When she turned the corner for Human Resources, Daniel blocked the path. Confusion and concern fluctuated over his typically cheerful face.

"Faye, what's going on? I'm the one who screwed up with too much testing—let me right the ship with Dr. Moskowitz."

She held him back with a kindly squeeze of his upper arm. "Working with you on dengue has been the most rewarding thing I've done in a while. But it's time to become an old cat lady submerged in Broadway musical matinees. I'm sorry you got dragged into my issues."

FIFTEEN

Albuquerque, New Mexico—Tuesday, July 20, 2021

Two cups of black tea in her stomach, caffeine headache brewing, Maya led Keegan to the nurses' station where she approached one of the staff.

"Excuse me," she said. "How is Mr. Burgos doing?" *Not dead, not dead, not dead,* she repeated in an internal pep talk to counter her own racing heart.

The clerk checked her computer screen. "Hello, Dr. Maguire. He had a high degree AV block leading to ventricular asystole, controlled with intravenous atropine and orciprenaline."

Medicalese, when good news, was comforting. Maya turned to Keegan. "Armand had an interruption of electrical signals between his heart chambers but it was managed with medications."

"Thanks," Keegan said. "All of that was a bit beyond my epi knowledge."

"I know you wanted to touch base with the patient," the clerk said. "I need to call his doctor and make sure it's okay at this point."

Maya hesitated, uncertain of the interview's importance. She could find other local relatives to get authorization for more mosquito collection on their property. "No need—we'll head to the cafeteria and reconnoiter."

In the line for soothing herbal tea, Maya yearned for a breath of fresh air. "Keegan, let's locate a picnic table so we're not overheard."

He grabbed a coffee and followed her outside. By the look of the overcast sky, they'd missed a summer shower. The temperature had cooled from several hours earlier when they first entered the hospital.

Maya pulled tissues from her bag and attempted to clean off water drops from the bench before inviting Keegan to join her. "I'd like to find out more about Arizona's response protocol for mosquito-borne diseases."

"We should call Lila," Keegan said.

Using FaceTime, Maya reached out to Dr. Becker, her best friend from her EIS class. On the phone screen, the new Arizona State Epidemiologist looked unchanged from their summer trainings in Hotlanta. Lila's short chestnut-brown hair was less frizzy in the Phoenix climate, but her lively expression was still accented by bright red lipstick and kohl-outlined dark eyes.

"Maya, it's good to see you. How are you doing?"

"I'm doing fine. If anything, I'm a bigger advocate of therapy than before. Both my physical and mental health are improving, thanks for asking."

She pivoted her phone. "Keegan's here with me in Albuquerque."

He waved a quick hello. "How's married life treating you? Do you recommend it for the rest of us?" He ducked his eyes. "Uh, sorry Maya, I wasn't thinking."

She hated everyone guarding their speech as if she were a fragile Ming Dynasty porcelain vase. "Lila's still in the honeymoon phase," she said. "I hope she's a fan of wedded bliss."

"Our life here in Arizona has fallen into place. We miss living close to the ocean, but Bretta's got family in San Francisco so we'll be back there for Thanksgiving. As long as COVID doesn't spike again."

"Fingers crossed on that for all of us," Maya said. "We're calling about the little girl from Puerto Rico who died from dengue in New York. Two of her family members are now confirmed: a young adult male who's hospitalized and their grandmother who also died. Neither of them traveled recently from their home in Corrales, a town along the Rio Grande where we tend to have more mosquitoes."

"Transmission's never been documented in our region—that's a big deal." Lila's face reflected her usual no-nonsense self-assurance.

"Based on a concern about Zika virus, Maricopa County developed our overall plan in 2015."

"What do you recommend?" Keegan asked. Maya whipped out a pocket notebook and started writing.

"Collect mosquitoes weekly within five miles of the residence. Sort them by sex and species, then batch test the females."

"How long should we keep that up?" Maya asked.

"Two months. I assume you're getting the whole genome sequence results from the human cases to compare with any positive mosquitoes."

"Yes, we already know it's DENV-1," Maya said. "Corrales is close to Albuquerque so I can ask their environmental health department for help."

"It's a challenge deploying sufficient staff," Keegan added, "but I'll check with my bosses in Fort Collins."

Lila continued. "In that same geographic area, go door-to-door and arrange for human blood testing."

Keegan straightened up. "Lab testing of those specimens for IgM and PRNT confirmation is something I'm sure we can offer the state."

"We'll get this going." Maya began planning—she could start quicker if staying at a motel or with Dave. A reasonable excuse to avoid her mausoleum apartment. "Any final suggestions?"

"Yes, reach out to the infectious disease docs about patients with similar symptoms. Track down their blood samples and test them."

"Will do," Maya said. "Thanks again for your advice."

Lila's tone sharpened. "Call me at home tonight about a computer problem here. Sorry, Keegan, it's a private issue."

Five hours later, Maya stood alone leaning on Dave's corral fence. She and Keegan had approvals from their supervisors to get Lila's recommended human and mosquito testing program underway the next day.

With Keegan comfortably ensconced at a nearby hotel, Maya

couldn't pass up another chance for an evening of Schwartz family life.

A slight breeze rippled the small stock pond's glistening reflections—the green of the cottonwood canopy and pink/purple stripes of sunset. Metallic blue-black wings and forked tail flashed when a barn swallow swooped to the water. Just as Maya was about to call Lila, a coyote loped across the field and paused at the pond for a drink. Then it sat, blue eyes locked on Maya's.

Blue? She'd heard about a *National Geographic* report of the mutation in California. The color was arresting, and spooky. Was it acting too tame, maybe rabid? If Bo raced out in defense of the property, it would be a nightmare. But the black Lab was nowhere in sight—likely indoors with everyone getting ready for bed. A nervous whinny emanated from the horse barn.

Maya dropped her phone in her pants pocket and waved her arms. "Get out of here," she yelled in her loudest voice. The animal remained focused on Maya, perhaps showing who was in charge, then trotted toward the Rio Grande.

The FaceTime call went through a few moments later. "Hi, Lila, your request for a private call got me on edge. I just saw a blue-eyed coyote—hope it's not a bad omen."

Lila's laugh was nervous and her expression didn't reflect mirth. "Coyotes don't catch dengue, all the better." She ducked her eyes. "We found a document when cleaning the backup computer files…"

"I worked in your Phoenix office during several outbreaks," Maya said. "Did I leave something that you need me to explain?"

"Not you. This goes back to Arizona's former EIS Officer who was harassing you," Lila answered.

"Enzo Russo—he's in Washington now."

"Yes, at NIAID, the National Institute of Allergy and Infectious Diseases." Lila hurried on. "Our deleted files are captured on daily system backups. One file titled 'Options' is a lengthy list of the jobs Enzo was considering. Also some road races, cultural events, countries to visit. But you were mentioned a number of times."

Maya gripped the fence rail to steady a wave of dizziness.

"What's the date on it? I thought his fixation on me was long gone. He was dating that vector control specialist."

"The file was last accessed before its deletion when he moved to DC."

"I don't understand how your staff has time to read individual files in your records cleanup. And what does Enzo's 'Options' list say about me?"

Lila brushed her fingers through her thick curls. "A different employee was caught writing a porn novel on his computer so our program screens for certain words. The backup of Enzo's deleted file was picked up on that."

Maya kicked at the dirt, forgetting she was wearing sandals instead of sneakers. She reached down one hand to stretch the leather strap and let out the pebbles. It sure seemed like Lila was taking her time to reveal the punch line. "Can you email it so I know what's going on?"

A frown creased Lila's face. "Sorry, no can do. The attorneys are deciding next steps. There may not be anything illegal in the document but it raises questions. And the language is rough. 'Fuck Maya Maguire' with vivid descriptions of how he'd like to do that. Nothing implying force, but physical contact I know you wouldn't welcome."

Maybe Lila was right. Seeing, talking to, and being touched by Enzo without her consent had been bad enough. Having a window into his mind would be worse. Shit, if only Nancy had fired him when it all came out.

"There are also items about car damage with nobody's name. Nail in a tire, smashed windshield. I don't know what those relate to."

Maya flashed back to the training program in Atlanta. "Remember when your car rental had the flat we fixed together? I had turned down dinner with Enzo to join you instead. Later that fall, Manolo's Corvette had a broken front window. I was in Phoenix recovering from my flash bomb injury." Her missing little finger throbbed and she twirled the rings on the fourth one to interrupt the sensation.

"There are no dates on his notes, nothing to tie them to you or me." Lila rubbed her forehead as if to clear her mind.

"I appreciate your letting me know," Maya said. "What happens next?"

"Once the attorneys complete their review, I assume we'll contact Enzo. As I said, I'm not spotting anything criminal in his notes, just creepy as hell. But you deserved a heads up."

Maya said goodbye and glanced at the pond, reflections now dark and dim with the sun below the horizon. On the far side, the coyote strolled toward the barn. Maya yelled at it again—no reaction.

Threat, threat, threat. She dashed for the house, Dave, and his rifle.

SIXTEEN

Manhattan, New York City—Wednesday, July 21, 2021

The grinding gears and brakes of the garbage truck woke Faye up as summer sun streamed around the edges of her blinds. Strong arms circled her torso and held her firmly in place. She glanced down to her pale, freckled leg sandwiched between Taylor's long dark ones. Just like the Day of the Dead eight years earlier when they first slept together after meeting on the Halloween parade float.

Dead—that's what her sodden head felt like.

How many bottles of wine did they polish off? She couldn't remember another time when she'd let go like that. Slurred rampages about the bumbling bureaucracy. Prejudiced tirades against the entire male sex. Mournful sobs about dengue-killed kids, menopause, and missed opportunities. Her skin flushed with the memories. Good thing Taylor was a known, safe companion to help her through all of it.

After slipping out from Taylor's embrace, she headed for her bathroom. Using both hands, she splashed cold water on her face. But when she pivoted for the toilet, she almost slipped on the damp floor. Past her prime, ready for handicap rails to prevent an old lady's broken bones.

She anchored herself with one hand on the pedestal sink and gazed into the mirror. Saggy jowls and permanent puffy dark circles under her eyes. Strawberry-blonde curls, who was she kidding? They'd morphed into pale-gray years ago.

Gentle hands massaged her shoulders. Taylor's sly smile in the mirror set off a sensual tickle in Faye's skin, reminiscent of lips caressing every inch of her body to distract her from the job loss.

"It's a beautiful new day." Taylor leaned down to whisper in her ear. "You're my Bernadette Peters songbird—free to fly for the first time in your life. Let's clean up and walk the High Line."

With embarrassingly chubby fingers, she stroked Taylor's prominent cheekbones. A long workday was always a convenient excuse for lack of exercise. Couldn't use that one again. "But you didn't run off at the mouth to your boss. Don't you need to get to the hospital?"

"My first meeting's not until one. Fresh air will do you good."

They hopped on the subway at Canal Street and off again at 14th. Walking the few blocks west along Gansevoort, they stopped short of the immense cantilevered entrance to the Whitney Museum.

Opposite the food truck advertising chicken kebabs, they climbed the stairs to the southern terminus of the former elevated rail line. Many of those enjoying the mid-seventies temperature followed the sign instructions and wore masks like Faye and Taylor.

Old rail lines peeked through variegated groundcover as they strolled the wide planks. In breaks from the foliage, historic and modern buildings provided a geometric cacophony to either side. Glare from glass behemoths prompted Faye to retrieve her sunglasses from her daypack.

At Chelsea Market, Taylor paused while peering down at the traffic. "Do you want to grab some breakfast? You didn't eat a lot before we left."

Faye sank onto a lounge chair overhung by shade trees. She pulled out her water bottle. "No thanks. My queasy stomach hasn't recovered."

Her head twisted to take in all the bird song, so much closer than the honking below. "Can you believe in thirty-eight years of being here, I've never done this."

"Played hooky? The High Line's only been open for twelve years. Not nearly enough time for you to squeeze in a visit."

Faye traced her fingers from the crown of Taylor's shaved head to their nose, then tweaked it. A deep breath of happiness filled her lungs. "You're good for me."

Two little girls raced past, dressed in bright orange shirts and shorts. Almost twins with dark locks. "Espérame," a Hispanic man shouted after them. They giggled and twirled, but waited for him to catch up.

The pain of Juana's loss crept in like Carl Sandburg's fog on little cat feet. A single tear slipped from Faye's eye and Taylor brushed it away with a fingertip.

"Am I betraying Juana's memory by jumping overboard?" she asked. "Daniel's on his own to fight for the dengue surveillance program."

Taylor sighed and took her hand. "You're having second thoughts."

"Maybe it's menopause. The hot flashes are behind me, but I can't sleep and that affects the brain."

"Might be me too when I change my hormone therapy," Taylor said. "Right now I'm on testosterone blocking pills and estrogen. But like cisgender women, estrogen at an older age can increase my risk of blood clots and stroke."

Faye pulled Taylor's arm around her. "I'll take you any way I can get you, even if we both end up temperamental."

"Sweetie, I like having tits, no matter how small. I don't smoke, I have a heart-healthy diet and lifestyle. Don't worry—when I turn fifty next year, I'll re-evaluate my treatment regimen."

Faye felt every muscle relax with the fresh breeze off the Hudson River. She and Taylor were so in sync—how did she get so lucky? She'd never taken the time to appreciate the benefits of a relationship with someone so intelligent, loving, and flexible.

Loving—not a big word in her vocabulary. It applied to her parents in a distant, obligatory way. Her only remaining Colorado connection was Devorah.

Would Devorah recognize Faye if she visited? On a recent Zoom from assisted living, Devorah remained elegant. Colorful clothing, dark hair with the Cruella streak, and a generous smile to neutralize any similarities to the Disney character. But a staffer helped with the technology and reminded Devorah of Faye's name.

Taking a permanent work break gave Faye hours to reflect and mourn. Parents who never accepted her, Devorah who didn't lure her back to the Rocky Mountains, Juana Gomez losing her life to dengue in a hospital far from home.

And others she'd never met in person, like Maya's husband and baby. It was time to smell the roses, or the fragrant white flowers they'd passed in the Gansevoort Woodland. Not getting any younger.

Taylor kissed the top of her head. "You're awfully quiet. Any regrets about quitting the job?"

"Surprisingly few, other than leaving Daniel in the lurch. But I haven't a clue what to do with myself. I assumed I'd focus on cats and culture, although your allergy has me rethinking."

Taylor's dark eyes widened with delight. "Well, that's huge news. I'm playing a role in your plans."

Faye averted her gaze to a tiny blue flower. "I guess so. But we have a pesky seventeen-year age gap. You've got a lot more years of vitality."

"Jane Fonda's over eighty and she's still hot. Let's worry about that issue in another decade or so."

Faye snorted. "If you haven't noticed, I'm no Jane Fonda."

"And I ain't no Laverne Cox. But every now and then, I doll myself up and pretend."

With the air getting warmer, between and around them, Faye pulled out her phone and checked the temperature.

"It's seventy-nine—no wonder I'm heating up. Or maybe it's the thought of your super glam look—the only time I see it is on the parade float."

"Dear, next time you want a private showing, just ask." Taylor tugged Faye to her feet. "I'm in the mood for a vegan dan dan mian at the noodle shop before heading to the hospital. If you're not too hungry, we can share a bowl."

As Faye shifted off the chair, her cell flashed the name of Juana's grandfather. "Señor Lopez, I'm surprised to hear from you. No dengue symptoms, I hope?"

He rushed on, his response a garbled language jumble.

"Just a second." She interrupted his torrent. "It sounds like you could use a clinical consult. Dr. Lewis is here—can I put you on speaker?"

With his rapid "Sí, por supuesto," she hit the speaker icon and he continued in English.

"My oldest grandson stayed in the PR with an aunt while the others traveled." His voice caught, then he choked out, "He's hospitalized with dengue, and I'm not getting answers. Maybe you can help?"

Faye gulped, uncertain whether they could offer anything from New York. "I chatted with the head of the CDC Dengue Branch there yesterday. She's headed out of town but I can call someone else."

Then she winced. She'd automatically gone into work mode, assuming she'd have access to a health department phone to dial San Juan. Even though Puerto Rico was part of the US, she was unsure about her personal cell phone plan.

"Why has my family been hit so hard?" It sounded like he was suppressing sobs. "Javier has hemo…phago…cytic lympho… histio…cytosis. Dr. Lewis, what's that?"

Faye was relieved they weren't on a video call with the severity of Taylor's grimace.

"HLH," Taylor said. "Inflammation is accompanied by a proliferation of white blood cells. Also spleen and liver problems. But I should talk with your grandson's physician."

Faye mouthed silently to Taylor, "Bad?"

Taylor nodded and Mr. Lopez continued. "Dr. Lewis, that would mean the world to me. My son said the *San Juan Daily Star* is reporting a surge of cases."

On her earlier call, Faye had intended to learn more from Siti about surveillance in Puerto Rico. Was Mr. Lopez's frantic concern reason enough to make nice with Moshe and rescind her resignation? Or maybe with Taylor, they could reach out to the San Juan hospital and authorities there. She needed to see this through, but crawling back to the NYC Health Commissioner wasn't an option.

SEVENTEEN

Corrales, New Mexico—Wednesday, July 21, 2021

Maya drove Keegan to a quaint Corrales restaurant for breakfast and initial planning of their dengue day. As she settled to the hard metal of a black patio chair, a hot-air balloon painted with Monet's water lilies floated overhead, close enough to hear bursts of fuel keeping it up in the postcard-perfect blue sky.

She and Keegan yelled "Good morning!" to the pilot and two passengers, a pair of senior citizens with arms wrapped around each other. In fear of the height, or in love? Their jubilant waves answered Maya's question.

Thoughts about Enzo Russo and dengue dueled for her mind's focus, but the spicy odor of Keegan's carne adovada and red chile drew her attention back to the table.

"Nothing beats New Mexican cuisine, am I right?" Maya asked.

"You ain't kidding—my lips are burning. But you took the easy way." He pointed to her slice of spinach quiche.

Using her fork, Maya toyed with the small pieces on her plate. She had supervised Keegan and Enzo on an Atlanta door-to-door survey of *Salmonella* infections. Keegan had been on the receiving end of Enzo's insults, so it was tempting to share last night's news about his computer file.

She took two quick gulps of black tea to offset a fuzzy brain from a sleepless night on Dave's couch. Sexy dreams of Manolo's tender caresses had been replaced by a loop of Enzo's rough touches at the Grand Canyon and the Atlanta hotel. His leering amber eyes had reminded her of the deadly movie clown Pennywise, and no tincture of time had softened the impression.

But Lila's insistence on confidentiality overrode Maya's instinct to confide in Keegan. She glanced around the small flagstoned patio surrounded by an adobe wall. Early on a weekday, they had the area to themselves, other than a chipmunk darting among the rose bushes. "I need to check in with my boss about our plans, then we can meet with local authorities."

"I'll verify with Fort Collins what resources they can offer," Keegan said.

Maya used FaceTime to contact Dr. Grinwold and angled her phone on the table so Keegan could also see the screen. Both Dr. Grinwold's and Nancy's faces popped up with violet morning glories behind them on a wooden trellis.

Nancy spoke first, always more chatty than her taciturn partner. "Maya, it's great to see you. Sorry I've been tied up with my move to Santa Fe."

She appeared more relaxed, the lines in her aging face less prominent. Her brown eyes sparkled, likely from a much-delayed commitment to her long-term relationship. And her graying bob now glowed auburn.

"What is it about transitions and changing hair color?" Maya joked, flicking her fingers through her own red-streaked locks. "I'd love to get together when we get the chance."

"Of course, dear, we'll have you to dinner soon. But I imagine you're calling Fred about dengue."

"Yes. Do you remember Keegan from CDC Fort Collins?"

"Thanks for giving Maya a hand," Dr. Grinwold said.

"I'm honored to be invited," Keegan answered. "Land of Enchantment—there's something magical about this area."

"Juana's local cousin, Armand Burgos, had a scare with arrhythmia yesterday," Maya said. "We called the hospital this morning and he's stable."

"That's good." Dr. Grinwold adjusted his stylish straw hat that blocked the slanting sun. "I'd hate to do a press release about another dengue death."

Maya shared his hope. "We have the Arizona arboviral plan."

"Yes, we practiced it during training," Nancy continued. "Implementation will be a lot of work with so many mosquito and human blood specimens."

"The *Albuquerque Journal* has Armand and his grandmother as their headline this morning," Keegan said. "Maya thinks the staff here will be motivated to offer assistance."

"Don't count your chickens," Dr. Grinwold warned. "Corrales is a small town with limited resources. It all depends on whether Albuquerque also feels the threat."

"We're headed there now," Maya said. "I think a Zoom with you and Albuquerque's Environmental Health director will help."

"Sure," he answered. "I'll be in the office shortly."

In agreement with her boss on the next outbreak step, Maya's dismay over the Enzo news shifted to the forefront. Why hadn't Nancy realized he was writing such vile notes on a network-linked computer? It was hard not to blame her old mentor for the lax supervision. But maybe Nancy could make it up to her.

"I heard Enzo went to Health & Human Services," Maya said with a casual tone. "Nancy, do you have any contact info for him?"

Dr. Grinwold exploded with a reddened face and a snarl. "Why in hell would you want to talk to that scoundrel?"

Maya appreciated Dr. Grinwold's protective stance yet still felt compelled to confront Enzo, just uncertain how and when to do it.

"Ah, it's nothing important. Someone asked me for his *Borrelia* article." Her toes tingled with the lie. Just like Enzo to make her feel compelled to tell one.

Nancy plucked at her widow's peak. "Lila may have those reprints in the office."

But asking Lila for Enzo's location wouldn't be wise—she'd warned Maya to stay out of it.

Dr. Grinwold inched away from Nancy, his body ramrod straight. "I never was comfortable with all the compromises worked out to keep his job. You'd be stupid to have any contact with him, Maya."

"Of course, you're right," she answered, prolonging her deceit. "I'll work through Lila to get the article."

As the call ended and Maya got up to pay their breakfast bill, Keegan took the check. "I'm on per diem, I'll take care of my half. What was all that about Enzo? Something going on that I don't know about?"

Unwilling to give Enzo additional footprints on her mind's roadmap, Maya shook her head and led them to her Prius. More important—getting local agencies on board with a ramped-up search for dengue infection.

Keegan held the door as they exited the headquarters of the Albuquerque Environmental Health Department. "Productive meeting—that extra local team will be crucial to supplement our door-to-door survey. Should we grab lunch before heading back to Corrales?"

Noonday sun searing her hair, Maya pulled her cap from her daypack. "Can we get by with a snack until dinner? There's a lot to get done. Those people we don't find home now, we can catch when they return from work."

"That's fine. I don't suppose you're going to break down and tell me what happened with Enzo."

"Keegan, I'd love to confide, but Lila swore me to secrecy." She unlocked her Prius in the parking garage and tossed him a box of mosquito repellent wipes. "If we think there's enough dengue activity to justify this surveillance, we should assume we're at risk, too."

Leaning against her car hood in the dank shade of the open-sided building, she checked her phone for a signal, then FaceTimed Faye. Expecting a cat-decorated cubicle as the screen background, she was surprised by the hospital corridor. "Hi, Faye, do you have another case?"

"No, Maya." Faye's face turned away as she continued, "Taylor, can we go back to your office?"

The scene shifted to a bookcase jammed with medical texts. The shot included the attractive, authoritative expression of a middle-aged Black woman in a white coat.

"Dr. Maguire, I'm Taylor Lewis, Chief of Staff here. Faye calls you her favorite protégé."

Unused to accepting compliments, Maya blushed. "I rely on Dr. Simpson's experience a lot."

Then she rotated her own phone. "This is Keegan Williams. He's an epidemiologist from CDC's Vector-Borne Diseases Division. We're about to set off on a serosurvey for dengue near Albuquerque and we wanted final words of wisdom."

"A challenge, but worth doing." Faye poked her head back in. "In 2000, I helped on one for West Nile virus. We selected about five thousand households, and less than half agreed to participate. However, we collected about twenty-five hundred blood samples. Five had antibody tests indicating recent infection."

"Small yield," Keegan said.

Faye shrugged. "But still valuable. Another ten new cases of severe neurologic illness were identified through hospital-based surveillance. Both sets of data allowed us to project the underlying background rate of infection and health impact in the larger population."

"We're following an Arizona plan," Maya said, "but it's never been implemented, only exercised."

"There are some developments here." Faye paused. "You won't be able to reach me at the health department. I quit."

Faye was almost a decade older than Nancy, but Maya was shocked by the announcement. Were congratulations or questions more appropriate?

"I knew that was coming at some point, and you deserve a chance to take it easy. But I'll miss working with you."

Faye shook her finger. "You're not getting rid of me so fast. Taylor's consulting on Juana's brother who's hospitalized in Puerto Rico with dengue. I'm unofficially in the loop."

Maya emitted a gasp before pulling herself together. "How much can one family take?" Then she remembered her own losses from COVID, and sighed. The bad news brought her down, and her mind flashed to the ominous blue-eyed coyote. The creature had vanished when Dave accompanied her to the stable. Had it been the product of her stressed imagination?

"If CDC wants to reactivate my Public Health Service officer status," Faye said, her face animated, "I'd be happy to give you both a hand. Good excuse to head back west—I've got some unfinished personal business in Colorado."

Thousands of miles apart, it never occurred to Maya she'd work with Faye again. She gave a quizzical look to Keegan—would he welcome Faye's help as well? "Our New Mexico study was announced in a press release. Let's see what kind of local cooperation we get this afternoon, then touch base later."

"Thanks for your offer, Dr. Simpson," Keegan said. "I'll mention it to my Division Director in Fort Collins."

Faye's service in the Commissioned Corps had been sometime in the nineteen eighties, well before Maya was born. But reupping had precedence, especially with the challenges of COVID. If CDC rehired Faye, Maya was confident they'd ferret out any dengue infections, human or mosquito, hiding in plain sight.

EIGHTEEN

Faye strolled down the tree-lined street from her hotel in Old Town. Fort Collins had a few landmarks she recognized from vet school. She was glad she didn't need a rental car for the meeting with CDC about dengue. Not that she'd forgotten how to drive, but the thought of doing so made her weak at the knees. Decades out of practice, living in New York.

Flying home to Colorado a day early provided a chance at closure with her intermittent lover, Devorah Abelman. Midday clouds tumbled over each other as Faye swung a compact umbrella from her hand. Right on schedule, thunderstorms built above the Rocky Mountains, soon to blow east over the foothills and plains.

Intermittent traffic and familiar old buildings slowed her tempo. A Classical Revival bank with a high arched entrance dominated the corner. Down the block, Art Deco bungalows flanked a Craftsman. The end of the street was anchored by the assisted living facility, an elegant two-story Colonial Revival fronted by four white columns.

Faye peeked through the front windows to the foyer, all contemporary angular lines of pine and stone. It was beautiful, catering to professionals with money for a high-class place to settle at the end of their lives.

When Devorah lived in her own home, they reconnected in her backyard hot tub, followed by mutual massages with Maude Oil on her king-sized bed below the mirrored ceiling. A sensual memory, but that level of connection wasn't possible in Devorah's current condition. Just as well, given her accelerating relationship with Taylor.

A brunette in a blue plaid cowboy shirt and jeans sat behind a desk in the glass-fronted lobby. Colorado mandated outdoor visits for licensed facilities, so Faye complied with the instructions on the door and pulled out her phone.

The young woman answered the call and cocked her finger to the right. "Dr. Simpson, can you head down the sidewalk and meet me at the garden?"

As Faye arrived at the opening, the receptionist punched numbers into a keypad, then held the ornate black gate open. "We're so happy you can visit Dr. Abelman. She's been asking for you. I'm glad to see you're wearing a mask—the state requires them, even when outside." She gestured to a lounge chair matching the vibrant foliage.

Faye sniffed the scent of almonds and myrrh from shrub rose blossoms until a white-clad nurse opened the building door, holding her client's elbow. As always, Devorah's entrance made a statement.

A sleeveless navy dress, shorter in the front, scalloped to her ankles in the back. Red camellias chased green leaves over the fabric, exposing the upper curve of her breasts. Devorah's mask matched the outfit.

The trademark ruby lips hidden away, Faye struggled to interpret her paramour's expression, until Devorah's arms arched forward as if to invite a hug. The nurse shook her head 'no' and guided her charge to a chair, six feet away from the one where Faye had dropped her umbrella.

"I'm sorry we can't allow contact," the woman said. "You both worked in health-related fields. I'm sure you understand."

Devorah's dark eyes, highlighted with deep blue eyeshadow and eyeliner, crinkled. "Faye," she shouted in her best college instructor voice.

Faye lowered to her own chair. "Devorah, you're looking hot." She glanced at the nurse, wondering if the woman would pick up her sexual implication. Deciding to direct the meaning to the weather, she added, "At least until this afternoon storm cools us off."

Devorah whipped her head from side-to-side, long brown locks covering, then revealing, her cleavage. "Airport?"

A flood of butterflies danced through Faye's inner vision— Devorah remembered more than she'd anticipated. Faye clapped her hands in excitement. "Yes, you always picked me up from the Denver airport when I visited. This time I took the shuttle— expensive but convenient."

Several years since Faye's last visit for her mother's funeral, she loved seeing Devorah again in person. But she hated that their faces were hidden.

"I checked with your State Epidemiologist before my flight," she directed to the nurse. "He anticipates your regulations being minimized or lifted in the fall. Do you really think we need masks out here?"

The nurse hesitated, glancing toward the building. "I'm impressed with your homework. Devorah, how do you feel about wearing a mask?"

"We're not at a masquerade ball," Devorah snapped, then yanked her mask off. Faye did the same. She was warmed by Devorah's longest sentence in months, but disturbed by the harsh, uncharacteristic inflection. Probably Alzheimer's aggression.

Devorah glanced at her watch. "Time for your Lyme disease talk."

Faye reached her arms forward to take Devorah's hands, but at the firm shake of the nurse's head, she drew back. "We did my Lyme presentation already."

"No, can't be late." Devorah squirmed in her chair, appearing ready to bolt.

Don't argue with someone who has dementia. Faye mentally kicked herself for forgetting that cardinal rule. "Yes, dear. Should we go after your nap?"

Devorah's tight posture relaxed as the nurse flashed a subtle thumbs-up.

"This time, I'd like to talk to the students about dengue, too." Faye attempted to keep Devorah's brain stimulated. "I remember your work with Lyme vaccine. Do you know we have one now for children at risk of dengue fever complications?"

"Lyme vaccine discontinued," Devorah answered, body deflated.

Again, a wrong conversational route to take. "You're right, but they're working on a new one. I bet your initial research will be invaluable."

Devorah's expression hollowed out and she yawned, then collapsed even further into the cushions.

"Are you getting tired, sweetheart?" Faye hesitated over the term of endearment—they'd never have an intimate relationship again. Were the words of affection leading Devorah on? *Meet the person where they're at. Reality is not as important.*

"Stay the night, please?" Devorah's expression changed to pleading while Faye decided how to respond.

"I'm meeting CDC to discuss our dengue work tomorrow, and I'll be back in touch when I know my schedule." Faye felt washed with guilt as raindrops pelted her arms, and the nurse helped Devorah to her feet.

Under the awning by the door, the nurse halted, holding onto Devorah's arm. "Thanks for stopping by, Dr. Simpson. Devorah doesn't have any family and she was looking forward to seeing you."

Faye opened her umbrella and pushed through the gate. So much more painful to see Devorah's decline in person. Phone calls had become impossible—Devorah never recognized Faye's voice.

But she had to accept the inevitable. Devorah was seventy-five, and sixteen percent of American women in their seventies got Alzheimer's, Faye remembered from her research. *Thank God we never committed to each other.*

Ashamed at the thought, she desperately needed a glass of wine. Devorah had bugged her repeatedly to take a CSU faculty position so they could share their lives and work. Faye was bonded to New York, and had abhorred the thought of living close to judgmental parents who condemned her to hell for her choices. Not a good excuse after their deaths.

Maybe she should avoid alcohol after the boozy night last week when she quit her job. But Fort Collins was known for craft beers. At a restaurant with bluegrass music emanating through outdoor speakers, she passed up the drenched patio chairs and headed inside.

Fort Collins, Colorado—Monday, July 26, 2021

Faye waited on the weathered wooden bench in front of the hotel until a Kia SUV pulled up. Keegan hopped out, then opened the back door. He hooked a leash to a small black-and-white dog, who jumped out with a friendly "Woof" to greet the stranger.

"Good morning, Dr. Simpson. Welcome to the Centennial State!"

"I was born here," Faye reminded him, then bent to ruffle the soft fur and floppy ears of the dancing dog.

"Of course. I forgot Colorado State is your vet school." He looked sheepish as he held the passenger door open and offered a hand to help her in. "This is such a quick trip home, my mind's a bit jumbled."

He hooked the dog's harness to the rear seat belt before joining Faye up front.

Faye enjoyed the dog's gaping grin. She'd been too long without the heart-calming drug of a pet's unconditional love. "And who's this?"

"Moki," Keegan answered. "She's an Aussie/border collie mix, six months old." He pulled south onto College Avenue. "I picked up some pastries from Verne's Place in Laporte. Should we stop by City Park?"

Faye's phone indicated they weren't due at the CDC offices for another hour. "That would be nice. It's been a few years since I last visited." She sighed and let the western ambiance seep in, savoring a respite from the heady charge of a New York street.

When they reached the city lake, they relaxed on a picnic table. A cinnamon roll triggered warm sense memories, but she left it for Keegan while she picked at the pecan bun, washing it down with black coffee. The contrast of sweet and crunch provided a happy jolt of food valium.

Keegan took several laps around the table for leash training with Moki, then rejoined Faye for their breakfast. "I feel guilty leaving Maya alone," he said. "The *Albuquerque Journal*'s treating the news of the three positive mosquito pools like the apocalypse."

Faye glanced at his earnest face. So young, so wracked with concern over any possible mistakes.

A honk prompted a bark from Moki, and Faye's attention was drawn to a pair of Canada geese shepherding their goslings in a flotilla on the pond, one parent in front and one behind. She recalled the defenders and alarmists dueling about goose overpopulation, with their risk of spreading *Salmonella*, *E. coli*, and cryptosporidium to people.

It would be a while before Keegan realized how many aspects of public health he couldn't control. "Why did you abandon Maya?" Despite her affection for such a polite young man, Faye's caustic wit wouldn't allow her to pass up an opportunity to needle him.

Clearly peeved, he scratched at his scalp. "Those mosquito results didn't come in until my plane landed in Denver yesterday. I wanted to show you around our CDC offices and see Moki again for the weekend."

"These field assignments can be hell on relationships, including with our pets. I'm sure Maya understands."

Faye appreciated Keegan's hospitality, but needed to get them back on task. "I don't want to be late for our meeting with your boss."

Keegan wrapped up his cinnamon bun, then detoured the SUV to his home, an older Victorian. He left the engine running as he greeted his roommate at the front door, handing over Moki and the pastry.

Driving west on Rampart Road, he waved his arm out his lowered window. "Over there is the Temple Grandin Equine Center, named after the autistic faculty member who did that research on humane treatment of livestock. Was she here when you were a student?"

"I never met her. Her doctoral degree is in animal science, not vet med."

Faye wondered if Keegan understood her sense of humor. Maya had to eventually look around for love. Faye wouldn't put her thumb on the scale for Keegan unless he knew how to go with the flow. "Temple Grandin made big contributions to the One Health initiative without a medical degree," she said. "Maybe you can too."

"That's my goal. CDC's on the One Health bandwagon, recruiting physicians like the New Mexico and Arizona State Epidemiologists, veterinarians like you and Maya, and environmental epidemiologists like me."

Faye beamed. "Each of us contributing our own area of expertise to the whole."

Keegan slowed for a truck labeled with the name of a medical supply company. "Good thing I have lots of experience catching mosquitoes. The first guy I tried to stick for a blood draw almost passed out, so I'm leaving that part up to Maya and the health department's team."

His rueful tone indicated his acceptance and respect of their different capabilities. Attitude adjustment—not needed.

Faye decided that Keegan was kind and respectful. When they got to Albuquerque, she would monitor whether Maya noticed at all. She gave a silent chortle. How did she, as a lifelong marriage skeptic, morph into a matchmaker?

The winding two-lane road climbed higher toward the concrete-and-glass multistoried building nestled into the hillside. After clearing security, they checked in with one of the staff near the conference room. "You're a bit early—Dr. Millichamp will be with you at nine."

"Tell him we'll be right back." Keegan led Faye out the back door to a series of metal poles that pierced the cloud-streaked blue sky. Large circular rings with dense netting were suspended on arms jutting out from the poles. "See these mosquitoes trapped inside? We can spray and evaluate the effect of adulticides at different distances."

"Sounds like that information will be helpful if we need to spray in New Mexico," Faye said. "How do you grow and maintain them?"

Back inside, he showed her mosquitoes feeding. "Pork blood is warmed to body temp and this membrane in the centrifuge tube mimics the skin."

Faye hadn't realized CDC Fort Collins maintained mosquitoes. She was more familiar with their surveillance and prevention efforts, not their research.

"We have entomologists to raise them," Keegan added. "We're looking at 3D printing to efficiently create customized artificial feeders."

Faye twitched with an illusion of them swooping onto her pale freckled skin. She'd never been close to such a dense concentration of the deadliest dengue vector, too small for her to see their markings clearly. Fingers crossed, they couldn't escape.

Some conspiracy theorists speculated that the abnormally folded prion protein which scrambled deer and elk brains in chronic wasting disease had escaped from a Colorado research study. Recent concerns about the prion's potential to infect humans and the lab leak theories for COVID in China increased press interest in the old story.

Dementia with inevitable death—had anyone looked at whether Alzheimer's rates were higher in Fort Collins?

She shook off paranoia. Typically, she scoffed at such rampant speculation, but Devorah's decline had her in a mournful mood.

The staff member invited them back to the conference room where Dr. Millichamp, the squat Vector-Borne Diseases Director, opened up Zoom on a wall-mounted computer monitor.

Good, Faye reflected, she wasn't the only example of pandemic compulsive eating and lack of exercise. Then she slapped aside her judgmental tendency—just because she slowly gained weight over the decades, then packed on extra pounds last year with more confinement, didn't mean others had the same issues.

Maya and Fred Grinwold popped onto the screen as they sat, backs rigid, on a leather couch. Nancy Bingham poked into view for a moment as she poured them cups of tea. "Don't mind me—I'm retired. Just lurking in the background."

Dr. Millichamp kicked off the discussion. "Thanks, Dr. Simpson, for joining our team over the next few weeks. Many of our staff are supporting COVID control, so it's helpful to have a senior person onboard."

Fred removed his glasses and dabbed a napkin at his face, looking strained. "One of our positive mosquito pools was collected on Sandia Pueblo. We're all too aware of the jurisdictional challenge that poses, and Maya's not the best to lead our efforts with a native nation."

Faye was surprised by Fred's slam—he had always supported his trainee. Then Maya's stiff posture and lowered eyes reminded her. In a freak storm, Maya's car hit the body of an elderly Jicarilla Apache. She was cleared of all charges when the autopsy confirmed he was already dead from exposure. But the accident had jeopardized state/tribal relations. Two years had passed, and Sandia Pueblo was in a different part of the state. How well known was the incident, and would it continue to dog Maya's reputation?

NINETEEN

Sandia Pueblo, New Mexico—Friday, July 30, 2021

As she drove west on Tramway Avenue, Maya was energized by the successful week of dengue surveillance after Keegan had rejoined her in Albuquerque, augmented by Faye's leadership. But the meeting with Sandia Pueblo had her worried. Edward Newton, an environmental scientist from the Jicarilla Pueblo, was their Indian Health Service liaison and her front seat navigator.

Maya hit the brakes and pulled off to the side of the road. "Is that a herd of buffalo?"

"The correct name is bison," Edward said.

Maya recoiled from the curt comment. Like other Jicarilla Apaches, was he still pissed about her car accident?

He pivoted to Faye and Keegan in the back seat. "Surprised to find bison in an urban area?"

"A herd was established not far from where I live in Fort Collins," Keegan answered.

"Do we have time for a picture?" Faye already had her phone out.

Edward checked his watch. "We're a bit early, so we can spare five minutes."

Maya parked next to the Bien Mur Indian Market, a huge circular arts and crafts center. Interrupted only by a couple of shade trees, the stark Sandia Pueblo lands stretched toward the mountain foothills.

Faye led Keegan to the fence line. "Those four calves look so cute, tagging along with their mothers."

Lingering behind, Edward looked at Maya with a wry expression.

"Aren't you into baby bison?"

"Not into baby anything," Maya said before thinking, then changed the subject. "I was surprised to hear about your new role with IHS. Why did you leave Dulce?"

"Your husband's COVID triage training gave me the motivation to expand my footprint. Tragic loss, my condolences."

"Thanks." Maya treasured hearing how people respected Manolo, but new reminders of his death were jarring. When would the painful stomach clenches and skin flushes stop? "I appreciate your help with mosquito collection." As Dr. Grinwold had reminded her, it solved a lot of jurisdictional issues.

Edward smoothed his dark hair. "It's good that your press release only listed the county for the positive mosquito pools, not Sandia Pueblo. That will make our discussion with the tribal leaders go smoother."

"I'm not sure this meeting would have happened if you weren't on our team," Maya said. "They have no women leaders—what's up with that?"

He checked his watch again, then his voice turned frosty. "I don't know, and I wouldn't presume to speculate."

Maya ducked her eyes. She'd hoped to impress him by researching the Pueblo, but instead she'd overstepped. With decades of experience, Faye was serving as their lead CDC representative, but she was too busy gushing over the fuzzy, lighter-colored bison calves.

"Dr. Simpson," Edward called out. "We should get going."

At the traffic light, Maya headed straight through to the resort area and parked. Multiple adobe hues glowed from the building, massed in front of the looming bulk of the Sandia Mountains, its peaks hidden under a massive cloud.

Edward led the group past the outdoor fountains through doors with a mask requirement sign and a staff person who checked their temperatures.

The casino had reopened less than a month earlier, and only a few patrons operated the noisy, colorful slot machines.

"Why did they want to meet here instead of the tribal administrative offices?" Maya asked.

Edward chuckled. "Never pass up an opportunity to part someone from their money."

"Believe it or not, I've never gambled," Maya said. "Not even a lottery ticket."

"Never tempted by OTB when you went to Columbia?" Faye teased. She turned to Edward. "That's off-track betting on horses or greyhounds—very popular in New York. But retired ladies like me also take the bus to Foxwoods in Connecticut."

Faye didn't look retired, Maya thought. And she'd not been forthcoming with the details on her jumping ship from New York. But whatever the complete story, Maya was grateful they were working together again.

"We need to go this way." Edward led them down a hall with the rug design matching the ceiling lights and the bright blue of the doors.

In the meeting room, he introduced the Sandia Pueblo Governor and their Environment Department director. Everyone sat around a circular wooden table carved with an image of the Pueblo flag, a black geometric pattern arching above a blue mound of mountain. The walls were covered with photographs and paintings of the local area.

"You came all the way from the Big Apple, Dr. Simpson," the Environment Department director said. "I guess we should be flattered."

Faye laughed. "That was a prior life. It's been decades since I worked for CDC, but I'm happily on board again."

"We're not comfortable with your finding dengue in mosquitoes near our Sandia Lakes recreation area," the tribal Governor said. "Only one mosquito pool—perhaps it's a mistake. What exactly is a mosquito pool?"

"For testing, a group of mosquitoes is pooled together, or combined, for a more cost-efficient process," Keegan said. "So we don't know how many mosquitoes in that pool were infected, but at least one."

Maya squirmed in her seat. "Our lab says there's no chance of false positives." She'd intended to let Faye take the lead, but Faye wasn't familiar with their state health lab.

"And our CDC lab confirmed it," Keegan added.

"I insist we keep that area open," the Governor continued. "Picnic sites, group shelters, a bait and tackle shop. The playground and nature trail along the Rio Grande are heavily used."

"We're not suggesting that you restrict those activities," Faye said. "The cautions about personal mosquito control for those near the Bosque should be enough."

"For our wetlands, do you anticipate any additional infected mosquitoes?" the director asked.

Faye shook her head. "We believe this was a single introduction of the virus."

"But climate change is expanding favorable mosquito habitat," Maya said, "and we have the most dangerous species here, *Aedes aegypti*."

"Explain what you mean by personal control, Dr. Simpson," the Governor ordered. "Are you putting the responsibility on our people? Does that mean you will do nothing to help us?"

"Of course not," Faye answered. "We'll identify the highest risk areas and get everyone on alert for rapid diagnosis and treatment if infected. But people can decrease their own risk."

"By reducing exposed skin with long sleeves and pants, or using mosquito repellent," added Edward. "Avoiding times of high mosquito activity. Maintaining intact screens. Emptying outdoor containers of water."

"The *Albuquerque Journal* reports just two human cases, from Corrales," the Governor said.

"Well, three with the index case passing through on her way to New York." Faye shook her head. "It's unusual that two of them died, but host factors probably played a role."

"Please explain that," the Governor said.

"They each had a chronic illness which made them more vulnerable," Faye answered.

"The blood draws in Corrales…" The director tapped his pen on the table. "I'm concerned about that here. We don't want our people feeling like they're part of a medical experiment."

Maya gulped. She hadn't anticipated opposition to human surveillance. Why hadn't Edward warned them?

With so many ethical violations in medical research, Maya understood the sensitivity. There still had been no government apology for the congressional act that resulted in the sterilization of thousands of native American women without their permission.

"Have you developed a tribal Institutional Review Board?" Faye asked. Maya remembered that the Navajo IRB could require research staff to come from their tribal members.

"Yes, but we haven't used it yet for this," the director answered.

"This is an outbreak investigation, not research," Faye said, "so it likely isn't required. It's not essential that we determine the rate of those infected without symptoms. Instead, we'll work with Edward to follow up on anyone coming through IHS with a compatible illness."

Keegan clenched his fists, signaling his frustration. "Are you sure? More than half of infections can be asymptomatic."

Faye cautioned him with a hand. "Forgive our eager recent EIS graduate. Dr. Williams is correct—infections can be mild and go unrecognized or unreported. But given the current limited results on the Pueblo, mosquito-borne disease education efforts should be sufficient."

"We're working on our messaging," Edward said. "We'll have information to recommend for your website and brochures by next week. All subject to your approval, of course."

Maya breathed a sigh of relief that they'd reached an agreement without too much rancor. She shared Keegan's concern about what they'd lose by skipping a larger serosurvey, but they were finishing one in Corrales. It wasn't essential to repeat it at the Pueblo.

"All right." The Governor reached over to shake Faye's hand.

"This is just a human disease—nothing to worry about with our livestock or the buffalo herd?"

"Because the virus isn't transmitted directly between animals and people, it's unlikely to be a problem," Maya answered, proud to show off her extensive literature search. "But lots of other species can be occasionally infected, including domestic animals like dogs, pigs, and horses. Also wildlife like bats, birds, and nonhuman primates."

"Those species may be dead-end hosts," Faye inserted. "Possibly susceptible, but with insufficient virus to infect mosquitoes or other animals."

Maya took a breath, fearing to contradict Faye but more afraid of being too reassuring. "For farm animals, pigs have been the most infected, 65% of those sampled in India." She glanced at Faye for confirmation. She hadn't intended to pontificate like an expert, but was pleased that her research could contribute something.

"We have different conditions here. Bottom line, there is no important nonhuman animal reservoir." Faye pinned Maya with her blue eyes and sat up straight with an authoritative 'end of conversation' tone.

Edward stood and shook hands with the two pueblo reps again. "Thanks for clarifying your positions on the plans. I'll be in touch to work out specific prevention and control measures."

Maya unlocked the Prius and settled behind the wheel. Faye grabbed the front passenger seat, then pivoted to the back. "Maya and Keegan, we must work from the same game plan as we move forward with the Pueblo. I know you're disappointed, but we needed to adjust when they started to get hot under the collar."

"I'm sorry if you think I alarmed them about the animals," Maya said.

Faye frowned. "I appreciate your thoroughness, but lay people can't cope with all the detailed possibilities. We need to address what's likely, not what's possible. Remember from vet school—when you hear hoofbeats, think horses, not zebras."

"I agree with Dr. Simpson," Edward chimed in. "If we freak them out, they'll throw up their hands and do nothing."

Maya's belly tightened as she held her breath. "That makes no sense."

Faye spoke softly but with emphasis. "This goes for both of you at the beginning of your careers. People are aching to find fault with public health, believing we're just out to expand our bureaucratic empires. We'll focus on tribal members with compatible symptoms. I realize they may be the tip of the iceberg, but we can't get overly ambitious without more justification."

Realizing she'd sat out so many months of pandemic response, Maya bit her lip and stayed silent. Her obsessive need to be thorough had to be modulated by Faye's more seasoned judgment.

Edward broke the tension. "Let's see where the positive mosquito pool came from."

After a short drive, they lined up along the edge of a tree-shaded expanse of blue water, cotton clouds painting the reflective surface.

"Guess we didn't get a storm after all," Keegan said.

Maya knew he was making small talk to ease the interpersonal electricity. She couldn't recall getting crosswise with Faye before. Her skin dampened—the humidity was high under the protective canopy of trees.

A mosquito bit her forearm beneath her loose blouse. Too late, she swatted it dead. "I hate that *Aedes* is a day-biter."

Keegan flapped his fingers at one near his shirt collar. "Hope my mosquito repellent's working."

Edward's eyes drifted from one to the other. "You guys don't wear permethrin-treated clothing?"

Defensive, Maya stiffened. "Neither of us do vector control full time, like you."

"I know," Edward said, "but you should set a good example."

"We've been a bit preoccupied trying to get shitloads of surveillance data collected." Keegan's height didn't rival Edward's but his voice cracked like a whip. "No time to think of ourselves."

Faye looked like she was about to calm the waters when her

phone rang. "Siti, we're making progress here in New Mexico. How about everywhere else—dengue still got you like a tiger by the tail?"

Faye didn't turn on the speaker and Maya heard nothing else of the conversation. It went on for a long time, Faye's face becoming tighter by the minute.

TWENTY

Honolulu, Oʻahu—Monday, August 9, 2021

New Mexico dengue under control with no more positives, Faye had agreed to Siti's request for help in Hawaiʻi. A pale sky tinged with pink lighted her walk from the Honolulu hotel.

She inhaled humid air and shared the joy of songbirds, greeting a dawn in paradise. From behind a blue-painted iron gate, she paused to admire the ornate ʻIolani Palace framed by palm trees. Too early for tours, and she'd likely not have time for Hawaiian royal history.

At the corner of Punchbowl Street, she turned and walked another block past the State Capitol building. No old-fashioned dome or turrets like Colorado's and New York's. Across the street, the Hawaiʻi State Department of Health appeared to be from the same brutalist era—all utilitarian concrete.

Once inside a DOH windowless conference room, Faye joined a Zoom meeting coordinated by Ino Kahale, a grizzled Hawaiian from their Disease Outbreak Control Division. He connected them up with CDC in Puerto Rico.

"Mr. Kahale, thanks for hosting at such an early hour," Siti Rahim said. "Faye, I thought I'd see you in a Public Health Service uniform like me."

Faye fingered her ocean-patterned loose pants, purchased to accommodate the heat and humidity upon arrival in Honolulu yesterday. "I re-upped as a civilian. Didn't want to take a chance someone could order me to Afghanistan."

Siti smirked. "Yeah, that's a cluster fuck. You did a great job guiding Maya and Keegan in New Mexico. Mr. Kahale, can you update us on dengue in Hawaiʻi?"

"Please call me Ino. We have more experience handling dengue than most states, but we're getting swamped by tourists. We need additional surge capacity for dengue on top of COVID."

Siti's Zoom screenshot froze for a moment, then she answered. "I'm alarmed that your confirmed infections have surpassed a hundred. We're stretched thin with a spike in San Juan as well."

Ino looked at his notes. "We had over two hundred persons with confirmed dengue in 2015-2016. Like tourists, *Aedes* mosquitoes are quite fond of our environment."

Faye was heartened he could joke despite juggling multiple disease outbreaks. The scale of the threat in Hawai'i made her dengue work in New York and New Mexico seem insignificant. But they hadn't known they'd get lucky and have those small outbreaks fizzle out.

Siti's serious expression relaxed. "Faye, you jumped into New Mexico at a critical time. Before you visited with him, the Sandia Pueblo Governor had phoned, threatening to ban CDC or state staff from their lands."

Faye was glad Maya wasn't on their Zoom call. She might have interpreted Siti's remarks as a criticism of her efforts before Faye arrived.

"Those human and mosquito infections related to Juana Lopez could have been the flame to ignite larger outbreaks," Siti continued, "but they never exploded exponentially like in Hawai'i. We dodged a bullet on the mainland."

Ino shifted his weight on his armless chair. "This year, our state lab didn't report any people with positive antibodies until July."

Siti tilted her pink-haired head down to consult notes. "Our San Juan lab is working on genetic sequencing to find out your type of dengue."

"It's been several weeks since our first patients had onset of symptoms," Ino said. "After our advisory to the medical community, the number of specimens overwhelmed our lab staff, who worked all weekend."

"So initially, cases may have been percolating with no one

seeking medical care, or clinicians not submitting samples," Faye said.

Tweaked by guilt that her New Mexico work delayed jumping over to Hawai'i, she hoped her remark didn't sound critical of the local health providers. Her early involvement in Juana's case benefitted from her relationship with Taylor, a muscular marathoner who was also an astute Staten Island clinician.

Ideally, public health proceeded along a science-driven path, but as in any human endeavor, connections made a difference.

Ino's friendly face morphed into a stony mask, like the bronze King Kamehameha I statue Faye had passed across from the Palace. "We weren't slow. Fever, muscle aches, fatigue—nothing unusual in initial patients to bring it to our attention."

Siti jumped in. "Over the weekend, the proportion of cases with severe dengue exploded."

"We'll do a new press release," Ino said, his tone less frosty.

Faye took another sip of her coffee. "I always thought my first visit to Hawai'i would be for relaxation. But being useful is more important." In New York, Moshe had implied she was over-the-hill, ready to join Devorah in assisted living.

She recalled Moshe's occasional drops of the professional facade, when he admitted that every death and long COVID case weighed on him like they were family members. Did anyone in his family die from a corona infection?

Ino interrupted her second guesses. "Faye, did you hear me? There's something that feels different about this outbreak."

Faye refocused. "I'm sorry, jet lag is catching up. At two in the morning, my body thought it was time to get to work, and now it wants to nap. You were saying?"

"Our 2015-2016 outbreak was fall-winter, so these cases are earlier. Of course, we have *Aedes* year-round."

"Where's the hotspot this time?" Faye asked.

"People living outside, whether unhoused or camping," Ino said. "Campgrounds reopened after COVID closures, and locals are charged less for campsites. So that's where cases predominate."

Faye had never gravitated to camping and couldn't imagine the heat and humidity, plus mosquitoes. Ranching as a child in Colorado was enough roughing it. "Which area's most affected?"

"At the moment, Hawai'i Island's Ho'okena Beach Park."

Armed with mosquito repellent and new permethrin-impregnated work clothes in her suitcase, Faye plunged ahead. "Well, I learn more onsite. Can we head there today?"

Siti smiled. "Keep in touch and let me know if you need additional resources." Her face disappeared from the computer monitor.

"I'll book us a flight to Kona," Ino said. "Then I'll text you the details."

Faye regretted having no time to wander Waikiki Beach, but starting the trip roasted like a radish wasn't a good idea. Dipping her toes in the Pacific Ocean for the first time in her life would have to wait.

Out her hotel room window, Faye glimpsed Diamond Head and its dramatic reddish-brown slopes, sparsely dotted with trees. She snapped a photo and texted it to Taylor.

"Are you headed up to the crater?" Taylor asked on the return call. "It was a highlight on my last visit. Paved trail, a bit less than two miles roundtrip, about five hundred feet elevation gain."

Faye settled into the armchair. "You know I'm not a hiker, even to a major tourist stop."

"Well, I dragged you out on the High Line."

Faye laughed. "I think those steps climbing up to the old railroad tracks were a hair less than five hundred feet. Hey, hope I'm not interrupting anything at the hospital."

"Nope, it's five o'clock—getting off at a reasonable hour for once. I'm headed out for my jog to the ferry."

Taylor's words triggered memories of a lean, athletic body in gym shorts and a sleeveless t-shirt. Faye sighed. "I was spoiled by seeing you so often. It's more than two weeks since I've been home, and I miss you."

"How long will you be gone?"

Faye sank deeper into her chair, exhausted. She yearned for her memory foam bed and her refrigerator stashed with Greek yogurt. "Sorry, no idea. When I left, I thought it was for Colorado and New Mexico. Never figured on hibiscus and surfboards."

"I checked in with the hospital in San Juan. Juana's older brother has been discharged. I recommended a re-evaluation of their treatment protocol, and that seems to have helped him."

"I'm jealous. In clinical medicine, you can see the direct outcome of your genius."

"Your efforts have a particularly quick impact on me when we make love," Taylor answered.

"See, you're even good at flirting on the phone. I still wonder why you have any interest in this dowdy old lady."

Taylor's voice continued its seductive tone, tinged with exasperation. "Sounds like this requires a deeper conversation, in person."

Faye stood up and used her free hand to slide her suitcase from the bed to the floor. "No can do. Dengue cases here exceed a hundred and I'm headed to Hawai'i Island."

"You sound a bit in the dumps, and have avoided the topic of your old flame."

Taylor was right. Ever since Fort Collins, she'd suffered from an underlying sense of futility, the grim reaper disrupting her sleep. Her mind couldn't adjust to the new normal for Devorah, so diminished from her fiery, flamboyant younger days.

"Did she recognize you? Did she enjoy your visit? That's all you can expect, at this stage in her Alzheimer's."

A text came in from Ino. **<In the lobby.>**

He was early, but she was ready to go.

"Sorry, Taylor, I have to catch my flight. I'll do better at keeping in touch."

"Maybe on your next trip to the Pacific, we won't need the phone. Traveling together, another item for our bucket list."

Taylor's warm humor melted an icy sliver of dread wedged

along Faye's spine. "You're good for me," Faye answered. *Love you* almost slipped her lips as she said goodbye.

She set down her phone. At no time had she felt accepted enough by her parents to use such an expression. With Devorah, she always feared escalating a commitment, and avoided the words.

Was there something wrong with her that it took sixty-six years to come close? Or something special about Taylor that she was finally tempted?

TWENTY-ONE

Manhattan, New York City—Thursday, August 26, 2021

Maya cradled the heavy urn in her arms as she gazed up at the Empire State Building from the hotel room window. The pinnacle with its antennas was a pale blue, the spire red, and the upper floors green, not unlike the colors swirling the earthen container of her husband's and baby's cremains.

"It's your thirty-fifth birthday tomorrow, sweetheart," she whispered. "I miss you so much. And you, little one, you break my heart."

She kissed the lip of the urn twice, set it on the end table, and curled up on the bed beside it until her phone rang.

"Maya, just checking that your trip to New York went smoothly." Mark's baritone warmed up the tiny room.

She adjusted a pillow behind her and sat up in the bed. "Some aggravating travel delays, but I'm comfortably nesting in Manhattan. Sorry to cancel our plans for horseback riding this weekend."

"Not a problem," he said. "Getting up on a horse would have violated my doctor's orders."

Maya mimicked her mother's strident tone. "I would have refused your invitation if I'd known it would jeopardize your health."

"Come on now, don't chew me out. My primary exercise lately has been swimming at the city pool across from the health department. I'd hoped to see you there."

"With all the dengue work in Albuquerque, I haven't been at home or in the office." Staying away from her apartment with its memories had been therapeutic—the nightmares had eased, a bit.

"I'm glad you're mending relations with your in-laws."

Goose bumps from the A/C spread over her bare legs and she pulled the sheet higher. There were no guarantees that this visit would thaw the Miranda freeze, but it couldn't hurt. They'd worked out the final details by email, not phone, so she couldn't be completely sure of their attitude toward her.

"And dengue has settled down?"

"Yes, here in the continental US." All the weeks of surveillance for infected humans and mosquitoes had turned up no new cases. "But Puerto Rico and Hawai'i are hotspots."

"Why the difference?" Mark asked.

"Warmer, wetter areas are supportive of mosquito breeding."

Infected *Aedes* mosquitoes and the dengue deaths in new areas had been a wake-up call that the climate was changing. But it appeared that Juana and her family were a one-off. Her blood infected some mosquitoes in the Corrales area, including the Sandia Pueblo—enough to spread the virus to her cousin and grandmother. But there wasn't sufficient virus to establish an endemic cycle with lots of infected mosquitoes.

"If we had more dengue, believe me, we would have found it," she added.

All those long sweaty days with Keegan installing and checking mosquito traps, all the late evenings interviewing residents. Many people had been reluctant to answer their doors to strangers, although having a senior citizen like Faye along had increased resident acceptance before she shifted to Hawai'i.

"I hope you'll get time off when you return to Santa Fe." Mark's words were tentative, begging. "It's been more than six weeks since we've seen each other. The staff would love it if you joined us for dinner at the ranch."

She was close with several of them but doubted that they were the prime motivation for the invitation. Mark was so accomplished at persuading judges and juries—using those skills on her generated a twinge of discomfort. She had shut down his flirting, but clearly his interest persisted.

"I could be pulled away for a bigger outbreak." She doubted

she'd be transferred to Puerto Rico even with their increased cases. But Faye had been assigned to Hawai'i, and if they couldn't get that outbreak under control, they might need an extra hand.

"I choose to be optimistic." Once again, he became assured, in command. "Some aspens are dropping yellow leaves, despite our recent heatwave. Touch base when you get back to New Mexico and we'll have you out to Pecos. I won't take no for an answer."

Maya ended the call without any promises. They'd made no mention of her biweekly checks to pay him back for the China fine. Ten thousand dollars—it would be the holidays before she ended the debt. Could they relax around each other and just be friends, with that looming?

She drew the drapes to block out the City. Something new—staying in a midtown hotel. During her two years working on her Masters of Public Health degree, she'd lived in a Columbia University dorm. When she visited with Manolo, they'd stayed with the Mirandas. No offer of that hospitality this time.

In his hometown for his family's Catholic funeral, she'd anticipated a sleepless night. Stephanie had recommended downloading podcasts and books on tape to her phone. *The Year of Magical Thinking* by Joan Didion was on her menu.

The book about the year following her husband's death won multiple awards. The author, in a fit of insanity, kept his clothes so he'd have them on his return. Maya hadn't been in their apartment long enough to figure out what to do with Manolo's.

As she hit **<Play>** on her phone screen, the narrator's intonation sucked her into the story, interrupting a nearly relentless cycle of Manolo lingering in her dreams.

The Bronx, New York City—Friday, August 27, 2021

The altar of the Romanesque Revival church was framed by a gold screen and an arch of celestial cloudy sky with Jesus and the angels. Faye had told Maya it was the same church where Juana's funeral was held. Small world, but Manolo was Puerto Rican like Juana, so not a total coincidence.

Maya spotted Manolo's sister and father in the first wooden pew. The Mirandas Zoomed to her wedding last summer, so she hadn't seen them in person for more than a year, pre-pandemic.

Like her, Ramona and Sebastian wore black masks and she couldn't confirm their expressions. But they ignored her when she held out her hand. She understood—touching still made some people nervous. She moved her hand to her heart, a greeting she'd picked up from Erika, who said it was used at her church in Santa Fe.

"You can't believe how wonderful it is to be with you again." Tears formed in her eyes, and she brushed them away. "Will Abdi and Johnny join us for the service?"

She missed Ramona's husband and son. Her heart pulsed with the tender memory of holding Johnny in her arms at the Bronx Zoo.

Ramona's skin and pulled-back hair couldn't be tighter, as if she'd had a botched face lift. Her grief made her robotic. Different ways to handle it, as Maya was learning from the Joan Didion audiobook.

Sebastian glanced at his daughter, then back at Maya. His eyes crinkled and he raised his open hand to his chest in response to Maya's gesture. He knew what it meant to lose a spouse too young. "They'll join us just before it starts. Johnny will be restless. He's only six—he doesn't understand about death."

Maya was happy with the more forgiving body language of her father-in-law, but the unnecessary reminder of Johnny's age felt like a body blow. Did Sebastian believe she'd divorced them all after Manolo's death? The toy firetruck she'd sent for Johnny's June birthday went unacknowledged.

"Did you forget the ashes?" Ramona's question sounded like it came from gritted teeth.

Maya lowered her daypack to the pew. "Of course not." She unzipped the pack and lifted out the colorful urn.

In the spring when her parents presented it to her, she'd been unable to look at it, let alone touch it. Now she hated giving it away, but the Mirandas wanted something beautiful to place in the burial vault. She'd already removed half the ashes for the outdoor ceremony she was planning.

"When you didn't contact us until seven-thirty last night," Ramona said, "we were freaked something had happened."

Maya welcomed Ramona's softer tone, but not the dig at what she did wrong. She tried to avoid a prickly response.

"I was upset about my delayed landing from the thunderstorm, too. All I could think about was the plane running out of fuel, or getting struck by a lightning bolt."

She exaggerated the last part in hopes of breaking the ice. "I would have hijacked the plane and ordered it to land before I'd disappoint you."

Sebastian picked up the urn. "We appreciate your making the effort in the face of your work obligations. We saw the news about the little girl who died here—it's ironic that the two states with dengue this summer have been New York and New Mexico."

"Well, except for Hawai'i and Puerto Rico, but they're so far away." Out of sight, out of mind. Other than her work colleagues, not many people thought about dengue.

Ramona put one hand on the urn. "We needed this for the wake last night." Her voice was mournful rather than accusatory.

"I'm sorry, Ramona. I tried to make it in time, but the weather conspired against us. Not everything is my fault."

"Don't worry about it," Sebastian said.

Maya took several slow breaths to release the stricture in her chest.

"If you had booked an earlier flight," Ramona said, "travel delays wouldn't have kept you from being here."

Maya opened her mouth to respond but Sebastian beat her to it. "The wake was wonderful—so many of his friends from school showed up. And some colleagues from his medical training in DC."

An elderly man in priest's robes joined them from the vestry.

"We're about to open the doors. Are you ready?"

"Yes, Father," Sebastian said. "This is Maya, Manolo's widow."

"Good to meet you," the priest said. "I hope you can take comfort in knowing that your husband is at peace with God. Do you have any last-minute requests for the service?"

"No." Manolo's nighttime visits didn't indicate he was at peace, but she respected the priest's job. She stroked the urn one more time. "I'm blessed by being here with Manolo's family on his birthday."

The priest placed the urn on a table in front of the altar. Ramona took the seat nearest the center aisle and Sebastian sat beside her. He invited Maya to join him. Then the nave filled with guests, many stopping up front to greet the Mirandas.

When Abdi and Johnny entered from the side, Johnny ran to hug Maya, then joined her on the pew. Just like a kid to ignore COVID protocols about touching. He didn't say anything, but Maya was filled with joy that he remembered her. Abdi bent to hug his wife, then sat on Johnny's other side.

Three people holding hands approached the pew. A dignified African American man in his fifties made a formal bow to the Mirandas, then turned to the petite Asian woman next to him. The third person, Manolo's age, was beautiful with straight black hair to her waist. She extended a hand to Ramona. "Again, my condolences. There will never be another like him."

Based on Manolo's descriptions, Maya realized who they were. Consolatory cadence with a renowned heart surgeon's confident bearing—it had to be Angela, Manolo's ex. The older couple were her parents, acting like Manolo's in-laws.

Sebastian turned to Maya. Before he could introduce her, she stood and offered her own hand. "I'm Maya. It means everything that you still hold him in your heart."

Angela briefly responded to the handshake, but Maya couldn't read her eyes above the mask. Perhaps she blamed Maya for Manolo's death, like the Mirandas. Or as a physician, did she understand the scimitar of death that struck down patients, no matter how hard the medical and public health world battled it?

TWENTY-TWO

On the picnic table under a palm tree, Faye reviewed her notes and popped arare rice crackers into her mouth. Ho'okena Beach Park was eerily quiet except for the rustling of foliage by a mongoose. The animal stared at her with deep amber eyes, then flashed scary teeth before it slunk away, like a meerkat on steroids.

Both CDC and the Hawai'i State Department of Health were satisfied with the number of adult and larval mosquitoes Faye and Ino Kahale had collected for dengue surveillance along Hawai'i Island's west coast for more than two weeks.

"I hate to abandon you, but these old bones need a break," he'd apologized yesterday afternoon as he posted the Park Closed sign on the campground gate. "This might be my last chance to see Alika dance with her hālau for a while."

Dengue's surge, in addition to more COVID cases with the delta variant, triggered Hawai'i's Governor to issue a proclamation discouraging tourism. Ino predicted Safe Hawai'i rules would restrict travel soon, so he flew home to Honolulu for his granddaughter's hula 'auana performance.

He'd ordered Faye to enjoy the aloha spirit, but her body was still New York-restless. She wasn't eligible to drive Ino's state vehicle, so CDC approved a rental for an additional day of work. Then Ino texted that Faye should expect a visit from Dr. Caren Oldner, a University of Hawai'i at Hilo dengue expert who'd just returned from the mainland.

Wondering when Dr. Oldner would show up, Faye kicked off her sandals and wiggled her toes in the warm sand. Elbow anchoring her paperwork, she eyed the gently crashing blue-green waves just in time to catch a long-beaked dolphin flip in the air, darker back and lighter stomach flashing as it spun.

Tomorrow or Sunday—she promised herself—she'd cool off with a snorkel tour to Kealakekua Bay.

"Just like the health department to leave you on your own."

It had been almost forty years since they were in vet school together, but Faye recognized the distinctly staccato voice. The clipped speech hadn't changed over the decades.

"Caren, I wondered if it could be you," Faye answered. The same angular build and thick hair, now a graying buzz cut. Caren's leathered skin spoke of a life in the outdoors. Faye glanced down at her own belly bulging above her dark shorts. Caren had no pandemic paunch.

"It's Cah-ren, not Care-en."

Shit, she should have remembered the woman's sensitivity about that, long before 'Karen' became a bad word for racially-biased white-ladies. "Of course, I'm sorry." They'd never become close, despite the small number of women in their class. So many excuses—Caren was a younger prodigy with different senior rotations and graduated a semester earlier.

"You'd think CDC's Dengue Branch would send an expert from San Juan," Caren said, "instead of dragging you away from New York."

Faye frowned. Was that a slam of her relative lack of dengue experience? But maybe it was sympathy for the challenges as Hawaiian cases exploded past three hundred.

"I can hardly complain about working in paradise," Faye said, "but I appreciate your help and insights."

Caren shifted off a khaki backpack, color-coordinated with her t-shirt and pants. A thermos emerged, then Caren poured two cups of a frosty yellow-orange drink. "A Lava Flow, but without those stupid umbrellas."

Throat dry from the salty snack, Faye took an initial sip. "Alcohol?" She set the cup down. "I'm trying to cut back."

Caren's face transformed with a scoff. "Come on now, I use more fruit than rum. Back in the day, I remember you downing one or two at Panama Red's."

Faye took a second sip. She'd escaped her Pentecostal parents for line dancing at every opportunity, but Caren didn't need those details. "I've forgotten—were you a Colorado native like me?"

"I grew up in Honolulu and attended CSU under the program for western states without vet schools."

"According to Ino, you're a dengue virologist with almost a million dollars in federal grant money—I'm impressed."

Caren raised her cup in a toast. "Come out to my lab in Hilo. There are tremendous benefits from contracting with research experts who work on these diseases full time."

A gust of wind ruffled Faye's notes and she grabbed for a sheet before it flew away. Caren reached behind to rescue a page that ended up in the sand.

"You should consider a laptop," she said. "It is the twenty-first century."

Faye shrugged. "I worried about damaging it on the beach, or losing power."

She stuffed the papers into her leather bag. "I'd love to see your research. So far, we've tried to reduce risk with public education and area closures, like this one. It's not enough."

Caren stirred her drink with her little finger. "I'm happy to give you a ride to Hilo this afternoon."

Faye glanced at her phone. "How long's the trip?"

"Two hours if we take the eastern shortcut from Kailua-Kona."

"Well, I'm done with my mosquito collections here at the campground. But I also need to check traps at the nearby historic site, then ship the specimens to Honolulu."

"They need to get one of those entitled Gen-Zers for leg work."

Ino had said that Caren was a faculty member, so the dismissive tone was surprising. "Do you work with students?"

"One undergrad biology lecture and lab this semester. My grants allow me to buy out of a second course, thank God."

Faye laughed. "I always assumed academics loved to teach."

"Teaching, research, and service—we're obligated to do all three, and there's always one of those we like to do more."

Providing only an occasional guest lecture, Faye never seriously considered a career in academia although Devorah had dangled the bait of a CSU faculty position. It would be enlightening to spend more time with Caren, if they could work out the details.

"I couldn't ask you to bring me all the way back to Kona after I see your lab."

"It's no bother—I love to drive. And I'm available to help you check any remaining traps. After we get the samples to the airport, we can head to Hilo."

Caren had always been results-focused, so her persistence wasn't surprising. "That's a lot to fit into one day," Faye said. "Maybe I should drive myself tomorrow morning." She immediately regretted the words. Her skills for navigating mountain roads were rusty and the car rental cost was exorbitant. She'd be crazy to pass up Caren's offer.

"I have an extra bedroom—issue solved. If you bring your swimsuit, we can go for a dip, and I promise not to admit that you played hooky."

Staying overnight with someone who was essentially a stranger, despite their four years together in vet school—not a comfortable concept. But balanced against driving curvy two-lane highways, the choice was plain.

"Caren, you're a super salesman. I can see why agencies give you all that money. You've got a deal."

Faye parked her car at the Puʻuhonua O Hōnaunau visitor center, next to Caren's Ford F-150. Low-hanging afternoon clouds dulled the sky to a metallic gray.

The almost fourteen-thousand-foot elevation of Mauna Loa to the east was barely visible, so she removed the sunscreen from her pack. But as a mosquito hovered near her nose, she swatted it aside and sprayed a second time with repellent.

Caren joined her, wearing a black cap emblazoned with **USS ARIZONA BB 39** in gold letters above a white ship and **PEARL HARBOR, HAWAII. DEC. 7 1941**.

"Your timing is perfect," Faye said. "Collecting these new specimens without Ino would have been challenging."

"Sorry I didn't stop by sooner. I was in Vegas helping my mother settle into a new place."

"Leaving the Aloha State for the Neon Capital of the World. I can't imagine." Faye split her supplies into two piles. "Can you carry some?"

Caren opened her daypack and loaded up. "Hawaii's priced out of reach for us regular folks. When Mom's taxes and homeowner's association fees jumped up on her Honolulu condo, I offered to pay them, or have her move in with me. But she has too much pride. My academic salary, even for a tenured position, doesn't go far here."

"That's rough. Ino said that Las Vegas is Hawai'i's Ninth Island because so many people have relocated there. At least she won't be alone."

Faye showed Caren her mask. "Do you have one? We won't be inside buildings, but the Park Service wants us to wear them in high-traffic outdoor areas."

Caren grimaced. "Public health Nazis. The government's always interfering in our lives."

Faye was astonished. Didn't Caren's dengue research make her part of the public health team? But it was challenging to imagine an invisible virus floating in the ocean breezes. In contrast, dengue had a visible manifestation in skeeters. She swatted another one circling her elbow and decided not to cross swords with Caren. "No problem, we should be fine."

The park restricted group size to ten and no school buses were on site, perhaps due to the storm warnings. Faye hiked left along the 1871 Trail toward the first trap hidden behind a black lava boulder. "Is your dad still living?"

Caren's eyes moistened. "Killed in Vietnam, when I was a child." Her grief seemed to war with her tough exterior.

An entire lifetime clinging to that pain—maybe he accounted for the military accent. "I'm sorry, it must have been difficult."

"He was a doc at Tripler Medical Center." Caren doffed her Pearl Harbor cap and studied it. "Just wish his final days had been defending the homeland instead of a bunch of gooks."

Prejudiced, much? Faye swallowed her reaction as she reached for the black canister.

Caren pushed her aside and shifted the trap to the path. "Let me. You don't look built for this kind of grunt work."

Faye laughed. "My partner agrees with you." Suspicious of her classmate's attitudes, she allowed the implication that the partner was Ino, rather than Taylor. The world had come a long way toward accepting gay marriage, but transphobia was increasing.

Caren replaced the catch bag with a new one. "You should consider alternate ways of mosquito surveillance."

Following her hand-drawn map, Faye led the way to the next trap behind a palm tree. "What do you recommend?"

"I helped with an overseas study using humans as bait. Two-hour shifts on a chair exposing your legs—another person collects them with a hand net and aspirator."

"Yikes, I can't believe we'd find volunteers for that."

Caren's face darkened. "The design was approved by Indonesia's Ethical Commission Board. But if it makes you squeamish, you can do the same thing with cattle."

"Let's talk about it with Ino." Faye and Caren alternated the next set of canisters until reaching a path in the developed park area, where they startled a brown goat with impressive horns.

"Escaped from someone's farm?" Faye asked.

"Feral, introduced by Captain Cook. The park had a removal program recently—guess they didn't get all of them."

Faye raised her eyebrows. "I can't imagine that killing cute animals is popular, even nuisance ones."

"Adoption this time, not euthanasia. But there are also hunting seasons for feral sheep and pigs, along with the goats."

The wind picked up force as the next trap came into view

between mounds of lava boulders forming the foundation for two thatched A-frame structures.

Inside one, a young man demonstrated wood carving, wearing nothing more than a mohawk and a red lavalava, the cloth skirt named by Ino in his local lingo lesson.

"Travel pono," he'd advised. "Show respect by learning some of our language."

Faye switched out the catch bag and led Caren close to Keoneʻele Cove, then paused at a towering cluster of kiʻi, wooden statues representing Hawaiian gods and ancestors.

"These carved faces are so dramatic," Faye said.

"They're warning that this spot within the Hale e Keawe temple is kapu, forbidden."

Caren's pronouncements seemed designed to provoke. "The Park Service approved the traps here," Faye answered, defensive.

"This is a spiritual area," Caren said, "a sacred burial site for chiefs and a place of sanctuary for those committing crimes. If they made it here, they were absolved of their sins."

The crash of a wave on the lava rocks and the splash of water on Faye's legs refocused her attention to the ocean, stirred up into a rage by the strengthening winds. "We'd better keep moving if we want to finish rather than get swept away."

"Yeah, this area is in the tsunami zone." Caren's dimpled grin softened the impact of her words.

As Faye pivoted for the walkway, she spotted a green sea turtle surfing the waves, its shell mottled with lighter spots. "Wow, my first on this trip. How big do you think it is?"

"Three feet," Caren said. "The honu is good luck—bodes well for our collaboration. If we get home in time, I'll make a Hawaiian out of you with a poke bowl."

Caren's pronunciation of poke rhymed with okay, indicating marinated raw fish. Faye had declined it once before, concerned about parasites. But Caren was going above and beyond with her hospitality, and Faye didn't want to appear ungracious. "Mahalo. I'll consider it."

TWENTY-THREE

Albuquerque, New Mexico—Friday, August 27, 2021

Wedged into a middle seat, Maya had plenty of time to fret during the five-hour flight from New York to New Mexico. Manolo's funeral and interment in the church crypt had been somber but celebratory, parts of it in Spanish which she didn't understand.

After the service, the Mirandas hadn't invited her to their home but Sebastian gave her a goodbye hug. When she got back to her midtown hotel, she checked out and headed to JFK.

Minutes after the plane touched down just before midnight on the Albuquerque tarmac, a text came in from Faye. **\<Call me?\>**

Faye started talking the minute the call connected. "I'm on the road to Hilo with a vet school classmate. Small world—she's a dengue virologist. Cases keep increasing, and I could use your help analyzing the data."

Like an automaton, Maya placed one foot in front of the other as she followed the other passengers through the Sunport concourse. "Faye, I'm too tired to think—I just got back home from Manolo's funeral."

"I'm so sorry I couldn't be there for you. Listen, don't worry about this now, but put it on your list of considerations. You may need an overseas investigation for your final year of training. Not that Hawai'i is really overseas, but think about it."

Maya heard a faint voice in the background, then Faye spoke again. "We're on Saddle Road that bisects the island. Caren's pulling over to show me hawaiite. It's a lighter gray lava from Mauna Kea."

"The active volcano in the national park?" Maya asked, envious of Faye getting to work there.

"You're thinking of Mauna Loa and Kīlauea. Let's touch base soon."

With only a carry-on bag, Maya headed straight for the arrivals curb where Dave sat in the cab of his truck.

"Getting to be a pattern for us," Maya told him. "It's good to know I can always count on the Schwartz family."

Her veterinary colleague gave her a sympathetic smile. "You flew back a day early—I figured things were rough. The next shuttle bus to Santa Fe isn't until two-thirty AM, and Emilia would kill me if we left you sitting here until then."

Maya wasn't in the mood to download the day's events, but felt blessed by a familiar place to spend the night. "Your couch must have a plaque with my name on it. And Bo's always up for a cuddle."

Nothing provided comfort compared to the happy grin and soft fur of a good dog.

Bernalillo, New Mexico—Saturday, August 28, 2021

The heat on Maya's face from the stove's gas burners softened her brain function like a congealed jar of honey set to boil. If tossing and turning on the couch amounted to three hours of sleep, she'd be lucky. In the beneficent light of a New Mexico summer morning, she repaid the Schwartz family by cooking her frittatas, perfected for Manolo during COVID lockdowns.

After breakfast, Emilia took the girls to a flamenco dance lesson, then Dave got a call from a nearby rancher about his sick goats. Bo hopped into Dave's front seat, his large Labrador head out the truck window and his dark fur fluttering in the breeze as Dave drove away.

"Aunty Maya, can I have some coffee?" Braxton held out a mug, his expression like Opie, the kid played by Ron Howard in the old *Andy Griffith Show*. Or one of those cat memes with monstrous eyes.

She pulled her hands out of the dirty water and turned to face him. "Are you sure Dave and Emilia would approve?"

He laughed. "You know my dad—he practically inhales the stuff. His limit for me—one cup in the morning as a reward for my chores in the barn."

She flipped the switch on the coffee maker. "Give it a minute to reheat. Dave mentioned that school's started. Freshman, right?"

"Yeah, they have this outdoor club. Backpacking, skiing. I can't wait." His cheeks pinkened with excitement.

Maya noticed he didn't talk about academics. She hesitated, then went ahead with her next question. "Did you ever do that kind of thing…in Freedom City?"

She'd never discussed with him his life in the polygamist cult. But it was awkward to pretend Braxton was a blank slate before Dave found him homeless in Utah and took on the father role.

"No. I couldn't leave the compound until I got thrown out." His slumped shoulders straightened up. "I know how to chop wood and build a campfire."

While pouring the coffee, she studied the Schwartz family photo, Braxton included, embedded in the mug. "I remember the time we had s'mores in your backyard."

He lifted the mug in salute and opened the door to the back patio. "If you're here tonight, maybe Dad will let us do that. See you after I muck out the barn."

Maya turned off the coffee machine and took another sip from her black tea. Normally she preferred a milder green, but needed the caffeine.

She added more detergent and hot water to the breakfast dishes in the sink and didn't rush through her task. A dishwasher was available, but the warm suds on her hands were soothing. The cups appeared to be souvenirs from family excursions to different parks and museums. She remembered Manolo's dad had an even more eclectic collection in his Bronx apartment. That's where Manolo had developed a yearning for adventure.

A vehicle engine sounded outside the kitchen window. Maya peeked through the curtains—perhaps Dave or Emilia forgot something important. They'd be in soon enough. She scraped cheesy egg scraps from Braxton's plate, hardened by his reheating.

When the tableware was dried with a dishcloth and replaced in the cupboard, she tackled the cast iron skillet. Wearing rubber gloves, she used the cut side of a white potato to scrub in sea salt and scrape away frittata particles. After dumping the mixture in the compost container, she set the skillet back on the stove, turned it to low heat, and rubbed in a light layer of canola oil with the second half of the potato.

She turned off the stove and glanced through the window again. Whoever returned home should have come inside already—perhaps she should find out what was going on. She'd check the barn first for Braxton. Dave might be there, retrieving some equipment for his goat herd inspection.

No barking dog to greet her with a lolling grin, wagging tail, and front feet on her chest. "Braxton?" she called out as she checked each of the three horse stalls. Lydia's and Teresa's ponies contentedly munched their grain. Braxton's rescue mare tugged at a hank of hay. The chickens poked at some lettuce scraps on the ground.

The blue-eyed coyote from her last visit flashed through her mind, but the animals didn't act like a rabid predator was stalking.

"Dave, Braxton?" She raised her voice as she rounded the outside of the house. No vehicles in sight—how could she hear one arrive but not leave? Maybe Dave decided to take Braxton on his farm visit while she was absorbed in the cast iron skillet. It would have been nice if they had let her know.

She took slow, deep breaths of the morning air, flavored with a hint of the cool autumn days on the horizon. There was a logical explanation. She whipped out her phone and FaceTimed Dave.

He was surrounded by goats which she recognized as Nubians by their long, floppy ears, round muzzles, and short, fine coats. Maya kept her tone casual. "How's it going? Did you come back here for Braxton?"

Dave's face became puzzled. "No, I left him feeding the horses."

"He's not in the barn. I'll recheck the house." She should have done that before calling Dave. Braxton could be playing a video game in his room. But there was still the car engine. Who was it, and where had they gone?

"Get back to the goats and I'll take care of your homestead

until you return." Maya's tendency to imagine the worst would not ruin the Schwartz weekend.

From the front porch, she tried the main entrance door—locked. They'd increased security since the confrontation with Braxton's biological father at Freedom City. She glanced up at the camera on the roof edge, then hurried back to the rear, calling out for Braxton.

Once inside the house, she beelined for his bedroom. The door was open to reveal a poster of skateboarder Nyjah Huston filling the wall. The other bedrooms and two bathrooms were all empty and haunting with the silence, not even the buzz of a fly to provide signs of life.

She glanced at her phone, then slapped herself in the side of her head. Braxton had his own phone—he'd used it to take photos when they explored the Petroglyph National Monument. But she didn't have the number. No other choice—she had to call Emilia.

"Hi, Maya." Emilia rotated her phone to show the two girls clicking castanets and arching their necks in time to the complex, emotional beat. "I wish you'd joined us—the kids are having a blast."

"Is Braxton there, too?"

"No, did you misplace him? Check the barn—sometimes he curls up in a stall with a book, listening to rap on his phone."

If he'd been relaxing on the floor with ear buds, could she have overlooked him? Unlikely—she'd been more thorough than that. "Emilia, I heard a car engine and assumed one of you picked him up. But he's not with Dave. Can you give me Braxton's number?"

Emilia's narrowed dark eyes and expression reflected Maya's own growing anxiety.

"Let me call Braxton," Emilia said, "then I'll reach out to Dave. Loop through the barn again—look behind the hay bales, just in case you missed him."

Maya raced back to the barn, shouting Braxton's name with no response except whinnies and shifting feet from his mare, startled by Maya's frantic motions. Then she spotted it near the mare's rear hoof—his dark brown coffee mug imprinted with the grinning

Schwartz family, Braxton's hand forming devil horns above Lydia's head. She didn't remember the chip out of the lip when she'd poured the coffee only an hour earlier.

She pried her phone out of her jeans pocket to answer the incoming FaceTime call from Dave. His face was contorted with a fiercer expression than she'd ever seen. That was saying something, considering the times he'd lost his temper on outbreak investigations.

"Maya, what the fuck is going on? You didn't mention hearing a vehicle when you called me. I don't suppose you've found him yet?"

Sheepish at her oversight, she spoke softly. "No—I've looked everywhere."

Her tone became pleading, filled with regret. "Dave, I'm so sorry, you know how I overreact. I just assumed he was around here, and didn't want you to catch my paranoia."

"If you've allowed anything to happen to Braxton…" The words ground out from his clenched jaw, lips tight. "I notified the county sheriff—they may get there before me. We need to check our video cameras." Then he hung up.

By the time Maya returned to the kitchen, her next call came in from Emilia. "Braxton isn't answering," Emilia said, "so I called Dave and we're on our way."

"All I found was his coffee cup in the barn." Maya sank to one of the chairs. "Dave's mad, blaming me."

Her head dropped to one hand. "Emilia, I feel terrible. If anything happened to Braxton on my watch, I'll never forgive myself."

Through her phone, Maya heard squealing brakes and Emilia swearing. "Fuckin' red light." Then Emilia added, "Girls, don't ever do this, but there's no one around and I'm going through it."

Seconds later, she said, "Maya, it's not your fault. You could have joined us at the flamenco class, and Braxton would have been alone. He's fourteen—we've left him by himself before."

"Drive safely," slipped out from Maya before the phone disconnected. A siren broke her incessant replay of Dave's harsh words, and she ran for the front door.

TWENTY-FOUR

Hilo, Hawai'i Island—Saturday, August 28, 2021

Faye cranked opened a jalousie window to let the fresh but humid morning breeze into the lower-level room of Caren's duplex. She ruffled her short, wet hair, then hung the towel on the hook next to the shower stall.

The previous night, after getting the mosquito specimens on the plane to Honolulu, they'd swung by the Kailua-Kona home of a health department nurse who'd been housing Faye. After retrieving Faye's things, she and Caren only had time for a gas station musubi snack—canned Spam marinated in a sweet sauce on white rice, wrapped with seaweed. Arriving late to Caren's home on the east side of the island, Faye had left her suitcase open on the floor.

Re-energized by a blissfully quiet night on Caren's guest bed, Faye dug out a clean shirt and pair of shorts. She disturbed a mottled brown lizard that snapped at her hand and chirped. It darted up the wall toward the window.

She ruffled through all her clothes after dressing, then zipped the suitcase tight to keep out the local fauna. Hearing footsteps above her, she stepped out the aluminum door to a patchy lawn, relishing the blades of fresh grass tickling her sandaled toes.

A palm tree soared above the rich foliage bordering the lot, almost touching the power lines. As Faye ascended the wooden steps of an external staircase, she held onto the rail despite its flaking white paint, probably loaded with lead.

At the landing, she checked the time on her phone—seven o'clock—and knocked.

The door swung open and Caren greeted Faye with a smile,

tanned lean limbs beaded with moisture beyond the sports bra and gym shorts. "Good timing—just got back from a run. Did you sleep well?"

Faye laughed. "Like the dead. I didn't even hear you go out. Hey, there was a lizard in my suitcase. How come you don't have screens on the windows?"

"We like our natural ventilation and being one with nature. One Health, isn't that what you epidemiologists call it?"

Caren removed a coffee pot from the electric burner and poured two cups. "The geckos have hairs on their feet called setae which give them a grip."

Faye couldn't get a reading on her colleague. Her educational messages always seemed to come with a dig. Was Caren a narcissist who didn't think anyone else was smart like her? Faye responded with an ironic tone. "In New York, we try to keep bats and rats, cockroaches and mosquitoes, out of our apartments."

She hoped the visit to Caren's lab would be worth the time spent with an acerbic colleague. If the dengue outbreak continued to explode, they'd be dependent on Caren's expertise to develop new ways to control it. Faye couldn't show her antipathy to Caren; it might jeopardize their working relationship. She slowly sipped the coffee, more bitter than the brew they'd downed with the gas station snack last night.

Caren gulped her coffee with gusto. "We don't mind geckos in the house. They feed on mosquitoes. You should get one as a pet—they also love roaches."

She pulled a plastic bag from the refrigerator. "I want to show off my lab as soon as possible, so I hope this banana bread will be enough. It's extra moist with pineapple and maraschino cherries."

Faye savored the mélange of flavors. She regretted her snark about the lizard and decided to go back to her well-honed political skill. "Mmm, if you made this, I need your recipe."

Caren shook her head. "It was a gift from a staff member. Hey, I'm jumping in the shower. Your clothes are fine—just wear your tennies."

Within thirty minutes, they drove past agriculture and forest research stations before the road dead-ended in a black graveled lot. "They insist on having my mosquito lab away from the main campus," Caren said. "Safer that way."

Faye noted the parking barriers formed from volcanic rock. "You're not too far from the active volcano at Kīlauea. Make you nervous?"

"We're in lava-flow hazard zone 3. Granted, that's just two zones down from the highest risk areas." She chuckled. "The last big Hilo flow was from Mauna Loa in the eighteen hundreds, so mai hopohopo. That means chill out." A light rain drenched them as they dashed for the building.

"If you want to keep your skin moist, Hilo's the spot." Caren flashed her badge at the electronic door lock. "Some nearby areas exceed two hundred inches of rain a year. Northeast trade winds collide with the mountains."

Inside, the metal-roofed dome soared over individual cargo containers. "Cheap and fast way to set up a lab with different experiments in each one," Caren said. The staff members strolling a concrete slab between the units were mostly young and casually dressed.

As Faye reached for her mask in her pocket, Caren wrapped her long fingers around Faye's wrist. "That again? I won't take you into lab areas with dengue-infected mosquitoes."

Faye jerked away. "Sorry, I'm a coastal elite." She slipped on the mask, more concerned about COVID than offending her host.

Caren shrugged. "Your poison. We keep it hot in here for the mossies."

"Mossies?"

"Mosquitoes, in Australian slang. I spent a lot of time there consulting."

Caren opened the first door to reveal shelves crammed with translucent white cubes, all filled with the insects. She cocked her head toward a young man who pulled on a short latex glove, then poked his bare arm into a cube through a flexible plastic sleeve.

"Good morning, Dr. Oldner. Who's our guest today?" As he kept his arm in the cage, the mosquitoes swarmed and began feeding. Soon, some became engorged with his blood.

"This is Faye Simpson, an old classmate of mine from vet school. She's out here from CDC, battling our latest dengue surge."

Faye suppressed a gasp. She noted that Caren wasn't doing the demonstration herself. "CDC in Fort Collins uses pig blood to feed their mosquitoes."

"This is cheaper and easier," Caren answered. "Depending on how eager these five hundred little females are, it should only take five to fifteen minutes."

Faye eyed the cubes lining the shelves and did a quick calculation. About two dozen with five hundred mosquitoes each—twelve thousand blood-thirsty insects in this shipping container alone. Her skin prickled, mimicking a sensation of their attack.

Caren removed rolls of heavy yellow paper covered with tiny dark dots from water cups within several cubes. "These are eggs deposited on sandpaper just above the cup water line, from mosquitoes fed a few days ago."

She dropped the strips into a shallow plastic bin near a new cup of water and sealed the top. "These eggs can be stored for several months until we need to hatch them to maintain our mosquito stocks."

Her staffer moved his other arm to a different mosquito cage. *You couldn't pay me enough*, Faye thought.

She assumed the protocol was approved by their Institutional Review Board, but still was amazed that Caren and her staff were so cavalier. Even if the mosquitoes weren't infected with dengue, the itching from five hundred bites on each arm would be unbearable. And how much blood loss?

"It's got to be uncomfortable," Faye said to the technician. "I admire your dedication to Dr. Oldner's work." She hoped the poor guy wouldn't submit his body for science more than once a day.

"Jorge wants to keep his job," Caren answered with a grin.

The guy's cheek twitched but he nodded.

Caren spent the next couple of hours demonstrating their detailed processes to breed mosquitoes and raise them through the egg, larva, pupa, and adult stages.

Stopping at a shipping container in the far back corner, she invited Faye in. "Let me show you our most recent accomplishment. Our journal article on methods to assess pesticide efficacy was published in the spring. We can assess them in the lab and in the field."

She greeted a dark-haired woman seated behind a dissecting microscope, then said, "New pesticides are desperately needed, as mosquitoes develop resistance to the current ones. Show Dr. Simpson how you evaluate this chemical against adult female mosquitoes."

The woman placed one end of a clear plastic tube through the sleeve of a round, covered pail of mosquitoes. The other end went into her mouth. She sucked up ten mosquitoes, which she then blew into a test tube.

Faye flinched—how did she keep them from flying up the tube to her lips? Or worse yet, did she risk swallowing them?

"They're anesthetized if cooled for five minutes," the lab tech said as she placed the test tube into the refrigerator and removed a different one from inside. She gently poured its dead-looking mosquitoes into a petri dish. She checked the time and wrote in her notebook.

"Next, another ten minutes on an ice bed." From one of the flat containers on the ice, the tech picked up a mosquito with fine tweezers, then held it next to a syringe and applied the pesticide. Treated mosquitoes were dropped into paper cups topped with mesh.

"She'll come back and assess how many are dead," Caren said. "We also find out if the ones that survive the pesticide application have any reduction in their ability to lay eggs. A lot more steps I could show you, but you get the idea."

"You mentioned field work," Faye said. "For the promising chemical formulations, you test them in real-world conditions, too?"

"Of course. That's why I'm famous. I go above and beyond. But let's catch lunch first, then the field work."

Caren's bragging was unsettling. But the wry tone may have indicated humor rather than arrogance—no reason to assume the worst about her apparently genius-level classmate.

Caren parked by a run-down building in an industrial area. "They have the best poke, which is raw fish, usually tuna."

This time, Faye didn't restrain her sarcasm. "I'm clued into a few Hawaiian foods and phrases since I've been in town."

Caren ignored Faye's retort and held the door wide open. As Faye stepped on a piece of utility carpet, a foot-long centipede scurried out to hide beneath the single chair. "Good thing you aren't wearing your sandals," Caren said. "A bite is excruciating, and your foot can swell up like a pumpkin."

Faye yearned for pizza-carrying rats rather than Hawai'i's peculiar wildlife, but she prided herself on an adventurous palate, as long as the meat or fish was cooked. The girl at the counter, bare shoulder exposing a red plumeria flower tattoo, didn't rush them.

"The Kalua pork nachos are calling my name." Faye studied the plastic menu. "Sorry to pass on the raw fish."

Caren smirked and said to the employee, "Make mine fresh ahi with soy. By the time we get to Kaumana Caves, I might persuade you to taste a bite."

"Do we have time for me to play tourist?" Faye asked as she was handed a paper take-out box. Caves connoted claustrophobia, and crawling through narrow openings was lowest on her list of recreational activities.

"This will be quick, and not far from my research site."

Faye held her food in her lap until they parked near the cave, then sat next to each other on a bench for lunch. She refused Caren's offer to share. A colorful rooster crowed his dominance and ventured near to pick up scraps.

"Remind you of New York pigeons?" Caren joked.

If truly on vacation, Faye might have broken her own rules and taken a chance on Caren's ahi. But she couldn't risk illness slowing her down from helping Hawai'i reduce dengue risk. Every case they prevented meant one less person to suffer and possibly die.

After dumping their waste in the trash, Caren led the way down steep yellow-striped stairs with bright metal handrails. At the bottom, she pulled out a flashlight as they approached the cave opening.

Concerned about her sneakers slipping on the fern-covered rocky floor, Faye wished she'd worn hiking boots.

Her plodding gait alerted Caren. "Don't worry, we're not going far." The temperature dropped as water seeped from the lip of the cave onto their heads. Red-tinted lava alternated with black and gray.

They stopped at a small stream tumbling along the path. "Pretty cool, huh?" Caren's demeanor became one of a little kid's. "This is a lava tube, formed by Mauna Loa pāhoehoe cooling on the sides and tops, but the fresh lava bores on through, leaving this hole."

"What's pāhoehoe?"

"It's the second most common type, with a billowy surface formed when the lava cools slowly." She shoved Faye's hand to the cave surface. "See, it's not as rough."

Faye pulled her fingers loose, appreciative of Caren's enthusiasm for her home state but irritated by her dominating personality. Maybe that's why they never bonded in vet school. "I'm not much of a nature girl—too infused with museums and music from decades of big city living."

Caren reddened, apparently done with their banter. "I won't put you out. Let's get back to work." She pivoted away from the cave opening and left Faye to haul herself, with all those extra pounds, up the slippery steps to the roadside.

TWENTY-FIVE

Bernalillo, New Mexico—Saturday, August 28, 2021

A county sheriff's truck skidded to a stop as Maya opened Dave's front door, frantic over the missing teenager. The burly young woman in a tan short-sleeved shirt and forest green pants doffed her cap and sunglasses when she joined Maya under the portal. "Is Dr. Schwartz here yet?"

Maya shook her head and invited the deputy in. "Dave's worried about Braxton's biological dad kidnapping him." Tears threatened as she regretted her part in allowing his disappearance. "When I was in the kitchen, I heard a vehicle but unfortunately didn't see who it was."

The deputy's tone was terse. "Ma'am, it's not kidnapping if it was the boy's father, but let's not get ahead of ourselves. Dr. Schwartz has a camera system?"

"I can't access it. Would you like to see the barn where I found his coffee mug?" As they pushed through the door to the back porch, Dave's truck roared up and he hopped out, Bo on a leash.

The dog gave one woof and Dave tied Bo to a porch rail. He asked the deputy, "Have you issued a BOLO yet?"

"What's a BOLO?" Maya asked.

"A 'Be On the Lookout' alert, ma'am. Let's talk first, sir. Any chance the boy wandered off, or was picked up by a friend?"

Dave rubbed his hand over his eyes. "He's never done something like that without telling us."

Fireflies of hope flitted along Maya's nerves as she remembered their discussion. "He wanted to build a campfire tonight for s'mores. He might be searching for firewood."

Dave led the way to the barn. "The axe is still here."

"Let me show you where he dropped his coffee mug." Maya headed toward the last stall and opened the gate.

The deputy eyed the horse with caution, then took a quick photo. After slipping on booties and gloves, she hooked the mug's handle with tweezers and dropped it into an evidence bag.

"It wasn't chipped when I handed it to him." Maya's voice weakened. "I'm worried there was a struggle."

Dave slammed his fist into a wood post. "Are you deaf? If he fought off a kidnapper, you should have heard it!"

Maya cringed. Last year, he'd turned his short fuse on her when they were blocked on the mink investigation. She'd warned Manolo about the risk of COVID in mink farmworkers and he'd alerted medical providers. Dave suspected that's how the information leaked to the farm ahead of their visit.

The deputy stretched yellow tape across the stall. "I want everyone out until my team inspects the area for more evidence."

Knuckles from his hand oozing blood from the abrasions, Dave scrubbed his face. "Can your team come soon? I need to get into the stall to care for his horse."

The deputy pulled out her phone and placed the request. "Now I want to review your camera footage."

Maya started to follow them into the house until Dave blocked the door. "We don't need your help. You suggested he's chopping wood—go check the property."

She opened her mouth to object, then realized she'd be no help to them. But if the sheriff's department sent out more officers to scour the area, she'd breathe easier.

She kicked at yellow-brown cottonwood leaves, dead beneath the trees from heat and drought. What would a real detective look for? Her disease detective skills were for data, not disturbed soil.

"Braxton," she shouted over and over.

A bright red salamander splashed with dark spots hugged the exposed lip of a rock. Maybe Braxton jumped the gun on his outdoor club and was exploring Bosque creatures. If the wetland had been saturated with its normal monsoon rains, she could look for footprints, but the soil was desiccated.

Despite the drought, purple loosestrife with three-foot spikes of magenta flowers proliferated as she got closer to the Rio Grande. No broken stems to indicate someone barging through.

Had he gone fishing? The logical solution was comforting, until she realized he could have fallen in. He'd never learned to swim at the polygamist compound, but Dave had brought the kids to lessons at the pool in nearby Rio Rancho.

Engine noise drifted through the invasive tamarisk and Russian olives. Anyone to distract Dave from his negative focus on her was welcome. She broke into a jog and met the three female members of the Schwartz family at the back door.

"Teresa and Lydia, go take care of your ponies," Emilia said.

"But stay out of the mare's stall—the deputy is checking it out," Maya added. Her arms instinctively reached forward and Emilia accepted the hug.

"Why can't we see Braxton's horse?" Emilia asked.

"I found his damaged coffee mug there," Maya repeated one more time. "The deputy is sending a team to look for evidence. I thought they'd arrived, but I'm happy it's you."

"Is Dave in the house?" Emilia asked. Under dark curls framing her face, sweat dripped to her tanned neck. Her early wrinkles were cemented deeper with stress.

"He's looking over the surveillance footage." Maya followed Emilia inside where they found the deputy and Dave at his desk in a corner of the living room. He leapt up to embrace Emilia.

"We know what happened." His expression warred between grim and relieved. "The back camera got a shot of a dark SUV. Braxton's father along with another man muscled Braxton into it."

Done in by the heat, Maya yearned for a drink of water. Thank God they wouldn't have to search the river. "I wonder why he didn't shout out for me. I'm sure I would have heard him."

"Maybe he was protecting you," Emilia said. "They could have threatened him."

"But the camera didn't catch a plate." Dave's voice was ragged and he sounded defeated.

"Cariño, does that matter?" Emilia squeezed her husband's waist. "We know where they're going."

"Can they force Braxton to go somewhere against his will?" Maya asked.

The deputy removed her phone again. "I'm calling this in. Someone may be able to intercept the vehicle and determine if Braxton is unharmed. But if he's okay, even if he doesn't want to be there, we can't remove him from his father's custody. I'm sorry."

Dave started to swing his damaged right hand toward the table lamp, then stopped short and leaned on the desk, tears in his hazel eyes as he spoke.

"When we started the adoption, I checked into the definition of an unfit parent. We need evidence of child abuse, domestic violence, substance abuse, or psychiatric illness that poses a risk to Braxton."

Maya couldn't believe he'd given up. She jumped to her feet and blurted, "Their leader is imprisoned on child sex charges."

Dave's head jerked up, eyes locked on Maya. "Unless we prove something similar for Braxton's father, that doesn't matter. So stay the hell out of it."

Emilia moved between them. Similar in height to her husband, she enveloped Dave's body with her own. But her gaze swung toward Maya. "Let me run you over to the Bernalillo station for the Rail Runner. You can catch an early afternoon train back up to Santa Fe."

Maya flushed. It was obvious that she'd be in the way while the Schwartz family worked with law enforcement. "I'll call a cab or Uber. Sheriff, can I go home? I'd do anything to rewind time so you could spend your Saturday on something else."

"Ma'am, I doubt we need you anymore, and there's likely nothing you could have done to stop Braxton's father. You might have been hurt."

Emilia pulled out her car keys. "No one's gonna pick you up out here. Dave, pull up a photo of Braxton on your phone for the deputy." She reached out to shake the woman's hand. "Thanks for coming to help our family."

Maya retrieved her suitcase and followed Emilia to the barn.

"Girls," Emilia said to her daughters, "it looks like Braxton's father took him home. He'll be fine—you don't need to worry." Her voice caught and she cleared her throat, then continued with a plastered smile. "Hopefully he can come back again, but for now, we'll adjust. We can write letters."

Wanting to accept blame, Maya considered adding her sorrow that she hadn't stopped them, but the girls were too young. She couldn't eliminate her guilt by confessing her sin to kids still in elementary school.

Emilia reoriented the teary-eyed girls to pony care. "I'm running Maya to the train. When you're done, Dad's inside with the sheriff."

In the front seat of the old sedan, Maya fastened her seat belt and word-vomited in an uncontrollable spasm of tension. "I don't know why they'd want him back, after they kicked him out. It's going to be so difficult for him to fit back into that society when he's tasted freedom. They discriminate against nonbelievers—is he going to be subject to endless rounds of punishment?"

Emilia's attention remained on the road but her eyes narrowed. "I'm not sure you're helping," she warned.

Maya slapped her hand on her pants leg. Lack of sleep, the funeral in New York only the day before—she could blame her loose lips on several factors.

Stick to your work, she chided internally. *You're up shit creek in your personal life.*

"I'm so sorry, Emilia. You guys should cut me loose as a friend after such a monumental screw-up."

"I don't think we need to get that drastic," Emilia answered. "You and Dave still need to work together, as long as you're here in the Southwest."

Was Emilia suggesting that Maya move on, their relationship permanently damaged? She had until June to finish her preventive medicine residency, but there was no rule that required her to finish it in the place she started. She'd done everything she could to avoid the Santa Fe apartment she'd shared with Manolo. Maybe this was the point to throw in the towel.

The white train painted on the side with a huge red-and-yellow roadrunner idled on the tracks.

"Good timing," Emilia said.

Maya unhooked her seat belt. "Words can't express how bad I feel about this. You will all be in my thoughts and prayers."

Emilia didn't answer as Maya yanked her suitcase from the back seat and waved goodbye. She hurried onto the train and grabbed a seat in one of the few empty rows. Excited tourists buzzed like a hive of bees about next Friday's burning of Zozobra, the wood-and-cloth Old Man Gloom effigy, and the Fiesta de Santa Fé starting Saturday.

Two years ago, on the road to recovery from anthrax, Manolo had joined her to write small notes of their troubles and burn them away with Zozobra's execution. But she'd never seen any of the events associated with the Fiesta—the music, art exhibits, or the Desfile de los Niños pet parade.

This year, she vowed to set aside all her mistakes and the bad things that weren't her fault, like Braxton. She'd fully embrace the traditions of her new hometown, before abandoning it forever.

TWENTY-SIX

Hilo, Hawai'i Island—Saturday, August 28, 2021

Faye placed her hands on her hips and fought to catch her breath after the steep, humid climb from Kaumana cave. Had Caren chosen a lunchtime excursion that would emphasize the differences in their fitness levels?

Caren held open the passenger door of her truck, her expression sheepish. "Sorry, I'm so addicted to nature that I assume everyone else is. I didn't intend to wear you out when I have so much more to show you."

Flushed with heat and embarrassment, Faye regretted less-than-grateful thoughts about her host. Caren was an enthusiastic tour guide for her home state—no different than Faye was for New York. "My body's not used to extensive travel," she answered.

Caren matched Faye's light-hearted tone. "No kidding, ain't aging a bitch?"

After hopping up into the driver's seat, she handed Faye a water bottle from the ice chest in the back seat. "Don't worry, I'm not contributing to the scourge of plastic waste. I keep these and refill them for years."

Faye gulped the refreshing liquid. "Thanks. What's next on your dengue demo?"

Caren glanced at the clock on the dash. "Two o'clock, we're right on time. My staffer demonstrated how to evaluate whether a spray of pesticide can kill a mosquito in the lab. Now we'll see how it works in real conditions."

She made a right turn after the elementary school and stopped at the side of a huge grassy field. Once outside the vehicle, she waved toward the volcanic mountain in the distance peeking out from the cloud cover. "That's Mauna Kea. I have connections—we can get a private tour of the thirteen telescopes."

Faye wasn't on duty 24/7 for her CDC assignment, but she rarely earmarked time for fun on her infrequent out-of-town work trips. "I read something in the newspaper about opposition to new telescopes."

Caren scowled. "Native Hawaiians are worried about expanded development on the mountain, which they consider a sacred site. The Audubon Society is concerned for the Palila, an endangered honeycreeper that nests on the slopes."

On her phone, she found a picture of the bird with a thick bill, yellow head and neck, white breast, and gray back. The wings and tail had a greenish tinge. "We must protect it—the San Diego Zoo has a captive breeding program. But ultimately, our astronomy program should be prioritized, don't you agree?"

Determined to keep the peace, Faye smiled. "I'm not here long enough to have an opinion." She noted the cluster of white poles dotting the field. "This looks rather elaborate. Tell me about it."

Caren stepped on one barbed wire strand and held a second up for Faye to crawl through. "We suspend twenty-five mosquito traps four feet off the ground and fifty feet apart."

She led Faye to the closest pole where a teenage girl was attaching a white cup. "These kids are part of the high school's environmental club."

The girl beckoned Faye closer. "We made these last week out of small ice cream containers." She rotated the cup, mesh on both ends and mosquitoes flitting around inside. "Dr. Oldner's staff put ten adult females in each one an hour ago." She marked **Pre: 0** on the side. "That means there are no dead ones before the experiment."

Faye was impressed by the team of students setting up the mosquito cups on the sea of poles. Half an hour later, they were done, and huddled in a shady grove.

Caren took notes on the wind speed and direction, then consulted with a white-suited spray operator who was protected with a full-face respirator. She drew a diagram and marked his path as he hauled a bulky machine in a straight line through the middle of the field. With little air movement, Faye's nose and eyes didn't detect the pesticide spray, but she reflexively slipped on her N95 mask.

The kids shared TikTok videos on their phones. Once the operator reached the other side of the field and rejoined them, Caren called the students back to attention.

"Grab a pair of nitrile gloves to minimize your pesticide exposure. Write the number of dead mosquitoes like this." She picked up an empty cup and marked **Post: 3**. "I'll show you how to layer cups in the coolers so the living mosquitoes can still breathe."

When the mosquitoes were all loaded up, Caren jammed a thick piece of cardboard under a corner of each cooler's lid to prop it open for air, then led the caravan of cars back to her lab.

"Do you worry about someone interfering with your experiment?" Faye asked.

"Nope, we finish each site all in one day. Some of the students stay behind to remove the poles, and by the end of the day, no one will know we were there."

"How about the impact on bees?"

"Naled, the organophosphate pesticide we used today, dissipates quickly, and when we choose the sites, we verify that there aren't any apiaries nearby."

Faye was impressed that Caren had been so thorough, but couldn't restrain herself. "So there's no chance of bees taking nectar from the chemical-contaminated plants in this area?"

Caren rolled her eyes. "Spraying for mosquitoes is widespread, sometimes by the health department. I'm not responsible for every bee colony death."

The students unloaded the coolers to shelves in another lab room, then Caren verified handwashing. She handed out coupons for a free ice cream cone. Most of the kids piled into their vehicles and sped off, except for those waiting for parental pickup.

"This is great that you're motivating kids toward science careers," Faye complimented Caren as they headed back into the dome.

"Yeah, get them when they're young and enthusiastic. Once they reach college, they expect paid internships. Our grant money won't stretch far enough to cover so many sites without the high schoolers."

"Is this your regular Saturday routine?" Faye admired Caren's work ethic. No wonder there'd been no evidence of a life partner. Like Faye, commitment to her profession seemed to be Caren's highest priority.

"You only got to see one of our test areas," Caren said. "I have staff today in two more challenging locations. With the varied topography and pesticides to evaluate, this definitely keeps us busy every weekend."

She led the way into a new lab. "The mosquitoes in this set were sprayed with a synthetic pyrethroid in a forest area at ten o'clock."

One bearded young man wearing gloves examined each container on a tray. He added the six-hour mortality to the pre- and post-numbers on the white side of each, then called the figures out to an older man typing on a laptop.

"Ralph, be more careful." Caren shoved her finger on his screen. "Correct that number to nine. You want to get us busted for fraudulent data?"

The man ducked his head and corrected his mistake. "All the containers will be rechecked for the death count at 12 and 24 hours post-spray," Caren added.

When they were back in Caren's office, she opened a colorful map on the screen. "The data is integrated using a geographic information system."

"Do your GIS maps only display control locations, or do you use statistics to analyze clustering of positive mosquitoes?"

"Both. This satellite image for 25 locations in a malathion spray area is superimposed with the mosquito mortality at 24 hours post-spray."

"What do the colors represent?"

Caren indicated a vertical legend at the bottom of the map. "Red means 91–100% of the mosquitoes were killed, shading all the way down to blue for 0–10% killed."

Faye pointed at a blue area in the right corner. "It didn't work here."

"Take a look at this bottom diagram. The wind was blowing in the other direction, so this area got missed. The pesticide applicator should have adjusted for that, but mistakes happen."

Caren displayed dozens of other maps to show varying effectiveness depending on pesticide and setting. Then she pulled up some of her scientific publications summarizing the study results.

Caren's productivity triggered a pang of envy. Faye had contributed leadership in many ways but never as the head of a research team prior to the current cases. Her deepest dive into dengue data had been for vaccines through the taskforce. Vector staff at the NYC health department decided on control measures, in consultation with Moshe.

A final paper showed a graph of efficacy over time. "This is the biggest issue now," Caren said. "Kill rates are decreasing because the mosquitoes are adapting to the pesticides. Those that survive are resistant to the pesticide effects, and their offspring continue with this resistance."

Faye ran her fingers through her hair. She'd been energized by Caren's success, but this latest news deflated her hopes like a popped balloon. She sank deeper into the chair, worn out by the intensive workload over multiple weeks. "Just like antibiotic resistance. The more we use antibiotics, the remaining bacteria become super-bugs with out-of-control spread."

Caren rested her hand on Faye's shoulder. "Come on, I didn't mean to be a Debbie Downer. We have more weapons in our arsenal, but we can save them for another day."

Faye squirmed at Caren's repeated invasions of her personal space, but again attempted diplomacy. "Definitely out of my field of expertise, but I want to learn all about it so I can advise CDC on their funding."

A grin flashed across Caren's angular face. "Just what a dedicated research scientist wants to hear. How about we decompress in one of the local hot springs before grabbing dinner?"

Faye almost said yes. Then she remembered Ino's brochures about *Leptospira* skin rashes from domestic and wild animals urinating the bacteria in Hawai'i's fresh water. Some unlucky patients died or developed months-long infections if the microbes damaged other organs.

"You're not worried about lepto?" Faye asked, guessing the answer from her fearless colleague.

"Oh, that's only in someone with an open cut, or who swims with their head underwater."

"I beg to differ," Faye answered. "Although those behaviors are associated with lepto cases, some get infected without those specific exposures."

When Caren didn't respond, Faye continued. "I need to verify when Ino is returning on Monday. Do you mind if we grab takeout and I retreat to your guest area?"

Faye was startled by Caren's forlorn expression. Perhaps she was sensitive to the feelings and ideas of others, after all.

"Of course," Caren said. "I forgot you're not a nature girl. You rest up tonight and let me know what you'd like to do tomorrow."

Faye wolfed down her fish tacos before reaching out to Taylor. With the six-hour time difference, she realized it was close to midnight in New York. She'd arrived in Hilo too late for a call the previous night. After she pressed the FaceTime icon on her phone, Taylor's face came into view.

"Aloha, Dr. Lewis, you look all dolled up. Anything romantic?"

Wigless, Taylor finished scrubbing their face with a washcloth and carried the phone to the bed. "I went to see The Boss tonight and dressed for the occasion."

"Bruce Springsteen? His Broadway stint is almost over."

"A group of doctors managed to score tickets. Fabulous show—I like him even more now than at the start of his career."

If home, Faye might have joined them. Was it worth trading retirement leisure for dengue virus? Then again, the disease paid for trips to Colorado, New Mexico, and Hawai'i. "Well, I might be on Medicare but I'm not over the hill. While you're gallivanting to musical performances, I'm working my ass off, and still haven't bodysurfed an ocean wave. Is my head screwed on right?"

Taylor frowned. "I'd prefer you not be worn out and frazzled when you get home. Tomorrow's Sunday—ditch the shoes for cool salt water on your legs up to your knees. Doctor's orders."

"I'll do you one better," Faye said. "If Caren's up for it, I'd love to snorkel. Although she's a worse workaholic than me, so I won't promise."

"I got a chance to scuba dive when I was in the Philippines for that big dengue outbreak. Have you ever considered it?"

"At my age? No thanks—those tanks are heavy."

Taylor dropped their robe and spread out on top of the bedcover. "Just a glimpse of what's waiting for you. Do good work but come back soon."

Faye sighed. Most of her life, sex was irregular, only once or twice a year. Not getting used to something meant not missing it when it wasn't there. But Taylor had upended all that.

Laughing, she said, "Maybe I'll get a tan, or more likely, a peeling sunburn."

She kissed the screen and hung up, placing the next call to Ino.

"How's your visit to Dr. Oldner's lab working out?" His gravelly voice was warm with the gentle lilt of a lifelong Hawaiian.

"Couldn't be better." Faye put the best face on the situation. "She's an old college buddy and granted me unbelievable access to the inner workings of her lab. Her program is incredible, and she wants more state and federal funding."

"Can you meet me Monday morning at our vector control office in Kahului? Fifty-three new cases on Maui in the last couple of days."

Faye noted that he hadn't responded to her mention of funding. "Of course, I'll fly over tomorrow. By the way, what's happening on the east side of Hawai'i Island? There's so much standing water, there should be a lot of dengue infections here in Hilo, too."

The call was silent for close to a minute, then Ino rejoined. "I just looked it up. The earliest cases were there, but the count has remained low."

Faye chuckled. "Well, all of Caren's pesticide work might be keeping the mosquito population in check. I'd like to do more detailed analyses on the human case data. You wouldn't object if CDC sends out another public health veterinarian to help?"

"I'll run it by our State Epidemiologist, but I'm sure the extra firepower will be welcome. See you Monday at nine."

Recalling that Maya was an early riser, Faye double-checked the time. Almost eleven in Mountain Daylight Time—she might be getting ready to turn in after the ten o'clock news.

Maya's face look strained when she answered the FaceTime call. In fact, Faye couldn't recall her looking worse except when Maya Zoomed while hospitalized with COVID, after her husband's death.

"What's wrong?" Faye asked, a constriction in her throat. She dreaded hearing about a setback in her protégé's recovery.

TWENTY-SEVEN

Despondent over Braxton, Maya dodged a complete answer to Faye's question. "This has always been my favorite time of year. I'm considering all kinds of cultural events."

Faye's expression on Maya's phone screen brightened. "You never know how long you'll be living there, so don't miss out on anything."

Maya remembered Faye's encouragement for New York activities during her internship. Dragon boat festival on Meadow Lake in Queens. Fourth of July fireworks on the East River. The Marathon from Central Park. She admired Faye's enthusiasm for her city.

"Are you making a dent in the Hawai'i dengue count?" Maya asked. "We're lucky—there's no new cases here in New Mexico." Corrales and Sandia Pueblo had temperatures in the fifties at night, turning mosquitoes lethargic.

"We target our prevention efforts based on surveillance, but the cases are jumping up rapidly." Faye shifted position to another chair, revealing a window and a palm tree highlighted by a streetlamp. "Now they're increasing in Maui. I could use someone to crunch data—we can respond better if we pinpoint the top risk factors in each area."

Maya had never been to Hawai'i, but after her bat work in Thailand and China, more heat and humidity didn't appeal. "Can I do the analyses from here? I've only been back on board with New Mexico for two months, and most of that on dengue. I can't imagine Dr. Grinwold wants me traipsing off again."

"Let me worry about that," Faye assured her. "We can touch base with him tomorrow. A lot of the information I want to analyze isn't collected on the routine case report forms, so I need someone on the ground, doing interviews."

Braxton's glowing expression when he waved goodbye shoved its way into Maya's mind. Maybe she should share the information about his abduction because it crowded everything else from her thoughts. But Faye already knew about Maya's previous fuckups. At some point, her mentor might run out of patience.

"Faye, I need a moment. It's getting chilly in here." Maya crawled out of bed to crank her bedroom window closed. At two thousand feet of elevation higher than Albuquerque, the Santa Fe overnight temp was forecast for 49 degrees. Usually she found the crisp air invigorating, but after the trauma of Braxton's kidnapping, her brain and body only wanted to sleep. What were those lines from Shakespeare?

> ...by a sleep to say we end
> The heart-ache and the thousand natural shocks
> That flesh is heir to...

But Hamlet was contemplating suicide, and Maya just needed a break. "I'm exhausted," she said. "Can we touch base tomorrow? If Dr. Grinwold approves it, I'll consider coming out to help you in Hawai'i."

Faye swatted away a mosquito from her nose. "Thanks. I'm such a night owl these days, I forget the whole world isn't. Get some rest."

When Faye disconnected, Maya tugged the comforter over her head and tried to quiet her mind. What was the rest of that Hamlet quote?

> To sleep: perchance to dream: ay, there's the rub;
> For in that sleep of death what dreams may come
> When we have shuffled off this mortal coil,
> Must give us pause.

Maya's right leg cramped and she rotated for a better position. Manolo-mirages now dueled with a fresh-faced teenage boy. At some level, she knew that she bore no responsibility for their fates, but an ingrained tendency to obsess kept winning out. If only she were more vigilant, on top of all the details, she could prevent the bad from happening. Admitting her latest anxieties to Faye wasn't on the table. But Monday morning, she'd make an appointment with her psychiatrist.

Santa Fe, New Mexico—Sunday, August 29, 2021

Tendrils of a cool breeze caressed Maya's cheeks as she relaxed in her tiny backyard, reading the Sunday paper. A streak of yellow on the Sangre de Cristo mountains triggered a yearning for a forest stroll. She could sit on a weathered log in a meadow and get lost in the quaking aspen leaves—nothing would be more calming.

In the newspaper's *Peanuts* cartoon, Snoopy inspired her. At loose ends, he went for adventure. She should emulate the dog's initiative and take Faye up on her offer of a trip to Hawai'i.

Her phone pinged with a text from Nancy. **<Sorry, last-minute invite. Barbecue at our place, noon?>**

Getting away from tangible reminders of Manolo through his furniture and photos—not something to turn down. And she could discuss with Dr. Grinwold another work assignment out of the office. Hitting him up after a few drinks, under Nancy's mellowing influence, was a sound strategy. Maya texted back. **<I'll bring beer and wine.>**

At 11:45, Maya parked her Prius on the street at the southside faux adobe. Cradling a soft-sided cooler, she approached the front portal, three-foot chile ristras accenting either side of the blue door. A handwritten sign directed her to the back gate.

The picnic table under the rear portal drooped with fall-colored streamers, reflecting the yellowed lawn from the drought. Nancy glanced up as she set out plastic plates. "Sorry we've let the yard go. Fred is serious about conserving water and doesn't think the turf deserves it. Maybe we'll dig it up and put in gravel, or desertscape."

Maya set her cooler on the concrete slab. First she pulled out cans stamped with the Zia symbol and SANTA FE BREWING CO. "I remember Dr. Grinwold loves Pepe Loco, this Mexican style lager." Next she showed Nancy a bottle of local Gruet Chardonnay. "This is what you like, right?"

Nancy gave her a warm hug. "You've paid attention to details, as usual. Thank you so much. By the way, you've worked with Fred for three years now. I think you can call him by his first name."

Maya blushed. "I, ah, it just wouldn't feel okay. Kinda like calling my dad Tom. Where is he?"

"In the kitchen, finishing up the potato salad. I hope you don't mind that we're staying outside. With COVID creeping up again, this way we can be unmasked."

As Maya admired a raised bed of petunias, Stephanie arrived with bottles of soda. "Good to see you again, mija. You haven't stopped by the office in a while."

"I know," Maya said. "I can't wait until we can hike again, maybe at a higher elevation for the fall colors, like the Santa Fe Ski basin. Hey, is Erika coming?"

Stephanie shook her head. "She and Rolf are taking Kyle on the Sky Railway, that old scenic train that goes out to Lamy."

Maya laughed. "Hanging out with us old folks wouldn't be much fun for an eight-year-old."

"You've got another year-and-a-half 'til you hit thirty—hardly over the hill."

Maya bent to smell the purple flower. "It just feels like I've already lived a lifetime."

Nancy slid open the patio door as Dr. Grinwold stepped through and set a large ceramic dish of potato salad on the table. "Ladies, thanks for coming." He dropped his arm to Nancy's shoulders.

His role as a gregarious host left Maya off-kilter. He usually was so formal—she didn't recall him having a work party in the three years she'd been assigned to New Mexico. Or else she hadn't been invited. In his late fifties, would he retire early like Nancy or stick around for a few more years?

A permanent position next summer would be more tolerable

with a familiar and respected boss, even if a bit crusty. She was indebted for his care when she awoke from the COVID coma.

Gray clouds clustered along the Jemez Mountains to the west. "Hope we can get this in before a monsoon hits," Maya said.

Dr. Grinwold scowled. "Don't go bringing us bad luck. Weather report says only a twenty-percent chance of showers." He opened Maya's cooler and pulled out a Pepe Loco. "You trying to loosen me up, Maya?"

He'd seen right through her, but she'd wait until the lagers kicked in. She grabbed the tongs and pivoted for the grill. "My dad taught me some skills barbecuing chicken. Can you put me to work?"

Several dozen health department staff stopped by the party, and some of Nancy's birder friends from the Audubon Society. She pulled out snapshots of the Elegant Trogon, a large black-headed, green-backed, and red-breasted bird with a long copper tail.

"Fred and I saw these thirty years ago in the Chiricahua Mountains of southeastern Arizona. But then I had a heart attack, and we haven't been back there since."

Dr. Grinwold took her hand. "Let's plan a repeat trip when they migrate back up from Mexico. Anyone want to join us?"

The birders clustered around Nancy as she opened up a paper map of the area. Dr. Grinwold frowned when his cell rang. "Faye Simpson, wonder why she's calling?"

Maya's breath caught in her throat. She assumed they'd sound him out together—sometimes Faye was a bull in a China shop.

Dr. Grinwold's first words were, "Faye, I hope you're not invading my New Mexico turf again."

Nancy left her friends and joined Maya. "He's always on the crotchety side with Faye Simpson. She defeated him decades ago to become CSTE President, you know, the State Epi group."

Maya thought that Dr. Grinwold's jealousy of Faye wasn't the type of information to be shared. Nancy's flushed cheeks and the almost empty bottle of wine perhaps accounted for impolitic speech.

Before Nancy revealed any more epi infighting, Dr. Grinwold waved Maya over to join him and hit the speaker icon.

"Dengue again?" he growled. "We just got it behind us, and it's not one of our public health priorities."

Faye's voice sounded tight. "Fred, your cases were a wakeup call. Some scientists believe that climate change will impact the risk of dengue more than any other disease."

"It's my job, not yours, to supervise Maya's preventive medicine residency." He glanced up to the darkening sky. "It's only a year, and there's a lot she needs to accomplish under my watch."

Maya interrupted their increasingly terse talk. "Dr. Grinwold, Hawai'i could use my experience with the dengue interview forms I developed here."

And a different environment would provide a major distraction from her helpless feeling over the Schwartz family.

"Fred, I'll be eternally in your debt if you and CDC approve this." Faye slipped back to the accent of a down-home Colorado rancher. "You can collect on the favor whenever it suits you."

Dr. Grinwold glanced over at Maya. "Well, I've got her at least until June, so go ahead."

Maya hadn't anticipated his immediate approval. Things were moving almost too quickly.

"Maya, I'll check with Siti Rahim in Puerto Rico," Faye said, "and get back to you about your travel plans."

No sooner had Dr. Grinwold hung up than a second call came in. "Damn, how come everyone's forgetting to rest on the Sabbath?"

Maya couldn't tell if her beers had released his inhibitions or lit a fuse. She headed back to the patio and Stephanie.

Minutes later, Dr. Grinwold returned. "Lila Becker's got a jump in meningococcal disease for college students. She wants to align Arizona's vaccine guidelines with us and other states."

Maya added the task to her phone. "Sure, I can help Erika pull up the policies." She headed to the front yard and dialed Lila's number.

"Hello, Maya, by the timing of this call, I'm guessing you're with Fred."

"Yeah, he's having a party. Listen, I've been so busy with dengue, I never checked back on what your health department decided about Enzo." She hoped they'd found a way to bust his ass.

"Sorry, the lawyers concluded we have no legal basis to act. He's no longer stationed here, and his computer rantings, although disgusting, don't break any laws. He didn't threaten you or anyone else in an explicit way."

Maya's legs weakened and she leaned against the hood of her car. "I've been too passive in the past. Can you at least give me his number so I can chew him out? You know me, it wouldn't go beyond that."

Lila sounded tentative. "I'm not sure if this crosses a line, but you and I have put up with his antics for several years." There was a short pause on the line, then Lila continued. "Take this down, but you can't tell him how you found out. Agreed?"

Maya jotted the phone number in her pocket notebook. "You're a good friend. I appreciate it."

Lila laughed. "Just remember, if his body turns up in DC's Rock Creek Park, you'll be first on the suspect list."

Maya stopped back to the patio and expressed her thanks to her hosts. She grabbed her empty cooler and hurried to her Prius. Unsure when and how she'd confront Enzo, she needed time to plan it out. But soon, very soon.

TWENTY-EIGHT

Lahaina, Maui—Friday, September 3, 2021

At the Paia Fish Market, Faye opened a corner of her takeout box. Famished, she sniffed the ono sauteed in butter, garlic, wine and lemon. She couldn't wait for the flavor of the mild white fish on her tongue. This was the first time the three of them would share lunch since Faye had flown into Maui from Hilo to meet Maya coming from New Mexico and Ino from Honolulu.

Faye eyed the restaurant's covered picnic tables lining Front Street, then glanced across the traffic to the verdant overstory in Courthouse Square. "Eating under that massive banyan tree looks like fun."

Ino Kahale glanced at Maya. "What's your vote? Almost a hundred-and-fifty-years-old, the tree has sixteen trunks. There are plenty of cool, quiet places to sit."

Maya patted a napkin on the sweat beading her forehead. "Your car radio said it's 88 degrees, so I'd welcome any place with shade."

Faye studied Maya's face, her skin color a bit washed out. Maya had been holed up at the district health office in Wailuku crunching data while Faye and Ino collected mosquitoes in the West Maui Forest Reserve and Lahaina. On her first day outside of air conditioning, no wonder Maya was hot and pale.

Looping her free arm through Maya's, Faye led them across to the park. "You can't come to Hawai'i and never experience its beauty, although I'm not one to talk. Dr. Oldner was pissed that I jettisoned her plans to be my scientific and tourist guide."

Ino chose a wooden bench on the east side of the two-story Old Lahaina Courthouse with its red-tile roof. Faye's heart warmed at the sight of a little girl scrambling up the banyan trunks. She looked like Juana Lopez, the New York dengue patient.

Glancing over to Maya, focused on her salmon burger, Faye wondered if the raucous laughter of children triggered traumatic memories of her miscarriage. Then she shivered, the contorted tree branches appearing to creep closer.

As Ino wolfed down his Cajun-style mahi-mahi, Faye's lips twitched. "With the risk of scombroid food poisoning, you couldn't pay me to eat that."

He shook his head. "This market knows how to keep its fish refrigerated to prevent elevated histamine and allergic reactions."

"In New York, we investigated a woman who developed acute pancreatitis twenty minutes after eating mahi-mahi. She was hospitalized for a week."

Ino patted his round belly. "Sometimes, I can ignore my public health paranoia for anything related to 'āina, our Hawaiian land and sea that feeds us."

Maya took a sip of her Waialua root beer, then set the bottle on the seat and opened up her laptop. "Would you like to hear my initial results?"

Faye nodded. "I realize you've only had three days to generate the data."

"From that list of fifty-two Maui cases you gave me, I completed interviews with forty-one. I'll email a more complete report tonight. Nineteen live within a mile of the Kahului airport and didn't travel anywhere in the past month. The West Maui Natural Area Reserve was visited by three separate groups of birdwatchers who remembered mosquito bites. Only one case resides in Hana on the east coast."

"Outliers can provide clues," Faye said. "Tell me more about that infection."

"He was the earliest Maui patient, with onset of fever and muscle aches on August 18. He'd been in Hilo giving a university lecture on August 12 and flew back to Maui on August 13. Along with two more reported Hilo cases, he could have been exposed there, or perhaps at the Kahului airport before driving home to Hana."

Ino jumped in. "I'm not sure one Hana case justifies mosquito surveillance with our limited resources. On the other hand, our Kahului work paid off. We've identified seven dengue-positive tiger mosquito pools. Five were *Aedes aegypti*, thought to be endemic only along the Kona Coast."

"But the other positives were *Aedes albopictus*," Faye added. "That mosquito is widely spread across the islands."

Maya collected their paper waste. "A Lahaina church offers services to the unhoused and they've seen several new dengue patients."

Faye checked her schedule on her phone. "You should have told me sooner about the church connection." Then she regretted her sharp words. They'd been too busy each day to reconnoiter and share all their findings.

Ino's truck slogged through the traffic crawl along Front Street. Amidst all the restaurants, tourist shops, and art galleries, Faye spotted a streetside stand of two-to-three-foot-high wooden statues, crowding a table under a red umbrella. Their fierce faces had similar expressions to the huge figures in the Puʻuhonua O Hōnaunau temple on Hawaiʻi Island.

Devorah would have loved one of those. Before her Alzheimer's forced her into memory care, she'd been a folk-art collector. Shopping wasn't one of Faye's favorite pastimes but it would be nice to bring something back for Taylor. What could you get someone who was a world traveler?

"Watch out," Maya yelled from the back seat as a pedestrian darted in front.

"Thanks for the extra set of eyes," Ino said.

Faye's pulse slowed with the relief of avoiding an awful accident.

"It's the same thing around the Plaza in downtown Santa Fe," Maya said. "Crystal-clear skies, quaint shops, scenic nature. Everyone's in their happy vacation mode, as if nothing bad can happen in paradise."

In the church parking lot, tables shaded by huge canopies dotted the graveled lot. Two ladies wearing surgical masks at the first table greeted them with the shaka sign—three middle fingers in the palm with the thumb and fifth finger extended. "Aloha, how can we help you?"

Ino's face lit up like a Maui sunset. "Pua, how wonderful to see you. I didn't realize I'd find my cousin here."

Leaping to her feet, the woman removed her mask and leaned in to touch noses. Honi ihu, an exchange of breath, Ino had explained to Faye when she first arrived in Honolulu.

"Palala, I could never forget my 'ohana," she told him. "Sounds like the Hula O Nā Keiki competition has been canceled. Maybe next year I can see your beautiful mo'opuna compete."

Faye tugged out her phone for a translation while the two continued to converse. Palala had multiple meanings, including slang for brother. 'Ohana was family and mo'opuna was granddaughter. She knew that keiki meant child.

Ino turned to Faye and Maya. "Pua, these are my colleagues Faye Simpson and Maya Maguire. They're both veterinary epidemiologists helping us with the dengue fever."

Pua grasped their hands. "Thank you so much. My good friend is at Maui Memorial Medical Center with dengue. He's only thirty-six years old, but he's had type 2 diabetes for several years. Now he has heart and liver problems—the doctor told me yesterday that his abdomen is full of fluid."

Her eyes filled with tears. "This morning, they put him on a ventilator. I wanted to go, but we only have this mission twice a week, and I can do more good here."

Faye turned to Maya. "Are you aware of new hospitalizations for dengue?"

"Yes, besides Pua's friend, a forty-year-old woman was admitted yesterday with a history of asthma and two days of vomiting and blood in her stools. I haven't been able to interview either of them."

"Let's check first on the people receiving services here," Ino said.

Pua turned to her notebook. "I have the names of seven people who signed in for showers and a meal last week, then talked to the nurse about feeling unwell. She took blood samples for COVID and dengue."

"Have the mosquitoes been bad?" Faye asked.

"We're only open midday, so I'm not sure," Pua answered. "But I live in Launiupoko and they've been awful there at dusk and dawn. I don't know of anyone in my neighborhood who's gotten sick, though."

"Pua, can you share with Maya all the information you have about those seven people?" Ino asked. "Faye and I will contact the hospital."

He moved to a quiet corner of the parking area under the fronds of a banana tree. After clicking on speaker, he held the phone toward Faye and connected with the chief of staff.

"Dr. Chang, this is Ino Kahale from the health department. Your staff has been in communication with Dr. Maya Maguire of the CDC about two patients hospitalized with dengue. Can you update us on their conditions?"

"Of course, Ino, happy to help. Let me pull up their records."

During the pause, Faye studied a sinister-looking Common Myna bird. Highlighted by a patch of bright yellow feathers, one dark eye pinned Faye. Defying her unease about some interspecies interactions, the bird hopped close to Ino's feet to grab food scraps on the ground.

Then it raised dark tail feathers to poop next to his open-toed sandal. *Salmonella* contaminating the soil where people gathered to eat—Faye urged the bird away. The curse of a public health veterinarian—the risk of disease spillover kept pushing to the top of her mind.

"Sorry to keep you waiting." The voice, now more somber, drew Faye's attention back to Ino's phone. "We just lost one of them an hour ago."

Faye crossed her fingers that it wasn't the young man Pua was close to.

"He had cardiac arrest and resuscitation failed."

The second patient had been female, so the deceased was Pua's friend. The five percent of severe dengue infections which resulted in death hadn't become personal until Juana. Now, after Juana's grandmother and this new tragedy, they loomed closer.

Ino's usually gregarious expression clouded. "My cousin is here at the Lahaina mission. She's his Aunty by affection but not related—can I let her know?"

"Yes, he's well-known in the community and I understand the family just talked to the press. Can you take me off speakerphone and we'll confirm the patient's name?"

Faye turned away to rejoin Maya and Pua. Waiting for Ino to finish his call, she focused on guarding her emotions. It was hard to believe in death when surrounded by brilliant blue skies and a sparkling ocean. "Get what you need, Maya?"

"I gave her the locations where they commonly hang out," Pua answered, "and their descriptions, as much as I can remember."

Maya smiled. "I'm here for the duration. Even though it's the Labor Day weekend, we can track them down and make sure they're okay."

Faye gave a supportive thumbs-up. "We'll test the mosquitoes from those areas."

She reached into her bag for some colorful trifold brochures. "Here are flyers warning about dengue and how to reduce risk. Ino also has mosquito repellent wipes—I'll ask him to leave you some to distribute."

At that moment, Ino rejoined them. Pua seemed to read his body language and started sobbing. Ino wrapped his long arms around his cousin and kept her standing when her knees buckled. Faye grabbed Maya's arm and stepped back to give them privacy.

A young staffer cleaned up after the lunch. He tossed a scrap of hamburger bun to the myna. Faye was too late with her warning about the risk of feeding birds in an area crowded with vulnerable people. The bird bobbed its head and croaked its thanks.

TWENTY-NINE

Lahaina, Maui—Monday, September 6, 2021

Carrying two lawn chairs from the car for her and Faye, Maya followed Ino and his cousin Pua down the narrow path between houses to Lahaina's Pu'unoa Beach. They emerged through the opening to the soft sand and crescent of calm water protected by an offshore coral breakwall. Ino set up an umbrella beneath a palm tree arching over the beach.

"Oh my God, this is paradise," Maya said. She kicked off her flip-flops and wiggled her toes.

"I've been waiting a month to do this," Faye answered, grinning under her floppy straw hat.

Pua dropped bags of Hawaiian hurricane popcorn and dried cuttlefish onto a red-and-white checkered tablecloth. "This is nicknamed Baby Beach—the shallow water's safe for families and new snorkelers."

Maya was distracted by a diapered infant crawling toward the water followed by a laughing young couple. *Should be me and Manolo.*

She shoved the yearning aside. "Thanks, Pua, for hosting our first day off. But before we decompress, I need to go over my updated numbers."

"Tell us what you've got," Ino said. "Sorry, Pua, we promise not to talk shop for too long."

Maya studied her notes. "The death rate for diagnosed cases who receive supportive care is typically one percent. Of 201 Hawai'i cases in my database, we're now up to sixteen deaths—six on Hawai'i Island, eight here on Maui, and two who died in Honolulu but were Maui residents. That's an eight percent case fatality rate."

"It's possible for the rate to reach ten to twenty percent," Faye said. "I'm worried, but we don't need to panic yet."

Ino stretched his legs out in front of his chair. "I agree with Faye. We've got no mosquitoes to harass us here at the moment, so let's pause the dengue discussion for an hour or two."

Air heating up despite the shade, Maya removed her loose blouse and shorts, happy to wear her swimsuit for the first time since arriving in Hawai'i.

She respected the decision to take a break, but her data hammered her consciousness like a southwestern summer monsoon. In New Mexico, a state only recently endemic for *Aedes aegypti*, they beat the bushes for more infections and didn't find them. In contrast, each new effort at surveillance in Hawai'i revealed an outbreak threatening to warp out of control.

Faye shed her clothes to reveal a deep blue swimsuit with a wide skirt covering much of her pale skin. She grabbed Maya by the hand. "Come on, kiddo, give your brain a break for a couple hours."

She turned to their Hawaiian hosts, kicking back on their lounge chairs. "Gonna join us?"

Ino glanced at Pua. "I think we'll catch up for a bit."

Maya followed Faye into the water, slowly reaching up to their waists as they waded deeper out toward the ring of coral reef. A dark shape approached underwater, then poked its head up to study them with enormous black eyes dominating a whiskered face.

"A Hawaiian monk seal!" Maya grabbed Faye's arm. "I can't believe we get to see one—they're highly endangered."

As the animal swam away, both women floated on their backs, rocking as if in a cradle. Maya closed her eyes to the sun warming her face. The only sounds were exuberant shouts from the shore until a group of teenagers joined them in the water, chasing and splashing each other.

"Faye, before the holiday crowds scare everything away, I want to snorkel. Are you up for it?"

Her mentor shaded her eyes with a flat hand. "You mentioned doing it in California. Can you teach an old lady some new tricks?"

Maya laughed. "You betcha." She raced ahead to the shore and gathered two sets of rental gear, dripping baby shampoo into the masks to prevent fog. "We could just spit in them," Maya told Faye, "but this is a bit more sanitary."

"That monk seal came close to you guys," Ino said. "We call it 'ilio-holo-i-ka-uaua or 'dog that runs in rough water.' Go closer to the reef for turtles."

Faye put her t-shirt back on. "I think I should wear this for sun protection."

Maya grabbed her fins. "I'd recommend a snorkel vest and swim noodle for your first time."

Pua lifted her cup in salute. "Faye, there's no need to dive under—you can see plenty just with your face in the water."

"Stay inside the reef," Ino added. "We've had deaths from Snorkel Induced Rapid Onset Pulmonary Edema, or SI-ROPE. First symptoms are shortness of breath and panic when someone can't touch bottom. It usually happens to people with recent prolonged air travel, which isn't you."

Faye's face creased with concern.

"I'll take care of her, don't worry." Maya reviewed one more time the rental shop's plastic cards with pictures and names of Hawaiian fish. Then she and Faye waded back into the ocean between standup paddleboarders and kids tossing Frisbees.

Once in waist-deep water again, she helped Faye adjust her snorkel. "Keep your feet on the ground and practice breathing as you look underwater through your mask."

Faye went a few seconds before popping her head up, coughing. "I can't keep water from leaking into my mouth."

"Just like now, raise your head, slip your snorkel out of your mouth, and twist the mouthpiece to dump out the water. Remember, you've got the life vest, your swim noodle, and me. We'll stick to these shallow waters where you can stand up for a rest break. Nothing bad's going to happen."

For a moment, Maya scanned the horizon in all directions, relishing their role reversal. Who would have thought she'd be the calm and experienced one, mentoring her older colleague in a new skill?

"Let's practice blowing out your snorkel," she told Faye. "I'll hold your arm to keep you steady while you dunk deeper to get water in it. Then bring your head back to level on the surface with your lips tight around the mouthpiece. Blow hard to expel the water or tilt your head back for a gravity boost."

Faye was a quick learner and soon was floating with her face in the water as Maya stood at the ready to help. A short time later, Faye leapt up, her face reddened and animated. "What are those psychedelic fish? Blue-green head, orange thorax stripe, and green belly and tail streaked with magenta."

"Saddle wrasses. They start life as females and change to males when they're older." Maya was pleased she'd spent a little time researching something besides dengue.

"So humans aren't the only ones capable of gender fluidity."

Uncertain if Faye's comment was general or personal, Maya agreed, then pointed with excitement to a school of angelfish. Too often, it seemed like nature was her enemy—deadly microbes, animals, ticks, lice, and mosquitoes all out to challenge her. She'd become a veterinarian because of a fascination with the world's creatures, but a duty to protect people from them colored her perspective.

The rocking swell of cool water, sun warming her shoulders, and camaraderie of colleagues who were also friends filled her with joy. Every muscle relaxed and her overactive brain cells slipped into something close to meditation. Life was worth living.

She donned the mask, snorkel and fins she'd clutched in one arm while teaching Faye. "Can you wait here while I snorkel closer to the reef?"

Faye frowned. "Ino said we should stick together."

"You're not ready for deeper water, but I'm a good snorkeler. I won't go on the other side of the reef." With a rapid flutter kick, she was off. The reef condition was disheartening—some spiky, cream-colored cauliflower corals were whited out or smothered with sediment and algae. Under a table coral ledge, a school of mamo, Hawaiian sergeant fish with black-striped greenish-white bodies, darted up to feed at the surface until they dove for cover.

A tiger shark cruised casually above the drop-off on the other side of the coral ridge. Keeping it in full view, Maya used her arms to edge backward to the shallower water. She wasn't shark-phobic but the sight still ramped up her pulse rate.

Rejoining Faye, she stood up and released a deep, calming breath. "I just saw a tiger shark, about my size. It wasn't aggressive but I've had enough of snorkeling today. How about you?"

"I'm fine with skipping sharks."

They ascended the sandy beach and joined their hosts, chairs tightly clustered under the umbrella as the sun burned high in the sky. "You ladies have a good snorkel?" Ino asked.

Faye almost tipped over her lounge chair as she dropped into it. "A carousel of colorful sea life. If I retire here, I'll be in the water every day."

"Near the reef, I spotted a small tiger shark," Maya added.

Pua handed Maya a water bottle. "I'm not a fan. Those sharks are fond of Maui, and we have 7-8 attacks each year."

"Just don't swim after heavy rains when the water is murky." Ino's expression was dismissive of his cousin's warning.

Maya wasn't surprised that his risk reduction hat wasn't ever far away. "The coral's in rough shape," she said.

Pua let the sand particles slip through her fingers. "We're not taking care of the coral that made this beach. Too much sewage promotes algal blooms. We've also had several thermal warming and bleaching events."

"It's not all hopeless—Hawai'i switched to reef-safe sunscreens," Ino said. "Listen, I'd like to treat our CDC guests and my cousin to lunch. Anyone hungry?"

A mosquito buzzed around Maya's ankles and she slapped it away. In previous times of stress, she'd seek solace in memories of childhood visits to the ocean off San Diego. Now she had a new happy place, a source of tranquility for all her senses.

At five o'clock, still full from her kimchi burger, Maya begged off dinner. Sitting at her computer in the Kahului hotel, she reviewed the data in her spreadsheet. A pregnant dengue patient at Maui Memorial lost her baby—tears moistened Maya's eyes for the young woman who'd nurtured a son in her belly for eight months.

The number of deaths might be within the high range of normal as Faye had pointed out, but perhaps something was off in the medical decision-making of the staff, or some weird patient host-factors were putting them more at risk.

Maya summoned up the restful rocking sensation of floating at Baby Beach. Even with Braxton's kidnapping never far from her mind, the ocean was a magic balm. But she'd put off the call to Enzo long enough.

Manolo had approached every challenge with energy and optimism, no second-guessing. He'd confronted Enzo when he learned of Enzo's sexual aggression toward Maya, although it almost cost him his job. After an insane year-and-a-half since she'd worked with Enzo, she would channel her husband's assertiveness.

Six-hour time difference but Enzo was a party animal and a night owl—she'd catch him awake. And perhaps he'd be more honest with the element of surprise, before he could craft a self-serving answer.

Maya typed in the phone number provided by Lila, and Enzo's tanned, lean face came into view on FaceTime.

"What a pleasant way to top off Labor Day," he said. In his early thirties, he had no wrinkles around his amber eyes. His unblinking gaze disturbed Maya, as always.

"It started with a morning kayak on the Potomac, followed by an afternoon string quartet on the grounds of the Washington Monument, and finally a barbecue at the home of the Finnish ambassador."

Just like Enzo to be so self-focused. Then he slipped on a mask of concern. "I was sorry to hear about Manolo's death. I never thought he was the right guy for you, but it must have been rough."

His remark was a gut punch, but Maya decided to be polite. She was determined to get on his good side before the confrontation about his computer files. "Thanks, I'm hanging in. How's your new job at NIAID going?"

Her strategy was working—his face lit up with pride. "It's wonderful. I'm in the Division of Microbiology and Infectious Diseases. We oversee grant funding—lots of influence on the direction of research and disease control. I love the big picture, and big impact."

Maya could see how that type of oversight and power would appeal to him—he'd never been skilled at the nuts and bolts of outbreak study design and statistics. "We had two cases of dengue in New Mexico," she said. "Now I'm helping with a surge in Hawai'i."

His fingers combed his brown hair, which he always cut short in the summer for his road race training. "We support a lot of dengue studies. In fact, we have a grantee in Hawaii, at a Hilo campus."

"Dr. Oldner? One of my colleagues visited her research lab last week." The coincidence reminded Maya of that old maxim—never burn any bridges. No matter how much a colleague upset you, it was imperative to maintain good relations. You'd probably cross paths to work with them again at some point. But she'd blow that up, once she broached the computer files.

"Yes, that's the one," Enzo answered. "Although we might need to yank those funds due to some study problems." He looked away, then rubbed his ear. "Sorry, Maya, I can't say more."

Faye would want details. Which was more important, finding out Enzo's allegations about Dr. Oldner or confronting him with the Arizona computer records? Feeling selfish, she decided to prioritize her personal concerns.

"Did you puncture Lila's rental car tire in Atlanta and smash the window of Manolo's Corvette in Phoenix?" She hoped the abrupt accusation would shock him into admitting the truth.

His expression transformed in an instant. "Jesus, Maya, where on earth would you get that idea?"

She hadn't figured out how to bring up his computer notes without revealing Lila as the source. But Arizona's health department attorneys had already talked to him, so Maya's accusations shouldn't be a surprise.

"And I don't appreciate having fantasy sex stories written about me." Her heart pounded and stars danced before her eyes. "I thought you'd moved on with the gorgeous blonde at the health department. After everything I experienced last year, I don't need to hear you still have some kind of perverse sexual obsession."

There were two ways he might go, based on her confrontations with him in the past. Either flaming anger or puppy-dog begging for forgiveness.

"Lila's gonna regret telling you that to her dying day."

THIRTY

Wailuku, Maui—Tuesday, September 7, 2021

Surrounded by bustling Maui Medical Center staff and visitors grabbing lunch in the cafeteria, Faye downed her third cup of coffee. "Two more dengue patients died here overnight," she said. "What a tragedy."

"I still don't see a pattern." Maya reviewed her spreadsheet on her laptop as Ino called the State Epidemiologist.

After he finished, he dropped his phone to the table. "The death count on Hawai'i Island also jumped up. Dr. Clark's flying there first, then here to talk with the staff."

Faye appreciated his involvement. "He may have suggestions about hospital procedures to improve survival. But the two deaths don't appear to be related. The grandmother died from acute renal failure and the retired firefighter with a secondary bacterial infection."

"Those are known complications of dengue infection," Maya said. "But deaths are coming sooner after symptom onset."

One hand on her coffee cup, Faye pushed back her chair. "We should touch base with Siti Rahim at CDC. Let's do it where we can use the speakerphone."

Ino held the door. As they rounded the corner of the multistory building, he directed them to a bench under a tree with an umbrella-shaped canopy. "Honolulu prohibited new plantings of monkeypod trees on city property because they're from South America."

Faye wiped her brow. "I appreciate its shade even if Hawai'i is stamping out foreign invaders." She patted the tree's deeply-furrowed gray bark and thanked it for protecting her tender skin.

"Do you sunburn?" she asked Maya.

"No, but my skin's darker today after only a couple of hours in the water."

"Me, too," Ino added. "You're just not meant to be here, Faye. You need to go back to Ireland."

You should head home to Tonga. Faye squashed her thought in response to Ino's grin and wink. Caren's 'us versus them' prickliness was seeping into her pores like a bad perfume.

In the gloomy face of an escalating outbreak, Faye welcomed Ino's jocularity and mimicked his expression. "You can keep your sea level rise, shark attacks, tsunamis, volcanic smog, and drought. I'll retire in Vermont."

Ino laughed so hard, his belly shook before he dropped to the bench.

Faye dialed Puerto Rico. Hearing the Branch Chief, she said, "Siti, I'm on speaker with Maya and Ino. Our dengue case fatality rate is up for no discernable reason, and we're still dealing with infected *Aedes aegypti* in new places, like here on Maui."

"Sounds like my decision to deploy you and Maya was a wise one," Siti answered. "We have an increase here too, and our proportion of severe cases is more than double other countries in the Americas."

"What's the situation worldwide?" Maya asked.

"I'm headed to Brazil later this week—their infections this year are threatening to top a million."

Ino's phone rang. "Sorry, it's Dr. Clark again. I need to take this call." Then he stepped away.

"Siti, what you're handling is orders of magnitude larger than our problem in Hawai'i," Faye said. "I hope our work here is making a difference."

"Apples and oranges," Siti answered. "I'm responding to areas where dengue's entrenched. Some would argue it's even more critical to knock it back when it surprises us. Keep me posted."

Ino rejoined them, rubbing the back of his neck. "Seven more deaths at Kona Community Hospital and Dr. Clark wants me to meet him there. He also said it's urgent to learn more about Dr. Oldner's study results that haven't been published yet."

Work with Caren felt like wrestling a porcupine, but she was the only expert nearby. Faye regretted the abbreviated review of Caren's research because of their shift to Maui. "It always feels like we're a step behind."

"Then it's decided," Ino said. "I'll catch a flight this afternoon to Kona, while you and Maya fly to Hilo."

Hilo, Hawai'i Island—Tuesday, September 7, 2021

Caren, dressed like a soldier in khaki pants and a forest-green polo shirt, ignored Maya's outstretched hand as Faye made the introductions inside the Hilo research building. Perhaps it was COVID caution, or maybe she was dismissive of someone so young—she'd made disparaging comments about her students on occasion.

Maya opened her laptop to an epidemic curve graphing the number of human dengue cases by date. "You can see the steep rise. Unless we reduce infected mosquitoes, they'll be in the thousands within a couple of weeks."

"But it's not all horrible news," Faye said. "The Health Department is considering more funding for your current work, if we can determine which techniques are most effective."

Caren's steely blue eyes focused on Faye. "I'm happy to show you our Sterile Insect Technique, or SIT. When we release irradiated males that can't reproduce, their competitive breeding with females reduces the mosquito population."

"If a female mates with a sterilized male, does she still lay eggs?" Faye asked.

"Yes, but they won't be fertilized, and won't hatch," Caren said. "Like chickens without a rooster."

She opened each door to the lab facilities that Faye had seen on her previous visit, as if to go through the motions of hospitality for Maya. When a young lab worker glanced up and grimaced, her arm in a container darkened by a swarm of mosquitoes, Maya spoke up.

"I was reading about a lab that feeds them using lambskin condoms filled with bovine blood."

Caren's laugh sounded more like a snarl. "I don't need to spend money on prophylactics more valuable to you young'uns."

Faye blanched with Caren's sharp remark but in the urgency of the outbreak, ignored it. The next room featured a water-filled vertical pair of glass plates. Caren pointed to three horizontal stripes of small dark shapes between them.

"Adjustment of the separator plate distance and angle determines which sizes are filtered out first. These closest to the bottom are the larvae that haven't pupated yet." The technician adjusted knobs and drained the larvae to a container.

"The next level has the male pupae," Caren continued, "which are smaller than the females." After collecting them, the tech handed the container to Caren, who sat down by a dissecting scope. She sucked out a few pupae and rotated them using probes.

"Faye, look through here," Caren ordered. "Can you see the genital lobe?"

The lateral view of the pupa was eerie. A monster head with a big dark eye dominated the small segmented body. No wonder people hated mosquitoes—they were gross even when unable to bite. "I can see the tail," Faye said.

Caren grabbed the container of females and dropped one by the male. "Check it again, the female's on the left."

With the larvae next to each other, the difference in genital probe shape and size was clear. Faye stepped aside for Maya and said, "It will take a huge amount of time to verify each one."

"We don't look at all of them under the scope," Caren answered. "This is just a sample spot check on our separator. Let's move on."

In the corridor, Caren tapped her foot as Maya lingered, studying the pupae. Faye hadn't realized Maya's scientific interests stretched beyond statistics. But magnification of tiny creatures brought the microscopic world to life, making it all the more real.

"Any day now," Caren said in a low voice. Maya scurried out to stand behind Faye.

In the next shipping container, Caren placed a stack of Petri dishes in a chamber with dosimetry film. "We irradiate the male pupae with cesium-137 for 5 minutes, 41 seconds." She turned on the machine. "Tomorrow, we'll read the irradiated film to verify the dose."

She shepherded Faye and Maya to another lab where a masked assistant rotated containers of pupae coated with red powder. "This is rhodamine B fluorescent pigment for the pupae," Caren explained. "We also feed it in a dissolved honey solution to adult males."

"Why do you dye them?" Faye asked.

"To identify them with fluorescent microscopy for mark-release-recapture studies," Maya answered.

Faye wasn't surprised by Maya's quick reply. Clearly, she spent her evenings doing more than mourning her deceased husband.

Caren narrowed her eyes. "Your trainee is correct. I don't want to overpromise on success because the irradiated mosquitoes could be less successful at breeding, thus reducing our aim for them to compete with intact males. By trapping after their release, we compare the mean distances traveled and average life expectancy of irradiated males versus wild strains."

Maya's face and posture turned back into silent, invisible mode. Faye bristled at Caren's tone when she said "your trainee." She remembered Caren's disparaging remark about gooks when describing her father's death in Vietnam.

Keep calm and carry on—the mantra Faye picked up on her coronavirus investigation in the United Kingdom. It wouldn't help to get in a spitting match with Caren on her antagonistic attitudes, but she needed to make clear her respect for Maya's abilities. "Dr. Maguire is scrupulous about sifting through hundreds of relevant peer-reviewed articles. What are the results of your studies?"

Caren angled her phone toward Faye with a table of data. "In our initial application, 18.9% of captured female mosquitoes had been mated by the marked males, compared to 52.6% mated by wild males."

"So you're making a dent, but not enough to overpower the natural mating," Faye said.

Caren frowned. "Any reduction in new mosquitoes is a benefit to public health. Why don't you join us on another release this evening? I'll add a cot to my basement apartment and both of you can stay the night."

Before Faye could answer, her phone rang and Ino's solemn face filled her FaceTime screen. "I'm at Kona Community Hospital. Early this morning, the Mayor of Hawai'i County collapsed during a meeting and had a cardiac arrest in the ambulance. Initial lab results just came in—it's dengue. She was only thirty-four-years-old, with several young children."

"My God," Faye said, "what does Dr. Clark want us to do?"

"He's sending a team to assist me with mosquito control. They tried to reopen the campground near the historic site but some of the campers are among those hospitalized here. Does Dr. Oldner have any recommendations on which insecticide to use?"

Caren moved in closer to answer. "I'll review the data with Faye. I'm also doing a SIT demo tonight—that's release of sterilized male mosquitoes. You'll have a full report of all options tomorrow."

"Make sure it's before ten o'clock." Ino's voice became stern. "That's when the Governor plans to show up for a press conference."

When Ino hung up, Caren turned to Faye. "We should get going. Our SIT is at Volcanoes National Park. Dengue risk is reduced at elevation, but with such a huge number of tourists, they want to make sure that mosquito counts stay low."

In less than an hour, Caren's assistant had loaded up the back of her truck with containers of the irradiated mosquitoes. As they headed south from Hilo, Caren kept the windows rolled down for fresh air but the ground-hugging clouds locked in eighty-degree temperatures like the lid on a boiling pot of water.

Faye tried to ignore the thousands of predators in the truck bed. Male mosquitoes don't suck blood, she repeated. They swarmed people but rarely landed. Caren said they'd reach the Kīlauea overlook by sunset to release their sex-crazed cargo.

THIRTY-ONE

Hawai'i Volcanoes National Park, Hawai'i Island—Tuesday, September 7, 2021

Mindful of Enzo's warning about the Hilo studies, Maya reviewed Caren's publications during the ride to the national park. While driving, Caren maintained a nonstop discussion with Faye of her plans for distributing irradiated male *Aedes aegypti* mosquitoes.

As they passed the Visitor Center, Maya opened a park service brochure on her phone. Pele, the goddess of fire, had shaped her home with red-hot lava which exploded in 1790 to form the volcanic caldera and crater. At the parking lot for the Kīlauea Overlook, the forest thinned to expose a pink-streaked sky at sunset.

Maya found a spot among the small group of visitors snapping photos. An earthquake swarm in August predicted future lava activity, but no spurts of golden fire danced from the sunken crater.

Caren scrolled through her phone messages, her back to the view. "Nothing dramatic tonight. That's good because tourists won't be around to freak out if they see what we're doing."

The parking lot emptied and became eerily quiet. The crater core glowed red when all the vehicle lights were gone, lighting up a low-hanging fog like pink cotton candy.

"Enough gawking, ladies," Caren chided. "We have work to do."

Each of them removed a light-weight container from the truck and spread out to release the irradiated males, recording the locations on GPS units.

Then Caren drove the length of Crater Rim Drive, stopping every few hundred feet for the team to disperse more sterilized adult mosquitoes.

"In other areas," she said, "we set out the irradiated larvae, but we can demo that for you at another time."

Caren was silent on the drive back to Hilo and the others followed her lead. Was she intimidated by the high political stakes of the Mayor's death and the Governor's visit? With Faye's complaints about Caren's overconfidence, Maya doubted that was the issue. Probably she was just strategizing about which approach would benefit her program the most.

At a market, Caren headed inside to pick up shrimp salad for all of them. Stepping out of the vehicle to stretch under the parking lot fluorescents, Maya said, "I talked to Enzo Russo."

Faye leaned against the truck bed. "The asshole who sexually harassed you? Why on earth would you do that?"

"Some unfinished personal business, but that's not why I'm mentioning it. He's involved with supervising Dr. Oldner's federal grant funds and said they might yank them due to study problems."

At the shocked expression on Faye's face, Maya felt a wash of guilt that she hadn't brought it up earlier.

"I wonder if he's a reliable narrator," Faye answered. "He and Caren are both so arrogant, I can see them butting heads."

Maya hadn't spotted a problem in any of Caren's published reports. "Dr. Oldner's expertise is critical to us right now."

Faye nodded. "We can participate in a real-world evaluation of her methods to see if they reduce dengue. I assume she'll be funded through a modification of current state contracts. Her federal monies couldn't be enhanced so quickly."

After returning to the vehicle with a plastic bucket of food, Caren hotfooted it to the lab where the grants manager met them in the conference room. While they ate, Caren wrote on an old-fashioned flipchart.

"Let's flesh out what we'll recommend to the Governor," Caren said. "Faye, you and the health department tried insecticides, but you may be running into mosquitoes that are resistant to them. So we should up the ante and implement my sterile mosquito program like you saw tonight."

Maya remembered the public opposition she'd seen on a YouTube video from Florida. "Anything with altered mosquitoes will get pushback."

Faye chimed in. "How can we find enough staff for a larger-scale application on short notice?"

Caren opened a deep cupboard along the wall and removed a drone. "This will speed up distribution."

Maya had been deferential to Faye in questioning Caren. But with dengue threatening to become another worldwide pandemic, she pushed aside her natural caution and respect for elders. "Drones are also used to distribute mosquitoes infected with a parasitic bacterium, *Wolbachia*, which blocks dengue virus from growing in *Aedes* mosquitoes. Any reason you're not considering that approach?"

Caren's lips pulled back around her exposed teeth like an alpha wolf. "You two are such neophytes. Australian studies showed promise but it was less effective in Vietnam."

"No technique is perfect," Faye said. "CDC tried *Wolbachia* in Puerto Rico. Now that the stakes are raised here, perhaps Siti Rahim would help us do that."

The grants manager frowned over her laptop. "It's not in our project plan. How does it work?"

Maya didn't wait for Caren to answer. "The bacteria are inserted into mosquito eggs."

Caren wrote *Wolbachia* on her chart and a thick line through it. "I found them too expensive to produce. So we're not investigating that here."

She joined them at the table and the hard planes of her face relaxed. "Look, I want to help you respond to this emergency. We've developed cost estimates to compare SIT with pesticides in separate areas, because the pesticides would kill our irradiated mosquitoes."

Opening her laptop to a map of the dengue cases, Maya moved between the older women. "I suggest the campground and historic site for the SIT. There hasn't been a spray event in almost two weeks. Both can be closed so no one's exposed to the altered mosquitoes."

"That's a stupid concern," Caren snapped. "Male mosquitoes don't bite."

Maya flushed but responded with calm to Caren's challenge. "People still understandably worry about things that are new and unknown."

"The Governor's addressing the press at the campground," Faye said, her tone conciliatory. "So he or the health department could introduce the sterile mosquito approach. We can compare it with an insecticide."

Maya re-examined her notes. "Kailua-Kona is at high risk. The residents are familiar with spray events and won't freak out."

"Good plan," Caren said. "Faye, let's choose the pesticide and review our available resources. Maya, develop the scientific proposal for the health department."

Maya started typing. Only three years out from being a graduate student, she knew she could pull an all-nighter, but it would be a greater challenge for her older colleagues.

"Aim for a draft to send Ino Kahale by midnight," Faye said.

Caren assumed the expression of a general. "We deploy at dawn to save the world."

Or at least Hawai'i, Maya muttered to herself.

Hilo, Hawai'i Island—Wednesday, September 8, 2021

FaceTime flashed on Maya's phone and woke her up. Two AM, and the call was from Dave, his first contact since Braxton was kidnapped. Her email and text attempts to reconnect with the Schwartz family were paying off. As a rancher, he was an early riser, so Maya wasn't surprised he'd be awake at six o'clock. Maybe he forgot about the time difference.

"Give me one second," she whispered to Dave. She tiptoed out the door, careful not to awaken Faye.

Braxton poked his face in front of the phone camera. "Hi, Aunty Maya, I heard you're in Hawaii. I want to try surfing someday."

Maya sank to the lawn chair, weak with relief.

"Get to bed." Dave's off-screen instruction was soft and

affectionate. Then he reappeared. "He's home—we've been driving all night. Emilia's arranged for a security service, so everyone's safe for the moment."

In the sticky breeze stirring the palm trees, Maya trembled, her skin prickling with goosebumps. "That's fantastic news. You've been in my thoughts nonstop."

"Look, I apologize for blowing up at you when Braxton disappeared. We know it wasn't your fault. There's nothing like losing a child—that's what he represents to us."

The regret on his face seemed genuine. Maya couldn't hold his over-the-top reaction against him. With time and effort, they'd regain personal trust. The Three Musketeers, they'd called their anthrax investigation team including Manolo. Now it was just the two of them.

"How did you get Braxton back?"

"He slipped out after dinner and stole a horse. Remember that Arizona café near the Utah border? The manager let Braxton use his phone and didn't turn him over to the sect."

He wiped a hand over his face. "I've been on the road for twelve hours—exceeded all the speed limits. I just needed to get him home."

Maya didn't know anyone else with the stamina to pull off that trip. He must have been worried every minute that the sect's militia would notice Braxton gone and chase them. Of course they would guess where Braxton was headed.

"Will you get in trouble for having him?" she asked.

He shook his head. "Emilia informed the sheriff, and Braxton came with me of his own free will. He decided to escape after unearthing some rantings in a drawer, indicating a possible bioterrorism threat. I'm calling Fred Grinwold and Lila Becker as soon as we hang up."

Maya recalled Sam Demille, his half-brother who deliberately infected people with anthrax. "Any chance they were written by Sam?" Her voice was taut and loud. She glanced over to Caren's house—no lights shone through the windows of either floor.

Dave shook his head. "According to Sam's diary, he wasn't living in the polygamous sect when he hatched his plans." His tone expressed his distaste for reliving the story.

The passages Maya recalled from Sam's diary swamped her senses, as if she'd slipped into a cesspool. The level of hatred for non-whites, including her personally, hit her again like a body blow.

"Braxton says the note mentioned a BT attack with ticks or mosquitoes to help disease spread."

Maya reswallowed the shrimp salad edging back into her throat. This evil was affixed to her skin like a bad tattoo. She couldn't imagine how Dave felt, having a public health threat once again associated with his extended family.

Global warming supported the spread of *Aedes aegypti*—no need to suspect BT. Juana Lopez was probably exposed in Puerto Rico and her New Mexico relatives were infected by mosquitoes that hitchhiked on her plane. But the CDC Epidemic Intelligence Service was formed in the 1950s to prepare for biowarfare, so her EIS training reminded her of the possible risk.

"The note made no mention of dengue virus?"

"No reference to any specific microorganism. Braxton didn't have a phone to photograph it but he's got a good memory. He wrote out everything he could remember as I drove."

"Other than dengue, we're not aware of any new diseases in the Four Corners area," Maya said. "But I'm glad you're alerting Dr. Grinwold and Lila. I assume they'll follow through with any appropriate legal investigations."

"Yes, I'll call them right now. Sorry to wake you up, but I know how much you care about Braxton. One more thing in his summary notes—he wrote the words 'genetic engineering.' Fred or Lila might have some guesses what they're planning."

He waved goodbye and Maya remained on the bench. Genetic engineering could be for good or evil, although the term always freaked everyone out. But Dave mentioned BT so he must believe the sect's intentions weren't good. Her deep breaths were timed to reduce her anxiety. The right people were in the loop.

She focused on the immense universe beyond. Caren had told her about Hawai'i's dark skies initiative with low-pressure sodium lights to decrease light pollution and protect the Mauna Kea telescopes.

The outdoor light fixtures, pointed down, didn't dim sprinkles of stars penetrating the cloud breaks. Even if Earth was the only planet with an environment supporting microbes and mammals, it was a big world, with never-ending public health surprises. But not all her responsibility.

With a deep yawn, Maya sucked in a lemon scent. She took several steps to a sprawling bush with clusters of red flowers and verified the heavenly source, slowly easing her tense muscles. Worry about BT and dengue wasn't worth a loss of more sleep. She needed to be rested for briefing the Governor.

THIRTY-TWO

Hoʻokena Beach Park, Hawaiʻi Island—Wednesday, September 8, 2021

The Pacific Ocean reminded Faye of a summer day at Lake George, one of her favorite upstate New York vacation spots. But palm trees replaced the pines.

She glanced up at the fan-shaped fronds, providing scant shade for Hawaiʻi's Governor as he huddled with his Press Secretary and Dr. Clark, the health department's State Epidemiologist. The lives of residents and visitors were hanging on the upcoming announcement.

No errant breezes disturbed the foliage or eased the sensation of a sauna. Standing next to Faye, Caren wore a brown fedora, safari shirt, khaki pants, and dark leather boots. She looked more like Indiana Jones embarking on a dangerous adventure than a University of Hawaiʻi professor putting her scientific reputation on the line.

Faye understood that the first major release of Caren's sterilized male mosquitoes would be an important addition to her colleague's curriculum vitae if the experiment reduced human dengue cases. Caren appeared so movie-actor cocksure, the only item missing from her costume was a bullwhip.

Faye leaned over to whisper in Caren's ear. "Perfect weather for mosquito control."

"Damn straight," Caren answered. "We can release the sterilized mosquitoes here first, then wait until dusk to spray in Kona."

Caren unfastened the top button of her shirt and mopped her neck with a handkerchief. "I hope we get approval for the entire proposal."

Faye studied Maya, near the Governor and Ino Kahale. Her features were reflected in so many of the officials and journalists. Did Maya feel more at home in Hawai'i with its population dominated by Asians and Pacific Islanders? Other than the considerable weight difference, Maya's complexion with the recent outdoor work made her look like Ino's daughter.

Maya had formed an easy bond with Ino—she appeared respectful and relaxed, in comparison to her muted responses around Caren. Was Maya particularly good at sensing a person's core values?

She'd certainly picked a winner of a husband—tragic to lose him so soon. Faye should ask how Maya knew he was the one. Like with snorkeling, it amused her to think of her mentee, not yet thirty, advising on experiences that Faye in her late sixties lacked.

Next to Faye, Caren's élan was slowly replaced by a tight, anxious energy. Of course she'd be nervous about her funding, but Faye warned her to avoid interrupting the Governor until he made his decision. Ino had justification to be close at hand, and Caren had ordered Maya to stick by Ino's side to report on any developments.

Dr. Clark, dressed in a black suit, waved Ino closer and Maya followed. With the mayor's death from dengue, the crowd buzzed in edgy speculation. Maya displayed a covert thumbs-up as the Governor stepped toward the assembled TV cameras.

"You heard from me last night about the premature loss of the wonderful young Mayor of Hawai'i County." Deep lines in his tanned skin radiated sorrow, and he spoke without a teleprompter or notes.

"We grieve along with her family and all of our state's residents. Our health department and CDC epidemiologists have been battling dengue for a month, but this tragedy reinforces the need to expand our war on mosquitoes. We are fortunate to have the expertise of a dengue expert in Hilo, Dr. Caren Oldner."

Caren beamed and tipped her hat as the cameras shifted, then the Governor continued.

"Our great university system is always poised to apply its

knowledge to real-world problems. Today, I'm announcing additional emergency funding of Dr. Oldner's work on mosquito control."

The Press Secretary began a wave of applause and Caren inclined her head in acknowledgment.

"She'll compare a Sterile Insect Technique or SIT in this area with enhanced adulticide use in Kona," the Governor said. "Dr. Oldner, how soon can you start?"

"As soon as you clear out, sir." The assembled group laughed at Caren's loud reply.

One reporter yelled, "So we can't be here when you release the modified mosquitoes. Are you saying it's dangerous?"

The Governor turned to Dr. Clark, who took the mic in his hand.

"Not at all. These are male mosquitoes that don't bite people. Based on Dr. Oldner's preliminary research in Volcanoes National Park, their mating will reduce production of mosquito eggs, larvae, and adult mosquitoes, and subsequent spread of the dengue virus."

The reporter continued. "So why does this beach park remain closed?"

"Sleeping outside is a dengue risk factor," Dr. Clark said. "We've only restricted access for a couple of weeks, and this will allow Dr. Oldner to accomplish her control tasks as quickly as possible. The sterilized mosquitoes will also be released at the national historical sites along the Kona coast, which will be closed as well."

Another reporter stepped out of the crowd. "Governor, some people in the spray areas worry about the chemicals on their kids' outdoor toys."

Dr. Clark again jumped in. "We always choose the safest treatments and will continue public notification of the nighttime spray events so people can bring in personal property and stay indoors."

No resentment of Dr. Clark's answer was evident in the Governor's expression. Faye admired a politician who allowed his scientific staff to take centerstage.

"If there are no more questions," the Governor said, "let's clear out so Dr. Oldner and our team can return to work. Dengue has reminded us of continual viral threats, their risk skyrocketing in a warming climate. We need to maintain our aloha for residents and tourists alike."

He stepped toward the parking area, guided by the Press Secretary.

Caren rushed forward to shake his hand, effusive in her thanks. "I won't let you down, sir. This will be a game changer."

Faye didn't extend her own hand to the Governor. She assumed he was vaccinated but didn't want to end her career by infecting him, on the small chance she was incubating the coronavirus with all her travel and contact with new people.

She yawned—Caren had dragged them out before sunrise to make the cross-island drive. As Caren unlocked her vehicle, Faye turned away from the gaggle of politicians and press to reach into the backseat. She gulped lukewarm coffee from her thermos despite its disagreeable taste. Along with Ino and Maya, they unloaded the male mosquitoes that buzzed with their annoying whine, energized to mate and with no clue they were shooting blanks.

At ten PM, Faye slid open the sliding glass door for the refreshing evening breeze, then kicked back to rest her swelling ankles on the bed. Not since her camel work in Saudi Arabia had she spent so much time on her feet.

She'd noticed the swelling during late summer in recent years, but neither she nor her physician had an easy explanation. Since it disappeared with cooler weather, no treatment had been recommended except for foot elevation.

Just a reminder of an aging body. Her take-out loco moco wasn't the healthiest of comfort foods with its mixture of rice, hamburger, egg, and gravy. Caren had driven back to her lab in Hilo to pick up supplies for a second day of control efforts. Dr. Clark had treated Ino and Maya to a late-night dinner but Faye welcomed the chance to recover from the day's efforts.

With reluctance, she reached for the remote to see how bad she looked on TV with its amplification of her weight gain. It was also important to see whether the local stations were getting the public health message right. But her cell rang with a call from the Fort Collins assisted living center.

"Dr. Simpson, we have some bad news about Dr. Abelman." Faye recognized the nurse's voice.

"Dr. Abelman passed away peacefully in her sleep this evening. You're listed as her next-of-kin—I'm so sorry for your loss. We typically don't have autopsies on our residents who die from dementia. Is that all right with you?"

Faye's muscles became so weak, she was relieved to be sitting down. How would her life have changed if she'd accepted Devorah's offer to interview for the faculty epidemiology position at CSU?

But there was no time for speculation—practical matters needed addressing.

"She's Jewish and they tend not to favor autopsies, although she was avowedly secular," Faye said. "Unless the state requires it for a disease investigation, let's not do one."

It was about six weeks since she'd visited the facility, so there was little chance that Faye had been a Typhoid Mary and infected Devorah with something. "She stayed healthy after my July visit? No evidence of COVID?"

"That's correct. We're very strict about requiring vaccination for all our staff and residents."

Brain fried from the long day, Faye tried to focus. "CSU will want a memorial for a longtime vet school faculty member. I have a job emergency and can't get back there now to arrange it."

She remembered Devorah's instructions. "Can you take care of cremation and I'll coordinate with the college?"

"Of course, Dr. Simpson. I didn't meet Dr. Abelman until she'd lost much of her memory, but I marveled at her sharp observations and flair for fashion. We'll miss her."

Grief hit like a wave, larger than the placid ones at Lahaina's Baby Beach. All of Faye's muscle power drained and she dropped her head into one hand, muffling her sobs. "Thanks." She mourned in silence until the nurse ended the call.

Unable to accept the news, Faye collapsed into the pillows as her eyelids closed. They never lived together, yet Devorah inhabited all her synapses. Memories crawled over each other. Beers at Panama Red's, hot tub sex, and a memorable hike to Longs Peak, one she'd regretted ever since.

Caught above the tree line during a lightning storm, Devorah had guided her down the mountain. Each rock sizzled Faye's fingers with static electricity at its touch. The sense memory was so vivid that she gasped. The fear had been overwhelming, and turned her off hiking for the rest of her life.

In her mind's eye, grief about Devorah made her so helpless that she couldn't stay upright on the hiking trail. Her flaccid body tumbled head-over-heels down the slope, thousands of feet to her death.

THIRTY-THREE

Kaloko-Honokohau National Historical Park, Hawai'i Island—Thursday, September 9, 2021

Near a partly submerged reef ringing the 'Ai'ōpio Fishtrap, a turtle the size of a hubcap rested on the beach. Maya tugged on Ino's arm to catch his attention. "Can you believe it's here with us around?"

Ino dropped his mosquito trap behind the thatched A-frame fish hut. "Sometimes they just like to sleep in the sand."

He rubbed one meaty fist on his lower back and sighed. "Glad we parked here at the boat ramp to shorten the distance."

Maya sipped from her bottle. "Yeah, I wouldn't want to haul these from the Visitor Center."

Ino checked his watch. "When's Dr. Oldner coming with more sterilized mosquitoes?"

"Midday." Maya set her trap in the shade under a bush.

"Good. We'll finish the mosquito surveillance first. I hope the infection rate is low—I don't want to close all the parks."

"*Aedes aegypti* is an urban mosquito, so why are several rural areas impacted?"

Ino shrugged. "Maybe Dr. Oldner will know, or Faye when she's up to joining us." He adjusted his hand on the heavy canvas bag and headed up the petroglyph trail.

Maya swung her lighter bag with three more traps over her shoulder and followed him away from the water.

She'd told him at breakfast that Faye was sleeping in, and he said she deserved it. They'd been battling dengue for a month with little time off. For Maya, her work in Hawai'i had lasted less than two weeks, so why did it feel like a lifetime? But the demanding work hours had a benefit—she'd been too exhausted for haunting dreams of Manolo.

Ino pointed out the petroglyph on a volcanic rock. "We think it's a musket. There are others that look like sailing ships, cannons, and figures with spears."

"War had a big impact," Maya said.

"Ancestor graffiti." Ino placed a trap under a spindly tree. "We'd bust someone for carving on the rocks in the park today."

He led Maya to a shallow lake separated from the ocean by a sand berm. "This is ʻAimakapā Fishpond, largest on the Kona coast. It was created to rear fish adapted to freshwater runoff mixing with ocean salinity. The industry mostly vanished with colonization from the mainland."

His voice was tinged with regret. After they placed their final mosquito trap, they settled on a bench overlooking the harbor. A light breeze twirled the boat sails and Maya's hair, reducing the day's clammy heat. Maya realized she knew little about her health department host beyond his granddaughter's hula dancing.

"Did you learn about fishponds in school?" she asked him.

He shook his head. "An aunty raises oysters on Oʻahu. When I close my eyes, I still breathe the fishpond ammonia mixed with salty air." His large chest heaved with a deep sigh. "If we ever get this damned dengue under control, I'll bring you there before you fly home."

His tongue traced his lips. "Cradle the oyster's rough shell." He held his hand palm up. "Then pour on a mix of shoyu and tabasco. Heaven."

He checked messages on his cell and frowned. "Is Dr. Oldner coming? Not only do we have the sterile mosquito release this afternoon, but we have another night of spraying in Kona. I'm worried about completing our work with Faye off today."

Maya was momentarily distracted by a seagull swooping within biting distance of her ear. Dave had jokingly called them sky-rats. Native Americans believed that gulls were wise grandmothers using cunning to protect those in need of it. Was the close call with a seagull a warning or a good omen?

Maya checked her own phone. "Caren promised extra crew after Faye texted she needed a me-day." Faye hadn't said what was going on. As the oldest on their team, she was probably just worn out.

Ino tapped his screen and the rich notes of a man singing in Hawaiian filtered out. "This is IZ—Israel Kamakawiwoʻole. I was one of his backup singers on this one."

His face beamed with pride as they relaxed into the long, slow notes until the song finished. "The song title *Kaleohano* is a sacred name for our home. Did you catch IZ mentioning Mauna Kea?"

Maya shifted to face him head on. "Your hidden gift! Do you still sing?"

Ino brushed the sweat from his forehead. "I wasn't that skilled, nowhere close to IZ. After his untimely death, I tried to focus on my own health and career. He was just a huge hunk of talent, at one point over seven hundred pounds. I'm no lean machine—you'll never catch me jogging—but I've already outlived IZ by more than a decade."

The image of fingers gliding over an ivory keyboard filled Maya's soul. She couldn't recall a single time since Manolo's death when she'd taken advantage of the church piano in Santa Fe. Who said that music soothes the savage beast?

Ino let the songs continue and Maya's entire body sank into the bench in relaxation, until her phone interrupted the reverie.

"Where the hell are you?" Caren's harsh tones disrupted the seaside ambiance. "I've looked everywhere here at the Visitor Center, scraping my ankles on the damned volcanic rocks."

Ino answered in his most diplomatic voice, "Are you okay?"

At sunset, a palm tree carved an artful stroke through the fire of magenta and pink in the darkening sky, reflected in the faint ripples below.

"That turtle we spotted earlier has a friend," Maya exclaimed to Ino as they spread out a blanket on the sand. The students had vanished into town for dinner at a local restaurant, paid for by Caren's hundred-dollar bill in thanks for their missing classes.

"Faye should have been here to help out," Caren complained. "I'm only a few years younger and you don't see me shirking."

Maya attempted to calm the waters. "We've had two days of success with the sterile mosquito release."

Caren stood at alert, eyes glued on the ocean. "I don't get over here at this time of day very often—watch for a green flash."

Ino rolled onto his stomach and stretched with a Cobra pose. Maya was surprised such a big guy in his fifties did Yoga. Then he turned over into an awkward Seated Forward Bend, only reaching his knees.

Manolo had been a bit of a health nut and had introduced her to the routine, which she'd continued under the supervision of Mark's physical therapist. She joined Ino in a brief Bridge pose before he grabbed a hot dog.

"Dr. Oldner," he asked, "why are we seeing dengue in these park mosquitoes more than any other year?"

Maya chimed in. "I've been wondering about that, too. *Aedes aegypti* are normally urban mosquitoes."

A monsoon of unclear emotions swept Caren's face. "First, Ino, you can call me Caren at this point."

Caren never said that earlier, perhaps because he didn't have a doctoral degree. Maya pushed aside that uncharitable thought.

"You do know about the association between mosquitoes and climate change?" Caren asked with a shade of disdain. "2019 was the hottest year ever recorded for Honolulu."

Maya nodded. "I saw coral bleaching when I snorkeled on Labor Day."

"We've also experienced dry spells and increased risk of wildfires," Ino added.

"Exactly," Caren said. "Droughts may increase exposure to mosquito-borne diseases because the little buggers are more concentrated in the limited water sources."

"My boss complains that the state legislature isn't prioritizing sufficient funds to help us adapt." Having wolfed down the hot dog, Ino started in on the coleslaw.

Maya, continuing with yoga, gently rotated her neck as she mused out loud. "Towns can't respond quickly enough to rapid growth. Inadequate drainage and waste management are a mosquito's dream."

A flock of seagulls sauntered close to their picnic and Maya waved an arm to discourage them. "*Aedes aegypti* prefers urban areas but Honolulu has few dengue cases compared to Maui and here."

"You're overcomplicating things," Caren snapped, gathering her trash. "*Aedes albopictus* have been infected too, and they're not as wedded to a city landscape."

Caren packed the containers of seafood salad into her ice chest. "Can we hit the road? We have that spray event scheduled for nine o'clock. I want to make sure everyone gets the warning and heads home before then. Last thing I need is another mom whining 'cause her child's ball got coated with insecticide."

Caren appeared to be one of those geniuses with poor social proficiency. If she was a mother, she'd understand a mom's panic over her kid playing with a contaminated toy. Maya only carried her child a short time until her miscarriage, but that was enough for her brain to absorb a La Brea tar pit of parental terrors.

Kailua-Kona, Hawai'i Island—Friday, September 10, 2021

A crowing rooster woke Maya as light filtered around the wall of curtains at six AM. Little reason to complain—Ino said feral chickens were more of a nuisance on Kaua'i. No sooner did she swing her legs to the side of the bed than the phone rang with a call from her New Mexico boss.

"Maya, I realize it's early but this couldn't wait." Dr. Grinwold said.

"No problem, the local fauna already told me to get ready for work." She yawned and rubbed her right biceps, sore from carrying yesterday's mosquito traps. "How's Nancy?"

"She's trying to make my backyard another Kew Gardens.

But with drip irrigation—she acknowledges the need to conserve water."

Maya moved to the armchair at the small table. "I'm happy Nancy's settled so well into retirement."

"You know how proud we are of our state lab in Albuquerque." Dr. Grinwold shifted to work mode. "Always going above and beyond the requirements."

"Their quality reminds me of the labs I worked with during my New York internship," Maya answered, "although not on the same scale."

"They've re-examined the positive mosquitoes you captured near the Rio Grande in Corrales and on the Pueblo."

Maya had thought their reports were final—were they going to retract the results? Blame it on lab contamination?

"The lab's curiosity was piqued by the note threatening bioterrorism," Dr. Grinwold continued. "The one seen by Braxton Farnsworth. It mentioned the Four Corners region, so all four of our states are doing enhanced surveillance."

"It's been only a couple of days since Dave told me about that."

"The FBI and counterterrorism teams are fully engaged. However, without any additional evidence, they're at a standstill."

Maya imagined how a federal search must have solidified the frosty feelings of Dave's mother toward him. Dave bringing Braxton back to New Mexico would only have deepened their mutual hostility.

"This morning," Dr. Grinwold said, "our lab called with disturbing news. Your New Mexico mosquitoes have genetic differences from the *Aedes aegypti* collected elsewhere."

Maya struggled to understand as she doodled zigzag lightning bolts. "But don't species in general have variations in their genome depending on geographical region? I know they can sometimes pinpoint the exposure location using that."

"I've consulted with Lila in Arizona and Dr. Rahim at CDC's Dengue Branch. They'll conduct more thorough comparisons of our mosquitoes with theirs."

She wondered whether to seek permission for sharing the news with Dave. He'd want to know about any connections to the BT note found by his brother. But at that level of threat, it wasn't her call to make. The more groups involved, the greater the chance of a news leak.

"Surely Braxton's family isn't capable of genetic engineering," she said.

"The press may blame Los Alamos or Sandia Labs—our federal research facilities are often the target of conspiracy theorists."

"Well, that's big news." Maya took several deep breaths to settle her nerves, then opened her laptop to search for scientific articles. She also planned to pick Caren's phenomenal brain for information about mosquito genetic engineering.

THIRTY-FOUR

Kailua-Kona, Hawai'i Island—Friday, September 10, 2021

At dawn, Faye tugged open the sliding glass door of her hotel room. She inhaled an odor that reminded her of damp wool socks. Not a bad smell, kind of cozy, like the time she and Taylor got caught in the rain after the Central Park play.

Mist curled in from the balcony and spritzed her wrinkled face. The moist air soothed her skin, leathered from a childhood working in the sun on her Colorado ranch. She could get used to life in a tropical steam room.

She stretched her body, stiff from yesterday's long hours in bed. She had binged on daytime TV amid memories of Devorah. If *General Hospital*'s Jason and Carly could overcome their baggage to plan a marriage, why hadn't she and Devorah?

Her current relationship needed tending—she settled back against the bed's headboard and FaceTimed New York City. Silhouetted against the office textbooks, Taylor had no wig, only that beautiful glistening buzzcut Faye loved to stroke.

"Good timing, darling," Taylor said. "I just got out of a staff meeting. Have you wrestled dengue to the ground?"

Faye assumed Taylor was alone. "Hawai'i's governor authorized a comparison of adulticide here in Kona with the release of sterilized male mosquitoes in parks near here."

Taylor's serene face brightened with a grin. "Cutting edge—who says us older folks should settle into our rocking chairs?"

"I've got almost two decades on you, so speak for yourself." Faye shifted her phone to show the king-sized bed. "Would you believe I haven't been out of this for twenty-four hours?"

Taylor's lips turned down in commiseration. "Did you need some downtime, sweetie?"

"Devorah passed away. I still hadn't adjusted to her need for the memory care unit."

"I'm so sorry. I know how important she was to you in your journey of self-discovery. That's a major blow—how are you handling it?"

Taylor never expressed jealousy over Faye's other connections—she marveled at her luck.

"I'm counting the hours until I settle into your arms," Faye said, "and a real retirement. While you're doing good work at the hospital, I'll help out at cat cafés."

She paused, concerned her words sounded like a commitment. They had never discussed it, not yet.

"Lots to look forward to." Taylor's tone was unclear, but Faye chose to interpret it as supportive.

"I'm treating my colleagues to breakfast in penance for ditching them yesterday," Faye said. "Keep in touch?"

Taylor blew her a kiss and disconnected.

<Meet you at Kona Coffee on the waterfront,> she texted her colleagues.

Under a stormy sky, Faye took a seat between Maya and Caren on a bench just off the beach, overlooking crashing waves. Ino commandeered his own bench next to them.

Faye sipped her Peaberry coffee, the café's 'golden jewel,' brewed from a rare bean. Flavors of milk chocolate merged with citrus and honey. She kicked off her tennis shoes and twisted her toes in the grass, a soothing tactile connection with nature.

Ino raised his Macadamia Nut Decaf in a toast and Maya licked her lips, holding a Strawberry Smoothie.

Buoyed by her tender call with Taylor, Faye felt that even someone with porcupine quills like Caren deserved to be embraced. "Caren raved about Kona Coffee during our first drive to Hilo. Thanks for suggesting it."

Caren cradled her Dark Roast. "Now that the students have headed home for Friday classes, I'm happy you're doing well enough to rejoin us."

Listening for any trace of sarcasm in Caren's voice, Faye chose to maintain the positive vibes. "Feeling tiptop, thanks, and I'm glad you could overnight here so we can start early."

Given the dire weather forecast for a powerful leeward storm over the weekend, they'd have to operate as a tight team to finish more mosquito surveillance plus sterile mosquito release. Evening spray events might be postponed.

"I got some unsettling news this morning." Maya jumped to her feet, looking agitated. "Dr. Grinwold told me that the New Mexico lab found genetic differences in *Aedes* mosquitoes near the Lopez home."

"That's the family our New York case visited before she died of dengue," Faye explained to Ino and Caren. Shocked by Maya's news, she was uncertain how to interpret it.

Maya's frame was like a lightning-struck tree, starkly outlined in front of the bubbly splash of waves over the coral breakwater. "And a bioterrorism threat letter seen in an Arizona polygamist colony mentioned mosquitoes."

"Those religious zealots will stop at nothing." Caren's disgust dripped from her words. "Or your lab made a mistake."

Faye realized that lab error was possible, and genetic changes could occur naturally over time. But Maya's mention of BT forced Faye to consider that as a clue.

"You're the dengue expert, Caren," Faye said. "What can you tell us about genetically modified mosquitoes?"

"We've never authorized GM research here in Hawai'i," Ino said.

Caren's skin darkened. "Well, you should consider it. An island is the safest place because if anything goes wrong, the risk is contained. Didn't you see the World Health Organization guidelines from May?"

Maya pulled out her pocket notebook before Ino could answer.

"After Dr. Grinwold's call, I reviewed information from WHO and other sites. A company released GM mosquitoes in the Cayman Islands and Panama. They're hoping for EPA approval of their use in the Florida Keys."

"What exactly are they modified to do?" Faye asked.

"They alter the males," Caren said, "like my sterilization technique. A self-limiting gene is passed onto females at mating and kills them."

Ino eased his bulk to his feet, joining Maya. "Climate change has gifted us this winter storm. It's called a Kona. Let's distribute your sterilized mosquitoes before the wind blows them all the way up the slopes of Hualālai."

Faye accepted Caren's hand up.

"I agree with Ino," Caren said. "We want my sex-driven males down here on the coast where they're needed to reduce human risk. Not up there buzzing through Kona coffee and macadamia nuts."

The wind's howling scream penetrated the seams around Faye's sliding glass door as she and Maya stared out, unable to see the ocean with the hotel's external lighting on the fritz. After Faye established the Zoom connection with Puerto Rico, she was startled by Siti Rahim's blue hair.

"Last time we talked, you were pink," Faye observed.

"My bit of rebellion," Siti answered. "The further I get past my intended retirement date, the more I need to rock the boat."

"Sever the rope to bureaucratic bosses. I did it." Faye peeked at Maya. "But look at us here in Hawai'i—guess I didn't really retire."

Siti raised her hand, fingers crossed. "I promise we'll only keep you on board until we sort out this dengue mystery. But Maya, you'll commit to CDC for at least twenty more years, right?"

Maya blushed. "Ah, I don't know. Trying to plan hasn't always paid off for me."

"Ignore my not-so-subtle pressure," Siti said. "Not many preventive medicine residents have accomplished so much in three years. Momentous outbreaks—anthrax, those unusual *Borrelia* strains, then coronavirus in China." She smirked. "Although that last one wasn't with CDC. Some at headquarters in Atlanta were none too happy."

Was Maya embarrassed by that remark? Faye was proud Siti recognized Maya's gifts and potential. Never having a child but working so closely with Maya, Faye felt almost motherly toward her.

Maya took the lead. "We want to touch base on the genetic variations in New Mexico mosquitoes."

"Quite unusual," Siti said. "They don't match anything we've seen before. We'll review the genome from additional mosquito pools collected in the Four Corners states."

"Has anyone done a thorough search of the compound where the BT note was found?" Maya asked.

"The FBI didn't find lab equipment capable of implementing a mosquito modification," Siti said. "Of course, it might have been hidden."

Faye had assumed Juana's cystic fibrosis made her vulnerable to death from dengue, but maybe there was something different about the virus or the mosquito vector. "New York City has an excellent vector control specialist named Daniel Toussaint who could send you samples we collected in July."

"Good idea. Ask Ino to forward your most recent Hawai'i collections as well."

"The only thing in common between New Mexico and Hawai'i dengue is me and Maya," Faye joked. "You're not accusing us of smuggling it in our suitcases, are you?"

Siti's expression darkened like the fierce clouds outside their window. "We all use macabre humor to handle an outbreak of the dead and dying, but it's not smart to make a joke about this."

Siti's warning was unsettling. In Faye's decades with the New York City health department, she'd violated agency expectations only on rare occasions. None of the times she'd teamed with the FBI and Homeland Security on potential BT threats led to anything, except for 2001 when Dr. Ivins spread anthrax through the mail.

Faye flushed. "I'm sorry, Siti. I didn't mean to make light of the pressure you're under. It must be tough sorting out these mosquito changes."

"You're working with Caren Oldner, right?" Siti asked. "I met her in June when she visited San Juan to request CDC help with her research."

During their weeks of Hawai'i work, Caren's trip to Puerto Rico never came up. She had complained of needing more support and was eager for Hawai'i to provide it. Perhaps she was ashamed at striking out with CDC after the issues with Washington funding that Enzo Russo had mentioned to Maya.

"Dr. Oldner is providing us tremendous resources and expertise," Faye said.

A puffy orange cat cruised Siti's camera and she pushed her pet aside. "Please forgive me. Tangerine thinks at midnight I should be cuddling." She leaned down, the top of her fluorescent-blue head filling the screen.

Faye regretted her own lack of commitment to new animal companions, but her postretirement travel ruled that out.

"We'll let you and Tangerine get your rest," Faye said. "I can fast-track additional Hawai'i mosquito samples. Keep us informed of any results."

"Will do," Siti said. "Thanks, both of you, for all your efforts on dengue this summer and fall. We realize it's not your usual gig but we're spread thin—it's comforting knowing that you're handling a few corners of our worldwide problem."

Faye glanced at Maya after logging off her laptop. How well they were controlling Hawai'i dengue was a big question mark. No matter what they tried, the infections and deaths were on a Mauna Kea-sized incline.

THIRTY-FIVE

Kailua-Kona, Hawai'i Island—Saturday, September 11, 2021

The hotel room door rattled in the Kona wind before dawn. Maya thrashed aside the bedcovers but didn't wake up from her Arizona nightmare.

Under a swath of blue sky so brilliant that it looked fake, she braced a hand on a Ponderosa pine to counteract a sudden swirl of dizziness. Then she followed Manolo as he climbed a thin fin of sandstone at the Sedona landmark.

A sharp whiff of butterscotch—she held her fingers to her nose and inhaled the soothing odor of pine resin. At the top of the span, Manolo embraced her in a tight hug to counter her shaking limbs. Taking deep breaths, she tried to focus on the glorious panorama of red monoliths.

With his goatee, he reminded her again of his distant relative, Lin-Manuel Miranda. His engaging grin after a quick kiss sealed it. Tucking a stray hair behind his ear, she leaned in for a mock grumble. "Here we are, married two years, and I still can't get you to rap or sing for me."

"Aw, come on. I sing *Hush Little Baby* to Lucas every night before bedtime."

"Croak is more accurate," she said, "and he's been squirmy lately. You need to modernize your playlist."

Manolo traced her lips with a fingertip. "Got any suggestions?"

A tingle from his feathery touch flashed all the way to her toes wedged in hiking boots. "Last night my dad tried *I Wanna Hold Your Hand*. Lucas was enchanted."

"I'm not a major Beatles fan."

She poked him gently in the ribs. "Don't let Dad hear that. He might rescind his approval of our marriage."

"Tonight I'll try *Goodnight, My Angel.* Billy Joel wrote it for his daughter."

With a sharp *caw, caw,* a crow swooped to the ground for a piece of popcorn dropped by a previous hiker. Startled by the dark wing grazing her hip, Maya twisted.

Manolo's grip on her waist loosened, and he tumbled over the edge. His mouth opened in a silent scream as his arms cartwheeled for anything to hold onto. But they'd been on a sandstone arch, there was nothing but air, and he fell to the arroyo a hundred feet below.

The shock of his crumpled body, blood darkening the red desert gravel, awoke her. She flailed her arms, knocking her phone off the room's bedside table.

"Fuck!" She felt a sudden flush with the unaccustomed curse. It had been weeks since she had a Manolo nightmare, why now? With the worsening weather, the door glass vibrated, emitting a shrill that pierced like the siren on a fire engine.

She climbed out of bed and adjusted the slider against the force, silencing the shriek. Taking a deep breath to reorient, she bent to the carpet for her phone. Undamaged, thank goodness.

The screen flashed **<Saturday, September 11, 7:33>**. Twentieth anniversary of the September 11 attack. Maybe that, and the storm, had her spooked. She tapped the phone to place a call.

"Good morning," she greeted Faye. "At least, I hope it will be."

"I'm not sure how much we'll get done with this weather." Faye's voice was more gravelly than usual.

Maya hoped she hadn't woken her mentor. She still didn't know why Faye had taken Thursday off work.

Maya checked the minifridge built into the credenza. "I have some leftover pastries. Want to stop by?"

She slipped on jeans and a t-shirt with the image of a bronzed young woman surfing a big wave. On the TV, a national news program presented snippets of memorial activities in New York,

Pennsylvania, and DC. Masked, white-draped dancers stretched their arms to the sky at Lincoln Center, accompanied by a violin. At the 9/11 Memorial, American flags dotted the bronze parapets bearing the names of three thousand victims.

Maya opened the door at Faye's knock as the TV picture changed to a picturesque park with a commanding view of the Manhattan skyline. Melancholic music replaced the anchor's commentary.

"That's Green-Wood Cemetery in Brooklyn," Faye said. "My friend Taylor should be in the crowd. They're having a chamber music performance called *Memory Ground*."

Maya spread out two Hawaiian cheesecake bars on paper plates. "Coffee or tea?"

"Tea is fine, I know that's what you like."

The blue teabag labeled Coconut Macadamia looked promising. Maya verified it was caffeine-free. "I'm jumpy after a horrible nightmare. Would you prefer a higher octane?" She held up a pink box of Guava Ginseng.

Faye nodded as Maya started the pot of hot water.

"Where were you on 9/11?" Maya asked.

"It was a gorgeous day. I was sitting on a Staten Island patio with a guy recovering from anaplasmosis. Two weeks earlier, he'd been bitten by a tick while working in his backyard woodpile. We rushed into his den when we spotted smoke from Manhattan. On the TV, we saw the second plane hit. He said, 'That's no accident.'"

At eight years old, Maya hadn't understood the day's events, not right away. Her parents had debated about school, but decided to maintain their normal routines.

The attack's enormity wasn't clear until a Memorial visit during grad school, where she'd traced her fingers over the etched names.

She handed Faye a tea bag. "When were you able to get back to your apartment?"

"A friend in Staten Island put me up for the night, and I returned the next day. No damage, but the acrid smell was pervasive. I wore a mask for a week, good practice for COVID."

"Did you get involved in the response?"

"I helped design the baseline survey of those exposed to the area. Thirteen percent of lower Manhattan residents like me had Post-Traumatic Stress Disorder." Faye accepted the cup of hot water from Maya. "What was your nightmare about?"

If anyone else had asked, Maya might have dissembled, but Faye was her longest and most trusted mentor.

"PTSD from the shock of Manolo's death. Instead of being sedated on a COVID ventilator when he passed, I visualized him falling from a Sedona landmark."

Her skin broke out in a shiver. Not being able to say goodbye before he died in the hospital room next to her was awful, but preferable to the horrific sight of his crushed body.

"The anniversary of his death is coming up, right?" Faye pushed aside her plate and rested her hand on Maya's arm.

"Next month." Maya hadn't spent a minute working on a memorial service.

"I'm in the same boat. One of the vet school professors died and I'm in charge of her affairs. That's why I ditched out work— needed time to adjust."

"I'm so sorry to hear that, was it anyone I knew?" Maya got up to peer out the curtains.

"Devorah Abelman, your pharmacology professor. Remember when she arranged for you to help me with Middle East Respiratory Syndrome?"

Maya rejoined Faye at the table. "How could I forget that London trip?" She'd been energized by her epi class in vet school, but applying the principles in a real outbreak hooked her.

The continuing storm could derail their dengue surveillance and control plans. "I'd love to share ideas for our memorial services," Maya said. "But first I need to touch base with the Arizona State Epidemiologist about the modified mosquitoes."

Faye opened her purse to retrieve a note pad while Maya placed a FaceTime call.

Lila's face came into view, unchanged in the two years since she and Maya had trained new Epidemic Intelligence Service officers in Atlanta. She still had frizzy chestnut hair, outlined dark eyes, and glowing red lips. Only her eyeglass frames were different, now brown. Perhaps she'd chosen a more sedate option in keeping with her new leadership role.

"Can you believe what's happening?" Lila's concern carved her face, making her appear older than her early thirties. "Just because some kid sees a bioterrorism threat letter in Arizona, your boss blames us for his aberrant mosquitoes."

"Dr. Grinwold is temperamental." Maya hesitated. It would violate his privacy to reveal his diabetes challenges. "I'm sure he doesn't hold you responsible."

"He thinks that if Nancy was still in charge, she would have sorted all this out by now."

According to Dr. Grinwold, Lila's predecessor Nancy Bingham walked on water. Maya couldn't recall that he'd ever criticized Nancy's public health decisions, his attitude likely influenced by their lifelong romantic relationship. With Maya, he'd been tough but nurturing after Manolo's death. He expected even more from Lila, however. She was required to function at a higher level as his peer.

Faye jumped in. "Nancy's a special case with their personal connection. I can tell you based on my own experience—it's harder for you as a woman to meet his standards."

Maya inhaled a deep breath, unsure what to add. "Give it a tincture of time, Lila."

Dr. Grinwold's mood was likely affected by New Mexico being the only location for mutated mosquitoes. Maya wondered if Nancy's diet modifications were improving his diabetes or making him grumpy.

"Has Arizona's mosquito surveillance detected anything like what Fred found?" Faye asked.

Lila's headshake was vigorous. "No, and our state troopers conducted an aggressive search of the compound where Braxton Farnsworth saw that note. The FBI's keeping the investigation open."

"How about Utah and Colorado?" Maya asked. "Are they coming up empty, too?"

"It's still early days. They had no reason to focus on *Aedes* surveillance this year, until this concern. But we'll have their test results soon."

Maya knew to respect the protocols and procedures in other states. Her reasons for wanting Dave's relatives exonerated were personal. Neither she nor the Schwartz family could cope with another bioterrorist in their midst.

Poor Braxton, uncertain which of his brothers' genetic predilections he would share. Dave was only a half-brother and a dedicated USDA veterinarian. In contrast, his dead brother Sam Demille had been a brain-damaged, vengeful maniac. Dave still regretted missed opportunities to set him on the right path.

"Keep us posted," Maya said, "and your relationship with Dr. Grinwold will improve, I promise you. I've got a related issue to ask about."

Lila dropped her head. "I can't handle anything else."

Maya had dismissed Enzo's tossed-away threat against Lila and now she regretted it.

"When I called Enzo about his diaries, he hinted that Caren Oldner's DC funding was in jeopardy."

"I never met Dr. Oldner." Lila's tone was acidic.

Maya, hampered by her kindergarten-level proficiency at handling interpersonal conflict, glanced at Faye.

"Caren's a world leader in dengue research," Faye said, "and our dengue control partner here in Hawai'i."

Emboldened, Maya jumped back in. "I was hoping that in your interactions with Enzo, he mentioned anything related to dengue."

Lila took off her glasses and rubbed her eyes. "Let me think. He lost his temper once, saying he didn't have time for Arizona crap when he was in the midst of busting a dengue researcher for academic impropriety."

Maya clapped her hands in triumph. "You got more out of him than I did. Now we have something to go on."

"One more thing," she added. "He guessed I got his number from you. He said you'd regret it to your dying day."

Lila slammed her laptop closed. "We'll see what our lawyers can do with that."

After Lila disconnected, Faye said, "I'm concerned about your safety and mental health. Enzo sexually assaulted you, so why are you the one who needs to sort this out?"

The storm slamming their hotel had Maya on edge. She should take Faye's warning to heart and avoid interactions with Enzo. "Dr. Oldner's trip to Puerto Rico got me thinking."

"But Caren wants to advance science and help people stay healthy," Faye said. "Just like we do."

Maya felt like she was rolling a boulder uphill to get Faye acknowledging any problems with Caren. "Enzo's hints to me and Lila are intriguing. Does Caren care about dengue control, or is she hoping we'll grease the wheels with Siti?"

Faye huffed. "Neither of us know what it's like to lose salary if we don't bring in outside funding." She reached down to retrieve her phone from her purse. "I'm calling Ino and Caren to settle our plans for today."

Maya pushed aside the unanswered questions. Both she and Faye were haunted by dead people, with personal obligations piled on work ones. But live Hawaiians were counting on their help in thwarting dengue.

THIRTY-SIX

Kailua-Kona, Hawai'i Island—Saturday, September 11, 2021

During a respite from midafternoon showers at Keiki Beach Queen's Bath, Ino's phone rang. He called Faye, Maya, and Caren over to huddle beneath a palm tree, its fronds ripped away as if by an invisible giant's hand.

"My boss has ordered everything shut down. A magnitude 7.6 earthquake was just reported off the coast of Japan and he's worried about a tsunami."

Faye's heart sank. She'd lived through Superstorm Sandy that decimated New York and killed more than a hundred people.

"Stop trap distribution?" Maya asked. "Or remove them all? We just spent hours putting them out."

Faye understood her despair. Between this park and the traps the team had distributed on Thursday without her help, she guessed there were at least sixty.

"Po'o!" Ino's shouted epithet slashed through a wind gust. "We need to pull them now. I'm not risking all this equipment, or our lives, by any delays." His words pounded Faye's chest like the bass speakers at a rock concert.

In an exaggerated whisper to Maya, Caren said, "He just called you a fool," then laughed.

"Do we have time?" Faye asked.

Ino's voice settled down to a lower volume but worry still caverned his face. "A bad tsunami hit here with a lot of damage in 2011. It was from the Japan earthquake that destroyed the Fukashima Daiichi nuclear power plant. But it took seven hours to reach us."

"That earthquake was magnitude 9.0, much worse than this one," Caren said. "Destructive tsunamis are rare at such a distance."

Faye wasn't sure who to believe, but the state health department had ultimate authority over their dengue investigation. Caren was just a contractor.

Caren held up her phone. "There's no official warning and the sirens haven't sounded. The traps we set out today won't have any mosquitoes—it's too soon to pull them."

Ino yanked a trap into his duffel bag. "Maya and I are heading to Kaloko-Honokohau while you two finish up here."

Faye appreciated Ino assigning her and Caren the smaller park, probably to spare two old women the extra work. But Ino at fifty was no spring chicken and it likely took extra effort to haul his weight around.

Caren scowled but cooperated with his orders. On their final trip clearing traps from under the beach foliage, Caren paused at a volcanic rock pool where a family with two toddlers floated and splashed. She waved the dad over to the pool's edge.

"You guys might want to head home, or at least listen out for the sirens. There was an earthquake in Japan an hour ago, and it could cause a tsunami."

"I'm not worried," he said. "The kids enjoy body surfing the waves."

Faye was impressed Caren made the effort considering her disagreement with Ino about the risk. "That was nice of you."

Caren flushed and placed her hands on her hips. "I don't want anyone to get hurt if I can help it."

"Me too," Faye answered. "I guess that's why we're both disease detectives."

They switched their focus to the dense hedges separating the public beach from multimillion-dollar mansions. On their fifth trip back from Caren's truck, Faye paused to scan the horizon, no sign of an impending giant swell. "All done with the ones we can access from the beach. Do we have time for homeowner approval before going into their backyards again?"

Caren checked her watch. "Anyone worried about the earthquake would have headed to higher ground." She gestured at the two-story, glass-fronted behemoth furthest north of the beach. "Let's see if these folks are home."

They shoved through a narrow strip between the bushes and a wrought iron fence to reach the double mahogany doors near the oversized garage at streetside. They were greeted by a muscled man in his sixties with an impossibly smooth, tanned face and jet-black hair.

"Dr. Oldner, back so soon?" he asked in the polished accent of a newscaster. "Come on in."

Eyeing the herringboned floor in the two-story entrance hall, Faye started to remove her sandy tennis shoes but he waved her off. "The maid's coming tomorrow—don't worry about it."

"Sorry to bother you again," Caren said as they entered the living room, walls splattered with European and Hawaiian art. One nature painting reminded Faye of Van Gogh with its thick bold strokes of color as if applied directly from the tube. The man who dropped to the black leather couch was a retired NBC anchor, so it could be an original.

"The health department wants us to remove our mosquito traps due to a tsunami risk," Caren said in an apologetic tone.

"We saw the news bulletin and Priscilla took the Yorkies up to a friend's house in Waimea. I'm dying to know whether my mosquitoes have dengue. Can we temporarily shift the traps to my garage? Then I'll put them back out when the storm and any wave threats pass."

Faye rested her elbow on the breakfast bar separating the living room from the high-end kitchen. The surveillance plan for a wealthy neighborhood made her uncomfortable. Those with clout shouldn't get preferential service when no dengue cases had been detected in the immediate area. But the homes were next to a popular public beach and the data could be valuable. She hated to see ocean access closed unless they found evidence of risk.

"I should check with Mr. Kahale—he's the state health rep in charge of our surveillance program," Faye said. "We can't assure trap integrity if you handle them, and your garage could be washed away if a tsunami hit." Afraid she'd been too blunt, she scanned the ocean's gray horizon through the massive glass wall.

Caren scoffed. "This place is a concrete fortress. Besides, the traps in this area are mine, so it's my decision."

Uncommonly parched, Faye gulped water from the glass the home owner offered. Caren was right. They'd save time if some traps were only moved to garages. By splitting up, they might complete every house on the street within the next hour. But if some residents weren't home, they'd have to find a way into the backyards on their own.

Faye, with little energy to make the effort, knocked at the door of the final home. No one answered, so she pushed through thick hedges behind the garage.

Before Faye placed traps in the morning, the owner had introduced her to their Doberman in the kitchen. Like any well-trained guard dog, he hadn't even growled, taking his cues from his master. With the man now away from the house, Faye hoped the dog went with him or remained inside.

She found the first trap under the back porch near the hot tub. When opening the pool gate to retrieve the second one, she heard a deep, ominous growl. She spun in the direction of the sound and spotted the dog. Head down, teeth bared, not a sound except the low rumble.

Apparently, he'd forgotten the introduction. She fended him off with the first trap as she backed away along the patio wall, then turned for an opening in the bushes. He took that opportunity to nail her calf and she fell through the foliage. All of a sudden, he sat on his haunches at full alert and didn't attack again. His collar likely meant they had an invisible fence.

After eyeing her wound, she limped along to the truck, single trap in hand. The one she didn't retrieve, and the Doberman, could wash away with the tsunami as far as she was concerned.

"I failed with my final house," Faye said. "The Dobie didn't appreciate my efforts to invade his territory." She showed Caren the tear in her pants.

"Shit." Caren dropped to her knees and reached for Faye's lower leg. "This isn't worth risking an injury, or your life."

Faye took a step back. "He didn't break the skin. I'll only have a bruise."

Suddenly weak with a flush of heat, she grabbed their paper map and fanned her neck, then pulled out her cell to phone Ino. When the call went to voicemail, she left a message that they were done. She tried Maya, with a similar result.

"Maybe they're in a dead spot," she told Caren.

"We'll drive over there to find his vehicle." Caren unlocked the passenger door and helped Faye up into the seat.

They filled up takeout salad bowls at a deli along the highway and headed north.

At Kaloko-Honokohau, Caren parked next to Ino's truck near the boat ramp. The area was mostly empty despite it being the weekend. The few remaining sailboats and motorboats surged up and down, as if tossed by a boisterous child playing in a bathtub.

Caren spread out a dirty blanket on the tailgate and invited Faye to join her for lunch.

"We're not blasted by blowing sand here. Want to share the breeze?" she asked with an ironic grin.

Faye winced with the pain of the bite wound as she climbed up to join Caren. She studied the jagged pounding waves. Could she recognize a tsunami crest? Not a catastrophic thinker, she was just in an existential funk about Devorah and 9/11.

"Getting lost in an ocean view never loses its appeal," Caren said, glancing at Faye.

"You don't seem worried about a tsunami anymore."

"Keep your eyes glued." Caren spoke with an ominous tone. "The water will abruptly recede and expose the reef before the big wave hits. At that point, run for your life."

Then she laughed. "Just pulling your leg—there's been no official warning and no sirens. Speaking of legs, you seem to be masking some discomfort there. We should check yours."

Faye tugged up her pant leg to reveal the reddened area on her outer calf. "Nothing to worry about."

Caren poured water from her canteen on her napkin and gently dabbed. "We should have done this right away."

She peered more closely. "There are some tooth scratches here. At least rabies isn't a problem with our quarantine and testing requirements."

Faye swallowed her grievance about Caren pronouncing on public health issues to a public health veterinarian. She rolled down her pants leg and reached for her salad. "Thanks, I'll be fine."

"Except for a nasty bruise over the next few days." Caren wasn't letting the subject drop. "You might not be able to help us again if it's too painful."

Trying to avoid more digs about her taking Thursday off, Faye decided to share her loss. "You remember Devorah Abelman, our Pharmacology professor? She passed away this week, and I'm the executor of her will."

"Huh. I didn't realize you were close." Caren's eyebrows peaked with an implied question.

"I was her research assistant during sophomore year, and we've kept in touch." That was all Caren needed to know. Faye wasn't about to reveal her bisexuality.

"Devorah certainly was dazzling," Caren said. "I always felt sorry for her, a female non-vet in a male-dominated vet faculty."

Surprised by the solicitude—Caren didn't often tune into other people's feelings—Faye redirected the conversation. "I'm still not seeing official tsunami warnings on my phone and we haven't heard sirens. I wonder if Ino changed his mind about the traps."

Then he and Maya strolled up with two full duffel bags apiece. He looked like a worn-out sheepdog who'd been rolling in the dirt. "I apologize for today. My boss just called and said not to worry— traps can stay out."

Caren leapt to her feet. She yanked Ino's bags out of his hands and tossed them into her vehicle.

"You public health types are always overreacting. I'm headed home to Hilo. You let me know if we can get back to saving lives tomorrow."

Faye looked at Maya, whose squirms telegraphed her anguish. After a high-stress and physically demanding day, everyone needed a good night's sleep to avoid killing each other.

THIRTY-SEVEN

Kailua-Kona, Hawai'i Island—Sunday, September 12, 2021

Maya wore a light sweater as she ambled along Kailua Pier, taking in the view of Ali'i Drive. With unabated high winds, the tree-lined route and its tourist shops were unusually bare of sightseers.

The pier looked undamaged. No vehicles or other debris were strewn across its deck, unlike the photos she'd seen of the 2011 tsunami. Last night, she'd obsessed over the team's rupture and the chance of a devastating late wave from the earthquake.

Ino had sent a text canceling all work for the rest of the weekend, then flew home to Honolulu. He apologized for insisting they remove mosquito traps on the basis of alarming data from deep ocean tsunami detection buoys. Later sensors in subsea cables didn't verify the threat, and all their efforts were for nothing.

Maya couldn't remember her last full day alone with her thoughts. She considered checking with Faye about breakfast, but an opportunity to wander and follow her own agenda appealed to her.

She headed toward the shore, then relished the massage of sand between her toes even as the waves tried to knock her over. A handful of people braved the rough surf in yellow kayaks, their shouts of excitement and frustration drifting in and out like a microphone on the fritz.

Along her stroll to Kamakahonu National Historic Landmark on a short peninsula opposite the pier, palm fronds littered the path, remnants of the storm. She found a bench in sight of the restored 'Ahu'ena Heiau, the thatched place of worship for Kamehameha I in the early 1800s.

In the distance, strips of gray clouds hugged the green slopes of Honuaʻula Forest Reserve and provided rare glimpses of Hualālai volcano. The culture and geography were so different from the American Southwest—maybe she should cauterize the wounds of her past and embrace a new beginning in Hawaiʻi.

A text from Mark made her smile. She hadn't seen him since July, and he hadn't pursued his romantic interest. But he'd kept her updated on his ranch and the close friends she'd made there during five months of COVID recovery.

This looked more like a poem than an ordinary message.

Enigma (Where are We?)
Death stalks you
a rabid bat
Your caution—
crime scene tape
But courage—
New Year's dragon
Hope flames
a fragrant kiva

During long winter months of joint physical therapy, they read poetry in the evenings. This one had to be his—it was too specific to their situation.

<Is it chilly enough to make a fire in your kiva?> she texted, ignoring the wistful tone of his creative writing.

<Yes, and some aspen leaves to golden the ground.>

She typed **<I'll have to visit when home.>** Then she erased the words. Mark was a welcome distraction from a focus on Manolo, but it was too soon for her yearnings to be satisfied by another man, no matter how accomplished and kind.

<How are your wonderful parents?> His text interrupted her thoughts about what to say.

<Doing fine. We keep in touch even from a distance.>

Her mom was incessant with reminders for Maya to see Mark again, and her dad didn't mind his wife's fondness for the wealthy attorney and philanthropist.

<Good. I'll let you get back to vanquishing dengue.> His message assumed her work was nonstop although she had the day off. Should she suggest a FaceTime call?

<Thanks, I'll do that.> She rose to her feet and began the fifteen-minute walk to her hotel.

Halfway back, her stomach grumbled at the scent of lemon slices wafting down from the Fish Hopper patio. She climbed the few steps and leaned in through the open window. Recognizing Faye at the nearest table, she asked, "How's the food?"

"Coconut shrimp are delicious!" With a flamboyant, silk-covered arm, she invited Maya in. "Almost no one's here today, so the service is phenomenal."

Maya sat to Faye's side, the choppy waters of Kailua Bay spread out in front of them. "You sure look relaxed."

"Damn straight." Faye dangled a straw from her fingers. "Want to join me in a Flaming Volcano?"

Maya lowered her nose to sniff the dark alcohol in a green-leafed crockery bowl, garnished with more lemons. "Rum?" She recognized the distinctive smell from her first college overindulgence with rum and Coke.

Faye took a slurpy sip using her straw. "You missed it on fire—fabulous."

Maya's stomach turned over. The drink looked way too big for a single person.

"I'm determined to plan a funeral today," Faye said, "and this won't hurt."

The waiter placed a bowl of risotto on the table and turned to Maya. "Would you like a menu?"

"Tell you what," Faye said. "My eyes are bigger than my stomach. If it's okay with my friend, she can share my order."

Maya had no idea what she was getting into but her tastes were eclectic. "I appreciate it, and please bring me an ice tea."

After the server returned, Maya helped herself to all the dishes, including mango salsa crab cakes and clam chowder. The warm and creamy spices on her tongue cheered her up despite the continued stormy weather and the memorials they both needed to plan.

"What type of commemorative service are you thinking about for Dr. Abelman?" she asked Faye between courses.

"Devorah didn't want any religious rituals, just something outdoors."

"Lory State Park is close to CSU." Maya thought back to vet school. "It's got a conference room in the visitor center and a picnic area with BBQ grills."

Faye tossed aside her straw and used a spoon to slurp down more of the drink. "You're right." Her speech was only slightly slurred. "I could ask her former students and colleagues to send me photos for a presentation."

When Faye's jacket sleeve dipped into the rum bowl, Maya helped her drape it over the back of the chair.

"Sounds like a great option," Maya said. She was thrilled that she had contributed to easing Faye's mind about an appropriate memorial. Now if only her own plans were so easy.

"I'm not under any time pressure," Faye said with a stern expression, "but you have only three weeks if you want something on the anniversary of Manolo's death."

"I know." Maya used a tissue to wipe her brow as sweat broke out in spite of the chilly wind. "He worked with staff at the Indian Health Service hospitals in Phoenix, Gallup, and Albuquerque. The IHS will want to honor him."

"Gallup's midway."

"Not really." Maya modulated her tone, controlling her irritation. She resented people thinking her home state of Arizona was all desert. Faye grew up in Colorado and should have known better. "With winding roads through mountains and national forest, the drive from Phoenix to Gallup is more than four hours. Albuquerque's only two hours on a straight-shot interstate."

She opened maps on her phone. The Petrified Forest National Park was a more central location and Manolo would have loved the rugged scenery. "This might work."

Faye struggled for her credit card, then Maya slipped her own card to the server.

"My treat." She grasped Faye's elbow to guide her back to their hotel.

"I know what I need to do," Maya said at the entrance to Faye's room. "Thanks for the kick in the pants."

"You too, dear." Faye collapsed on her bed without undressing, and Maya quietly closed the door.

An hour later Maya had reserved a picnic pavilion for early afternoon on October 6. The rangers were happy to support a service to honor an esteemed federal colleague. She'd call his supervisor in Albuquerque tomorrow to work out invitations.

Then there was family. It was only two-and-a-half weeks since she'd attended the Miranda funeral in New York, but their rejection still tormented her. She hadn't a clue if they'd fly all the way out to Arizona, but she texted them anyway.

No immediate answer. Next, she phoned her parents, and they promised to drive over from Flagstaff. They had adored Manolo, even if her mom might be angling for Maya to find a new lover, or as her mom might say, a new beau.

Dengue guilt crept back in. She could spend only so much time on personal matters. She ran another statistical analysis for the cases on the state's secure intranet. The incubation period from mosquito bite until symptom development, averaging a week in earlier years, dropped to five days in 2021. And the case fatality rate for hospitalized patients had inched up to eleven percent, although either difference could have occurred by chance.

What worried her most was the number of cases, finally exceeding one thousand, four-fold higher than the Hawaiian outbreak five years earlier. Small potatoes compared to an estimated hundred million worldwide, but it was the responsibility she'd been handed.

This early in her career, she couldn't afford to fail. More hospitalizations were a struggle for the health care system, and each represented a real person whose infection she hadn't prevented.

After emailing her latest report to Ino, Faye, and Caren, Maya stretched with tai chi and woke up her brain with Guava Ginseng tea. Then she returned to her search for dengue peer-reviewed studies.

Higher mosquito infection rates had been associated with naturally occurring genetic differences—the changes in New Mexico might not be unusual. Perhaps the only reason to suspect otherwise was the timing of the threat note Braxton found.

Some labs supercharged the genes to spread rapidly in future mosquito generations. The altered genes were designed to reduce the mosquito's ability to transmit diseases or to reproduce. In contrast, Caren's research study just sterilized a certain batch of mosquitoes, creating a more limited opportunity for impact.

The power to disseminate gene changes excited scientists about the potential benefit and freaked out others about the risks. Groups had protested everything related to genetically modified organisms, including inadequate international standards for shipping GMOs.

Maya understood everyone's fear. Between climate change and newly created organisms, humans leaned hard on the balance of nature. But her unrelenting drive as a medical scientist to make things better widened her perspective. Scientific discoveries usually gave her a jolt of joy, not panic.

Except for this one. Mutated mosquitoes, natural or manufactured, made her skin crawl.

She picked up her phone to FaceTime Dr. Grinwold. Nancy answered, a gardening glove on her left hand.

"Hi, you caught us in our fall yard cleanup. Fred's wrestling with the wheelbarrow so you got me."

Maya welcomed a chat with Nancy. She'd been a motherly mentor even though she never married or had children. Like Maya, Nancy had formed a powerful love relationship at a young age. Having seen the price that Nancy paid for decades apart from Dr. Grinwold, Manolo had insisted they only consider jobs where they could live together. They'd pulled it off for a few months, until he died.

"I'd like to run something by you," Maya said. "Lila's worried that Dr. Grinwold is angry at her. She hasn't connected the Arizona bioterrorism note to the New Mexico modified mosquitoes."

Maya felt awkward referring to Nancy's partner as Dr. Grinwold—he'd never told Maya she could call him by his first name. Manolo, as a fellow physician, had called him Fred. Maya started out self-conscious about her status as a veterinarian and never relaxed around him. Perhaps once he was no longer her supervisor…

Nancy frowned. "Oh, that poor girl. I'll talk to Fred. It's a life-long battle with him—he's too intimidating to female colleagues."

Especially veterinarians, Maya thought. But Lila was a human doctor like Dr. Grinwold.

"I don't want to get her in trouble, as if she's complaining." Maya felt foolish bringing it up, but hoped Nancy could be a bridge.

"Not to worry. Lila is my successor and it's only natural I can remark on how Fred works with her." Nancy glanced away. "Let me find him for you."

When Dr. Grinwold appeared, his broad face was like an overripe strawberry. "How's your dengue work going?"

"You're lucky you haven't had more cases," Maya said. "Over here, we're not keeping up, especially after losing a day to a tsunami threat. False alarm, though."

"Well, I can't begrudge your temporary placement to Hawaii where the need is greater."

Maya hated to ask her question, hoping to avoid an implication that he'd overlooked something. "Are the federal labs in New Mexico doing any GMO work? Maybe they're responsible for what the state lab found."

Dr. Grinwold paused for a drink from an ice-filled glass. Was it Maya's imagination, or did he take time to compose an answer? "Of course we asked about it. No relevant GMO research here. After all, the Southwest isn't the highest risk area for mosquito-borne diseases."

Those labs might not have been completely transparent, but Maya wouldn't press him on it. "A lot of groups are on high alert, wanting GMOs banned outright."

"This might be an anomaly. I'll call if we find any more mosquitoes with a similar genome."

"Thanks, I'll let you get back to your gardening."

After Maya disconnected, she realized that she had no information about GMOs in Hawai'i. Caren had dismissed the modified New Mexico mosquitoes as a nonissue, but she might be a valuable subject matter expert, worth consulting when they met tomorrow for work. Unless the hints from Enzo meant she was not to be trusted.

THIRTY-EIGHT

Kailua-Kona, Hawai'i Island—Monday, September 13, 2021

A breeze twirled Faye's curls at the hotel entrance. She relished the crystal-clear water, a delicate undulation instead of crashing whitecaps. Finally, a day with magnificent weather. The sun baked her bare arms and face like a heating pad, soothing and sleep-inducing.

"Did you get enough rest?" Maya's eyes narrowed. "You still look tired."

A day in paradise avoiding alcohol would solve that. "I'd love another snorkel like we had on Labor Day," Faye said.

Her mind drifted to an underwater scene of colorful fish and a green sea turtle. If only Ino decided to play hooky for one more time, she and Maya could do the same. But no such luck.

He pulled up in his state truck left at the airport during his brief family reunion in Honolulu. "I apologize again for Saturday's screwup."

Faye climbed into his front seat followed by Maya, then Ino tugged out his phone. "Aren't they remarkable?"

The short video showed a group of girls, all with long black hair crowned by light floral hats that matched wrist and ankle bands. Each blue dress, draped with a leafy green necklace and a pale grass skirt, swayed like ocean waves in time with resonant male voices singing off-camera.

"You must be so proud." Faye tried to focus. "Which one is your granddaughter?"

"I centered my picture on her. That's Alika, right up front."

"Maybe if I retire in Hawai'i, I could learn to hula." She poked

Maya in the ribs. "Want to join me in some lessons?" Maya just smirked.

At Keiki Beach Queen's Bath, Ino moved mosquito traps back to the beach area and left Faye and Maya to handle the wealthy neighborhood. Maya reinstalled traps to the bushes surrounding the newscaster's pool as Faye relaxed on his patio. Overheated and queasy, she welcomed a cup of their host's passion fruit juice.

Then he headed out for a round of golf and graciously allowed them to stay until Ino picked them up.

Maya opened her laptop. "I'd like Caren's insights on these genetic modification articles but don't know if I can rely on her perspective."

"Jesus, you're like a dog with a bone."

Flinching at Faye's harsh tone, Maya put her laptop back in her pack.

Faye spoke again, careful to modulate her words. "So you think we shouldn't use Caren's expertise because of Enzo's allegations of study problems."

She leaned her head on the back of the patio chair. If Caren had a cat fight with Enzo over her work, he was likely at fault, given his history with female colleagues. Not that Caren was young and pretty like Maya, but sexual harassment was about power, not attraction.

"We're short-handed if Caren's done something wrong and loses support." Maya fingered her phone.

Maya was like an orb-weaver patterning all its silky threads. CDC and Hawai'i had their own resources, even if tiny compared to NIH. And the NIH priority was research, not the immediate public health threat. Faye refused to fret about the endless turf wars between NIH and CDC.

"Enzo's her NIH contract manager, so he's the best source," Maya said. "But I understand why you think my talking to him could be risky to my mental health."

"Damn straight. Ask Nancy Bingham to handle it—she was his Arizona boss." Suddenly overcome by chills and shakes, Faye pulled a windbreaker from her daypack. Feeling lousy didn't seem fair on a spectacular day following hours relaxing in bed. Taylor had serenaded her to sleep with a rendition of Beyonce's *Love on Top*. Who knew they were such a tender tenor?

"Nancy is retired and has no sway with him." Maya interrupted Faye's blissful rewind of the song lyrics. "Despite my toxic history with Enzo, maintaining relationships with coworkers can have some benefits. A simple text will let me avoid his leering grin and voice."

"Hmmm…" The last thing Faye felt up for was an argument with Maya. The girl was an adult, after all, and if she wanted to cross swords with Enzo or Caren, Faye was disinclined to get involved. Not on a day when her brain was stuffed with pillow foam.

Maya read her message out loud. **<Enzo, you hinted about a problem with Caren Oldner. Our dengue work relies on her. As her funding sponsor, you need to tell us if we should be worried.>**

Faye watched Maya click **<send>** before she could form words in comment. Then Maya dug for a banana in her bag and offered it to Faye. "Eat something. The potassium can give you a boost."

By eleven, Ino had picked them up and they headed south to Hoʻokena State Park. Caren texted she'd meet them there with students to help disperse sterile mosquitoes. If Caren wanted to restart that work instead of collecting mosquitoes for dengue testing, Faye wouldn't argue. Sometimes it was challenging to figure out who was in charge.

Right after Ino parked, Maya's phone dinged. With a shaking hand, she held it out to show Faye and Ino the text from Enzo. **<Caren screamed at a student sleeping in class, who filed a complaint including an allegation of fudged data. It's still under investigation. You owe me.>**

"Way to cast a shadow on a lovely day," Ino said.

Not a lot more detail than they knew before, Faye thought. All hearsay, nothing proven.

"What do you think we should do about Enzo's note?" Maya asked.

Ino rubbed his chin. "Dr. Clark can use his channels to find out more through the university system. If the data problems are verified, we could lose resources for our partnership."

Caren parked her own vehicle next to Ino's and climbed out with three students. "I'm jammed to the gills with sterile mossies. Hope you're all ready to get to work."

Her gung-ho attitude irritated Faye, whose mind and body were on a go-slow mode. Now she imagined a dyspeptic worm whose wriggles through her brain made her weary. She wanted to shove Enzo's text in Caren's face.

"We have to get all these out today," Caren continued. "My grad students can distribute half here and the four of us will head up to Pu'uhonua o Hōnaunau."

After unloading one mosquito container onto a picnic table, Faye settled to the seat and contented herself with watching everyone else handle the rest. Then Ino started for his own truck before Caren stopped him. "These guys can't be stuck here without transportation. Leave your vehicle for them—we don't need it."

Ino handed his keys to the older female student. "No one except a state employee is permitted to drive this. I'm not using my mosquito traps at the moment, so you kids can have my truck for an emergency." He winked at Faye. "Like a tsunami."

"Not funny." Caren's expression and tone were frosty. "We'll all meet back here at sunset."

Faye followed Maya as she climbed into Caren's rumble seat. With Ino's bulk, the only logical place for him was on the truck's front bench with Caren.

When Caren pulled away from the shore, Maya spoke up. "I've been researching genetically modified mosquitoes. You know, 'cause our New Mexico lab found them near Albuquerque and our human dengue cases."

Faye kicked at Maya, out of Caren's view. Undeterred, Maya kept going. "My boss said federal labs in New Mexico can't be the source. Dr. Oldner, is there anyone doing GM work in Hawai'i that we can consult?"

Caren braked for a car pulling out from a driveway, then

continued down the narrow tree-lined road. "No one here has funding for that type of research," she finally said.

The answer didn't address Maya's question—the research could be conducted if monies were siphoned off from other studies. Faye pulled together thoughts for her own question. "Do mosquitoes here have much natural genetic diversity?"

"Of course," Caren answered.

Faye's radar bumped to higher-beam. Caren had never mentioned the capability to monitor mosquito genomes. Or perhaps she was answering on behalf of another lab.

They rode in silence as Caren navigated the heavy traffic. Everyone on the island's west coast headed to the ocean for fun. Not Faye, still committed to hard labor as the death toll climbed. A long way from home, she was crazy to be doing this in her late sixties. With no regrets, this would be her final stint.

Faye's phone rang with a call from the Dengue Branch in Puerto Rico, and she pressed the speaker icon out of habit to keep her team in the loop. Siti said, "Faye, we need to talk in private."

"Shit." Faye pressed the symbol again. "Sorry, speaker's now off. We're headed out to distribute Caren's sterile mosquitoes."

"This can't wait," Siti said.

Through her phone, Faye heard men arguing in the background, then Siti resumed. "Just listen and don't respond. It's important that this remains confidential."

"Okay."

Seated behind Caren, Faye could see her colleague's neck muscles tighten. The whole carload had to be intensely curious about the call.

"Multiple mosquito specimens were fast-tracked. We now have matching genome patterns for New York City, San Juan, the Albuquerque area, and Hawai'i. What do all those locations have in common?"

"Me?" Then Faye stopped—she'd been ordered to remain silent. Ino turned in his seat and Maya's dark eyes locked on Faye's phone. Maya had been in most of those places too, although San Juan was an outlier for both of them.

Faye yanked on her hair, hoping the slight pain would wake up her brain. Why was she so dizzy and nauseous? Sitting in the back didn't help.

"No, estúpida. It's Caren." Siti's voice was harsh.

"That makes no sense." Faye was unaware of Caren making trips to New York and New Mexico.

"You're certain she can't hear me?" Siti asked.

"Affirmative," Faye answered.

"We have a theory, and Caren's a common element. But how it all happened, we're not sure."

Faye couldn't process Siti's news. There was still nothing to go on, other than Siti finding someone to blame. "What's next?" Faye asked.

"Continue your work as scheduled. Others will intervene—it's out of my hands." Siti sounded as exhausted as Faye felt, and hung up.

Caren pulled into a parking spot near the closed visitor center and turned to nail Faye with a glare. "What's going on?"

"I, uh, I told Siti yesterday I wasn't feeling well and she's requiring me to take a break." Telling a lie with a grain of truth was easier. She was fading fast.

Caren reached across Ino's belly to open the glovebox and retrieved a first aid kit. Removing a thermometer, she handed it to Faye. "Take your temperature."

When it beeped, Maya read its digital display. "102.7."

"I agree with Siti," Caren said. "You shouldn't be working with a fever."

"What are your other symptoms?" Ino asked.

Faye hugged her windbreaker tighter, skin twitching with the fever's chill. "Fatigue, dizziness, sore muscles." She glanced at Maya. "I overindulged yesterday on food and drink."

"That doesn't explain your fever," Caren said. "Any signs of infection with your dog bite?"

"Just a bruise, no redness."

"It could be COVID." Maya's eyes appeared wide with alarm. "We haven't exactly been perfect about masking around each other."

Faye had been vaccinated with a booster and had no respiratory symptoms, but it wasn't surprising that Maya would bring it up with her personal history.

"All of us were bitten by mosquitoes." Ino refocused Faye on dengue. Dengue would make sense given all their time outdoors chasing and combatting mosquitoes teeming with virus.

She'd made an effort at disease prevention with permethrin-treated clothing and mosquito wipes, but her own health hadn't been top-of-mind. Working with something every day, it was only human to forget the risk. Otherwise, no one could ever function in situations that had any possibility of illness or injury.

Caren unfastened her seat belt. "Stay with the truck. The three of us will disperse the mosquitoes."

Almost tender in her solicitude, Caren rolled down the windows and handed Faye her canteen. She insisted that Faye swallow two acetaminophen tablets to see if her temperature would lower. "We'll be back for more containers. Text me immediately if anything worsens."

An unusual tone from the brittle researcher, but Caren had flashed empathy on occasion. Faye watched Caren and Ino head toward the sacred temple at oceanside. Maya rounded the visitor center, maybe headed to the royal fishponds.

Siti's explosive allegation deserved more discussion. She clicked on her most recent call—no answer. Siti had sounded stressed and might be tied up.

Faye used her daypack as a pillow and reclined in the back seat. Despite the pain, she dozed, eyelids fluttering when someone opened the back of the truck. As the minutes ticked by, she glanced out the window through the palm trees to the sky, a lovely shade of mauve. The jackhammer behind her eyes intensified, and she pulled her cap lower on her face.

THIRTY-NINE

Pu'uhonua o Hōnaunau National Historical Park, Hawai'i Island—Monday, September 13, 2021

Maya placed her mosquito container in Caren's truck and opened the passenger door to find Faye stretched out on the back seat.

Behind the wheel, Caren asked, "How are you doing, amiga?"

Maya was surprised at Caren's affectionate use of Spanish. She didn't think of Faye as Caren's friend, just an old college classmate. But Faye had been tolerant of Caren's eccentricities. Was there anyone from Maya's vet school class of 2016 that she'd be close to after forty years?

Faye struggled to sit up. "Don't worry…'bout me." Her words were weak and garbled.

"Let's recheck your temperature." Maya inserted the thermometer between Faye's lips.

After the beep, she handed it Ino, seated in front of her. "102.9, a bit higher."

"We can swing by urgent care," he said. "It's only a half hour back up to Kona."

Faye shook her head. "Need…good night sleep." She leaned forward to put her hand on Caren's shoulder. "Why Siti say you are conn…ected to outbreak?"

Caren twisted in the driver's seat. "What the fuck?"

Ino frowned. "Faye, I'm worried about you." He looked at his watch. "Damn, urgent care's closed by now. We should go to the emergency room."

"I agree with Ino." Maya was stunned by Faye's provocative question but her health took precedence.

Caren shrieked like a captured wild animal, then appeared to gain control. "I'm treating the students to dinner in Hilo—we all have early Tuesday classes. Take Faye in your own truck."

Maya's body flooded with electricity. What was wrong with Caren? It might not be safe riding with someone so erratic. The shorter trip to Ino's truck would give them a quicker escape from Caren's poisoned fog of energy. And with Ino driving, Maya could call Siti to clarify what she'd said to Faye about Caren.

Ino's face transfigured to one of the historical park's fierce ki'i wood carvings. "The students can wait while we take care of Faye."

Caren pounded her steering wheel, triggering a loud honk. That startled Faye, who flinched to the side until Maya caught her.

"You're so damn shortsighted, always focused on the here and now," Caren shouted. "I've got decades-long commitments to my research which you fucked up with your freakouts about fake tsunamis."

In a battle of wills, Maya would place her bets on Ino, who always exuded a benevolent but forceful authority. As Caren started the engine and headed toward the park entrance, Maya was unsure of their direction.

Flashing lights approached at high speed and a white sedan marked **SHERIFF** blocked the narrow road ahead. Caren slammed her brakes to avoid a front-end collision and jerked the steering wheel to force a skid in the opposite direction.

"What are you doing?" Ino shouted. "That cop can give us a high-speed escort to the hospital."

Maya stretched her arm across Faye's body to protect her, despite both wearing seat belts. At the end of the visitor center's parking lot, the truck became airborne as Caren flew over a raised speed bump, then caromed off a low volcanic wall and slammed through a small white gate at the horse trail. The sheriff's car was on their tail within seconds.

"Can't shake them." Caren pivoted, scanning the thicket of palm trees. "Refuge, I need the Place of Refuge."

Faye looked like she was ready to vomit with the violent twists and turns of the vehicle. "Caren, please let us out," Maya pleaded. "You're making Faye sick."

She'd seen Caren's volatility before, but nothing like this. The only explanation—Caren was paranoid about the sheriff's flashing lights.

They all lurched left as she swerved a sharp right onto a lava stone walkway through the vegetation. Maya glanced out the rear window and saw the sheriff slow. A sedan without four-wheel-drive might hesitate to follow, but Caren's route in the direction of the ocean provided no escape.

With one hand, Caren flipped off the truck lights, dimming the view ahead in the darkened landscape after sunset. Did she think the sheriff couldn't see her? The path of destruction was all too obvious.

"Caren, I order you to stop now or someone's going to get hurt!" Ino's hands clenched into fists, like he was planning to punch her or grab the steering wheel. Maya held out hope that Caren would follow his command before he tried to gain control of the vehicle.

Outlined against a sky of deep purple, the consecrated thatched house emerged. "Hale o Keawe," Caren muttered.

A loud bang from a flat tire—she struggled to maintain control as her truck raced for the volcanic Great Wall, looming twelve feet high.

Maya smelled burning rubber when Caren slammed the brakes. The truck ploughed into the wall at an angle, right corner first. When Maya's head whacked the support for Ino's headrest, the sudden shock momentarily blackened her view. The sound of metal crunching was punctuated by Faye's cry. Like a silk scarf unraveling, time scrolled out in a languid wave.

Drops of liquid oozed down Maya's cheek. She felt a gash on her forehead, then she opened her eyes to find fingertips red with blood. Her head throbbed from the headrest blow. In front of her, Ino was quiet. Too quiet, with the engine pinning his legs in the compartment. He ought to be screaming in pain.

A rusty smell of fresh blood, too overwhelming to be her own, made Maya nauseous. She found her phone to dial 9-1-1 but the sheriff was already trying to open Ino's door. Faye appeared unhurt but confused, pointing out the side window.

"Who's that?"

Maya recognized Caren crawling over the lattice fence surrounding the historical hut, the glowering faces on ki'i statues barely visible as they towered over the Hale o Keawe. Were the akua, Hawaiian gods, aghast at the invasion? Or did they have compassion for the invader seeking sanctuary after kapu, a breaking of sacred laws?

The driver's side door hung open and sirens overpowered the sound of gentle waves splashing on shore.

"I have immunity in this sacred place!" Caren's screams from behind the fence pierced the siren din.

The sheriff, unable to open Ino's mangled door, raced to the driver's side and leaned in. "Are you ladies okay?"

Maya looked at Faye whose hand shielded her eyes from flashing lights. "I'm not sure about Dr. Simpson, but I'm fine. Ino's the one I'm worried about."

The sheriff crawled through the narrowed opening in front of the airbag and placed his fingers on Ino's neck. After releasing her seat belt, Maya peered around the headrest, unable to detect any motion in Ino's chest. The sheriff glanced up and caught Maya's gaze, then shook his head. A torrent of tears mixed with the blood seeping to her chin.

FORTY

Kailua-Kona, Hawai'i Island—Wednesday, September 15, 2021

Faye awoke from her afternoon nap to find Taylor studying her electronic chart. After two days in Kona Community Hospital, Faye's brain was finally engaged. Everything in the room glistened white or stainless steel—too monochrome even if it emphasized good sanitation. Previously healthy as the horses on her family ranch, she'd never experienced a medical setting from the patient point of view.

Taylor brought the room to life in a red pantsuit and shoulder-length dreads. Faye grabbed a cup of tea from the hospital tray and gulped it.

Maya entered holding a small paper bag. "These cinnamon rolls aren't as good as the ones in Fort Collins."

"Can you believe Taylor flew all the way from New York?" Faye asked her. "I'm hardly at death's door—I don't need the Staten Island Chief of Staff for a mild dengue infection."

The tea was lighter on caffeine than coffee but she felt like the toy bunny in the battery commercial, ready to march off the edge of the bed.

Taylor angled the laptop toward Faye. "Not only dengue. On top of the truck accident, you were diagnosed with high blood pressure. I had to make sure you're getting the best care."

Faye tore off her first bite of Maya's treat, the glaze comforting her mouth, and she noticed the stitches on Maya's forehead. One more scar as a reminder of the occasional hazards associated with public health investigations.

But Ino was the only one seriously affected by the crash. He bled out from a lacerated femoral artery before the ambulance arrived.

Tears formed in Faye's eyes. Ino's death seemed like something in a movie, not experienced first-hand during his last moments.

"Ino's funeral is scheduled for Saturday in Honolulu." Maya choked up.

Faye's heart rate on the monitor shot up. "We need to be there. Do you know what's up with Caren?"

"Siti Rahim may tell us more at the health department on Friday." Maya ran her fingers through her hair, a perplexed look on her face. "Everything's still circumstantial. They're looking deeper into Caren's work with altered mosquitoes."

Faye's old friend had never mentioned experimenting with genetic modification during their weeks of fighting *Aedes* together. "She sure acted guilty when I asked her if she had anything to do with the outbreak."

"I'm surprised you remember," Maya said. "Dengue definitely had you down for the count."

"My first infection on the job. Taylor, did you ever catch a disease at work?"

"No." Taylor turned to Maya. "My condolences on the COVID loss of your husband. I understand you're working on a memorial."

With all the talk of death, Maya slumped and her eyes dropped. First her grandmother, Manolo, and her baby. Then Devorah Abelman, vet school instructor and mentor for both of them. Now, Ino.

Faye couldn't imagine so much loss in a year. She hoped that Maya wouldn't drown in depression again.

"Faye and I need to finish our arrangements." Maya straightened up with a pasted-on smile. "We'll get it done, somehow. No matter what's happening personally, our work is a priority, when we can do something to prevent people getting sick and dying."

"I'd lose my capacity for mercy if Faye had been injured." Taylor's voice was taut. "Is Caren Oldner in jail?"

"Yes, she was arrested for the accident," Maya answered. "But the press still knows nothing about her research on genetically modified mosquitoes."

"Sheltering in the sacred place wasn't a 'Get Out of Jail Free' card after killing Ino." The monitor reminded Faye to take deep breaths as she spoke. She didn't want to complicate her dengue recovery by exacerbating her high blood pressure.

Caren hadn't intended to harm Ino. No one else was seriously hurt—it was a fluke that a leg laceration from a piece of the engine led to his death. Yet Caren's irresponsible driving was the immediate cause. Despite their vet school ties, Faye prayed that a vehicular homicide charge would stick.

Honolulu, Oʻahu—Friday, September 17, 2021

Faye squirmed when Taylor reached down to envelop her in a bearhug. The crowds in Honolulu's airport bustled around them, one harried man almost knocking over Taylor's roller bag. Sweat beaded her neck as other travelers glanced at them, an elegant RuPaul enveloping an old hag. That's what her father had called her mother during their frequent fights.

"I'm mad you left the hospital after only four nights." Taylor massaged the back of Faye's skull. "You're still having headaches. That makes me nervous to abandon you for my work."

Faye checked the time on her phone. "I bounced back quickly under the care of my concierge physician. Thank you."

A high-level meeting was starting at eleven o'clock in health department headquarters and Ino's funeral was set for tomorrow. She was determined to attend both in person.

Initial dengue infections were rarely fatal and she was confident about her recovery. If she hadn't been hospitalized, she might have suffered for months the insidious effects of untreated high blood pressure.

"Please, wrap this up so we can cuddle in bed together soon," Taylor insisted.

Faye appreciated Taylor's patience and had agreed this would be her final assignment. Her health scare was a wakeup call to prioritize personal relationships. She'd never given theirs the time and attention it deserved.

In the swampy late-morning heat, Faye's long-sleeved blouse was damp from the taxi ride between the airport and the health department. Her pants and blazer were dark like Dr. Clark's black suit. Others in the room were somber, COVID masks hiding their faces. Quiet greetings reflected their mood.

"I'm so sorry for your loss," Faye directed to Dr. Clark. "Ino was the most diligent yet compassionate of colleagues." Her eyes teared up with the words, and she swallowed to gain control.

Maya looked haunted and Faye squeezed her hand. Then she nodded to Siti Rahim, newly arrived from Puerto Rico.

Next to Siti was Keegan Williams, the Epidemic Intelligence Service officer from Fort Collins who'd been so helpful in New Mexico. Faye assumed that Siti wouldn't do any fieldwork, so Keegan was evidence of CDC's commitment to the dengue investigation.

"Now that we're all here, let's get started." Dr. Clark turned to Siti as Faye flushed, embarrassed that they'd been waiting on her.

"Federal agents scoured Caren's lab," Siti said. "We confirmed that she's been conducting unauthorized research with genetically modified mosquitoes."

Faye had even more reason to feel chagrin. She'd toured Caren's facilities but wouldn't have recognized the equipment or processes.

"Are you alleging she deliberately disseminated dengue to multiple states?" Maya's tone was alarmed.

"We don't know," Siti answered.

Compared to the phone call in the truck, Siti sounded less confident about Caren's link to other dengue outbreaks. Faye emitted a deep sigh—she hadn't missed a signal that her colleague might be a bioterrorist.

Dr. Clark twisted in his seat. "Dr. Oldner's actions were criminal—reckless driving in an insane effort to escape capture by hiding in the sacred grounds. The area's history and cultural status are still respected, but why would she expect that to protect her?"

No matter how long Faye had known Caren, she had no answer to Dr. Clark's question. Shifting their focus back to dengue, she asked, "Is Keegan here to replace Ino on the team?"

"I'm happy to help out." Keegan was a Labrador Retriever, all eager to please.

"We're working on multiple fronts," Dr. Clark said. "Not only do we need to determine Dr. Oldner's culpability, but the dengue outbreak continues to plague us. We appreciate Dr. Williams joining the effort until the case count starts to drop."

Maya appeared restless in her seat. "How can you tie Dr. Oldner to mainland cases if she didn't travel there?"

The question sparked a memory of Faye's conversation with Caren when they reconnected. "She visited her mother in Las Vegas. Maybe she went to other areas, too."

"All her trips are being tracked." Siti ruffled her blue hair. "She could have transported her GM mosquitoes to Puerto Rico when she visited in June. That might explain Juana Lopez's infection."

"If infected mosquitoes snuck into Juana's flight to Albuquerque," Maya said, "that would account for dengue in her two family members and the few mosquito pools with the modified genome."

"We got lucky in New York," Faye said. "No cases other than Juana, even though our staff found some positive mosquitoes after I left."

Siti checked her notes. "But only one matched the genome of concern. Perhaps the local mosquitoes became infected by biting Juana before she was hospitalized."

"New York dodged a bigger outbreak," Faye said. If that had happened, she could have jousted with the virus from the comfort of her home. But she wouldn't have wished the disease on New York just for her convenience.

Besides, if dengue was winding up her public health career, the locations had been movie-set magnificent. She'd become too entrenched in her routines, fond of her *New York Times* while cuddling on the couch with a cat.

An overseas trip with Taylor that didn't require lugging around mosquito traps—that was something to look forward to.

"Most of the GM mosquitoes were found on Hawai'i Island and Maui, not O'ahu or Kaua'i," Dr. Clark said. "We don't know if it was accidental or deliberate."

"Lab errors can happen," Siti said. "We've had a few at CDC as well."

"Have you checked her computers?" Maya asked. "Are there any records to support one theory over the other?"

"If there's anything like that," Dr. Clark answered, "we haven't found it. However, we're making progress on the other allegations. We have corroboration on her mistreatment of several students, and she compelled them to keep silent about her poor results with the sterile mosquitoes."

Faye shook her head in dismay. Why would someone so brilliant need to change data and pressure students to cover it up? Then she remembered one of their fellow CSU classmates. Fearful of failure despite good course grades, he'd broken into an office and stolen answers to a final exam.

"Caren claimed it was too soon for a reduction in mosquito counts from our sterile mosquito distribution," Faye said.

"She's right." Siti pointed her pen at Faye. "You can verify its success without her thumb on the scale, if you and Maya are willing to stay on with Keegan's help."

Above her mask, Maya's skin darkened. Faye was certain she was thinking of Manolo's memorial. At least for Devorah, there was no real time pressure. A spring service before graduation would give Faye and CSU plenty of time to organize something.

Faye considered her words in light of Maya's reaction. "We can re-evaluate after next week's work with our new team."

"Your leadership is much appreciated after your own dengue infection," Dr. Clark said. "I hope you're feeling up to the job."

Faye hadn't recovered all her strength and had slight elevations in temperature late at night, but she was still committed to identifying and stamping out dengue hotspots.

Dr. Clark continued. "I can spare a couple of our local vector staff—it's a lot to manage without Ino, Dr. Oldner, and her students."

"Are you staying on, Dr. Rahim?" Maya asked.

"I'm trying to find out if Caren's experimental mosquitoes escaped the lab," Siti said, "or if it was intentional. She might have been trying to get more funding for her research, or perhaps was angry at the NIH threat to cut it."

Decades earlier, Faye had shed her family's Pentecostal faith, like the skin of live rattlesnakes occasionally used in their rituals. But the instinct to pray was baked in, and she winged a prayer to heaven that the lab leak theory was true.

"What about the bioterrorism threat note in Arizona?" Maya's voice was low as if she was afraid of the answer. She'd been petrified that Dave Schwartz's family would be tied to another BT attack.

"We need to verify whether Caren had any connections to that group," Siti said.

When a secretary pushed into the room with a message for Dr. Clark, he ended the meeting. "Thank you for your help with our crisis."

Faye placed her hand on her heart and made a slight bow, to replace her normal instinct to shake his hand. She was exhausted by this pandemic world.

FORTY-ONE

Honolulu, Oʻahu—Saturday, September 18, 2021

The massive crowd gathered on Waikiki Beach at noon. In the sand, a traditional lūʻau had been set up. Tables were laden with kalua pig, huli huli chicken, and lomi lomi salmon.

The heavy meat aroma triggered pulses in Maya's stomach that bordered on uncomfortable. Fingers crossed, she wasn't coming down with dengue like Faye, recovering in her hotel room from a severe headache and fever spike. Siti and Keegan, never having met Ino, were in Hilo inspecting Caren's lab records.

A laptop cycled through photos and video clips of Ino. Maya hadn't realized he'd been a surfer in his younger days. Graceful, for someone larger than life. A man wearing only a malo, a loincloth made from tapa fabric, strummed a ukelele and sang *White Sandy Beach* by IZ, Ino's favorite Hawaiian singer.

Maya visualized squishing her tears into a tiny ball to bury on the beach. She'd only known Ino for two weeks, but surrounded by his grieving friends and relatives, she couldn't help but identify with them. She sighed. Anticipating Manolo's service on top of the reality of Ino's could be contributing to her volcanic emotions.

Gravitating toward a food more easily digestible by a tender tummy, she ladled some Molokai sweet potatoes garnished with grated cheese onto her paper plate. After her first bite, she sensed a shadow in the sand and looked up to recognize Pua, Ino's cousin from Lahaina.

"Thank you for coming," Pua said. "Ino was so passionate about his job. He'd appreciate people he worked with showing they valued him."

A young woman stopped by to give Pua a colorful paper brochure. "Aunty, will we see you at next month's drug awareness walk? Without Ino to lead us, we need to represent."

Pua smiled. "Ino made promises to God and all of us that this movement would keep going—we'll carry on for him."

Maya's surprise must have registered on her face. "Growing up with little," Pua said, "he gravitated to trouble, including drugs and alcohol. But after his second hospitalization for an overdose, he got his act together. With AA and his leadership for our walks, he maintained his commitments to everyone, and then some."

Maybe that's why he chose a caring career, Maya thought. He understood what it meant to struggle, and to serve. From the little she'd known him, money wasn't important, or achieving high status.

"I recognized immediately that he was a person deserving the greatest respect," she said.

"Mahalo." Pua turned away to embrace a boy tugging on her arm.

Sarah, the new addition to their dengue team, strolled up to greet Maya. "I hope you remembered your swimsuit for the remembrance ceremony at sea, Dr. Maguire."

Maya flushed at being addressed that way when their ages were similar. "Yes, I'm wearing it under this. Please call me Maya."

She fingered the navy muumuu decorated with leaping dolphins, bought yesterday afternoon at the hotel gift shop. Along with a t-shirt, the only souvenir she'd take home from the challenging trip.

Doubt mixed with the sweet potatoes and congealed in her stomach. "I have experience snorkeling but I never tried a surfboard."

Sarah waved toward the flat blue surface, sparkling with sunlight. "No waves today, nothing to worry about."

They shed their outer clothes and Sarah draped a lei of yellow roses around Maya's neck. Then they picked out small boards from those jammed upright in the sand like an army of soldiers standing at honor. Paddling on their bellies, they joined a rainbow connection of people circling a large, anchored catamaran.

Maya sat up on her board, holding hands with Sarah and a man to her right, water sparkling in his long white beard.

Under a crystal sky streaked with delicate ribbons of clouds, Maya rocked gently, bare legs tingled by the cool ocean. A middle-aged man on the boat, his dark locks crowned with a ti leaf lei, raised a clear plastic bag of Ino's ashes.

"We are gathered here today to honor Ino Kahale," he said. "Husband, father, grandfather, uncle, brother, and revered public servant." He handed the bag to a woman with silver hair cascading down her back, who bent down to a little girl Maya recognized from the hula dancers on Ino's phone.

"We send his spirit to this safe place," the man continued, "which we can share whenever we join him here in the moana."

He dove into the water, then the older woman and her granddaughter emptied the cremains into the sea. The surrounding crowd on surfboards began to cheer and sprinkle their lei flowers across the ocean surface. The sun's benevolent rays on her skin and her rose petals strewn on the oscillating blue carpet transfused Maya with serenity.

Back at the lūʻau, Maya's mood shifted with the memory of Caren's raging recklessness. She expressed her condolences to Ino's family and headed up to her hotel room for a quick shower. Then she delivered to Faye a food plate put together by Ino's widow.

"Sorry I couldn't make it." Faye reheated her chicken long rice in the small microwave next to the TV. "Ino's wife is so sweet, just like him. Imagine, thinking of me today."

"Are you feeling any better?" Maya asked. Faye tended to push herself, perhaps beyond what was wise for someone her age.

"No fever and my blood pressure's back to normal."

Maya hoped Faye would be healthy for their return to Kona. "We'll be fine with Keegan if you need more time. This morning, I thought I might have dengue symptoms, too."

"Paranoia is understandable when we spend all day capturing infected mosquitoes."

"Not to worry, I checked my temp." Glancing at her watch, Maya estimated that her parents would be cooking dinner soon. "If you're okay, I'm going to touch base with my family."

"I'll see you in the lobby at eight AM. Can't wait to finish our work on Hawai'i Island and confront Caren."

It wasn't surprising that Faye, as Caren's vet school classmate and recent dengue control partner, would want to find out what the hell Caren had been thinking. Not that Maya expected Caren to be honest. And depending on the legal situation, Faye might not be allowed to see her anyway.

In the shade of languorous palm leaves, Maya settled on a lounge at the empty pool. Everyone else must have escaped to the beach on a day reflecting Hawai'i's reputation for glorious weather.

She clicked on FaceTime and her mom's blazing red hair came into view.

"Hi sweetheart, are you on a mosquito break?" Her mom tilted the camera to show her dad browning hamburger on their gas stove.

"I'm making sloppy joes." He waved his spatula, then dropped a morsel to Hypatia, their sable Persian.

Her mom refocused the camera on herself. "We've been so upset since you told us about that car accident. When are you coming home?"

"Unsure, but I made progress with the Indian Health Service on a service for Manolo. They're working on a presentation about his contributions to Native American health."

"Wonderful news, dear. We're glad you don't have to make all the arrangements from Hawaii." Her mom was supportive, unusual for someone who too often seemed like she was telling Maya what to do.

"I'm not sure how to handle the Mirandas." Maya was thinking out loud, not expecting that her parents would have a solution. "I texted them the details but haven't heard anything back."

Her dad raised his voice over the cooktop fan. "Perhaps they'd appreciate a direct invitation. Have you tried to call?"

She sighed. They'd ignored her phone calls in the past year, but she should make the effort. "I'll do that. Thanks for the encouragement."

After hanging up, she took a drink from her water bottle, hoping to wash away her guilt. She'd said nothing to her parents about the fact that she'd been working with a possible bioterrorist. If she revealed that, they'd hop the next flight to drag her home.

Bite the bullet. She thumbed her screen for a FaceTime call to Sebastian. At Manolo's funeral, his father had been a shade more friendly than Manolo's sister.

He answered from his art studio wearing his Yankees ballcap. She waved her own, a gift from him before Manolo's death. The brim felt gritty after weeks of salt and sand.

"I'm out in the hot Hawaiian sun." She decided to break ground with humor. "What's your excuse for the headgear indoors?"

His warm eyes crinkled. "Yankees-Indians game this afternoon. We got crucified, 11-3. I'm mourning in solidarity for my boys."

Maya took a deep breath, deciding to use his words as an opening to the dreaded subject. "Speaking of mourning, can you come out for Manolo's service at the petroglyph park? It was one of his favorites. We'd hoped to go camping there."

She almost said "with the baby" but held back, not wanting to compound Sebastian's sense of loss. He'd been ecstatic at the possibility of a second grandchild. She and Manolo should have waited until the end of her first trimester to tell everyone she was pregnant. But by then, he and their baby were both dead.

Sebastian's face twitched and his words were halting. "Ramona says the Catholic mass was sufficient. Johnny's back in school and Abdi's working on a new environmental lawsuit."

Maya uncrossed her legs to ease her tension. He was making excuses for his daughter, grandson, and son-in-law, not himself. Last year, he'd discussed moving nearby to help them with child care. She tried to guess what might be holding him back now.

"You haven't flown since the pandemic, but you can mask to reduce the risk. You're vaccinated and boostered, right?"

"Yes," he answered, "but the idea of clustering with possibly infected people on a plane is causing family strife. That's why I didn't respond."

Ramona still blamed Maya for Manolo's COVID infection and death—that was clear. "Manolo was your only son. He'd want you to hear all the wonderful accolades from his colleagues."

She was reluctant to play the guilt card, but yearned for a renewed connection with others who loved Manolo. Attending his service alone, without any of his relatives, would reinforce her isolation from what could have been.

"If Manolo and your baby had died of something else…" He trailed off as he rubbed his eyes. "Ramona says that dreadful disease can't rob her of another person. She's forbidden me to fly."

Ino's death was a reminder that relationships need nurturing—they could be all too brief. "Sebastian, lots of people are driving and camping, reducing human contact. You once mentioned buying a van to tour all the states."

The service was less than three weeks away, possibly too short to locate an RV and drive alone cross-country, depending on his stamina. Her own parents limited their travels to the Southwest, but they were a decade older than Sebastian.

"Maybe it's worth considering." His response surprised her.

All the highway accident statistics flashed through her public health brain. She searched for other options. "A private compartment on Amtrak? Might be expensive but could reduce COVID risk."

"Long drives are fun. I plug in my Bruce Springsteen cassettes and rock the road."

Maya laughed. "And where will you find a vehicle that still plays cassettes?"

They concluded with a commitment to explore the possibilities, even if not a guarantee he would make it. Regardless of the outcome, they'd tiptoed out onto a narrow branch of the family tree, testing to see if it would support them both.

FORTY-TWO

Kailua-Kona, Hawai'i Island—Monday, September 27, 2021

Faye sat at the small table in the police jail, her feet restless beneath the uncomfortable metal seat. A door opened, and Caren's face brightened with a desperate smile as a guard led her to the opposite chair.

"Thank God you came." Caren reached for Faye's hands but the guard stopped her. "I've been stuck here for two weeks and my attorney has no answers on why I can't get bail."

Faye tried to work up some sympathy for her classmate. She'd never seen Caren so unkempt and distraught. Before her incarceration, she'd always appeared in total control with no personal commitments to interrupt her work.

"Why the hell do they have you on suicide watch?" Faye asked. "You're not going to spend the rest of your life in jail."

Caren gulped down a moan. "I just…there's nothing without my research…the university will fire me…all my work, gone."

Unsure how or whether to reassure her, Faye hesitated. Despite Caren's mosquitoes having a matching genome to other locations, no notes indicating a deliberate act had been located. The agencies worried that Caren might take the truth to the grave, but Faye's sleuthing mission in the jail was unauthorized.

"Your attorney's doing some good," Faye said. "He got the charges reduced from first-degree to second-degree vehicular homicide."

Faye had been surprised by his success, but Caren had cleared all tests for DUI impairment. If convicted, her sentence for the felony could be up to five years in prison with a ten thousand dollar fine.

Losing her faculty position would be life-changing for someone in her sixties whose self-worth was based on her scientific reputation. She had too few years left to find other work and redeem herself.

Faye waved at the guard standing a foot away. "Could we have some privacy, please?"

He leaned against the wall without taking his eyes off Caren, and Faye reduced her voice to a whisper.

"The judge hasn't set your bail because they're hoping to make bioterrorism charges stick."

Caren's blue eyes melted with tears that coursed through deep lines carving commas around her nose. "I'd never do anything to risk someone's life."

Driving like a madwoman into a volcanic rock wall and killing Ino must not count as risky. Every day that Faye worked on mosquito control with Maya, Keegan, and health department staff, she revisited memories of Ino's grace and humor.

The guards had said that no one visited or called except Caren's attorney. Her mother was a ninety-year-old invalid in Las Vegas—unlikely to be a confidante. Faye was convinced she had the best shot at getting Caren to reveal what happened.

"They should have honored my seeking refuge." Caren's face twisted into a scowl. "If I'd been native Hawaiian, they would have."

Surely Caren didn't believe that the ancient tradition would apply to this modern world. For the first time, Faye wondered if Caren was showing signs of early dementia like Devorah. She remembered advice to validate feelings and avoid arguing over altered perceptions.

"No one has your passion for productivity." Faye wanted to believe that Caren didn't intend to infect anyone with dengue, although the racist remark gave her pause. "You've been working nonstop to make a major contribution to dengue science. Did some of your experimental mosquitoes escape your lab?"

Caren violently shook her head, then issued a sharp retort. "Not me—fuckin' students let 'em out."

Faye glanced at the guard, whose expression didn't change. She hoped that Caren had forgotten about him. "I'm surprised you'd trust undergrads with such groundbreaking work."

"Of course not." Caren spat out the words between tight lips. "But they were sloppy about doors. You know, holding one open while saying goodbye to friends. That kind of crap."

"When did you realize some of your modified mosquitoes escaped?"

"When Maya mentioned the New Mexico lab results, I checked some I collected in Hilo, Kona, and Maui." She cupped her face with her hands, shoulders slumped. "I couldn't believe they were the same genome as the GM mosquitoes I'd developed in my lab."

"How did they get to Puerto Rico?" Caren could have brought them on her June visit to the Dengue Branch for a real-world field test, or perhaps as revenge against the federal government threatening to withhold her funding.

"Hell if I know. Got into my bag, if I had to guess." Caren looked bewildered.

Even with a perception of friendship, Faye probably couldn't persuade Caren to admit instigating bioterrorism. But she was determined to find out anything that might help.

"Maya's analyses indicate a more rapid onset of illness and a higher death rate. Which of your mosquito changes might have caused that?"

"Outrageous—that would come from genetic manipulation of the virus, not the mosquito."

Caren was right. *Aedes* modification could increase or decrease its ability to transmit the virus, which would affect the number of cases, but not the dengue virus incubation period or case fatality rate. Perhaps what Maya found was only due to increased surveillance.

"Why is Hawai'i experiencing so many dengue cases this year?" Faye asked, then lowered her voice again. "I assume you didn't intend to enhance their ability to spread dengue."

Caren's fingers etched a pattern in the Formica table top. "Damned if I know. My genetic research aimed to make *Aedes* less effective at breeding, similar to my sterile mosquito work. Something got screwed up and a few of them got better at mating."

Faye struggled to understand the geographic pattern. Probably through vehicles and planes, altered mosquitoes had established themselves on Maui and Hawai'i Island, but not the more distant islands of O'ahu or Kaua'i. Hawai'i Island's location as the focal point of the lab leak, plus its warm, wet climate, provided perfect outbreak conditions.

The few GM mosquitoes found in New Mexico and New York didn't result in larger GM colonies there. Even in Puerto Rico, the GM mosquitoes couldn't out-compete others.

Faye leaned back. The idea that her classmate wasn't a bioterrorist finally relaxed her jaw muscles, clenched from anticipation of the meeting.

The guard gestured toward the clock on the wall.

"You haven't explained this to anyone," Faye said. "If you want my support, you have to come clean."

Caren frowned and Faye realized she needed more convincing.

"For someone with your admirable life and work ambitions, this is a major mistake. You weren't approved or funded for GM research, and I assume there will be penalties. But the courts might go lighter on the charges if they understand what you were trying to do."

The guard stepped forward and Caren broke down with wracking sobs. She hunched over, then the guard took her elbow.

In all their years of contact, Faye had never seen Caren cry like this. Should she recommend Caren get a psych evaluation and cognitive function test?

Maybe she would broach it with her attorney, not Caren herself.

"It'll be okay." Faye used her most soothing tone for consoling a cat owner whose favorite pet had just died. "I'll do everything I can to help."

And she meant it, if nothing else surfaced to contradict Caren's version of the story.

Hawai'i Volcanoes National Park, Hawai'i Island—Tuesday, September 28, 2021

Faye waved at the Steam Vents road sign as Ino's vector control specialist drove the state truck along Crater Rim Drive. "Sarah, let's take a quick break—I want to check these out."

"No problem." The ponytailed blonde beamed in her role as local tour guide. "The pillars of hot water vapor are created by groundwater seeping down to magma deep below."

Once Sarah had parked, Maya dug in her daypack for small bags of chips and handed them to her colleagues.

"Working here is a blessing—maybe we shouldn't get paid," Faye joked.

The chatter filtering in the open windows from tourists visiting the steam vents reflected the team's mood at getting back to the battle against dengue. It was three weeks since Faye and Maya had visited the national park for Caren's sterile mosquito demonstration.

Faye had shared everything she'd learned from Caren on a call to Dr. Clark last night. Maya, listening in, expressed skepticism that Caren had revealed the whole story so easily. But it was out of their hands—Dr. Clark would follow up with the authorities. Faye was just happy to be sufficiently recovered from dengue to evaluate a new scientific weapon.

Sarah handed her an apple. "It's exciting to pilot test the *Wolbachia* mosquitoes Dr. Rahim got for you."

"Do you remember when Caren said they failed in Vietnam?" Maya asked.

"She probably hoped to get the big bucks for *Wolbachia* diverted to her work with mosquitoes she was researching, like the sterile ones," Faye said.

Maya shook her head. "Pretty cutthroat competition."

"Unlike Caren, we have government jobs with dependable salaries and benefits," Faye replied. "Many academic salaries are dependent on submitting grants with a small chance of ever getting funding. I wouldn't trade places with her for anything."

She was careful about any further comments. Sarah wasn't in the loop yet about Caren's possible role in starting the dengue outbreak with GM mosquitoes.

"Do you think we'll get any public protests about this new technique?" Sarah asked.

Faye understood her question. To hinder mosquito reproduction, *Aedes aegypti* eggs were injected with *Wolbachia* bacteria from *Drosophila* fruit flies. Injecting mosquitoes with a strange-sounding bacteria before releasing them sounded more dangerous than the mosquitoes which had been sterilized in Caren's lab, even though both techniques were intended to reduce mosquito numbers.

"*Wolbachia* is naturally occurring in butterflies and other mosquitoes," Maya said. "It doesn't infect mammals, including humans."

Faye hoped that their use of a modified mosquito would generate less pushback than their insecticides, which had raised concerns about possible human and environmental impacts. Unlike Caren, they weren't altering any mosquito genes.

"It's daunting doing this work without Ino." Sarah had a somber, respectful tone. "He was a terrific boss."

Faye couldn't recall many people who garnered such an adoring response. She didn't hold that crazy Saturday placing and removing mosquito traps against him, and she'd even forgiven Dr. Clark for ordering it. Maybe being overworked that day made her dengue symptoms worse, but she'd never know for sure.

The Governor had approved distribution of *Wolbachia*-infected mosquitoes with a late Friday news release, the best time to dampen the reaction. Because of the truck accident, newspapers already questioned whether he should have been funding someone as unstable as Caren. Her GM role was still under investigation, so he didn't comment on that aspect, yet.

Faye wished that Siti had supported a dengue vaccination campaign. But overall vaccine acceptance had dropped precipitously since the COVID vaccine rollout.

Dr. Clark's initial assessment of blood samples stored at the lab found little evidence of previous infections in children aged 9-16, the target group for vaccination. Maybe they could roll out the vaccine later if the rate of seropositive kids ticked up.

She opened the truck door and hopped out. At the edge of the parking lot, she peered into a steam vent. Tourists were protected from falling in only by a metal pipe railing. The fog was uncomfortable on her skin after a day of sweaty work.

Sarah tossed in a penny. "Better cut that out," Faye warned. "Pele, the volcanic goddess, might get pissed at you."

"Just paying my dues," Sarah answered with a grin.

Faye took small breaths of the rotten egg fumes, not wanting to risk her aging lungs. She spun to admire a row of volcanic flumes on the far side of the road, then headed back to the truck. "Let's get going. The lodge desk clerk recommended the Ohelo Café for dinner."

Sarah gestured to a bush with cranberry-like fruit. "These ōhelo berries are a favorite food of the nēnē, our endangered Hawaiian goose. It's kapu to pick any—Pele could engulf us with a volcanic vapor and we'd never find our way out."

Faye flashed to Caren, breaking kapu by climbing the fence at the Hale o Keawe sacred site. She had raced there for a place of refuge; instead, she killed Ino and gained a jail cell.

No, Faye wouldn't taunt fate. She'd leave the ōhelo berries for the nēnē.

FORTY-THREE

Hawai'i Volcanoes National Park, Hawai'i Island—Wednesday, September 29, 2021

On their second day of *Wolbachia* mosquito distribution, the team took a breather overlooking the Kīlauea caldera. The stubby trees and sparse ground-hugging bushes reminded Maya of her beloved Southwest. But the dark dirt, reflecting its volcanic origins, wasn't warm and welcoming like the red desert of northern Arizona.

If she slipped on the slick pavement, the railing seemed like minimum protection from tumbling into the lunar landscape of Halema'uma'u crater. She regretted not getting to see any volcanic activity but their days in the park were limited.

"We're almost done here." Her mind drifted to Arizona's petroglyph park and all the planning for Manolo's service.

Faye turned to Sarah. "Did you confirm arrangements for us in Lahaina?"

Sarah nodded. "Dr. Clark's secretary has weekend plane tickets to Maui and more *Wolbachia* mosquitoes waiting for us there." She tugged on her ponytail. "Ino was so capable in his role of coordinating all this. I hope I'm up to replacing him."

Faye patted her arm. "You're doing fine, dear."

Maya sucked in a calming breath. "Don't forget, I'm flying home on Saturday." She prayed there hadn't been any misunderstanding. Only recently recovered from dengue, Faye was handling a lot, including the suspicions about Caren's potential role in bioterrorism.

"Oh my goodness, of course." Faye flushed bright pink. "Sarah, verify Maya's flight to Albuquerque."

Maya smiled. "I can handle it. I just didn't want you expecting my clone in Maui. Is Keegan almost done with the *Wolbachia* mosquitoes south of Kailua-Kona?"

"It's going well," Sarah answered. "Everyone's overjoyed that those parks and beaches can reopen soon."

The ground vibrated beneath Maya's feet and she rested a hand on the metal railing. "Do you feel that?"

Sarah checked her phone. "The Hawaiian Volcano Observatory is reporting increased earthquake activity."

Just then, a fluorescent tower of lava exploded from the dark crater floor and gray steam billowed up into the sky. Multiple volcanic vents burst into flame and the vapor clouded their view.

"I'd been hoping to see an active volcano," Maya exclaimed, "but I didn't expect it to happen."

Sarah's voice became high-pitched as she showed them a live closeup video of the new lava lake. "Now there's a volcanic alert warning. This is the most activity since lava destroyed seven hundred homes a few years back. But we're not in any danger yet—I'll keep an eye on the status."

The increasing clouds of volcanic fog might be unhealthy for the insects in the back of their truck. Maya chuckled at the unusual thought of wanting mosquitoes to live. These were special ones, intended for dud matings to reduce the dengue threat.

With a violent cough, Faye bent over, resting her hands on her knees.

"Are you okay?" Maya was ashamed that she'd been thinking more about mosquito health than Faye's.

"My lungs are just a bit sensitive." Faye raised up to rest her hands on the railing again. "My parents were smokers."

"The vog—that's what we call volcanic fog—has sulfur dioxide gas and particles that irritate the lungs." Sarah studied her phone. "No road closures yet."

"Before that happens," Faye said, "we need to distribute our remaining mosquitoes closer to the commercial areas to protect the largest number of people."

The unpleasant odor reminded Maya of July fourth fireworks.

She knew that older people were more sensitive to respiratory irritants. "Maybe we should check out of the lodge and save these last ones for Kailua-Kona."

Faye led the walk toward the parking lot as the path filled with people rushing to the viewpoint. In the truck's front seat, she said, "If the Volcano House has to charge for the late checkout, we're staying here. I won't run up the government's tab with two hotel bills for the same night."

Even when she wasn't feeling up to snuff, Faye continued to provide a shining example of a dedicated public servant.

"You're the boss," Maya said. Another plume of smoke drifted over the truck and Faye leaned back, wiping her eyes.

The hotel desk clerk was confident no life-threatening eruptions were imminent, so they enjoyed the caldera glow on the low-hanging clouds through the restaurant window during dinner. After a throat-soothing bowl of vanilla ice cream, Faye said, "Busy day, I'm turning in."

"I'll walk with you," Sarah said. "An early night will have me fresh for tomorrow's drive."

Maya stepped through the door to the Crater Rim Trail along with dozens of other guests. Lava danced from the crater floor and she opened the US Geological Survey's live webcam on her phone for a close-up view.

The massive flames of fire reminded her of the annual Zozobra burning in Santa Fe. Dangerous and scary, but cleansing at the same time. Out with the old, in with the new—the world required removal of detritus to allow room for growth. The electrified conversations from other tourists warmed her heart with nature's magnificence, although Pele could turn vicious and drive them away from the crater's rim.

She'd been in Hawai'i for almost a month, the longest of her work assignments so far from home. In spite of her mourning for Ino, she couldn't help but feel renewed by Pele coming to life. Already thinner from the weight loss following COVID and

Manolo's death, her body was athlete-tough with the physical labor of their war against dengue.

A pang of guilt pinched in her chest over abandoning Faye. But with the resources Siti provided from CDC's Dengue Branch, they might start to see a reduction in new cases. New Mexico had disease outbreaks, too, and she owed Dr. Grinwold her statistical expertise. He didn't have anyone on staff who loved deciphering data.

According to legend, Pele died in an epic fight with her sister but her spirit lived on within the crater. She sure was dancing tonight. Someone's phone played IZ, Ino's favorite singer, crooning his mashup of *Somewhere Over the Rainbow* and Louie Armstrong's *What a Wonderful World*. Maya turned her back on Pele and headed to her room, grateful for a heart filled with peace and acceptance.

FORTY-FOUR

Kailua-Kona, Hawai'i Island—Saturday, October 2, 2021

Faye stroked her bare feet through the sand as she reclined in the beach chair. She raised her piña colada in a toast to Maya on one side and Keegan on the other. "Here's to a productive couple of weeks."

She wasn't just putting an optimistic spin on it. Their reconfigured team without Ino and Caren had gelled. All their mosquito collections to monitor dengue had gone well, including their control efforts with *Wolbachia* and insecticides. No more interruptions from storms or threatened tsunamis.

Keegan took a swig from his mai tai. "My first time away from the mainland. I know it's 'cause people are sick and dying, but I couldn't ask for a prettier place."

"Ditto." Maya clinked her mimosa glass against Keegan's. "Did you have fun on our snorkel?"

"Did I ever! Two green sea turtles, a dolphin, and whale song underwater." He sighed. "You're a first-rate teacher, Maya."

She laughed. "That's what you said two years ago during your training."

"Thank God I don't have Enzo Russo as a partner again." Keegan shuddered.

"Yeah, he's far away in DC," Maya said. "But he did me a favor by providing some information about Caren."

Faye thought that Maya gave Enzo more credit than he deserved. His information didn't make a difference. Caren was still successful at multiple years of clandestine research into mosquito gene modification, using monies intended for sterile mosquito work.

Enzo and NIH moved at the pace of a sloth on their investigation of the student's allegation about exaggerated data. They should have sent a team to monitor Caren's studies and discover that she'd inflated the sterile mosquito results.

"Is she still locked up?" Keegan asked.

"Yes," Faye answered.

"It's weird that we know about Caren's association with the mosquito mutations but almost no one else does," Maya said. "Just Dr. Clark and some higher-ups."

"I avoided that discussion when working with the state staff this week," Keegan added. "Do you think it's wrong to keep all this a secret?"

Faye shrugged. "Damned if I know, but the decision is above my pay grade."

Decisions about the release of public health information were sometimes controversial. Hopefully they were made to optimize the mobilization of public interest and protective measures. Once the GM mosquitoes were announced, subsequent panic might encourage emptying containers of standing water, covering the skin, and using mosquito repellent.

"Dr. Clark will get heat about how long he sat on the information," Maya said.

"And CDC too," Faye replied.

With a visible shiver in the late afternoon breeze, Keegan dropped a second towel to his legs. "Enzo might go for a big splash by announcing his discovery of Caren's forged data."

"Just like him to go for the credit." Maya looked at her watch. "Time for me to catch the airport shuttle."

Faye propelled herself up from the lounge chair to give Maya a long hug. Her eyes threatened to spill. The decision, or lack of it, to have children weighed heavy on her heart. Hugs like this were few and far between. But she could form a close attachment to an extraordinary teammate like Maya.

"Are you okay if I hang out here with Keegan and don't see you off at the airport?" Faye asked.

"Of course."

"I'm sorry to miss Manolo's memorial." She should have insisted to Siti that her old bones needed a break from mosquito work. But with Maya leaving, Dr. Clark was short another person. It wasn't the time to bail, but soon.

Maya shoved her bangs out of her eyes. With limited time for personal care, her pixie cut had grown out. "You never met Manolo, and I'll have family and friends for support. It will reduce my guilt about jumping ship if you and Keegan are still in the good fight."

Keegan leaned in for his own awkward hug with Maya. Faye realized she'd never seen them touch. Maya blushed—perhaps it meant something to her.

After Maya was out of sight on the boardwalk, they dropped back to their lounge chairs. "Keegan, have you got a girlfriend somewhere, or a boyfriend?"

Keegan choked on his mai tai. "Not hardly. There's never a free moment."

"What do you think of Maya?"

"She's great. I loved getting to know her and Lila at my training course. Now we're all working in the Southwest, and I couldn't ask for better colleagues."

Faye noted his slipping in a mention of the new Arizona State Epidemiologist. So Maya wasn't special—he lumped the two young women together.

Disappointed, Faye let the subject drop. She'd hoped that Keegan and Maya would bond over their dengue work in New Mexico and Hawai'i. Despite her nerdy stats inclinations, Maya was too warm and loving to follow in Faye's footsteps and live her remaining years alone.

"Did Sarah confirm our flight to Maui?" Faye asked.

Keegan nodded and finished his drink. "I'm going to clean up and take care of emails. Meet you in the hotel restaurant at five?"

Faye shook her head no. "This old lady has FaceTime calls. Check with the health department staff. Have a great night out on the town before we restart our work in Lahaina tomorrow."

Keegan looked like a younger and shorter version of Taylor. Maya didn't know what she was missing by ignoring him. Faye wished she was back in the nineteen-eighties, fresh out of vet school. It would have been fun to explore other options besides the long-distance, intermittent relationship with Devorah.

Then she shook herself. Keegan wasn't even alive then. What was she thinking?

"Sorry to call so late." Faye had slaked her hunger with room service opakapaka before placing the FaceTime call to Taylor. A few morsels of the baked pink snapper remained for a snack.

"Don't worry about it." Taylor was resplendent in a rose robe dappled with white carnations. "I just finished watching *Saturday Night Live*."

"Thanks again for flying all the way out for my recovery," Faye said. "I think your consultation with my doctors made a difference."

Taylor leaned their head, free of the lush black wig, on the padded headboard. "I'm thrilled you're feeling better. When are you coming home?"

"Siti's making noises about winding up our work here." After two months, the hotel and food expenses were accumulating on Faye's credit card, and she wouldn't be reimbursed until she filled out the paperwork after the trip.

"At least you figured out what caused your outbreak. Any progress on nailing your college classmate?"

Faye shook her head. "I still think she's innocent of any bioterrorism attempt. Her whole life is devoted to solving infectious disease problems. I can't think of any reason she'd want to hurt someone."

"Yes, but a scientist sent anthrax through the mail to gin up his research budget. Then there was that copycat several years ago in Arizona. Maybe your friend did something similar."

With a sigh, Faye sank deeper into her bed pillows. "Some people believe Dr. Ivins's role was never proven."

She understood that professors had different expectations than those in frontline public health at CDC and state health departments. Epidemiologists like Faye and Maya were responsible for solving actual outbreaks in real time. Perhaps farther removed from the consequences of their basic research, scientists like Caren could justify cutting corners.

The ends justified the means, Caren had said when she spoke with Faye on a phone call. Her GM work had the potential to make a major dent in the worldwide scourge of dengue. If NIH or CDC wouldn't fund it, she'd do it on the downlow. She admitted that her sterile mosquitoes were disappointing, and a new approach to knocking back the mosquito scourge was crucial.

"Will you get in trouble for sitting on the news about the connection between Caren's GM work and Hawai'i's outbreak?" Taylor's dark brows lowered with concern.

Faye's own responsibility for the coverup never occurred to her. But it didn't make a difference at this stage in her career. "After this, I'm retired for good, so no one can withhold a job as punishment."

Taylor's face lit up as if engulfed by the Hawaiian sun. "I can't believe you made that decision. Will you stick to it?"

"You betcha. What do you have planned for us when I'm back?"

Taylor waved the Sunday *Times* in front of the camera. Faye missed her routine of picking it up on Saturday night at the street corner.

"The Wine and Food Festival is coming up in a couple of weeks," Taylor said. "I planned to buy a ticket to the Drag Brunch hosted by Neil Patrick Harris and his husband. Can I buy two?"

Faye hesitated. They'd done the Mets game and the Shakespeare play in Central Park as a couple, but those were informal. Was she ready for a splashy event, surrounded by others who were trans like Taylor or bi like Faye?

"Go for it," she answered.

What the hell—she'd stop giving other people power over her options when they didn't approve of her beliefs or activities. She never had the chance to deepen personal bonds because public health always took priority. Robert, her externship supervisor, died of AIDS and *Toxoplasma* infection before they could work out what they meant to each other. Then a relationship with Devorah would have required moving home to Colorado, something she was reluctant to do while her parents were living there.

Taylor had hung in for eight years of occasional sexual evenings while Faye used her job to avoid a deeper connection. No longer would she ignore her need for a committed partner, although they'd never discussed it.

"I'll call Siti to finalize my return date. And buy me something glorious to wear for the Drag Brunch—I want everyone aghast at our impact as a couple."

FORTY-FIVE

Petrified Forest National Park, Arizona—Wednesday, October 6, 2021

Maya stretched her restless legs and bumped the back of Nancy's seat in Dr. Grinwold's sedan. Her boss and his life partner were providing a ride from Santa Fe to Manolo's memorial service.

"Sorry, I'm jumpy from sitting so long." She rolled down her window and inhaled the clean, high desert air.

Nancy turned around as Dr. Grinwold parked at the Rainbow Forest Museum. "We're happy to do this, dear. We loved him too."

The words eased the tension in Maya's spine. Manolo had impressed everyone with his dedication and compassion. Although Puerto Rican, he'd committed his life to Native American health.

"Are you checking with the visitors' desk?" Dr. Grinwold asked.

"Yes, see you in a few minutes."

Inside the museum, Maya verified that a ranger would meet her at the picnic pavilion, then peeked into the Blue Mesa Room with its diorama of an ancient crocodilian in a verdant river basin.

"Sweetie, there you are!"

Maya usually didn't hear such a girlish squeal from her mom. She spun in time to be sandwiched by both parents.

"We ran into Fred and Nancy outside." Her dad released his grip. "We've been so worried you'd catch dengue like Faye Simpson."

In a teasing tone, Maya said, "You can relax—Arizona doesn't have it. I missed you guys."

Her mom stood back with her hands on her hips. "I'm still not fond of the short hair."

Maya fluffed her bangs. "It's growing out."

"You've changed, and it's not just your hair."

Her mom was right—Maya felt transformed. Mournful, but stronger. More willing to embrace a new life without Manolo. Before, she'd dreaded the moments in her apartment. After the Hawai'i trip, she welcomed getting home to Santa Fe with its terracotta adobes, vibrant blue skies, and gray-green piñon pines.

Maya led the way to the museum door. "I'll introduce you to Manolo's coworkers."

With Dr. Grinwold and Nancy, they walked around the corner to the covered pavilions. The four senior citizens, who'd bonded during Maya's COVID recovery, chatted like old friends.

Dave and Braxton stood at the periphery of the mostly masked crowd. She wanted to greet them, despite her nerves over seeing them in person for the first time since Braxton's kidnapping. But so many Commissioned Corps officers came up to offer their condolences, she never got a free minute.

The ceremony kicked off with a Navajo elder offering a prayer while a younger man began a slow drum beat. Then Manolo's Albuquerque supervisor stepped to the front.

"We all know about Dr. Miranda's expertise as an infectious disease specialist. He'd pick up a diagnostic clue that the rest of us missed. And he was generous with his personal time. I remember when he drove a patient several hours to get a lab test not available locally."

Humita Nampeyo spoke next as medical director of the health clinic where Maya first worked with Manolo and Dave on anthrax. Dr. Nampeyo's Hopi prayer shared that Manolo was one with nature—to be envisioned in the birds and the snow and the wind.

Her artist husband gave Maya a beautiful figure, dark horns curved back over a blue-painted head and wooden body cloaked in a multicolored ceremonial skirt.

"This Mountain Sheep Katsina represents strength and protection. We hope it provides you the courage to soldier on, knowing that Manolo's spirit guides and guards you."

Maya wiped away tears as she cradled the gift.

One by one, they took turns sharing funny tales of Manolo on the job, pretending to be a feeble old man when he accidentally dropped a medical chart, choking down an inedible birthday cake at an office party, and bursting into a clown dance to brighten a crying child. Maya's dad slipped her a handkerchief to absorb her rivulets of sorrow and joy.

Finally, Maya pulled a simple wood box from her bag and caught Sebastian Miranda's eyes as she stood. He must have arrived during the speeches. Her heart swelled with joy that he made it. Maybe she hadn't lost the entire Miranda family.

"If it's okay with Manolo's father, we'll go to a spot near a special juniper where we can sprinkle Manolo's ashes." No matter his answer, she intended to go ahead with her plans, but getting him to participate felt like the right thing to do. When he moved to the front and embraced her, she used her dad's handkerchief again to stifle her sobs.

"This is the end of the official memorial." Between deep breaths, Maya managed to eke out the words. "We know that many have different religious traditions, and cremation may not be among them. But you're welcome to join us while we complete the ceremony."

With Sebastian, she walked in procession to a hole dug in the tawny dirt under a large tree at the corner of the road.

"Manolo was such a social guy," Maya said. "He'll get a kick out of being here where there's so much traffic from people enjoying the park." But she kept back some of the ashes for other treasured spots.

A ranger filled in the area using a shovel and Maya led the group in placing colorful small stones in honor of Unitarian Universalist traditions and the minister who'd married them.

Maya reached out her hand to hold Sebastian's. "I was scared you wouldn't make it when you texted about engine failure."

He adjusted his gray ponytail sticking out of the band of his Yankees cap. "A Texas businessman took pity on a scrawny New Yorker and fast-tracked the part I needed."

Nancy hovered nearby. "Sounds like the Texans I know."

Dr. Grinwold shook Sebastian's hand. "We never met on your earlier visits to Santa Fe. It's good to close the loop."

"Same here," Sebastian said. "You must be an inspiring leader 'cause Maya's such a fanatic about her job."

She knew Dr. Grinwold would be flattered by the compliment but she flushed with Sebastian's choice of words and sharp tone. Despite his long-distance drive to support her at Manolo's service, he clearly harbored some resentment that she prioritized the overseas mink investigation when pregnant.

"We've benefited from her contributions, off and on." Dr. Grinwold winked with his dig about her frequent jaunts to new places for strange diseases. "Maya, I don't want to rush you, but when would you like to head home?"

Dave stepped up, black cowboy hat pushed back to reveal his piercing hazel eyes. "Emilia and the girls would love to see you if we can offer a ride to New Mexico."

Her friends and family were a pride of hungry lions, each wanting a piece of her. She'd meet their needs, one at a time. But she prioritized the Schwartz family for in-person peacemaking, overdue since Braxton's kidnapping.

"Dave, I'd love to spend time with you again—thanks for the offer. Mom and Dad, can we commit to Christmas in your Flagstaff apartment? I won't be off playing medical detective for any outbreaks then. Right, Dr. Grinwold?"

He shrugged, but doffed his cap to her parents.

"You get Maya home safely, Dave," her mom admonished, but Maya knew she was fond of him. They'd met Dave before Manolo and had tried to tout his praises, not realizing he was married with kids.

As they left, Maya turned to Sebastian. "What are your plans? Want to stay with me in Santa Fe for a few days?"

Her heart soared when he shook his head yes.

"You know the way," she said. "Here's my house key. I'll text you when the Rail Runner train from Bernalillo gets in tomorrow."

Finally alone with the Schwartz men, Maya was engulfed by

Dave's strong cowboy hug. Braxton shuffled his feet awkwardly to the side.

When Dave let go, Maya reached out to shake Braxton's hand. She remembered that he fled on horseback and rode for miles through the night until he could find help. "I was ecstatic when I heard you escaped."

Dave squeezed his half-brother's shoulder. "We now have a horse thief in the family."

"Aw, Dad," the teenager muttered. "I didn't keep it." Even though Braxton's real father was the cult leader, Maya loved hearing Braxton call Dave 'Dad.'

"We should get going," Dave said. "I want to make a couple short stops along the way."

Maya followed them to Dave's pickup. Seated in the middle of the front seat, she cradled the katsina and kept quiet with her thoughts. Ten minutes north, Dave pulled over to the Crystal Forest parking area.

Afternoon clouds crept in from the northwest, threatening to drown the parched landscape. Thrilled by an angry sky hovering low over the colorful striations of desertscape, Maya inhaled the storm's electric sharpness, a smell and feeling like nowhere else.

"We'll take a short walk," Dave said. "I want Braxton to see a petrified log."

He stopped at a six-foot hunk of wood at least a foot in diameter. Its texture and color reminded Maya of the California redwoods she'd visited as a child. In the remaining shafts of sunlight, it sparkled with quartz crystals. Dave showed Braxton the tree rings preserved as solid rock.

"Am I allowed to touch it?" Braxton asked. Dave nodded and Braxton stroked its smoothness.

"We can't remove any of it, even a small piece for a souvenir," Dave said. "A lot of these are tropical trees from two hundred million years ago."

"They're mineralized from volcanic ash." Maya beamed with her knowledge from working near Kīlauea.

"What's the color from?" Braxton's fingers traced the lines.

"Carbon is the black, manganese the pink and orange, and those tiny stripes of green—chromium." Dave stood, straight-backed, relishing his role.

Raindrops plopped on their heads and they dashed for the truck as a lightning bolt streaked west to east, followed by a thunder boom that vibrated the vehicle.

Maya flinched. "Wow, that's close." Cocooned between Dave and Braxton, she was comforted, but not enough to counteract overwhelming grief from memories of camping with Manolo. She reached into her leather jacket and drew out her dad's handkerchief.

The guys remained silent until Dave slowed for a turn onto a side road. "Quick stop to see Blue Mesa."

In short pauses of wiper blades tackling sheets of rain, Maya glimpsed the colorful cake-like hillside. From a frosting of creamy sandstone, the rusty flood streamed down horizontal layers of purple, blue, black, and white rock.

"That's fire!" Braxton pounded his fist on the dash.

"Teen speak for awesome," Dave said.

"Dad, Maya knows that. She's not ancient like you."

Maya's sorrow dissolved in a laugh. Dave was thirty-four. A different decade than Maya, but Braxton's attempt to put his new dad in his place amused her.

During the long drive home through the pounding storm, Dave focused on the highway and Maya delighted in teenage tales of school and extracurriculars.

The sun had set when they pulled up to the small adobe in Bernalillo. Maya's nose filled with the rich aroma of Rio Grande vegetation released by the assault of hail and rain. Inside, Dave started a roaring fire in their kiva as Emilia and their daughters greeted Maya with excited hugs, all tension forgotten.

Emilia apologized that she couldn't take time off at her restaurant or pull the girls out of school for Manolo's service. At the dining table, she dished out chicken enchiladas. Maya loved all the great fish meals in Hawai'i, but nothing triggered endorphins like Hatch green chiles.

The downpour eased after dinner as Braxton helped Emilia with the dishes. Maya caught Dave alone in the barn, grooming Braxton's mare.

"Are we good now?" she asked. "I would have protected Braxton's life with my own if I'd realized what was happening."

"You were a convenient target when I went out of my mind with worry. I'm sorry—it wasn't your fault."

"Thanks for saying that." Maya glowed inside with happiness. One of her deepest friendships hadn't been ruined, after all. "I've been dying to find out more about that note Braxton found at his father's home."

"This is home, not that incestuous cesspool." Dave whacked his curry comb against a wooden post.

"It must have been so painful when he was locked up there and you couldn't go get him." Maya picked up another comb to groom the pony in the next stall.

"How did Braxton feel being back with his mother and other siblings?" Out of Dave's line of sight, she felt comfortable enough to probe on the dicey subject.

"You mean my mother?" Dave replied with a harsh laugh. "Of course he enjoyed seeing them, but it didn't make up for the lack of freedom. He was astonished that his father wanted him back, considering he'd kicked him out before."

"How did Braxton find the note?"

"He went snooping for a map to help his escape, then found the note in his father's things. But Aaron Farnsworth could have taken it off someone else."

"I heard the FBI didn't locate the note or any evidence that the cult could carry out the BT threat."

Dave stepped out for a brush, then rubbed it over the mare's withers. "Now they're acting like Braxton made it up."

Maya lifted the pony's front foot to remove packed soil with a pick. "The FBI investigation is concentrated on Caren Oldner, the academic researcher working with us. She created genetically modified mosquitoes without authorization. Similar altered mosquitoes were found in San Juan, New York City, and here."

"Holy shit! How did she spread the mosquitoes around?"

"Faye and I don't think Caren did it on purpose. Perhaps the mosquitoes stowed away on her flight when she visited Puerto Rico in June. Same situation when Juana flew from San Juan to Albuquerque, then New York."

"I hold a dimmer view of humanity. I bet Caren Oldner planned a grand experiment to see how many places she could infect."

Maya finished up with the pony and brushed dirt from her jeans. "Puerto Rico might be the ideal place to sneak in modified mosquitoes. They already have so much dengue, more dangerous mosquitoes wouldn't be detected right away. Anyway, she's locked up in jail for a car accident that killed our Hawaiian colleague."

Dave closed the stalls and dimmed the lights. "She sounds like a piece of work."

Maya didn't mention being in the accident, and her bangs covered her latest scar. Talking about it brought back the awful moments when they struggled to get out of Caren's truck, leaking diesel, and Ino not moving or breathing.

"We'd see larger numbers of the GM mosquitoes in more places if Dr. Oldner tried to increase infection rates," she said.

"But if her study aimed to reduce mosquito reproduction, why was there an outbreak?" he asked.

"Caren admitted that something went wrong with her experimental technique. The FBI's scouring the polygamist cult's computer files for any communication with her."

Dave joined Maya on the porch swing. "My estranged relatives live there so I'd sure like to have the truth about all that."

"Faye Simpson went to vet school with Dr. Oldner and wants to believe she's not a bioterrorist. We don't feel that many scientists would harm people just to increase the urgency for funding."

Dave punched his hat and set it between them. "Makes us look bad, even if our agencies are less involved with academic research."

"Yeah, we have no reason to generate more work for ourselves." Maya's laugh was tainted with regret over her own professional ambitions leading to COVID infection that killed her husband and her baby.

"What I told you is confidential," she continued, "so you can't share it with your colleagues until CDC brings USDA into the loop."

She hesitated. Their relationship was based on trust built over countless hours of joint investigations, and she hoped his personal loyalty would trump a sense of obligation to inform his superiors.

She attempted to rekindle their perpetual banter. "I'm thrilled to be home in the relative quiet of New Mexico. Promise not to spring any zoonotic cattle diseases on me?"

Maya knew she was poking the bear with her joke. Public health prioritized humans whereas agricultural agencies were responsible for farm and ranch animals. Their interests didn't always perfectly align.

Dave's face froze in a tight grin. "We do everything we can to reassure people when our livestock diseases don't pose a health risk to them."

Maya stood with her hand on the back door. "And I'll keep puncturing your complacency about new ones that are a human threat."

Inside Dave's home, she bedded down on the couch with Bo, his Lab Retriever. Not as exciting as a Hawaiian hotel room with a postcard view of the ocean, but some familiar things were worth treasuring.

FORTY-SIX

Santa Fe, New Mexico—Thursday, October 7, 2021

Sebastian picked up Maya from the train station at noon in his battered station wagon. She climbed into the passenger seat, eyeing the tent and Coleman stove in the back.

He patted the steering wheel. "The old lady's got a quarter million miles on her. I figure this'll be her final excursion."

Typical of the Southwest, the sunny day showed no sign of last night's storm. Maya felt warmed by the sunlight reflecting off the black dashboard and by Sebastian's easy conversation. Once back at her apartment, she was startled to see his sleeping bag next to the couch.

"I texted you to take the bed. You must be exhausted after your cross-country drive."

"Not a problem." He pulled a plate of roast beef sandwiches from the packed refrigerator. "I have good memories of visiting you here with Manolo."

Maya joined him at the kitchen table. "As always, you're too generous. I should have picked up the groceries."

"You're a bit short on supplies. Not much time after you returned from Hawaii?"

She shook her head. "I focused on the memorial, not eating." She set the sandwich down. "I hope your coming hasn't caused friction with Ramona."

"No disagreement will ever break up our family." Sebastian held Maya's restless hand. "Ramona needs someone to blame so she can cope with her grief. The two of them were best buddies after my wife died."

In desperate need of fresh air, Maya opened the sliding door to her back patio. "I wish I could forgive myself."

Talking about it felt like slipping down a slide backward. Her life with Manolo wasn't all one rosy glow. They had major blowups, sometimes her fault, sometimes his, often over a misguided notion to protect each other by keeping secrets. But he'd be pissed if that's what she dwelled on.

She sat back down, determined to regain the strength earned in Hawai'i. If Ino could fight his way out of addiction for a highly successful personal and professional life, she had no excuse.

"I'd like to renew my friendship with Ramona. Please let me know if anything would make a difference. But in the meantime, I'll honor Manolo's memory by continuing the path we planned. Love, dedication to work, and family."

She squeezed his hand. "I'm glad you're part of it."

"Me, too," Sebastian answered with an affectionate smile. His magnetic Hispanic features, similar to Manolo's, warmed her heart.

"I'm taking the couch." Maya got up and tossed Sebastian's sleeping bag into her bedroom. "Dr. Grinwold's given me the whole week off. Let's do some tourist stuff and we can spread Manolo's remaining ashes in his favorite spots."

Sebastian signaled his agreement with another long hug. "Sounds like a plan."

Pecos, New Mexico—Thursday, November 25, 2021

As Carmen placed a platter of sweet potatoes and honey on the table, Maya noticed her conspiratorial whisper with Mark. She envied the casual rapport between her attorney and his longtime ranch manager. Mark caught Maya's eyes and grinned.

Maya passed the cheese cauliflower to her mom as Carmen giggled, unexpected from someone her age.

"I want to know what's so funny." Maya pointed her knife toward Mark, then Carmen. In a morning of playing board games before Thanksgiving dinner, they'd relaxed into the camaraderie formed over months of living together during her COVID recovery.

"You're nosy." Tone hushed, Maya's mom leaned forward.

"I want to know, too." Lukas chimed in as if he owned the table. Maya stifled her own giggle at the authoritative posture of the table's youngest person, Mark's college student aide.

"Okay, okay." Mark paused from carving the wild turkey. Maya was thrilled to see him standing at the end of the table, several years of physical therapy paying off. But his wheelchair and crutches loomed nearby.

"Now that I'm on my feet," Mark said, "Carmen thinks I should take you dancing."

"He's a *tramposo*, a trickster, putting his idea into my mouth." Carmen put her hand on Maya's arm. "I only asked if he liked your hairstyle."

Maya fingered the bangs which constantly got in her eyes. She hated that growing-out period when they were too short to be pushed behind her ears.

"You know what?" her dad said. "Before we head home to Flagstaff, let's make a night of it, line dancing at La Fonda."

"I'm not recovered enough for that," Mark answered with a plaintive tone. "But I could manage a slow waltz if Maya's interested."

"How long have you two been line dancing?" Maya directed the question to her parents, postponing Mark's invitation until they were alone.

"A new pandemic hobby," her mom answered, "and your dad's become quite good at it. We're trying it out in public, masked of course."

They all lingered over dinner for another hour, friendly jokes continuing. Thanksgiving last year had been grim with both of them in wheelchairs, Maya barely able to stand or speak. It will get better—that had been their mantra, and they were right.

As Maya helped clear the table, her phone rang and she grabbed her coat, excusing herself to the front porch. Beneath a sparkling Milky Way, she shivered as ice crystals pricked her lungs.

Faye's face filled the screen. "Hi Maya, I'm checking in. Did your family accept Mark's invitation for a country Thanksgiving?"

"Yes, it's been wonderful. What are you and Taylor up to?"

"Just finished dinner and the Rockettes. Then Taylor was called into the hospital for a late-night consult."

Maya was thankful to find Faye's life back to normal. She'd felt guilty that Faye and Keegan had to stay on in Hawai'i for a few more weeks after Maya left, but there were worse places to be stuck working hard.

"I heard the dengue cases have dropped in Hawai'i," Maya said. "Either it's the cooler weather or all our efforts paid off."

"It needs to get below fifty to discourage the mosquitoes. Not cold enough in Hawai'i for that, so I'm giving our team all the credit."

Maya hated to interrupt the good mood, but was dying to know. "What's happening with Dr. Oldner?"

"She copped a plea deal on the vehicular homicide charge—eighteen months instead of a potential five-year sentence. The prison health care system isn't great but I lobbied for a full psych evaluation."

Without evidence to support a BT attack, Caren would be free again in 2023, although unlikely to be eligible for another university or government job. But her unique skills and obsessive focus might be valued by a private research firm.

Maya pulled her wool coat tighter. She prayed that Faye's assumption was correct—Caren made a colossal lab error with her GM work in creating mosquitoes more deadly rather than less, then allowing them to escape.

But like Dave suggested, Caren might have distributed mosquitoes bioengineered to trigger a pandemic. The idea of Caren back in a dengue lab triggered another wave of chills.

"Great news," Faye said. "Siti drafted a journal article for the dengue data. She'll send it for our review."

Would such a report ever include someone posthumously as a coauthor? For all the countless hours Ino spent organizing their work and outperforming everyone on the physical labor, he deserved to be credited. Certainly he'd be listed in the acknowledgments.

Maybe the news of a dengue lab error wouldn't cause much of an uproar, with new COVID variants still popping up and wreaking havoc. She and her parents had received their fall boosters, and fingers crossed, no one else in her family would come down with it.

Faye's face scrunched in a mischievous grin. "I have some personal news. Taylor and I are discussing commitment."

Maya almost dropped her phone. "That's amazing! Are you getting married?"

"No, and we're not giving up our apartments. Taylor's schedule at the hospital is too crazy and I need my space. Plus, I'm adopting a cat from the shelter and Taylor's place doesn't allow pets."

"So what are you talking about?"

"We're each other's one and only. With any luck, we'll keep going along that path for years to come." Faye's expression bloomed.

Maya didn't know a lot about Faye's romantic history. "Congratulations, I'm thrilled for you."

Her phone buzzed with a text message from Mu Jian, her Chinese study co-conspirator. "Faye, thanks for sharing your news. I need to head inside. I'm thinking 2022 will be a fantastic year."

After she hung up, she checked her messages. **<Happy American Thanksgiving. See, I didn't forget.>**

Unsure if Jian was still in the doghouse with the government over their illegal bat sampling, she typed, **<If you're allowed to Zoom, we can schedule it. I'd love to see you again.>**

Then she re-entered the warmth of the Great Room where Mark stoked the kiva fire with a poker. "Where did everyone go?" she asked.

"Carmen and Lukas took your folks out to see the animals in the barn."

"Thanks again for having us over. You and your staff have cheered us up two years in a row."

Mark offered his hand, leading her to the couch. "I'm happy to host your family, and get some time alone with you."

"This ranch is one of my favorite places." Saying it out loud made it clear to Maya that it was true, even though she'd finally adapted to her empty apartment. Her job at the health department fell back into routine, alternating office and home hours to reduce COVID spread.

Maya adjusted a pillow. "Most winters, you work in Phoenix. Is that your plan?" It felt like prying, but she wouldn't mind seeing him again if he stayed in New Mexico.

He nodded. "I've got some Arizona cases and the warm weather will be wonderful for these aging bones."

Maya laughed. "A man in his early fifties is still in his prime." She blushed, afraid he'd think she was flirting. "And if you want to go dancing, we can try it sometime."

"Good to know," he answered with a twinkle in his eye.

Checking for a twinge of guilt, she felt none. She was a sucker for swarthy men. Hawai'i had done its magic and grown her resolve to embrace a new life without Manolo. And the memorial brought closure, more than she expected.

"In May, there's a legal conference in Paris. If you have vacation time, consider joining me."

Maya gasped at the shock of the invitation. Mark never hid his attraction but had made a major effort to go slow after Maya rebuffed his advances in the spring.

"I, um, let's see what the New Year brings." At that point, she'd no longer owe him anything for the bribe to get her released from China. "Can I give you my answer then?"

"Of course. If you decide to come, I'll reserve an extra room for you before they're sold out."

Good. He wasn't assuming they would sleep together. She poured herself some eggnog spiked with Mark's favorite bourbon, then handed the second glass to him.

They clinked in a holiday toast. "I appreciate having time to think it over," she said. "I always wanted to get my feet wet with another language besides Spanish."

Mark's expression was hopeful as she kissed his cheek, roughened by evening whiskers.

"Merci, mon ami," she whispered.

CODA

Afi Mountain Wildlife Sanctuary, Nigeria —May, 2022

The 420-pound silverback pokes at the stiffened body of his twelve-year-old son on the forested hillside near the Cross River. The stench of diarrhea and vomit permeates the ground nest of sticks and clumps of grass. The patriarch can't linger. It's time for him, as the dominant male, to lead his small troop in a search for fruits and herbs.

A three-month-old gorilla, blood dripping from his nostrils and staining his reddish fur, lies inert in his mother's arms. The young mother opens her mouth for a high-pitched scream, and another female gorilla joins in.

The silverback twitches his ears and stretches up to his five-foot height, glancing into the canopy as the deluge begins. They must rebuild their nests in the treetops for the rainy season.

The torrent cascades off the leaves and triggers a swarm of flies, already invading the dead gorilla for their own nourishment. The silverback roars and pounds his chest, startling a greater long-fingered bat, roosting upside down from a branch of the bloodwood tree. The nocturnal carnivore shakes its wings and defecates more guano shiny with fish scales, and Ebola virus, to the nest below.

Emitting a low-pitched growl like a deep rumble, the silverback heads off into the forest to find their next meal. Reluctant to leave, the others glance back to the dead body. The mother cradles her infant, the baby already in transition to the spirit world.

[Ebola: A Microbial Mystery, 2025]

About the Author

MILLICENT EIDSON is the author of the alphabetical Maya Maguire microbial mysteries. The MayaVerse at https://drmayamaguire.com/ includes references and links to prequel and side stories. Author awards include Best Play in *Synkroniciti* and Honorable Mention from the Arizona Mystery Writers.

Dr. Eidson's work as a public health veterinarian and epidemiologist began as an EIS Officer (like Maya Maguire and Faye Simpson) with the Centers for Disease Control and Prevention, and continued at the New Mexico and New York state health departments. She has authored over a hundred scientific papers, articles, and book chapters. Currently, she is a public health faculty member at the University at Albany and the University of Vermont, and teaches a UVM course on zoonoses and climate change in its Larner College of Medicine.

With formative years in the Southwest, Millie enjoys reconnecting with Arizona family, heritage trips to Norway, Ireland, and China, and wider travel worldwide. In retirement from full-time public health work, she has settled in Vermont with her husband Tom Henderson and daughter Lian Henderson, inspiration for Maya Maguire.

Other interests are photography, painting, hiking, and bicycling along the beautiful Burlington, Vermont waterfront.

Social media links:

www.linkedin.com/in/eidsonmillicent

Maya Maguire Media | Facebook

Millie Eidson (@drmayamaguire) • Instagram photos and videos

@meidson-author.sky.social Bluesky

Acknowledgments

COVID-19 made epidemiology and public health more visible. However, animals and the environment are still under-recognized for their part in microbial life and disease transmission. Veterinarians play a key role in public health, agriculture, and environmental agencies, universities, and corporate and private practice. Our work is always in partnership with others having diverse backgrounds.

The MayaVerse would not be possible without my initial training in research design and statistics at Michigan State University and the University of Colorado. The 40th reunion of my Colorado State University veterinary class reminded me of the dedication forged during four years of challenging but supportive training.

Ultimately, the greatest inspiration for the MayaVerse comes from collaborative work at the Centers for Disease Control and Prevention and the New Mexico and New York state health departments. If these stories capture even a small part of their ceaseless devotion to excellence and duty, I'll be happy.

The MayaVerse benefits from my family team of Lian Henderson, inspiration for and feedback on the Maya Maguire character, and Tom Henderson, audio and visual media advisor for Maya Maguire Media.

"Dengue: A Microbial Mystery" has been critiqued in its entirety by two writers' workshops. One includes multi-genre authors and the second includes independent authors associated with the national Sisters in Crime (SinC) group (https://www.sistersincrime.org/). Initial sections benefitted from feedback from additional author groups affiliated with SinC, the Burlington Writers Workshop (https://burlingtonwritersworkshop.com/), and the

Green Mountain Writers Group (https://greenmountainwriters. com/).

Additional organizations contributing education and support are the Sisters in Crime local chapters: Grand Canyon Writers (https://grandcanyonwriters.com/) and the Tucson Old Pueblo Chapter (https://www.tucsonsistersincrime.org/). Membership in the Alliance of Independent Authors (https://www. allianceindependentauthors.org/) is also invaluable.

My continued growth is fostered by academic affiliations as a language and creative writing student at Champlain College, emeritus epidemiology professor at the University at Albany, and instructor for a zoonoses class at the University of Vermont.

Provision of information by agency employees or workshop participants does not imply endorsement by those individuals or groups.

Scientific nomenclature, including when to italicize organism names, can be confusing. For more information, see: https://wwwnc.cdc.gov/eid/page/scientific-nomenclature.

Most website and book cover photographs are the author's. The CDC Information Portal provides a wonderful source of public domain images. For this novel, the mosquito on the cover is based on https://phil.cdc.gov/Details.aspx?pid=20139. The Maya Maguire Media logo is based on https://phil.cdc.gov/Details. aspx?pid=2871.

Dengue fever may be the most complex zoonotic disease addressed to-date in the alphabetical novels or short stories. Hundreds of nonfiction resources were consulted. A curated list for general education is provided at https://drmayamaguire.com/.

DENGUE Discussion Questions

Book groups interested in discussions with the author should email <u>drmayamaguire@gmail.com</u>.

"DENGUE" crosses genres, with multiple themes in the framework of a zoonotic disease. The following questions may help in thinking about and discussing the novel.

1. The genre elements include medical thriller, crime fiction, mystery, women's fiction, and romantic suspense. How do each of these elements contribute to the overall arc and your enjoyment of the story?

2. The initial point-of-view character is a recently widowed Chinese American woman adopted as an infant by an Irish-heritage family living in the Southwest. What elements of the character's background enrich the story?

3. The other point-of-view character is an older bisexual public health veterinarian raised on a Colorado ranch but working her entire life in New York City. What elements of the character's background enrich the story?

4. How do the alternating POV chapters expand your identification with the story?

5. Geographic locations are intended as characters in themselves. How do geography and history influence the story?

6. Both characters are changed by their work in Hawai'i. In what ways do you think exposure to other ways of life impact us?

7. What do you think of both characters' choices for handling personal grief?

8. What are the roadblocks to achieving a work-life balance based on gender and economic status?

9. Zoonotic diseases are those in common between humans and nonhuman animals. How are transmission, investigation, prevention, and control more complex for zoonotic diseases than those infecting only humans?

10. What is the role of climate change in the story and for zoonotic diseases?

11. How can someone with a veterinary medical degree contribute to disease investigations?

12. For authenticity, writers often rely on personal experience, while protecting the privacy of those sharing life events with the author. Writers also use research and close consultation with others to create characters, plot events, and settings not their own. As a reader, do you have a preferred balance of work informed by an author's imagination, research, and representation of their background?